FENCE/JUMPERS

FENCE/JUMPERS

R O B E R T   L E U C I

ST. MARTIN'S PRESS ❧ NEW YORK

Design by Junie Lee

Library of Congress Cataloging-in-Publication Data

Leuci, Bob
    Fence jumpers / Robert Leuci.
        p.   cm.
    "A Thomas Dunne book."
    ISBN 0-312-13073-2 (hardcover)
    I. Title.
    PS3562.E857F4   1995
    813'.54—dc20   95-846
                                        CIP

First Edition: May 1995

10 9 8 7 6 5 4 3 2 1

For my brother, Richard Leuci.
One more of life's regrets,
that I never really knew you.

Help came from several directions in the writing of *Fence Jumpers*. Mostly it came from my experiences during the twenty years I spent with the New York City Police Department. My childhood, the years growing up in Ozone Park, friends who I can still call friends from those years. Arthur Monty and John Pisciotta, Arty for his great cop stories and John for being John.

My agent, Esther Newberg, who has been a friend and advocate for more than a decade.

The International Association of Crime Writers, who brought me to Spain. It was there, in that wonderful country, where I was to meet my new editor and dear friend, Ruth Cavin.

And, my loving family. Those that are gone and those that remain.

Jesus! I could have been a dentist! I could have been a nice person. But I didn't do that. I chose to run a crap game and make you feel superior. Schmuck.

Look after your friends, and take care of your enemies. You'd be surprised how that simplifies everything.

—Joey Gallo

FENCE/JUMPERS

CHAPTER ONE

1969, Queens, New York

The telephone rang in the brick row house on Eighty-fourth Street, and Jimmy Burns looked at his watch; it was just before two, five minutes before two. He gave the ringing phone his shrewd look and bet himself twenty bucks it was Dante on the other end of the line. He turned away, thinking you can wait and let the phone ring for two reasons, one major and one minor.

The minor reason was that he was vigorously combating a need to pee and at that moment on his way to the second-floor bathroom. The major reason was Dante's undisguised urgency. His buddy's frenzy made him nuts, the guy always moaning and groaning about being left alone with JoJo. The damn phone kept ringing, which meant that Dante was not going to give up. Christ, he'd just hung up with the numbnuts, told his pleading pal that he was on his way. Running his fingers through his hair, he stared at the phone, studying it. For a horror-filled moment he thought he might pee on the sofa.

Jimmy made for the stairs, counting how many rings it took to pee, flush, and return. Nine.

He took his time picking up the receiver and listened to that slow voice. Out of the corner of his eye he saw his brother Josh standing in the kitchen holding a cup of coffee, watching, his face perfectly still.

In the kitchen of a railroad flat some twelve blocks away Dante O'Donnell held the phone between his shoulder and chin. He raised a bottle of Bud to his lips and swigged, saying whataya doing? Jimmy said talking to you. I'm coming, whataya think I'm doing? Dante said ey buddy, you've been coming for three hours. How long you think we're gonna wait over here? Jimmy told him that he just now scored, and that the pot was top quality. No twigs or seeds, it's clean, looks smooth. You'll like this, he told Dante.

"Get down here, will ya," Dante said. "We'll be on the roof."

Jimmy said is JoJo still off the rails with this Nancy business? Dante said yeah! Sure. The boy's in love, man. It's a real headache. The guy's bummed, saying crazy shit. Nobody can talk to him, except maybe you.

"Talk to him goddammit, reason with him," Jimmy said.

Dante thought of saying to him you're kidding me right? His mind telling him that nobody can talk sense to JoJo Paradiso. He would be willing to bet some money that before this day was over JoJo Paradiso would make some oddball move, come up with something eerie, something only JoJo could do. He saw that look on JoJo's face, that smirk saying you ready? You're gonna be with me or gonna be gone? Dante paused, thinking a moment, asking himself that very same question over and over. Since they were in sandbox, JoJo made him wacky.

Jimmy examined himself in the hallway mirror, listening to Dante, hearing him but thinking about JoJo, wondering why his buddy had been so quiet that past week. What the hell was wrong with him? Even when they were alone, JoJo gave him his Mexican bandit grin and said nothing. The last damn thing he'd said was, "Jimmy, it's time you discovered the life of the mind. You need a fantasy, or a trip to London." The guy was spaced out lately, nothing was registering.

Jimmy told Dante he'd be right there, then left his house at a run, the tremor in Dante's voice and the nickel bag of Panamanian red in his pocket putting a fire on his tail.

He quick-walked crossing Pitkin, then Sutter Avenue. It was mid June, a perfect New York day, about eighty-five degrees, warm for June. The sky was alight, pale blue and clear. In a couple of weeks he and the guys would be able to hit the Whitehouse down in the Rockaways. It was one of those Irish joints, a spot where you sucked down tap beer from paper cups, got loaded, then pulled chicks under the boardwalk. At night, if you got lucky, you could watch JoJo fistfight off-duty cops. Like JoJo and Dante, Jimmy was nineteen, and he loved every hour of every day of each week of his life.

At a half jog, Jimmy scanned the street and spied that handsome bastard Bobby Fives with Tony T and the Twins. They were sitting on their usual perch in front of Rosen's candy store watching him, and the cards were out.

Tony shouted, "Jimmie B, you gonna be around later?" Tony had a behind the size of a Volkswagen and he never got off it. "Ann Marie," he said, "my girlfriend, she don't come around anymore either. Says I'm depressing. It's probably the same with you."

Tony T grinned like a retard, but when you considered the amount of dope he ingested, you had to figure it would be a goddamn miracle if the guy had three working brain cells. His father owned Morton's, the drugstore, which gave the T easy access to all the pharmaceuticals. The guy'd remained seated and stoned his entire teenage life, and the monotony of it all made Jimmy woozy.

"I'll come by later," Jimmy lied.

The way Jimmy saw it, pot smoking was no big thing. But pills and powder frightened him. You could jump out of your skin with some of the crazy dope people were bringing around lately. It had been banging around the yom and Rican neighborhoods for years. South O.Z., South Jamaica, and Brownsville were flooded with the stuff. Now it was coming here. It was in the air, it was coming for sure, people were talking about it all the time. Junk, they called it, heroin. It turned people into gerbils on exercise wheels. He wanted no part of that shit. But pot, pot was cool, weed was harmless, no problem there. The worst it did was make him hungry for Clark Bars, Mounds, and Almond Joys. Jimmy Burns loved Almond Joys.

He carried his pot in a manila envelope, a small one, about the size of his palm, in the back pocket of his jeans. Angrily he thought of something that sent a roller coaster from his brain to his feet. He broke into a lope, feeling unsettled, wondering why it was him that always carried the pot, always him that was out front? He guessed it was because he was kind of, well, the slickest guy around. He never slipped up. Never had a problem getting through this life. Mr. Slick, Dante called him.

Jimmy Burns was born handsome and never thought much about it. He wasn't sure if he was born slick, cocky, and quick or if it was the Queens streets that had taught him. But he knew he was a smooth piece of work, probably more polished than JoJo and far more slick than Dante. Jimmy Burns was not given to modesty.

Jimmy paid money for the dope to his brother Josh, who was at the school of dentistry at NYU. Sometimes, when he was thinking, Jimmy wished that when he was in school he'd spent more time there. He flashed on his brother, the way Josh handed him the smoke with the tips of his fingers, saying, "You and your friends' tiny brains will light up with this stuff." Jimmy figured that it was a toss-up whether Josh was stoned more often than Tony T.

He jogged down two blocks and turned the corner near the Hornet's Nest Bar and Grill. Carmine Joey came out of the bar, grabbed at his crotch, and held up his hand like some kind of f'n traffic cop, stopping Jimmy cold.

Carmine Joey was a skeleton in a pale blue Hawaiian shirt, aviator sunglasses. He had stringy shoulder-length hair the color of dead grass. Carmine was always grabbing at his crotch. He thought it helped develop his street image as a James Dean type.

Carmine asked Jimmy where his hippie brother was. Told Jimmy he'd like to get some 'erb. 'Erb was what Carmine Joey called pot.

A blue-and-white with two uniforms in it turned the corner, slowed; the uniforms both gave Carmine Joey and Jimmy a drawn-out stare. Carmine Joey did look sinister, grabbing at his balls and squinting. You'd cast him as a child abuser or a serial killer. The cops were smart to keep an eye on Carmine. For his part, Jimmy smiled and waved at the cops, because part of being cool and slick was thinking that you were, and he was. The cops drove off. Carmine didn't smile. He seemed genuinely disturbed by the cops' scrutiny, his cool damaged. He told Jimmy to tell Josh to give him a call and Jimmy nodded and loped off.

Josh was one year older than Jimmy and in the neighborhood people called him a hippie. Adhering to that custom, he read poetry aloud and smoked a ton of pot. He'd score ounces across the street from the university in Washington Square Park. His connection was this black guy who wore a dashiki, beads, and sandals and had one of those wall-to-wall Afros. They called him Razor, and a few weeks back Jimmy stood by and watched him grab Josh, digging his fingernails into his arms and hissing, "Jew boy, you have a nice way about you. But underneath you hate my black ass. Remember," he'd told Josh, "I ain't no tame nigger, so you best be careful."

Josh had turned over his money, saying, "Are you kidding me man?" Then he laughed a stupid little-boy laugh. Razor turned on Jimmy and Jimmy told him, "You remember, I ain't no tame Jew, so back the fuck off."

His brother Josh tried, but the guy just could not be cool. Violence terrified him for reasons Jimmy never quite understood.

In two years a mortar round will pick Josh up and toss him into the sky, and one day his name will be engraved on a black wall in the nation's capital.

Jimmy hurried along the sidewalk on Eighty-fourth Street, by the Jewish cemetery. He was feeling intense, on a mission, the rhythm of music in his head. Underneath the El at Eighty-fifth and Liberty Avenue he ran into Howie Blutstein, the baker's kid. Howie had a smile pasted on his face like he was happy or something.

Howie told him that he had lined up three chicks from City Line. Had his father's big-ass four-door red Buick and was gonna run over to the Pizza King, maybe grab a feel, play a little stinky finger. Howie was standing hip-cocked, grinning like a real dumbo, biting at a thumbnail.

Howie saying there was room for him, room for him and Dante too. The guy was real thin, you could say frail, and he didn't like JoJo Paradiso. JoJo terrified Howie, scared Howie to death since the day he saw JoJo beat the shit out of a school bus driver who was as old and as big as his own father, bigger.

Jimmy told Howie that he and Dante were real busy.

Howie kept talking and Jimmy heard him in a distant way, as if Howie were talking to him through some sort of f'n drug haze. Jimmy massaged his stomach and started to walk off.

Carmine Joey, showing up from nowhere, yelled from across the street, "Hey!" Then he grabbed his crotch with both hands, laughed, and turned and walked away, looking slightly disappointed at Jimmy and Howie's lack of amazement.

"I'm gonna tell you something Howie," Jimmy said, wanting to get going. "I'm gonna tell you that you got no talent with chicks. None. And second, you invite me and Dante you'd better invite JoJo. Because you don't want JoJo Paradiso to think you're disrespecting him. He just might want to kick your skinny little ass you treat him that way."

"You'll see man," Howie was saying, jumping up and down like somebody just nailed his toe with a hammer.

Jimmy spread his hands palms up like he was about to surrender. He'd had it with this jerkoff. "Seeya," he told Howie, and was gone.

Howie called after him, "A Jew's gotta be a nut to hang with the wops. Those greasers down on One-hundred-and-first are bad fucking dudes, man. You're gonna see, they're gonna get you in a jam. You and Dante too."

Jimmy turned down Eighty-fifth. The sun was high now, no clouds in the sky, heat came off the pavement making him sweat. Jimmy jogged on toward 101st Avenue, thinking that it was true, the more time he and

Dante spent with JoJo, the greater the chance of some real trouble finding them. Nobody else from their neighborhood was brave enough or stupid enough to come down to 101st. Only the truth was he liked the craziness and figured that Dante liked it too. Nevertheless, he wasn't all that sure that he was ready for real trouble yet. Not just yet. Not today anyway.

Shit, it wasn't smart to fool with the bad guys from 101st in their stronghold. And that, he was certain, was exactly what JoJo had in his wigged-out mind.

The day before, down at the Eighty-third Street park playing a little handball, JoJo had told him that he needed to smoke some pot, feel feisty, and then go and lock horns with a pair of badasses. Forget it that they were his girlfriend's father and brother. Forget it that they were known hard guys, probably gangsters with mob connections to boot. Give JoJo a little smoke and he had all the energy in the world.

Jimmy was moving real fast now, grateful for only one thing: Dante would be there. When Jimmy thought of locking horns with tough guys, he was reminded of how fortunate he was to have Dante at his side. Dante was tough, as savage as they came, except for maybe JoJo, who was demented. He figured that Howie was probably right when he said you're gonna get jammed up on 101st Avenue. Funny thing was, Jimmy wasn't sure right then if he cared. As crafty as he was, how bad could things get?

In five minutes he hit the avenue, slowed and began to walk toward JoJo's apartment house. He checked his reflection in the storefront glass as he went. He was slim, and tall, two inches over six feet. In spite of the hot weather, watchful men stood on the corner of 101st Avenue and Eighty-fifth street with their arms tightly wrapped around themselves as if they were cold. They eyed Jimmy as he walked past, with the patient interest of tourists observing some alien custom.

Greasers, he had this notion that the whole f'n block was choked with greasers. He looked up the street, then back again. A vast army of Guidos appeared, and the looks they shot him gave Jimmy a case of the creeps, made him feel like an intruder. He took care to ignore them. Guidos and Guidettes everywhere. It was how he referred to the Italians from 101st Avenue. Guidos and Guidettes and greasers.

Jimmy stopped in front of a four-story woodframe walk-up and looked up at the roof. Suddenly he felt great relief that he had made it. He was there, moments away from his buddies, the only two people in the world that gave him real emotional feelings, buddy feelings, whether things were going good or not. The good buddies were there, the closeness was there. Except people could change. And that was something that Jimmy Burns didn't like thinking about. Didn't like those kinds of thoughts at all.

Inside the building he moved up flights of stairs, passing open apartment doors. The air was heavy with the fragrance of basil and olive oil, garlic and simmering meats. These were the homes of hardworking men with big families and bad-tempered women who were lashed to gas stoves and looked it. Through the open doors he could hear soft curses and the clatter of pots and pans.

Somebody screeched after a kid named Paulie.

On the second-floor landing he ran into a girl he remembered from high school. Her name was Victoria, and she stood in the hall doing her nails with an emery board. Victoria was so wrapped up in herself that Jimmy felt invisible as he passed her. She was the type that always sat in school with spread knees and never said a word. Like she was waiting for someone. She smiled at him like a bad actress; her look said what the hell are *you* doing here?

The Paradisos lived in the top-floor apartment. When Jimmy passed their door and mounted the stairs to the roof a surge of optimism flooded his heart. He was ambushed by the smell of Louise Paradiso's cooking. JoJo's mother, with that high-gloss white skin of hers and those black eyes that would make heavy eye contact with him, never let him head for home without a bite of something. A sandwich, a plate of pasta. He'd eat her food and say very tasty, very tasty. She had a pair of legs like a world-class sprinter, and sometimes Jimmy would think about her in a certain way and freak. Christ, man, he'd think, thoughts like that could get you killed.

"Jimmy," she'd say, "you way too skinny, have something to eat." The basic trouble with the Italian food she pressed on him was that hardly any of it looked familiar. In the beginning, when he first met her, he felt uncomfortable taking the food she'd offer. More often than not he'd decline. He was not a big eater to start with. No thanks, he'd say, all courteous with a nice smile. Once JoJo told him, "Ey, you insult my mother one more time I'll bust you up. She offers you food, you eat!"

After that, Jimmy ate everything Louise Paradiso offered. One time she gave him a sandwich of hard-boiled eggs wrapped in pigskin. It was a hard moment. For a Jew from a family that kept kosher, a very tough moment. He recalled the way JoJo grinned, how they made a contract that day. It made him smile, the memory of it. That smile was still on his face when he stepped from the stairwell out onto the roof.

Jimmy and Dante had come to the conclusion that JoJo's obsession with Nancy Vanzetti was the worst thing possible. Since Nancy threw JoJo that puckered I'm-ready-for-you look their buddy hadn't been the same guy. Listening to Sinatra and Peggy Lee, et cetera, for chrissake.

Jimmy crossed the flat expanse of the roof and slid to the edge. He said to Dante, "What's up? How's he doin'?"

Dante looked at JoJo and spoke quietly to him.

"Real great, he's been standing here for two hours, talking under his breath. Hang around awhile and see for yourself."

JoJo and Dante were leaning over the parapet of the roof, inspecting the street. They were waiting for Nancy, with those knockers of hers, to get off the Q-10 bus. Nancy in her brown Dominican Commercial Catholic school outfit. Nancy, who half the men and all the boys on 101st Avenue would give their right arm to plug.

The sun was hotter on the roof than in the street. Jimmy breathed in and out. He took off his T-shirt and stood next to Dante, who seemed relaxed and poised at the roof's edge, looking down at the ground.

JoJo was hunched over, his chin in his hand, his elbow on the parapet. No one said a word for a couple of minutes, and Jimmy felt just a little self-conscious. Dante draped his arm around Jimmy's shoulders. He said, close to his ear, "It's him that wants the weed."

Jimmy said, "Will you catch the look of him. The guy's in orbit, man."

Dante, his head still close to Jimmy's, said, "Love man, love. It'll happen to you too someday."

"I ain't got time for this bullshit," Jimmy said.

JoJo said, "The hell you two talking about?"

"I chased my brother for two days for this weed. Okay! I hustled my ass over here, and what are you doing? I'll tell ya what you're doing. You're standing on the roof like some kind of depressing kid, gaping down into the street, waiting for some chick to get off a bus."

JoJo shrugged, he said to Dante, "You hear that?"

JoJo had perfect skin, never a blemish, and long hair that was so black in certain light it appeared blue. He had a habit of running his fingers through his hair, and when he did it would fall back perfectly in place. Tony Curtis, people said JoJo resembled the movie actor Tony Curtis.

Jimmy heard JoJo say, "Throw me a break, will ya?"

He didn't look at JoJo or at Dante. Pretty soon he too was caught up in street watching.

"That's him," JoJo said.

"Where?" asked Dante.

"Coming out of the sandwich joint. That's him with the hat."

Down the street near the corner an immense fat guy wearing a broad-brimmed gray hat and carrying a black cane came out of Carlino's, the sandwich and pizza joint. He stood in the center of the sidewalk, one hand firmly planted on his hip. The other held the cane in the air. A cigarette hung from his lip.

Dante grinned from one ear to the other. "The Ice Man," he said.

"Nancy's father?" asked Jimmy.

"One and the same," said JoJo.

Jimmy's stomach grew knots. "That guy'll kill you," he said. "He'll catch you and tear your head off. That guy's a gangster, ain't he?"

JoJo said, "A gangster? What's a gangster?" He began walking around the roof, dragging a foot like he'd had a stroke. "She's killing me. Nancy kills me."

Across the street the Q-10 bus rolled gradually to the end of the block and stopped. Nancy got off the bus and stood at the curb.

"Nancy," the Ice Man called out.

They watched as she nodded and ran across the street to greet her father. All the neighborhood guys standing around would go freaky for a week and have tears in their eyes from watching her tits bounce.

Dante took the cigarette he was smoking out of his mouth and stared at the long tube of ash at the end. He said, "I bet Nancy got no idea what she does to fellas when she runs like that."

"I bet she doesn't neither," JoJo said. "Roll me a bone, will ya Dante? I gotta think."

JoJo stood for a moment at the corner of the roof, absorbed in the sight of Nancy walking. He took the joint from Dante and lit up.

JoJo Paradiso was having a wild party in his head, recalling his last conversation with his sweetie, with his Nancy. She had been tense, worried about him, the way she worried over everything. Nancy passed on the threats from her family, and at first he figured that the warnings from her father and brother were just some silly shit on their part, some dumb plot to keep Nancy in line. When he thought about it later, he felt a real tug for his girl and knew he had to do something. Show her shithead father and brother who they were fooling with when they scared hell out of his baby. He'd make them pay, drop some heavy shit on their asses for ter-rorizing Nancy in their goddamn greaseball way. Nancy, the only woman in their house, treated like some kind of black African slave, cooking for them, cleaning that dump of an apartment, to say nothing of ironing and washing, and still catching slaps when they drank that guinea red and felt tough. He'd show 'em, show 'em what tough means. Them saying they were the bosses around here and were going to spank a Paradiso, laughing when they said it, take him home by the ear and throw him down in front of his father, huh? Zip bastards should have stayed on the other side where they belonged, always talking about fucking Naples like it was a goddamn paradise.

He turned away from the street, angry. He looked over at Jimmy and Dante.

Jimmy was lighting up and Dante was sipping another beer. Dante glanced over at JoJo and seemed to smile. When he finished the beer, he rolled himself a joint and looked JoJo in the eye, JoJo reading it clear: you ain't so tough.

He couldn't figure Dante, never could and didn't much care where his wacko head was at. As for Jimmy, in all the years he'd known him he'd never seen the guy lose control. He was as cool as they came, and sharp as a f'n razor. You wanted Jimmy with you, you got Dante too and that was that, the two having been attached at the hip since first grade. Only his hanging with Dante, a cop's kid, didn't exactly put joy into his father's heart. Still, the guy was tough as nails and wildass crazy, so JoJo didn't mind hooking up with him so long as he got Jimmy in the bargain. Except how could you really trust a cop's kid? Sure, a crooked cop, but a cop nonetheless.

"Whataya gonna do, tough guy?" Dante said.

"Think," JoJo said. "I'm gonna think this through. I make my move, you guys with me?"

And Jimmy said, still gazing down into the street, "What do you think?"

"I'm asking."

Jimmy pushed himself off the parapet and moved toward him. He got up real close; JoJo could feel his breath.

"We'll be with you. We'll be there," Jimmy said.

Dante and JoJo had been his closest friends for as long as he could remember. He'd cut off a hand before he'd hurt either one of them. The three of them were, in other words, simply as close as three teenagers could be. You screwed with one, you dealt with all three. That's the way it was, the way Jimmy figured it would always be.

Dante saw Nancy talking in front of her building next door with her brother. "Hey Jimmy," he said. "C'mere will ya, and look at the size of the brother."

"JoJo," Jimmy said. "I hope you got those baseball bats in your apartment."

JoJo didn't say a word, just sat on the parapet at the corner of the roof. Dante sat down next to him.

"I ain't met a wop yet whose ass I can't beat," he said. And JoJo smiled at him.

After they'd sat and smoked for close to an hour JoJo said, "What's richer than love, I wonder? Whatever it is, that's what I feel for Nancy. My Nancy with the laughing face."

Jimmy turned away from him mumbling, "This guy's blowing me away. JoJo," he said. "One of these Italian witches around here put a curse on your ass, buddy."

They sat stoned and still, their legs stretched out, moving their feet a little this way, a little that.

"It's time," JoJo said. "I'm going down, I'm gonna go over the roof and I'm going down." He felt confident.

"No you're not," said Jimmy. "Whataya, nuts? These are big guys. They're likely to kill us."

Jimmy and Dante got to their feet. Talking past JoJo, Dante was saying that some things are worth dying for, 'specially a girl like Nancy.

JoJo told them he was not going to die, he was destined to go and love Nancy with the laughing face. "We got no plan," Jimmy said.

Dante told him JoJo got this all worked out. He goes over the roof onto Nancy's building and down her fire escape. No one is ever home in her apartment. He knocks on the window, she opens it, and okay, no problem, our boy's inside. Into her room, close the door, forget caution and common sense, all the other bullshit that slows down mere men. JoJo is an ace. JoJo wants to go down a hero.

"F'n nuts is what you are," said Jimmy. He cocked his head, watching a flock of pigeons swoop, waiting for them to settle or fly off. For a moment they seemed to be hovering just over his head.

JoJo forced himself to look Dante in the eye. "Tough guys drop like everyone else, you catch 'em right," he said. His voice was calm.

"We'll back you up," Dante said. "We'll be there. They show up we'll kick their asses good and proper."

With his pot grin in place Jimmy said, "I don't want to inhibit you two. But the way I see it, that fat bastard of an Ice Man looks like he'll go nuts and maybe grab a gun, he snags JoJo lying between his sweet daughter's legs. And forget the brother, that guy's a monster."

"Don't talk like that," JoJo said.

"Like what?"

"Don't talk dirty about Nancy."

Jimmy said, "Ey, come on, I'm serious now. You ain't really going over that roof to her apartment? C'mon, be serious. They catch you in there they'll chop you up."

"Just watch me," JoJo said. "You two pay attention and be there when I need you."

"All right, don't worry pally," Dante said. "Everything will be fine."

"And Jimmy B," JoJo said. "Nobody inhibits me. Dante," he said, "you know what 'inhibit' means?"

"Whataya think, I'm brain dead like you, you wacky asshole?" He took hold of JoJo's shoulder and squeezed. "I could inhibit the hell outta you if I had a mind to."

The guy was so f'n strong JoJo felt a tingle of pain shoot down his arm to his wrist. Dante kept talking and JoJo could barely hear his words, just the sound, like steam from a busted hot-water pipe.

"That's the weed talking," JoJo said.

"You ain't such a tough guy, you little guinea bastard," Dante said. "You're not so tough."

"You shithead you," JoJo said. "The weed. That's the weed talking, Dante, not you."

JoJo got to his feet and began pacing like a tiger. "I don't believe I let you smoke so much. You can't handle your high, never could."

"I could handle you in a f'n heartbeat." A mean hot whisper from Dante.

JoJo was about to say oh yeah? Can you handle this, you big dumb Irish bastard? but thought better of it. Chest pumping, he reached behind him and felt the butt end of the pistol he carried stuck in the waistband of his jeans at the small of his back, hidden by his sweatshirt. JoJo stood there blank with quiet rage, thinking no, that's my surprise, and surprises are best kept hidden.

———

Jimmy shut his eyes, closed them real tight.

He saw the moon full in hard silver light over the Eighty-third Street park. A candle burning on a park bench. A yellow-white flash. His brother with a rifle slung across his shoulder, smoking a joint the size of his arm. One more flash, a blue triangle. Josh again, now dancing the hora with Howie Blutstein. And Howie, that scrawny bastard, was grinning. Then a circle and square, neither of which could hold their shape. The circle within the square, blazing yellow now. Then he was on the park swings, pumping, but his lungs were empty, he couldn't find breath. The grass around the park was dingy gray, lifeless. His eyes flashed open, and he was suddenly afraid. His right arm was dangling limp at his side.

This was some mighty stuff he was smoking. Possibly it wasn't pot at all, maybe it was opium, or hash or some other insane shit.

"Guinea bastard," Dante said. "Thinks he's the toughest man in the valley. Tell him he's mistaken, Jimmy."

Jimmy shook himself loose from the high and thought it was possible that these two could go at it. See who was the heavyweight champion. JoJo, he knew, would not sit still for this "guinea" bullshit too long. Dante was powerful as an ox, a few inches taller and thirty pounds heavier than JoJo. Nevertheless, JoJo was the craziest man in the world. And he feared no one. Jimmy tried to say something, something amusing to take the edge off. He took a deep breath.

"It's the weed," JoJo yelled. Then he pulled himself free of Dante's hand, bent, and kissed him. Jimmy watched as JoJo put his hands alongside Dante's cheeks and kissed his lips.

Dante's voice mellowed. "You're a f'n nut case JoJo," he said. "And this is what worries me for you."

JoJo grinned at Dante. He looked at his watch. "Will you look at this? It's four thirty already."

"So?" Dante said.

JoJo stood and stretched, reaching for the sky. To Jimmy his eyes were extraordinary now. They were treacherous, they were tranquil. Jimmy wanted to say *damn!* loud as he could. Damn let's not do this! Scream it out. This is evil shit. Shout in JoJo's face. Only he bent his head and clenched his jaw to keep from making a sound. The weed was having its way with him. There was a film festival in his head. Josh, what in the hell did you give me?

"I don't want to be late for my Nancy," JoJo said.

Dante told him, "Just be careful, I'm too young to go to funerals for my friends." To Jimmy, it came out phony and forced.

"You want to tell us your plan or do you want it to be a surprise?" Jimmy said.

JoJo turned to look down into the street. Through an open window a floor below them they could hear shouting and laughter. JoJo's brother John was watching cartoons.

JoJo whispered hoarsely, "I'm gonna jump the roof to Nancy's building. Then I'm going down the fire escape, through her window, and into her room. I've done it plenty. I know what I'm doing."

"And us," Jimmy said. "What are we supposed to do?"

"Watch my back." JoJo went to the parapet and swung his legs over, climbing onto the roof of Nancy's building and starting down the fire escape. At the gooseneck of the fire escape he winked.

Dante called over, "I'll check the street, make sure her old man and brother don't slip up on you."

JoJo didn't answer, he waved his hand and climbed down, smiling that smile at Jimmy, showing those beautiful teeth. And Jimmy Burns nodded. In a moment JoJo came scrambling back up.

"I'm counting on you two. I don't want no shocks when I'm loving my Nancy. You see those two mutts coming, get down there, get down there real quick. It's apartment three-A."

Jimmy said, "We're here. You got nothing to worry about." Thinking you crazy bastard.

JoJo advanced down the ladder cautiously. "You do the right thing and fate will be kind to you," his father had told him. "You're a Paradiso, you teach these Vanzettis some respect, something they won't forget."

In front of Nancy's window JoJo sighed. He was thoroughly stoned. He tapped on the window, saw the curtains move and there was Nancy, still in her high school uniform. He watched as she bent to open the window. It was not easily done, and he gave her a hand. JoJo wanted his dolly, he wanted his Nancy, and he could give a shit if it killed them both.

They stood there, JoJo on the fire escape, Nancy in her room, looking at each other. They stood for a long time, a five-minute scorpion dance.

As JoJo took that first step down onto the fire escape, Jimmy leaned against the parapet and drew in a mean, deep toke on the joint he held and started thinking about a lot of things he didn't like to think about. Like what he and Dante were going to do, for one.

Dante was hawking Nancy's father and brother. The two men had walked back to Carlino's. He kept a close eye on them as they stood and chitchatted and looked around. If they had a mind to head for home, what then? Run down three flights and come up behind them in their building? Why not?

Jimmy figured that he, Dante, and JoJo could take care of business. Kick these two guys' sorry asses and then split. He walked around the roof. He felt funny. He stood near Dante, put his arms around his shoulders, and looked down into the street. Funny again. Like on the street in front of

JoJo's apartment building. Feeling like he didn't belong here. His stomach was twisting, his hands sweating.

He hated this. If JoJo knew the kind of person he really was, would they be friends, be tight? How about that one? Because the truth was—and he stood frozen, as nearby a siren wailed—the truth was, he was no gangster. No street fighter, no hard guy. He wasn't Dante, didn't get off on fistfights. He didn't run from them, could remember losing one, maybe two his entire life. But punching shit out of somebody was just not his favorite thing. No, he wasn't Dante. He'd rather suck on a titty or a joint than bite some guy's ear off. And he sure as shit wasn't JoJo, the guy had violence in his genes.

JoJo's father was a well-known wiseguy. Had had his picture on the second page of the *News* and the *Mirror* more than once. But it always followed a front-page story about a couple of other wiseguys slumped in the front seat of a car with holes in their heads.

This crap was dangerous. Maybe, Jimmy thought, he'd get Dante and run. Leave JoJo to handle his own shit for a change. Better yet, he'd just leave and tell Dante to walk with him or stay and do JoJo's dirty work. He didn't want to be part of JoJo's craziness anymore.

Or maybe what he should do is go over the roof to Nancy's building himself and drag JoJo out of there. Out of that apartment, away from the bullshit. Take JoJo on, face to face, tell him what a lunatic he thought he was. JoJo used to listen to him. Respected what he had to say. Maybe JoJo just pretended to listen, the guy's blood was fired by something Jimmy knew zero about, and that was the gospel truth. JoJo could have such rage in him. He loved to see people shit their pants when he came at them. How healthy was that? How sane? Maybe JoJo was truly a nut case? Jimmy flashed again on the newspaper photos of the two wiseguys with blood running down their cheeks.

Maybe it was time to cut it short. Stop the pretense. He wasn't JoJo, and Dante wasn't either. They weren't from 101st Avenue, where half the people had arrest records, and guns, bats, and chains in their cars. It was conceivable that all the good times were kid games and were over. Maybe it was time to make a move before some real wicked shit came down. Then again, possibly it was already too late.

"Look out," Dante said suddenly. "They're walking toward the building, coming fast, walking like fucking Mussolini with their jaws stuck out."

"Whataya mean they're coming?"

"Whataya mean what do I mean? The two morons are on the move, man, and they're coming straight here, looking pissed and mean and man, this is gonna be good, this is gonna be some shit."

Jimmy felt his heart fly around inside his rib cage. "We should go, then," he said.

"Yeah," Dante said. "I mean we can't tell our quote-and-unquote buddy we were called away on business."

With a fear knot in his belly the size of King Kong, Jimmy followed Dante down three flights of stairs to the street. Nancy's father and brother were nowhere to be seen. They went through the street door, into the darkness that was Nancy's building, and started up the stairs. Jimmy could hear the father and brother climbing the steps ahead of them. "The bats," he said, "Dante, we should have brought the bats." He felt energized and was pretty sure the energy he felt was in no small way fueled by fear.

"We don't need no bats for some fat-ass wops," Dante told him. "We'll kick their f'n asses."

Jimmy was aware that Dante was laughing; he knew a hallucinatory circus was taking place in his friend's head. I'm gonna get slaughtered, is what he thought.

Jimmy felt a terrific spasm in his chest that fanned out in a wave down into his stomach, leaked to his groin, and tightened his ass. Then he felt a rush of elation and got a giggling fit. He was strong as a bull and had a sense that something good was about to happen. He heard the door to Nancy's apartment open. The sounds that came from the two men a flight ahead of him were not of this planet.

Inside Nancy's bedroom JoJo was looking closely at his sweetie, deciding.

Her black hair framed her schoolgirl face. She was seventeen, but to him she always seemed older. He leaned close to her and put his face in her hair. Nancy smelled of strawberries and clean cloth. She had thick, full lips and they pursed for him. Sweet Nancy's pucker. Her brown eyes had never been so brilliant. She gestured sharply for him to be quiet, they had, she whispered, at the most fifteen, twenty minutes. His mind slid off to her father and brother, to his two buddies on the roof.

Nancy pulled him out of it by reaching for the front of his jeans and grabbing at him. JoJo ran his hand up and down her back and Nancy closed her eyes.

Then as gently and as quietly as he could he moved her across the room, turning her. She pulled down the zipper of his jeans, then knelt.

"Hurry," she said aloud.

Nancy put her hand inside his jeans, and JoJo parted his lips and began to breathe through his mouth.

All this past week he had told himself that what he needed to do was as obvious as neon. He'd planned it out, now everything and everyone was in place. From where he stood in Nancy's bedroom he had a perfect view from down the hall to the apartment's front door. It was good—no, better than good. It was perfect.

He closed his eyes, thinking of Nancy's father, and that mook brother of hers, Rocco. And of the look on their faces when they opened that door. He opened his eyes and gazed around at the walls and ceiling of sweet Nancy's room. Then down at the top of Nancy's head, and what he wanted, what he truly wanted was respect. Bullshit—what he wanted and what he would get was white-hot fear in the throat of an enemy. How much, though? He grooved on fear. How much was enough?

Nancy brought him from his pants to her mouth, holding him with strong hands, stroking him, kissing him and licking him, making that sound he loved, that slow, long and pretty goddamn loud mewing. He took hold of her head and caught sight of himself and the kneeling Nancy in the mirror on her closet door. He let his gaze linger. As he watched their reflection he saw his penis disappear into her mouth.

It was somewhere in there that JoJo first heard the footsteps advancing up the stairs, or thought he did. In spite of the danger or because of it, he wanted to raise that uniform skirt of hers and get deep inside her. Her panties, bra, and stockings were laid neatly on the chair by the bed.

"On the bed," he drawled. "Get up and get on the bed."

This was how he gained respect, this was how he'd have all he needed. Except he couldn't last another minute, he knew it.

Nancy moved her head away from him, smiling. She stuck out her bottom lip and said, "No time." Then she returned her mouth to his penis, coming at him with a certain amount of fury.

That's when he heard the key in the door.

Then he felt something else, felt the heat of it perceptibly in his chest. JoJo didn't have the slightest acquaintance with any kind of fear. He never once thought that he could die fairly soon. But suddenly a wave of fear the like of which he had never experienced washed over him. In this, his first moment of clear thought in the past three hours, he remembered his father's words: "It's our way before anything else. Remember, people respect only what they fear."

Nancy's bedroom was at the end of a long hallway that led to the kitchen and the door of the apartment beyond. There were people at that door, of that he was certain.

With the exception of Bruno Greco, his father's driver, no one knew that JoJo carried beneath his sweatshirt, tucked into his jeans at the small of his back, a .32-caliber revolver. "It's a small gun, a woman's gun," Bruno had told him. "But it makes a big bang and will kill you as good as anything else. Little guns bring you to God," Bruno said. "That's what little guns are for."

JoJo shifted himself and moved Nancy so that they would be clearly in view from the front door. He felt her lips, her greedy schoolgirl's mouth on him, and he leaned his head back.

At that very moment JoJo Paradiso realized that he must have accepted God. For it was God's name he was calling when they strolled through the door.

He came like Mount Etna, pulling her head to him, rising on his toes, flying with the fear, the danger, the magnificent joy of his Nancy's sucking.

It was Rocco Vanzetti that screamed first.

"Lookitcha, you dumb bitch! Look watcha doin'!"

Instinctively JoJo reached behind him where his pistol was waiting. Down the hallway he saw Nancy's father standing with both arms in the air, his cane touching the ceiling. Rocco pushed past his father, screaming as he came, and the old man too let loose a scream and some other horrible noises and followed his son. They had him just where he wanted them. JoJo held the back of Nancy's head in a death grip with one hand and with the other he pulled the pistol from his jeans. He made a sweeping motion with his arm and leveled the pistol.

———————

Jimmy knew two things from the sound of the first pistol shot: that JoJo was probably dead, and that Howie Blutstein, skinny bastard that he was, was clairvoyant. The second shot erased some of that.

He could hear JoJo's voice shouting over the screams of the Vanzettis.

Dante for his part was running stumbling up the stairs. And the guy was laughing, laughing so loud he was gagging. The dope they had smoked had done little for Dante's air-gathering ability.

The door to the apartment was open wide; Jimmy and Dante charged through it. The Vanzettis, father and son, sat on the hallway floor, their hands on their heads. JoJo had fired two shots into the ceiling, and he gave Jimmy a wide-eyed crazy grin.

Jimmy's first impulse was to run toward JoJo, but before he could he found himself flung aside by Dante. He collided with the hallway wall, banging his head, and staggered back, his face bleeding.

JoJo stood over the Vanzettis in an animal crouch. Nancy had locked herself into the bathroom. The father was screeching, loud and rough, almost a cry. Jimmy felt humiliated by the sound.

"Who's shot, who got shot?" Dante shouted.

JoJo said, "Nobody's shot. Not yet anyway."

"Okay, okay, cool down," Nancy's brother said.

The father shook his head in utter confusion. It was clear to Jimmy that he couldn't understand anything that was going on.

"Cool down?" JoJo yelled, "I'll cool down—after I put a fuckin' bullet in your heads."

JoJo lovingly stroked the pistol in his hand, ran his hand along the barrel, put a finger in the snout. He's finger-fucking the gun, Jimmy thought. A nut case, the guy's a total wack job. "Cool down," Jimmy said, and slid down the wall to the floor.

Rocco was banging his head against the wall. JoJo shoved the pistol into Rocco's ear.

"I should blow your brains out," he told him. "You were gonna beat me like a dog, drag me home, were ya? Well this is one fucking dog that bites. Maybe you've learned that now. Maybe that's all you've learned."

To Jimmy, JoJo looked as though someone was playing field hockey with his brains. They guy was over the edge and going down. He was tightening his stomach, banging on his gut, curling his shoulders. Jimmy was entirely focused on him. The rage in JoJo's eyes was total.

Dante reached under Jimmy's armpits and lifted him. "C'mon," he said, "we're outta here."

"Where the hell you goin'?" said JoJo.

"Outta here."

"You too, Jimmy?" JoJo said. "You're gonna split on me too?" He moved toward Jimmy.

Dante said, "Don't."

"You got this under control," Jimmy said. "You never said nothing about any guns. You said guns, JoJo, we wouldn't have been here. We're not about guns."

Nancy began shouting from the bathroom. "Leave, why don't you all just *leave*. Please," she cried, "you scare me, you all scare me."

"C'mon," Dante said, touching Jimmy's arm. "Make it quick, let's get going."

"All right, g'head, split. Beat it, just go, go on. You're a couple of bullshit guys anyway," JoJo said.

Nancy's father and brother weren't listening. They looked like they were lost, gone off somewhere in their own heads.

Jimmy and Dante went out through the apartment door, Jimmy holding his head. Dante had his hand on Jimmy's shoulder. He kept himself between Jimmy and JoJo.

"A couple of punks is what you are. A couple of ball-less bastards. I don't need you two."

Jimmy stood for a moment in the hallway, peering back inside the apartment. "See you around, JoJo," he said.

"Not if I see you first."

Dante led Jimmy down the stairs. Jimmy's head hurt like a bitch. "Whataya think he's gonna do to those two?" he said.

"Who gives a shit," said Dante. "Like my father says, the best thing to do with wops is give 'em guns and knives and then stand back and watch the blood fly. Fuck 'em all."

"Ey," Jimmy said, "isn't your mother Italian or am I nuts?"

Dante laughed and threw his arm around Jimmy. "Christ, did we almost get in a jam or what?"

Jimmy smirked. "I guess we won't be seeing JoJo for a while."

Dante laughed so hard he began to drool. Jimmy put his arm around Dante's waist and held him hard.

"Jimmy," Dante said, "you gotta talk to your brother. He sure is getting some weird shit lately."

They walked along 101st Avenue and turned right at Ninetieth Street, toward Liberty. Jimmy had a terrific and horrible feeling of letting go. Like nothing was ever going to be the same again. He compressed his lips and shook his head, the way Nancy's father had, sitting on the hallway floor.

"JoJo," he said, "is a f'n nut case. The guy really is bad news."

Dante raised his head to check the sun. He turned to Jimmy, a wide grin on his face.

Suddenly it dawned on Jimmy that Dante hadn't heard anything he was saying, or if he had, he didn't much care. The guy was seriously stoned. At least, Jimmy thought he was seriously stoned. Or maybe, just maybe, Dante O'Donnell didn't give a rat's ass about JoJo Paradiso and the wackiness that made up his life. As they walked along the street, Dante slapped him lightly on the back.

"Don't worry about JoJo, he's totally insane. We're from different worlds. Tell you the truth, I've felt like that for a long time. But today did it. For me the guy's history."

Jimmy shrugged. "We'll see him again," he said.

"Sure we'll see him again. We're gonna be cops, ain't we?"

"Cops?"

Dante imitated Jimmy's reaction and cracked up. "Right, cops," he said. "We're gonna be cops. I like running around playing this cowboy shit, but I want a gun of my own."

"Cops?" Jimmy said. "We'd make a hell of a pair of cops, now wouldn't we?"

"I ain't kidding," Dante said.

"Oh, I know you're serious. And that's what worries me about you."

CHAPTER TWO

twenty years later

Joseph Paradiso was an inch under six feet, powerfully built, black-haired and handsome, and when he looked straight at you and fixed you with a squint from those black eyes, if you were like most people you would turn away. There was much that was intimidating in his manner. He was spotlessly neat, and in the shops along Madison Avenue where he bought his clothing and along 101st Avenue in Queens where he walked with friends discussing the business of his business, he was very popular.

On the morning in June when JoJo left Queens for Florida, a dwarf whose name was Karl Marx Syracusa walked into a barroom on Knickerbocker Avenue in Brooklyn carrying instructions from JoJo in his head and a 9-millimeter Beretta in his pocket. The dwarf put a slug into the mouth of a man who had dared to mention JoJo's name to a grand jury.

That afternoon JoJo stood in an airport lounge at LaGuardia with a can of peanuts in his hand, watching the local news on TV. He smiled when the reporter, a redheaded man that JoJo called a mook, said, "My police department source tells me this killing was the handiwork of a Mafia shooter."

"Brilliant," JoJo said to the man on his right.

The man turned and began to move off, looking back over his shoulder at the TV. "C'mon boss," he said. "We gotta catch a plane."

Thirty hours later, JoJo sat in the passenger seat of a rented white Chrysler parked on the street midway between the Orlando Hotel and Wet and Wild Water Park.

Outside there was a warm wind; a heavy rain was due. The few palms that lined the parking lot of the hotel were shaggy and windblown. Bizarre white birds that reminded him of sea gulls but were not sea gulls walked into the light of a streetlamp. JoJo studied them, then glanced at the water park, resting his hands on the oversize attaché case in his lap. It was ten o'clock at night, and there were no people on the water rides.

JoJo was dressed casually in jeans and a blood red cashmere sweater, and on his feet were Banfi loafers over fawn-colored socks. His skin looked tanned, but JoJo was naturally dark; his jet black hair was slicked back. He had left New York City and come to Florida to meet a man whose name was Luis Valero. A man who was not a member, a man who was not an Italian. JoJo considered the fact that he was about to be part of a sitdown arranged by a Jew lawyer from South Miami, a merchant prince who owned condominiums, sailboats and airplanes, two Rust Belt congressmen and a Sunshine State senator and went to country clubs where he played golf and did business with some of the world's leading drug smugglers.

JoJo felt as though he were in the hands of strangers. He was apprehensive, more than a bit fearful. In the attaché case he carried two hundred fifty thousand in hundreds and fifties. Cuban drug dealers, he knew, can become crazy with greed and use machine guns and chain saws when they want to take your money. And they don't give two shits if you're a connected guy from New York. JoJo believed with all his heart and soul that he was at the lowest point of his life, sitting here ready to meet and do business with some rice-and-beaner in the land of sun-and-fun seekers.

They had come up from Lauderdale Airport, driven the four hours on the Florida Turnpike in the rented Chrysler, watching endless saw grass sweep by. Bruno Greco, the Paradiso family *consigliere,* drove. JoJo was big through the shoulders and appeared powerful, but Bruno dwarfed him. Both men's Mafia roots ran generations deep, and although Bruno was twenty years JoJo's senior he complied willingly and happily with any instruction JoJo gave him.

JoJo was an "under," the underboss of the Paradiso Mafia family, a family with problems, a family whose financial base had eroded. A family in the midst of losing their influence and power. The Paradisos were in need of an ongoing heavy-duty cash flow, and they needed it quickly.

JoJo's father, Salvatore, was a somber man with a dying heart. The elder Paradiso didn't make any distinction in his mind between people who tried to shoot or stab him and those who played him for a fool. The Skipper, as JoJo referred to his father, like all the old-time mafiosi, damned the blacks and Latins with one breath for their drug trade and commended their ability to earn money and squash enemies with the next.

JoJo figured that his father was past wanting drink or smoke or women. The man had paintings of Jesus and the Virgin Mary and one of Sinatra hanging on his bedroom wall. After the death of JoJo's mother, the Skipper had found Jesus.

In his youth, Salvatore was known as Sally Blue Eyes, and he had buried more than a few people. But that was when the family was young, and Sally was wild and ran in the streets. Now he was an old man in a business where people didn't get old. The last of the old-time New York dons, he was death on drugs and forbid any family member to become involved in what he called "the loathsome business."

JoJo was of a different generation and had his own view of things. He understood that Mafia money flowed upward. Family members, mafiosi who were made men, did what they had to in order to earn in the street. They brought shares of their earnings to capos, captains. The capos in turn delivered tribute to the don in the form of envelopes stuffed with cash. In a well-run and strong Mafia family there was order and efficiency. People made fortunes.

But lately the street money for the Paradisos was drying up, and Salvatore Paradiso didn't even know it. And if he did, he didn't seem to care.

The FBI and intelligence units of the NYPD described the Paradisos as an old-time family with traditional rackets: loan sharking, gambling, some union money and sophisticated hijackings and robberies. They were known as a non-drug-dealing family, a distinction that earned them no small respect from law enforcement. The family owned controlling interests in two restaurants, a trucking company, and a Rhode Island construction firm headed by JoJo's brother John. John Paradiso permed and tinted his hair, played golf and tennis, and steered clear of his younger brother. All his life JoJo had done things that John was afraid to even think about.

JoJo knew that if his father heard of the drug move he was about to make it would put leaks in the old man's heart. However, he believed with all his being that he had no options. Their family was being outmanned by the other New York families, who went about mocking the drug ban. His capos—there were five—all were hurting from seriously reduced incomes. Fading incomes and difficult times breed revolt, JoJo told his father. Christ, it was like having a conversation in a dark room with a deaf man.

The Skipper heard zero, listened to zilch; his face was crimson with fury when he told JoJo, "Right or wrong I lead this family. And I say no, not maybe. I say no." Then he threw JoJo a pretty snappy "You had better forget this shit. Use your head, that f'n business is not for us."

Recently when he spoke to his people, JoJo noticed that there were some that would move away from him. He had sniffed the unmistakable odor of a coup in the air. If that came to pass, a load of loyal people might be denied the luxury of dying in bed. For weeks he had gone about imagining a scene where he and Bruno, shot and stabbed, were stuffed into garbage bags and then dropped in a Canarsie landfill. But most of all he suffered over his father. The man had become old and sloppy, was an easy and available target. For JoJo this was not a pleasing thought. He gave himself over to the notion that for the family's survival as well as his own, the ban regarding drug dealing had to be reviewed. And to this end, two weeks earlier, he had met with his father again.

JoJo suggested that a limited entry into the cocaine business would prove worthwhile for the family. Its old power might be restored with such an expedition.

You could say that the Skipper was not impressed. "Ey dummy," he'd said, "for once and for all, I say it's a dead issue. And the reason is simple: the drug business is a business of stool pigeons, a business that gives birth to traitors. Restraint," his father told him, "is a hard notion for many of our friends, but with our thing, our *borgata,* moderation means survival." There were times his father could hold an expression of such rage in his blue eyes that JoJo could scarcely speak to him without lowering his head.

It was one week to the day after their second conversation regarding the drug move that JoJo turned to Bruno Greco.

Greco was a powerful man in his own right, with a crew of ten made men and fifty noninducted members. JoJo figured that Bruno loved the Skipper, he'd been with him from the start. His argument had to be strong. "The family will come apart," JoJo told him. "There's gonna be a war. You tell me how we're gonna come out if all the captains line up against us. We'll blow everything. I'm telling you, Bruno," he'd said, "the major event of the coming months is gonna be a mass funeral, with me, you, my father, and a batch of the others the star attractions." This exercise in reality convinced the *consigliere,* and he sullenly agreed that a drug move by JoJo was in the best interest of all.

The connection was made through a New York attorney, a Harvard graduate who had a brother that practiced international law in Miami. They were dope people on the highest level. For the first time in his life, JoJo

Paradiso had taken a step away from his father. And now he found that between his own desperate need to keep the family intact and his fascination with the business of the business of drugs, he was moving to a dismal place from which he would be unable to return. In all his life he could not have conceived that he could oppose his father's judgment about anything, and yet he was doing it. In a manner of speaking he had joined those who were turning on the family. He was off on his own, a renegade. A fence jumper.

Through the windshield JoJo could see the moon high and full, but dark and heavy clouds were moving quickly from the east, casting a dreary light. JoJo had a keen eye for approaching storms.

"I don't know how you feel Bruno," he said. "But I got a knot in my chest the size of a grapefruit."

Bruno gave a nervous sniff and a small laugh, showing smoke-stained teeth, which just made JoJo anxious, and he was already anxious enough. The idea pushed its way into JoJo's brain that the most courageous man he knew was as frightened as he was.

"Look," Bruno told him, "this thing of ours is going down the tubes. You had to step in."

"It don't matter. The Skipper gets a whiff of this I'll get no pass."

Bruno gripped his shoulder firmly. "You'll talk to him again. Try harder this time."

"Talk to him? Yeah, I'll talk to him, sure I'll talk to him. Then I'll run to you for cover."

Bruno laughed again, and JoJo smiled.

"Joseph, when it's a done deal he'll have no choice but to give his okay."

"Sez you. What if I told you that it wouldn't surprise the shit out of me if he put a rocket in my pocket?"

"C'mon, you're his kid. He lives for you. The question here, buddy of mine, is what about me?" Bruno bit at his thumbnail. "You think maybe he'll let me slide? Aw, Christ, what am I gonna do? I gotta count on you."

"He knows that you do what I tell you to. You got no problem," JoJo said. He regretted it immediately.

"You ain't so sure," Bruno said. "No more than I am. With all respect, if Sally Blue Eyes goes nuts, I better leave the planet, you know what I mean? I mean, I seen the man go, you ain't never seen him go, I seen it and it ain't pretty. Your father's got this thing with hammers and hatchets."

"I'll make the man understand. He gave me no choice. I got no options here."

Bruno lit a cigarette, tilted his head back, and blew a perfect smoke ring off the ceiling. JoJo watched him evenly with wary eyes.

"Whatta we talking," Bruno said then. "You're the man. You're the next in line. This is a new day, a whole new world. You said that, and you're right."

"I know," JoJo said. "Still, I can't shake the feeling that I'm running a sham on the old man." Clearing his throat, putting on his quietly inquiring face, JoJo said, "You wanna tell me why I should feel this way? I'm doing what's right for the family. And that's what he told me, that's what he always told me."

Bruno said, "For chrissake why are you so tense?" He sounded both rational and crazed. "What's the worst that can happen?"

"We could both wake up dead with our hands cut off and twenty-dollar bills stuffed up our ass. Waking up dead is something worth thinking about." Although the night air through the open car window was hot and humid, JoJo felt himself shiver. "Death," he said, "is not the worst thing that can happen to you, just the last."

JoJo looked at Bruno's face, sure he saw there deep interest in what he was saying. He was constantly in awe of this power he had on someone like Bruno and felt pleased with himself.

"I'm counting on you to carry this off," Bruno said. "Ain't no reason for anybody to get hurt here." He wiped his hand across his face, looked over at JoJo. "Every other family is in the business. They're making moves to pull our people away from us. The Ramminos, the Biscoglias, that psycho Tommy Renina. All of 'em sitting together counting dope money. I don't know about you, but I don't like that picture." Bruno took hold of JoJo's shoulder again and JoJo felt the power of the man; he held tight until JoJo nodded.

Bruno smiled and shook his head. "What you are doing," he said then, "is saving us. Joseph," he said, "you are the one who came to me with this."

JoJo didn't say anything. It was true, this move had been his idea. He set it up, arranged the meeting, and put the money together. But at that moment his guts were cooking. He felt like shit, felt like he was doing everything wrong.

"This boss should step down," Bruno said softly. "He can move to his place in Boca, right? The man doesn't have to prove nothing. He's seventy years old, for chrissake." He poked JoJo's shoulder and let his hand drop. "It would kill me if some renegade reached him. But we can't go on like this. Just can't."

JoJo looked at his watch and opened the car door. *"Sangu di me sangu,"* he said.

"Yeah, right, you and your father are of the same blood, that's true. That don't mean you love him any more than I do."

JoJo said, "The Italian word for drugs is *babanya. Babanya* in Italian means garbage. One time my father told me, he said that there is a difference between trash and garbage. Trash, he said, you throw out. Garbage you kill."

"Eyyyyy Joseph, give me a break, will ya? This f'n meeting we got here was a bitch to arrange. Now, we came a long way, and before we took this step we talked this through. Chrissake, it's all we been talking about this month. *Babanya* is heroin. The deal you're going to make here is for cocaine. There's a difference."

From JoJo came a deep sigh. "C'mon," he said.

"Hey, you wanna say g'bye, we leave. You're the boss."

They sat in silence for a long moment. JoJo held the car's door ajar with his knee. "When I tell my father, it's going to be interesting, don't you think?"

"We don't need interesting things," Bruno said with a strange grin. "That's not what we need. You got grumbling capos reaching for guns and knives." He looked with distaste at the parking lot and hotel. "That is what the fuck brought us down here." He gazed for a moment at the ceiling of the car, the smile still on his face, and then licked a fleck of tobacco from his upper lip.

JoJo cleared his throat. "I blame these moaning and groaning capos for this." He had hesitated to say this, fearing that such thoughts might produce silence, and worse, fear in Bruno that he might be threatening him too.

"It's their fault that I have to walk into this shitstorm. That I have to lie to my father and play him for a fool."

"There's no money out there," Bruno said.

"Is that what we're all about? Just money?"

Bruno smiled politely. "You're kidding me, right?"

"We got fence jumpers in this family," JoJo said. "More than one."

"Times are difficult. Don't think that they want to turn on your father. And don't think that they won't. Business is business. But Joseph, you know all this. You're not some wannabe on a corner somewhere."

"Maybe if we clipped a couple of these bastards, like Tony Yale and Lilo, the others would see the f'n light."

Bruno's astonishment was unsettling. "Wonderful," he said. He lit another cigarette from the tip of the one he was smoking and waved it about. They could hear disco music coming from somewhere inside the hotel. "A small family war is just what we need now. That's brilliant."

Keep your thoughts to yourself, JoJo reminded himself.

"This deal you'll make here will save your father. In truth it will save all three of us. And this thing of ours will hold together. Your father cannot win, he can only die."

"If I didn't believe that I wouldn't be here," JoJo said.

As JoJo got out of the car Bruno called after him, "Don't let that spic take you to school. Make a good deal for us."

JoJo shook his head. He glanced in at Bruno and smiled at him. "This life of ours is fun, hah?"

"Sure Joseph," Bruno told him. "It's a gas. Get going."

It was a two-minute walk to the hotel's entrance, and by the time he got to the archway the storm broke. The rain darkened the night and glistened on the pavement of the hotel's parking lot. It came in sheets, making it impossible for JoJo to see the Chrysler or Bruno, who sat behind the steering wheel pulling on his cigarette and his fingers. Blinded by the rain, Bruno Greco knew that when the truth was known, there would be no goddamn way he could talk himself out from under the rage of Sally Blue Eyes. He contemplated his remaining two options, as he had been contemplating all his options during the past month: he could run—South America or maybe Europe would be good—or he could strike first. Bruno considered that he was not and never had been much of a runner.

JoJo entered the hotel through the front doors and walked as casually as he could past the desk. The weight of the oversize attaché case he carried caused his shoulder to ache. Families in swarms crowded the narrow hall-way—exhausted tourists returning from a day's outing at Disney World on their way to their rooms. A British family of three walked slowly in front of him. The father displayed a four-foot Mickey Mouse to a party of red-faced friends.

At a bank of elevators JoJo stopped and looked around him. He felt himself shiver, this fear that ate at him was awful. He knew instinctively that this was his moment. His life had led him here. And as part of the same thought, that this life he had chosen was a madhouse life. He recalled his twenty-first birthday, the night he was inducted. How he took a gun and knife from his father's table. All the capos were there, and it was Bruno Greco who placed a picture of Saint Ignatius in his hand and with the half smile that goes with knowledge put fire to that paper and asked him to recite the incantation.

" 'I will use these tools for the benefit of the people at this table and for any friend not present. May I burn in hell, hand in hand with other lost souls, if I betray anyone here, or any friend not present.' " It was like joining the goddamn Elks or Rotary. Ridiculous shit.

It was Bruno's lips that he kissed second only to his father's. He remembered the panic later that night when it came to him that he was then and forever, like his father and both grandfathers, an inducted member, a made man. Standing, dreaming or imagining in the hallway of the Orlando Hotel, he recalled all the hugs and kisses. How he allowed the mood to move him along that night. He remembered too, how a man roars and no sound is heard when you make a clean head shot. He flashed on the first time and freaked. Afterward Bruno found him and told him, "Don't let it get to you. The man was an enemy of your father's. A drug dealer, a man without honor."

On the second floor, in front of room 237, blinking and breathing deeply as if trying to decide something, he knocked twice, then once again and waited.

CHAPTER THREE

While JoJo Paradiso was dealing with the most important moment of his life, New York City Police Detective First Grade Dante O'Donnell was screaming obscenities at his lifelong friend and partner Saul Burns, who for the past twenty-five years had been called Jimmy. That was because back when Dante was twelve his father, Big Dan O'Donnell, a sergeant in the Public Morals Division and a citywide bagman, would not allow a son of his to have a best buddy and hang out with a boy who had a pansy Jew name like Saul.

"You're not going to make me drive that big crazy tobacco-chewing son of a bitch to another one of those scenes," Dante told Jimmy. "I'm not going. You wanna go, g'head. Take the car, have a party. I'll wait here."

"You're coming."

"I'm not."

"I promised the man."

"Then go. Freddie Miller is the only cop in the f'n world that doesn't drive a car. The man's a nut factory. Did you know that the Internal Affairs Division is investigating him for murder of all his neighbors' dogs and cats?"

"He said it was an accident."

"Yeah, an accident. Did he tell you about the pigeons?"

Jimmy began to smile, those bright blue eyes shining at Dante. "What about the pigeons?"

"The stiff's learning to be a taxidermist, right. I had to be drunk, or on drugs, I don't know. Anyway, he convinces me to help him round up six of these gutter eagles. Says he needs the birds so he can practice. Me and him, we snatch a half dozen down near the courthouse, use this big old net."

Jimmy's expression didn't change, though the amused look in his eyes seemed to grow.

"So the loony takes the birds home. Now, what he tells me is that he doesn't want to damage the filthy things. So he stuffs them in his refrigerator, figures he'll freeze 'em to death. New York City birds're used to cold weather, you know what I mean? The next morning he opens his refrigerator door and they all zoom out. Fly all around his kitchen, shit on everything in sight. Freddie, the wack job that he is, rounds them up and tosses them into a plastic bag. He takes the bag into his garage and attaches it to the exhaust pipe of the family Toyota. The loony figures he'll asphyxiate them. Only instead the bag catches fire, the birds fly out, and he burns down half his house. The guy's f'n nuts, he's always had half his lights out. How this city in all its wisdom gave Freddie Miller a gun and badge is beyond me."

Jimmy gave a short mean laugh and slapped the oval edge of the bar with both hands. He cleared his throat. "I need to make a call," he said loudly. "Get us a couple of beers and bring them to the table."

They had worked late, missed supper, and stopped in at Monahan's on Pitken Avenue to have a sandwich and a brew. For a Friday, the place was slow. A few regulars stood at the bar, old-timers like Fat Willie, Ronnie P, and the Twins, and of course there was man-eater Katie the Greek, wearing her prescription sunglasses, playing "Blue Velvet" for the six billionth time, whining about Bobby Fives, the way he'd skipped on her. The bartender, whose name was Sam Mosca, was an inordinately short man whom Freddie Miller called Treetop.

When Jimmy left him standing alone at the bar, Dante had two beers and a ball, forgot the sandwich and did it again, two beers and a ball. Freddie Miller, who weighed just a little less than the jukebox and who could put a serious hurt on you with the tips of his fingers, bellied up to the bar. He called on the bartender for a Bud on tap, finished it off, and, giving a belch that came from his toes, squinted those crazy green eyes of his and said, "Jimmy tell ya that I need a lift to the One-four-four?"

Dante was thirty-nine, two years younger than Freddie Miller, and he came from a row house in Ozone Park that was one block down and two blocks over from the one in which Freddie had been born. One of his first memories, from when he was five or six, was of watching in horror as Freddie taped the tails of two cats together and flung them over a clothesline. Now, looking at demented Freddie, Dante could see his luck changing from disagreeable to desperate right before his eyes.

"Later," Dante told him.

Freddie looked concerned and bug-eyed. He was a wild man, a legend among cops for twenty years. "I'm supposed to be working," he said. "But I'm here hiding out."

"We'll drive you," Dante told him. Then he subjected Freddie Miller to a sustained barrage of verbal abuse, telling him what a wacko son of a bitch he was. Hoping beyond hope that at some point Freddie would fly off the handle and tell him to forget the ride, that he'd find his own way to the Bronx. But Freddie just fixed him with his nonsmile and said, "You just don't understand me. You never did." He drained his glass and called to the bartender, "Hey Treetop, jump up on a chair and give me another."

Five minutes later, his hands wrapped around two glasses of beer, Dante moved across the barroom. He wondered where Jimmy was, at their table certainly, but where was that exactly and how would he get there? Dante O'Donnell had had a few too many, more than a few. He finally made his way to the table to find Jimmy staring at him, holding back, trying to appear casual.

"According to my sources, Dante, which are A-one reliable, I'm told you've been hitting the sauce pretty regular again."

"Where'd you hear that?"

"It looks to me that they were right on. You're drinking full time again, ain't ya?"

Dante moved a chair out and sat down at the table. "I don't like you checking up on me."

"Since we've been friends for about thirty years, I figure I got the right."

There was a long pause before Dante said, "I don't like it. I don't think it's any of your concern what I do."

"That's bullshit," Jimmy said.

"Whataya mean?"

"You want me to rephrase it? You're drinking too much."

They sat in silence, Jimmy staring at Dante until Dante said quietly, "I miss my kid, I didn't think I'd miss my boy so much."

"I know," Jimmy told him. "You'll take the oath, make promises you won't keep, and Judy will take you back."

Dante squinted at him, thinking, Maybe if I'm lucky she won't. "You think so?" He spoke slowly, judiciously. "I got this feeling that this time she might be through with me. And who can blame her?"

Jimmy patted Dante's hand and smiled sadly. "Judy's put you out what, five, six times? The women I know wouldn't put up with your shit for a minute. Judy's different, she's a neighborhood woman, one of the last of her kind. Got a heart as big as Shea Stadium."

And an ass to match, Dante wanted to say but thought better of it. Instead he told Jimmy that the women he knew were sluts. "Far as women go, Jimmy, you haven't made any great strides since you were a kid."

"Not sluts, independent is what they are. But you're right, I have no luck with women. And that's why I'm not married."

"I know."

"But I'm happy."

"So you say. Listen," Dante said, "you don't really expect me to drive Miller to the Bronx."

"Sure I do. I promised the man. 'Nuff said."

At times when he'd seen his luck go all to hell, Dante would walk the streets of the old neighborhood. He'd stand on the corners and watch the kids play. Now and then he would walk to the Eighty-third Street playground, climb the monkey bars and ride the swings. Sometimes he'd get to the park late at night and ride the swings till dawn.

Looking around the bar, Dante sighed. Jimmy had it all wrong. He wasn't drinking because Judy wouldn't let him back in, he was drinking, in fact, because he didn't want to go home. At least he thought he didn't want to go home. He was thinking that he didn't know what to think. When he'd left his house two days before, he felt something powerful click in him, something that had been building for a long time.

From time to time at home he would stand in front of the mirror and pull at his lip with his thumb and first finger, vaguely afraid that he was becoming his father. Now and then he would imagine a shape lying in the street and would see in his mind's eye his own death. Lately he'd been troubled by dreams.

"You know," Dante said. "What I'd really like to do is get a couple of six-packs and yeah, maybe even a joint, drive to the park, down the ramp, throw the Five Satins, Dickie Do and the Dont's, and why not? maybe a little Joanie James into the tape deck. 'Crying in the Chapel' would whip my ass. Put on a little buzz and listen to tunes. How's that sound?"

"A joint? That's just what you need now. Will you stop trying to go back. How many times do I have to tell you that going back ain't healthy?"

"Going back sometimes is the best thing I have. At times I feel like it's all I have."

"That's it," Jimmy announced. "He's cut off. No more for him, Katie. Dante," he said gently now, "you're loaded, and you look terrible."

"Thanks."

"You looked fine yesterday."

"Judy didn't tell me 'I never want to see you again' yesterday. I've been trying to stay drunk, this is what I look like when I drink."

Katie, a little crazy behind her gay smile, placed bowls of chips and peanuts in front of them. Freddie Miller waved from the bar, pointing to his wristwatch. He seemed merry and held a glass of beer in the air.

Leaning back, Dante lit a cigarette and stretched. "So we'll go to the Bronx. You promised the guy, we'll go. But I'm telling you, and I'll tell him later: this is the last f'n time."

"Freddie never goes home," Jimmy said. He glanced around the bar and shook his head. "What a life, the guy's got no life."

Dante shook his own head slowly and rested his chin on his fist. "He ain't the only one. Cops make the worst husbands, the worst fathers. You tell me who could be worse."

"You want an answer?"

Dante gave him a thin sad smile. "I didn't ask you a question."

"You certainly did."

"Go on then, who could be worse than cops?"

"Wiseguys, wiseguys make the worst husbands. You don't know what problems are till you marry a wiseguy."

"But you got cash."

"That's for sure. Then you got to figure how much value you place on money. Money versus sanity. A wiseguy would definitely drive any normal person wild."

Dante's elbow collapsed. "The way I see it, you marry a wiseguy, you ain't normal. Screw wiseguys."

"No, no listen," Jimmy said. "Say you're married to a wiseguy. You've got to know the guy's got one, maybe two women stashed. He's paying their bills, taking care of them. Wiseguys don't carry life insurance, and sooner or later they end up in a trunk of a car wrapped in a carpet. Marry a wiseguy, you end up broke and alone."

"They're bums, Jimmy. They're all bums. Fuck wiseguys."

There was something slightly contemptuous about the way Jimmy looked at him, and Dante didn't like it. Jimmy seemed preoccupied. Dante was no dummy, he thought of himself as a thinker. And he was in pretty good shape, but around Jimmy he always felt a little slow and too heavy. Jimmy Burns had the features and the kind of sandy curly brown hair that old hippies had. And on the police test when he'd taken it, the guy scored a near perfect ninety-eight. Ten points higher than Dante had. Since they were kids on the block, women always chased Jimmy.

"Wiseguys aren't all bums, Dante. You know that, they're not all bums."

"This is a dumb conversation," Dante said. "I hate talking to you when you're in this frame of mind."

"You asked a question and I answered it. Simple. I guess you don't like the conversation because you're drunk."

"I'm not drunk," Dante said tilting back in his chair. "I've been drinking. I don't get drunk, goddammit."

"That's the worst kind of drunk."

"I'm not so bad," Dante said, startled.

"You're the top-of-the-line human being," Jimmy said. Then in a soft voice he said, "Speaking of wiseguys, I guess we're going to see a whole lot of JoJo."

"I guess."

"With the bug at the social club and the wiretap on the old man's phone, just no way to avoid it," Jimmy said.

Dante smiled as Jimmy frowned. He made a quarter turn in the chair he sat in. He was an ace at sizing up his partner. Suddenly jumping up from his chair real quick like he had sprouted wings, he caught sight of Katie waving at him. "Wait," he said. "Katie, bring us another round, that's a good girl."

"Just rinse your mouth with soda this time, will ya," Jimmy said. "You're beginning to smell."

"No, wait, wait, let me think about this. I figure you're in this weird frame of mind because of the Paradiso case. Because we took this case and got those wires."

Katie brought two beers and a shot of Jack Daniel's for Dante.

"You're gonna have another beer and ball? What are you, losing your mind? A beer and a ball, you're drinking like some old Irish barhound."

"Well that's what I am, ain't it?"

"That's true."

Dante sucked thoughtfully on a peanut. "You're on my case," he said, "because your head is twisted over this Paradiso thing. Am I right?"

"No. I don't give a flying fuck about JoJo."

"Sure you do," Dante said. "Look," he said, "me, you, and JoJo haven't exactly been skintight over the past years. And this is what we do, we work wiretaps on wiseguys. That's our job. Been doing it for thirteen years for chrissake." Dante whisked the Jack Daniel's from the table and downed it without flinching. "I hate the bastard. Always have."

There was a long pause.

Dante said, "I should have known you'd pull this shit. We talked about this case before we went in. You said fine, fine let's do it."

"Well maybe I'm changing my mind. We used to spend time at the man's house, for chrissake. His mother fed us. How can we work this guy?"

"Whoa! Hold it. That's when we were kids. We're not kids any more Jimmy. JoJo went bad, he followed his old man and went to bed with the wiseguys."

"JoJo," Jimmy said. "Good ol' JoJo. Listen buddy, this city is full of wiseguys. If we needed to work one this badly why not pick some asshole we don't know? Someone we didn't grow up with. What kind of people are we?"

Dante sighed and decided that he needed another Jack Daniel's. "Listen, hotshot," he said, "it's too late now. We're on the lines and going in."

"What crap," Jimmy said. "What kind of country is this anyway where we put bugs around people and tap their phones?"

Dante fixed his eyes on Jimmy the way he would on some bad guy giving him a ration of shit. But Jimmy's eyes didn't waver or lower. After a long moment Dante said, "The kind of country where it's a serious crime to be a member of a Mafia family."

Jimmy's face got a dreamy look. "Right," he said. "C'mon, let's me and you run Freddie up to the Bronx and forget JoJo for a while."

"God," Dante said. "I hate the f'n Bronx. If I had to work there I doubt I'd survive an hour." Dante smiled at Jimmy, feeling good.

"C'mon, let's get going."

"I don't like going into any station house when we been drinking," Dante said. "It's a bad policy. Dangerous is what it is. And I'm gonna tell you something else, pally. JoJo Paradiso is a shithead."

"I'll tell *you* something *pally*," Jimmy said. "We all ate shit growing up—but we ate shit together."

By the time Dante got to his feet, Jimmy was already heading for the door. "When you go to the ol' One-four-four," he said over his shoulder, "you're better off a little ripped."

Katie took off her sunglasses, she gazed at the ceiling and started to sing. Freddie Miller was perched on the edge of a barstool. One side of his mouth twitched in a weird smile. "I need to get to the One-four-four," he said.

"We'll take ya," Dante said, thinking hard. Jimmy was nodding. "I'm just trying to find the bright side of this f'n trip," Dante told him.

"You do that Dante," Katie said. "Remember, no matter how bad things get there is always one bright side."

Dante smiled. "That's nice Katie, nicely put. You're a sweet woman. A ditz, but a sweet woman."

As the three men walked out the door Katie called after them, "As for me, I can never find it. I can never find that part. The bright-side part."

Jimmy said, "You're a big girl Katie, keep trying."

Dante swung his arm in a broad gesture. "We are out of here," he said. "Off to mambo land. The dark side of the moon." He held the door of the parked squad car open while Jimmy looked the street over. Freddie climbed into the back seat.

Dante stretched, throwing his arms into the air. "De dark side of de moon is where we're going. Let all peacefulness vanish." He got into the driver's seat and waited for Jimmy to get in next to him. "This is it for you Freddie. You hear me?" Dante said as he drove off. "This is the last f'n time. You make me crazy. You know that, don't you, you demented bastard?"

"Aw c'mon," Freddie pleaded like a ten-year-old.

They rode in silence for a time, then Freddie said with a warm and frisky grin, "Did you guys know that every year we throw away enough aluminum to rebuild the entire American air fleet, enough paper to build a twelve-foot wall from New York to L.A., and enough iron and steel to rebuild every car that comes out of Detroit for a year?"

Dante and Jimmy cross-fired Freddie with frowns in the rearview.

"Yup," Freddie said. "One hundred and fifty million tons of shit comes out of this country every year. You guys know that? You read *Time* or *Newsweek,* you guys read anything? Watch a little PBS?

"I bet you don't know that street-prowling, rock-dwelling scumbags take no responsibility for their acts," Freddie went on. Dante bit at his fist. "They are no different than machines without feeling or conscience. My God, we live in an age of impersonally cool aggression. The skel, the perp, the street pariah feel no kinship with their victims. Did you know that?"

"We know," Jimmy said. "We've heard that."

"Did you guys know—"

"Shut the fuck up, Freddie," Dante said.

From Freddie Miller came a disgusted hiss.

"You know shit," Freddie said. "Dante you're just a dumb fucker that don't know anything."

Dante knew that he prayed for Freddie to roll out of the back door and die.

"Dumb, blind asshole. That's you Dante," Freddie said. "You ain't changed in twenty-five years."

"Enough!" Jimmy said.

"Anyway, I love you Dante," Freddie said. "I always have."

Dante tried to smile but he couldn't. He drove, staring blankly at the Grand Central Parkway, the Triborough Bridge rising before him. Mid-span he thought he could hear gunshots and screams from the dingy streets of the South Bronx.

Twenty minutes later they arrived at the 144th station house. It was a South Bronx precinct that bordered northern Harlem, a precinct whose population was totally black except for a sliver on its eastern edge that was mixed South American and Puerto Rican. The place was a war zone.

Freddie bounded from the back seat, carrying a sack slung over his shoulder. He appeared to Dante to be in a downright jovial mood. Freddie took the steps of the ancient precinct house two at a time, went through the door, and disappeared.

After a moment Dante and Jimmy got out, and Dante started to go up the steps, but Jimmy put his arm around his shoulders and squeezed him hard.

"We've got to talk about JoJo," Jimmy said. "I don't feel right about what we're doing."

"Ey, it's a done deal, man. Forget JoJo, goddammit. We've got this crazy bastard Freddie to deal with now."

"You remember the summer of 'seventy-three? Right before we came on the job? You were down at the Linden Café and ran into those guys from City Line. Remember that?"

"Yeah, I remember. Sure I remember. So what?"

Jimmy fixed his jacket, tucked in his shirt. "So what? So those grease-balls were gonna take you apart. You going in that dive telling everybody you could kick the ass of any guinea there. You remember that?"

"So?"

"You remember who showed up and marched you out of the place?"

They stared at each other for half a minute.

"You know what Jimmy? You blow my mind," Dante said softly, shaking his head in amazement. "Let's not me and you get into a heavy thing here. We talked about this case, we both decided to go with it."

Jimmy shrugged and pulled a box of Marlboros from his breast pocket. He flipped it open with his thumb and extended the pack to Dante.

"Fine," Dante said. "JoJo probably did save my ass that night. Only to tell you the truth, if I hadn't been half smashed I probably would have done all right."

"All right? You're kidding me, right? The way I heard it, not for JoJo they would have taken you out of the Linden in a bag."

"Oh yeah?" Dante said flatly. His guts were starting to cook, Jimmy always standing up for JoJo. He felt like saying the bum's a no good killer, you dumb shit. He ain't your friend, how could he be. Instead he grabbed Jimmy's shoulder, gave him a little shove. "I'll tell you what I remember about the guy. I recall how he got himself a blow job from some kid and set it up so her father and brother could watch."

"He married that kid, pally."

"So what? That doesn't change what he did. The guy's a half-assed nothing. Period. And I'm gonna lock his ass up."

"Sure, sure."

"Snap out of it, will ya Jimmy? C'mon now, we're gonna go in this f'n station house and watch your other friend, nut factory Freddie, do his stuff."

He held out his hand for a slap. Jimmy gave him a half swipe that ended in a quick grab, and they marched up the stairs into the station house.

––––––––––––

Freddie Miller put on a show, and he presented that show in a converted storage room known as Bugsy's room.

A couple of years back, the city had decided that it would be a whole lot wiser and far cheaper to refurbish the antique precinct house than to build a new one. At the time, Freddie worked as the detectives' clerical man. Along with the detective squad commander, who was as nutty as he was, they somehow convinced the construction workers to build a trapdoor in the second-floor storage room closet and to put a two-way mirror in the wall that separated the detectives' squad office and the storage room. The trap door opened into a hallway that ran from the detectives' office to the stairway down to the front desk and the muster room beyond. The dilapidated storage room was cleaned and painted Bulgarian precinct gray, and a stout oak chair was bolted to the floor. And so it was that a storage room became an interrogation room. When the squad detectives ran into an unusually tough nut and were in need of information, they called on Freddie Miller. Just a few chosen people were allowed to catch his act, and they would bust a gut watching Freddie work.

For most of his twenty years in the department, Freddie Miller had been a clerical officer. But like most police officers, he had a passion for interrogations. Which was perhaps why, early in his police career, crazed Miller had been taken from the streets and hidden in an office. He was six feet four inches tall and two hundred eighty pounds of nut job, and few things in life gave him more pleasure than to do a soft shoe on the head of some tough-ass street slug. Only times had changed. Protests from pounded prisoners brought attention and neverending problems from the Internal Affairs Division, who just loved to come down with righteous indignation on the back of some overzealous cop. So it was the tenor of the times that drove Miller to come up with a scheme that would make him a Bronx legend.

Dante and Jimmy were standing in the detectives' squad room looking through the two-way glass mirror at two black detectives, one small and one tall, a real Mutt and Jeff team. They spoke calmly and reasonably with an overweight killer who had been nabbed leaving the scene of a drugstore robbery after having blown away the store's West Indian owner and his twenty-four-year-old son. The prisoner, a black Hispanic, was handcuffed to the oak chair, and from a speaker connected to a transmitter in the interrogation room, Dante and Jimmy and the detective squad commander could hear their conversation quite clearly.

The tall detective dropped into a squat next to the prisoner and spoke to him softly. "We know you ain't no genius. But you got a good memory. We want the names of your crime partners."

The prisoner was thirtyish, a fat man in a loose sweatshirt and camouflage pants. "I was out shopping," he said, "these fellas did this robbery, there was shooting and shit. Man, I crashed, man. I rolled to the floor. Didn't see a thing."

"Pigshit, we got two witnesses that spied you holding a gun," the tall detective said. "It may not be the killer weapon, but you were in on this, and you were armed."

"Uh-huh, see what I mean? I wanna tell the truth but you guys don't wanna hear it. What you wanna hear? Tell me what you want me to say and I'll say it."

"The truth, pigshit," the short detective whispered. "Just the truth is all we want to hear."

The prisoner slowly and incredulously wagged his head.

"Well, you think about it," the tall detective said. "We're gonna go out and get some coffee. We'll only be a minute, you sit here and think about questions and answers."

ROBERT LEUCI   •   4 2

They left the interrogation room and joined Dante and Jimmy and the squad commander in the detectives' squad office. The five detectives stood in the darkness of the room staring through the mirror at the prisoner, who was at that moment stretching his neck, rolling his shoulders, trying to touch the tip of his nose with his pointy tongue.

Then the closet door in the interrogation room opened slowly, and what the prisoner, whose name was Domingo Valdez Cruz, would later claim he saw was enough to have him admitted to the psycho ward of Lincoln Receiving Hospital for observation.

Whispering obscenities, two hundred eighty pounds of six-foot-four-inch beefy white rabbit came through the door carrying a sap. He hopped around the room, twirling the sap over his head as he went. The prisoner shot erect in his chair and gazed in shock as the gigantic white rabbit bounded in front of him and swung the sap recklessly, hitting him first on his right shoulder and then on his left. The next few seconds involved several panic-stricken shouts from the prisoner. Then the rabbit did a neat pirouette and whacked Domingo Cruz with a nice backhand across the cheek, ending in a high faultless followthrough, a blistering shot that made the giggling detectives shudder. Freddie Miller skipped playfully in his rabbit suit to the closet, opened the door, and went inside, whispering, "The truth will set you free."

The Mutt and Jeff detectives went back into the interrogation room to find the prisoner squirming, kicking his feet, and screaming, "Hurry, hurry man, a big fuckin' rabbit just went into that closet. No shit, I'm telling you it went in there." His voice boomed through the walls and echoed around the station house.

"Excuse me?" said Mutt.

"You've gone nut job," said Jeff.

"Just open the fuckin' closet, he's in there. Be careful man, he's got this blackjack, and big crazy green eyes."

The tall detective opened the closet door while his partner stood with arms folded, repeating over and over, "Nut job, you've gone batshit on us."

The closet was about as empty as a pimp's heart, wacky Miller having made his retreat on hands and knees through the trapdoor; he stood now in his fluffy outfit with Jimmy and Dante and the squad's commander, who were at that moment doubled over laughing.

"Ey, pigshit," the tall detective said, "don't try and pull that psycho bullshit on us."

"He needs more time," said the short detective.

"This is a crazy house," said the prisoner. "I'm telling you fools that there's a rabbit in that closet. He went right in there. I seen him go, a big white motherfucker of a rabbit."

"That right?" said the tall detective. He opened the closet door again cautiously and smiled with satisfaction while Domingo Cruz strained in his chair, trying to get a looksee into the closet.

"All right man," said the short detective, "we'll be right back." He smiled patiently and started for the door, followed by his partner, who spoke slowly and deliberately to the prisoner.

"You poor tormented asshole. You really think you saw a rabbit in here. See, ya see what guilt can do to your head? Cleanse yourself!" he bellowed. "Tell the truth."

"Don't go!" cried Domingo Cruz as they left. "That fuckin' thing is gonna come outta there. Man, I know he is." Alone again, the prisoner laughed, but the laughter was more than a little strained.

Suddenly the closet door flew open and Freddie Miller, now armed with two slappers, bound into the room. Dante stepped back away from the mirror and went to a cluttered desk covered with files and photos and fingerprint forms. In the clutter was a stained and smudged Polaroid photo that had been taken at the robbery scene by members of the Major Case Squad.

Taking care so that the other detectives would not see, Dante palmed the photograph. The picture in his hand was unbearably gruesome. Holding it at arm's length, he stood transfixed. As the laughing, chattering detectives watched the creative antics of crazed Miller, Dante studied the results of a point-blank shotgun blast. A middle-aged black man spread-eagled in a corner, a gaping hole in his chest; the dead man's son, his arms crisscrossed over his face, a crater where the back of his head had been. There was urine and vomit, splattered blood and bone on the walls and floor behind the store's counter. Dante thinking, this is hell, this is what hell's all about.

Dante looked up and saw the backs of the squad commander and the Mutt and Jeff detectives and was actually glad to see Jimmy's smiling face. He stood with his arms folded, head cocked to the side, looking at him.

"Bad, ain't it?" Jimmy said.

"The worst."

A horrible scream came from the prisoner as Freddie Miller took the man's chin in one of his furry mitts, held the back of his head with the other, and then quickly, with a certain amount of passion, bit the side of his neck. Then he slapped the prisoner across the face with one gigantic paw and bounded off into the closet joyfully screaming, "The truth, truth will set you free!"

When the pair of detectives reentered the room, the prisoner literally tried to tear himself from the bolted oak chair. He was bawling; crazy madhouse sounds were coming from him.

"Christ, man," he said. "G'head, ask me them questions. I'll tell ya what happened, man. It weren't me anyways. It was that gangster Blue Moon. It was him what capped those people. I'll tell ya where he's at. Just don't let that crazy motherfucker of a rabbit back in here."

The Mutt and Jeff detectives looked knowingly at the mirror, silently agreeing with their giggling lieutenant, who was beaming as if he were proud of Freddie.

"They call him Satan," Dante said. "That's what's on those print cards there. They call this dude Satan in the street."

The squad commander was creeping closer to the mirror, singing softly as he went. It was a Doors tune, one of Dante's favorites.

"Hey Lieutenant," Jimmy said softly. "Can you see to it that someone runs crazy Miller back to Queens?"

The lieutenant turned and smiled a smile of anarchy.

"Don't call him crazy," said the squad commander. Then he turned his back on Jimmy again and got up real close to the mirror, not wanting to miss a single second of the personal retribution of the law. "Don't ever call that man crazy. It's my theory that Officer Miller is the Avenging Angel of the Lord."

"In a rabbit outfit," said Dante.

"Zingo bingo bang. Whatever works," said the squad commander. "This is the South Bronx. If you're looking for sanity you're in the wrong place." He turned with a big smile, which was met by Jimmy and Dante with stony silence.

"You guys can split," the lieutenant said with a certain amount of gusto. "We'll take Officer Miller home."

"Good," said Jimmy.

"Great," said Dante.

"But before you leave," the squad commander told them, "stop in the captain's clerical office. There's a narco detective named Pope."

"Felix Pope?" asked Dante.

"You know him?" the lieutenant said, his lips parting over a crooked smile. "Tell Detective Pope that I would very much like to see him."

The lieutenant stopped smiling; bobbing his head, he began pacing, talking to himself, scratching at his groin. Then he began to hum a tune that neither Jimmy nor Dante could identify.

CHAPTER FOUR

Detective Felix Pope sweated behind a large olive green desk. The only furnishings in his office besides the desk he sat behind were a wall of file cabinets, an old-fashioned wooden coatrack, and a percolator. Laid out across the desk were stacks of money; Detective Pope sat in back of rows of stacked tens, twenties, fifties, and hundreds. In a cardboard box on the floor alongside his leg were singles rolled into barrels held tight by brilliant red rubber bands.

"I'd offer you guys a chair," he said, "but as you can see there is only one and I'm in it. Bad luck."

"Felix! Jesus Christ, old pal, you went and hit the lottery," Jimmy said. "Buddy of mine, you be careful in here. Keep the lights on and your gun handy, you could be mugged, it's not unheard of."

"We took down a crack house with a group of kids in it." He said this loudly and repeated it.

"How much?" said Dante.

"Plenty," said Jimmy.

"I'm up to twenty-five big ones. There has to be, shit man, I don't know, at least three times that much here."

He told them he and his team took down a drug plant on Southern Boulevard. The money was a surprise. Whack, just like that, down comes a door, boxes of money on the floor.

No one spoke.

The moment Dante set foot in Felix's office and saw all that cash, he convinced himself that the loop-de-loop taking place in his stomach was physical, brought on by maybe a gallon of beer and a few JDs. Yet standing there, the feeling intensified. He'd been around money before, seen plenty of cash seizures. Only he'd never been quite this broke before. He was unaccustomed to this feeling that grabbed at his throat and suffocated him. Say the truth, he told himself. Under the right set of circumstances, if the moon and planets lined up just the right way, you'd grab some.

He was constantly broke, it was a fact of his life, always had been. He fought endlessly with Judy over the necessity to squeeze the dollar. The house he'd bought last year way the hell out on Long Island, the taxes on that house, the second car for Judy, the insurances, and that commuter gas bill were whipping his ass. He was seven days from the next payday and he carried, what, twenty bucks in his pocket. His checking account was bouncing off zero. A black hole is what he called the new house. A hole, a pit, a money-eating machine.

As if reading his thoughts, Jimmy said, "One hit like this, partner, there goes your cash-flow problem."

Dante winced inside. "Anytime you want to become an outlaw, Jimmy, let me know. We can work it out."

"Just like that. You make it sound easy."

"Joking. You know I ain't serious."

And Jimmy said, "Sure I know. I know you." He seemed relieved, though, with a hint of suspicion.

Felix Pope said, "Ain't this a bitch? The oldest perp in this crew of dealers is eighteen. Imagine that, an eighteen-year-old spitting, stuttering kid with close to a hundred grand in his kick."

"He did his thing, you did yours," Jimmy said. "He's inside eating cheese sandwiches, you're out here counting his money. Who's the winner?"

Felix hunched over the desk, leaning on his elbows. "You tell me," he said. "This dunce will be out tomorrow and I'll be ducking bricks with twelve bucks in my pocket till payday." He paused a moment, studying the piles of cash. Then he shrugged. "This war on drugs is lost," he side-mouthed. "It's time to accept it. The people cannot be changed. If I were another kind of man, I'd keep a pile of this good cash as a reward for showing up in this zoo."

Dante smiled. "Yeah, I know what you mean. Believe me, this being-poor shit is starting to get old." He winked at Jimmy. "You tired of being poor Jimmy?"

"Nah," Jimmy said. He smiled too and shrugged, embarrassed.

"Just kidding," said Dante.

Jimmy said, "Good. Then I don't have to worry about breaking in a new partner because my old one's brain fell out his ear." He gave Dante his I'm-tired smile. "And I'm not kidding."

———

The precinct house was a red brick building that sat among the ruins of the South Bronx on Bathgate Avenue. Lit by streetlamps and a full moon, the street took on the characteristics of the main drag in downtown Beirut. Standing in the street on the driver's side of the squad car, Dante absently toyed with the car keys. "I'm gonna punish Miller for this damn trip," he told Jimmy.

"It's over," Jimmy told him. "Get in the car and bring us back to Queens. I'm wasted. Wake me when we get there."

The thought of a lost night in the Bronx watching crazy Miller jump around in his rabbit outfit while a trio of just as nutty detectives laughed and clapped made Dante's insides boil. And Pope, when they told him the lieutenant needed him in the squad room, confirmed his suspicions that the squad commander too had fallen off the edge. "The lieutenant's nuts," he'd said. "The squad commander talks to Elvis and Malcolm X. The Bronx is crawling with madmen."

The 144, Dante kept thinking, was always a kick. Blown-up and burnt-out people and buildings, the whole place was lost and condemned. Something had gone wrong.

Driving back to Queens in the squad car, Jimmy quiet, asleep on the seat next to him, Dante wondered about the shape of his life. Back at home in Ozone Park with his mother—talk about your downward mobility. At least the ten-minute emptying of his bladder proved that his body chemistry, together with his father's Irish heart, could still handle a gallon of beer and a few hits of booze.

At least they still have each other, he said to himself, his mind going back to Judy and his son, Danny. If he had enough cash, just a bit more money, if they weren't always squeezing the buck . . . Like he told his mother, "If I allowed myself to turn a dollar once in a while, things would not be so bad." His mother didn't understand what he was talking about. Even though she was married to big Dan O'Donnell for thirty years, a cop who'd take a hot stove and go back for the smoke, she still didn't understand. But Dante, who had been thinking a whole lot about money lately, knew exactly what he was saying.

At the Triborough Bridge toll booth, he thought of Jimmy. The man was always flush. When they were kids and ran the streets together, Jimmy had cash. Jimmy told him it was a confirmation of his frugal attitude toward life in general. Dante preferred to regard it as dramatic proof of a Jew's ability to remain solvent when everyone around him was going bust.

He drove back to Monahan's, taking care so as not to wake Jimmy, who slept with his head resting against the passenger-side window. They arrived at two A.M. to find Jimmy's car parked in the bus stop where they had left it. Jimmy came awake, the natural response of an ex–patrol cop when a rolling car rocks to a stop on the bricks of a city where someone might shoot you if you're not moving.

"Whataya thinking?" Dante asked.

"I'm thinking that at least you don't have to make that hike out to the boondocks tonight."

That sat together in the front seat of the squad car. The street was deserted, no one walking, no cars moving along Pitkin Avenue. The empty feeling made Dante fidgety. It was their neighborhood, the streets they grew up on. People lived there. Still, Dante had this odd feeling that it was empty.

"I'm gonna stay here at my mother's," he said.

"It could be worse," Jimmy told him.

"You know, on the ride back I was thinking."

"Oh shit, don't do that. I didn't give you permission to do that."

"No man, hold it. Listen, I'm serious. Maybe if we had the shot, we should think about it."

"What in the hell you talking about?"

"You know, say if we had a shot at some real cash, maybe we shouldn't turn away so fast. I mean we've been in this job for thirteen years, and we've never done a thing. Never made a dollar."

Jimmy threw back his head and laughed. "I see. You were thinking you'd like to be a thief."

"No, not a thief. You know what I mean. I'm always broke. I don't have a goddamn dime to my name."

"I'm so sorry," Jimmy said gravely. Then he cleared his throat and said it again, stronger this time.

"Money is a problem," said Dante.

"You do make fifty grand a year, that ain't hay."

Dante watched Jimmy carefully, tried to check out the mood of his voice.

"Who told you," Jimmy said, "to go out to Stony Brook, Long Island, and buy some ranch house in the middle of nowhere?" To Dante he looked flushed and exhausted, like a detective that just finished a straight twenty-four chasing bad guys.

"You don't know, Jimmy," Dante said. "That house is a black hole. I'm telling you, I can't see how I can make it anymore."

Jimmy Burns listened as Dante spoke of the dilemma of the city cop who splits for the burbs. Why he'd run out to Long Island, to a town where his kid could grow and prosper away from crack pipes and street muggers. And shit man, he didn't make fifty grand. His take-home was a whole lot less. Dante told Jimmy that he felt like a dying tree in a forest fire, what with pension loans, cars, taxes, a monthly gas bill that could choke a horse.

"I want to remind you of something," Jimmy said. "You've been drinking. You're drunk. I never should have let you drive, as drunk as you are."

Jimmy smiled for a moment. Dante shrugged, tried not to smile.

"C'mon, look," Jimmy said. "You find the door, I'll go through it with you. We stumble over neatly stacked piles of fifties and hundreds, then we'll talk about it."

Dante sighed, playing with the car's cigarette lighter. "I can't tell if you're bullshitting or being serious."

Jimmy held out both hands palms up. "You are completely full of shit. Who you kidding? Me? You trying to kid me? I figured you quit trying to kid me when you were fourteen. Since when you've been down for making a buck? Since when?"

"Since I ran out of money and started hitting up my mother."

"If you're that goddamn broke, why not come to me? Or better yet, tell Judy to get off her ass and find a job, why don't ya."

"Right, sure. I've only asked her about a thousand times. And you? When did I ever come to you for money? You know I couldn't do that. Big spender that you are, I'd never hear the end of it."

"That's crap. You're desperate, you come to me. I'll always find you money."

"Sure."

"I mean it."

They sat in silence, nodding and chuckling. On the one hand Dante felt like he could tell Jimmy what a hole he had climbed into with the credit cards and loans and so on. His MasterCard was over four thousand, and now there was a hold on it. His gas card was topped out, and American Express was calling him every other day. What he was thinking was that he should tell Jimmy the way Judy stood around with her thumbs up alongside her head, saying, "I don't think that I should be going out to work, not with Danny still in school."

On the one hand he could tell Jimmy that Judy's got no time for a job, not with Little League, driving Danny everywhere, music lessons and all. On the other hand talking to Jimmy about family financial problems would not win him an award for cleverness. It would just get Jimmy more tense, if that were possible. Yet he was about to let it out, get to it, tell his best friend how he actually felt about his marriage, living in the suburbs, cutting grass, planting shrubs, talking bullshit to neighbors about this and that.

Dante sat back and watched Jimmy's smile. He said, "I feel like I can't be myself anymore. How about that? You understand what it's like when you can't be yourself?" He could see Jimmy's face gathering force for the reply. Dante was suddenly overwhelmed with shame, revolted by the sound of his own voice. "I'm all right," he said. "I'm feeling a little nutsy is all."

Jimmy went through his wallet. "Take a peek," he said.

He held out a small color photograph. In the picture Dante could see the side door to Monahan's. The shot had been taken one hot summer's day a long, long time ago, after the Korean War but before the time of Vietnam and the Rolling Stones. There was a brick wall and on that wall a VFW scroll, its frame gilded with imperial red and gold. There were names in blue script; alongside several names were gold stars aglow in the afternoon sun.

The three boys in the photo stood in street-corner style in celebration of the spirit of the sixties. They were fourteen years old, the year was 1964.

Dante looked at himself, the way his hair was buzzed on top with long sides, which had waved together on the back of his head in a deluxe and sensual duck's ass. His smile was wide and brilliant and thoroughly phony. Jimmy was smiling a smile of studied nonchalance. His hair was more near blond than its current light brown, and curly enough to quality as a Jew-fro. JoJo, dark and straight-haired, stood with his thumbs hooked into his jeans. He stared at the photographer with apparent distaste. In the shot Jimmy was holding fast to JoJo's shoulder. We were thicker than brothers, Dante thought, and well drilled as to the culture of the neighborhood. We weren't brothers, we hadn't come from the same blood, but we sure as hell came from the same place, and in that time that counted for a whole lot. Dante smiled, remembering.

Jimmy sat stone-faced and stared out the windshield, watching Carmine Joey emerge from Katie's ground-floor apartment. Carmine glanced at the squad car. He paused for a second, as if weighing options, then grabbed his crotch.

Jimmy said, "That dumb shit ain't never gonna change, is he?"

Dante nodded solemnly. "Carmine's Carmine," he said.

"Whataya got in your pocket?" Jimmy asked. "Twenty bucks? I got forty. But I don't have a house, a kid, a wife. Whataya wanna bet our old buddy JoJo's holding a few thou right this minute?"

"Fuckin' A."

"Whataya wanna bet that tonight when he goes home and lays his head down, first he's gotta make sure his gun's under the pillow? And his heart—you know JoJo's got a big heart—well I'll bet you that heart of his lives in his throat. It lives in his throat because he sleeps waiting to hear a rap on the door."

"C'mon," Dante said.

"Shut up and listen," Jimmy said pounding on the dash with his fist. "You see, when that rap comes—and come it will—it's going to be me, or you, or someone else telling him it's time to go. That's if he's lucky and don't get himself all blown t' shit on the street."

"All right, all right, all right. I was thinking out loud, man. If I can't think out loud and talk to you, who can I tell it to?"

Jimmy tilted his head and beamed at Dante as if he were proud. "Now that's him, that's JoJo's life," he said. "You hear me? Are you paying attention?"

"What am I, deaf?" Dante said. He couldn't tell if Jimmy's anger was directed at Dante or at himself.

Jimmy sighed, started playing with the car's cigarette lighter. "That life," he said, "is a criminal life. It's not mine, and it sure as hell ain't yours. I know you, partner, you'd last about two minutes in the can."

"Me? Hell, I'd suck on my gun long before they'd lock me up, pally."

It was an immediate thing, a total presence, the thought of being busted, taken out in handcuffs. They'd come before dawn, bang on the door, show him their warrant of arrest. An awkward embrace with Judy and Danny when they took him out. Neighbors, commuters heading for car pools would grab their Instamatics. Get a shot of the cop going to the can while he tried to cover his condemned head with Danny's Little League jacket.

"Blow yourself away? Oh right. Now that would be great, perfect. Marvelous for your kid, fantastic for Judy, and just a thrill for me."

Dante lit a cigarette and took a drag. He forced himself to sound casual. "C'mon."

"C'mon my ass. Like your old man, you'd pop a cap in your head. And you want me to go through a door with you, find some cash, and help you do it?"

"Whoa! I'm just kidding."

"Well, fuck you Dante. Find another partner, partner."

Dante was badly shaken, letting his mouth overrun his brain. "Just a joke," he said.

"I know you. You ain't kidding. And what's the joke? What's so funny? I don't know, sometimes you say the most moronic shit. But you see, I know better, I know what you really mean. For you it's all daydreams and bullshit, all make-believe."

"Will you give me a break?" Dante said. "Don't be so heavy. Everybody's doing it."

"Yeah, like who?"

"Everybody."

"Bullshit."

Dante looked up, studied the squad car's ceiling for a second. Then he smiled. "Kidding, kidding, kidding. Calm down, man. Forget what I just said, just forget it."

They fell into silence. For Dante, thinking of boxes of money had been exhilarating a moment before; now thoughts of his father were terrifying. His mother had told him, when she'd tried to explain it to him, things led to things, then things got out of control. Your father just could not handle it. The shame and all. All out of human control.

"See," Jimmy said. "I let you drink, I get what I deserve."

Dante slid down low in his seat. Jimmy threw him that I'm-tired look again and then opened the squad car's door.

"Used to be we never talked about money. That's not us, you said. I seen what it did to my old man, you said, and it ain't going to happen to me. That's what you told me."

Jimmy got out. He closed the door and put his hands on the car's roof, leaning down to talk to Dante through the open window. "Tomorrow we get back to work. The wires went in tonight, and tomorrow we go. I wasn't crazy about this case from the get-go. But I'll tell ya, now I want to do it. I want to get up real close and personal to JoJo. See what his life's like."

Dante was furious at himself, sorry he ever opened his mouth. "Look," he said, "maybe you're right. Maybe we should bail out of this case."

"No, no, no. Hey listen, I want to get on JoJo now. I think it's real important we get next to him. Maybe you'll learn something Dante," he said with an eerie grin. "Brother of mine. Under the right set of circumstances, possibly, just maybe, I'd think about grabbing a few bucks. Who don't need money? But I know you couldn't handle it. You talk big, big ol' hotshot Dante. But you couldn't take it, the big dumb Irish Catholic that you are."

"Okay, okay." Dante paused, wanting to end on a different subject. He hesitated, thinking about what else to say.

"All that guilt, all that bizarre shit that eats at you would drive you up a wall," Jimmy came back at him, "and I'd be left to pick up the pieces. I know you. I know you better than *you* know you."

"Ey Jimmy," Dante said. "Maybe I shouldn't have mentioned money, huh?"

"Go to your mother's, get a good night's sleep. Forget it."

Dante laughed. "You know," he said, "when we were kids you usta say that all the time. Go to your mother's. When we were out late, I'd wanna go bouncing, maybe smoke some dope, you'd say forget it, go home, forget it. And I'd do it, go home just to please you. I did a whole lot of shit just to please you."

"I know buddy, I know. And I know how weepy you get when you drink too much and try to go back. You love to go back and get weepy."

Dante shook his head, laughing at himself. He felt the gallon of beer and shots of booze raging through him now. "I wanna climb a roof and throw golf balls at the moon," he said.

"Shit Dante, we ain't kids anymore. We're a lot of things, but we ain't kids."

Dante pursed his lips and glanced upward. He put the car in gear and drove off, he drove surprisingly well.

———

JoJo stepped back as the motel door opened. He saw the Cuban, face well lit, eyes glancing up at him, nodding with a faint smile. The guy had good white teeth and he showed them. He held a pack of cigarettes in one hand and a gold lighter in the other.

"Joseph?" was all the Cuban said, and he said it softly.

Hearing the Cuban say his name with the slightest trace of an accent was a fearful thing for JoJo, bringing as it did visions of his father. JoJo remembered that even in the best of times, when he made a move on his own it could tighten the old man's jaw. And the best of times for him and the Skipper were over, and he knew it. He could hear the old man saying, a spic? You, my son, you're doing business with a mambo dancer? Is that what I taught you? Is that how you arm yourself with good friends? You fool.

The Cuban held the door open and watched him come in, then his smile broadened and he held out his hand as though they were in some way old friends.

"I am Luis Valero."

JoJo smiled. "I know who you are."

The room's fragrance was that of cologne, new linen, and leather. And JoJo detected the smell of scented candles. The aroma in the room was so severe and lush that for a moment he thought of Barney's men's store. The light-skinned spade broad with spiked hair that worked there. The bitch had yellow eyes and a gorgeous ass.

When JoJo pictured a Cuban drug dealer he put it on pretty heavy, imagining a shifty-eyed dark-skinned guy with oil-slick hair pulled tight into a ponytail wearing some kind of white outfit unbuttoned to the waist. Gold chains lying on mahogany skin, wild black eyes ablaze with speed, a machine gun in one hand, a golden bowl of coke in the other. Some wild, hot-tempered guy who'd blow you away in a heartbeat. A guy, he was certain, that always plotted treachery. Except then he would see Don Johnson sail into a scene on a yacht with those *Miami Vice* guys, doing business with men who wore Armani suits and had trailer trucks full of cash. It was a pure bitch to figure who these people were and what they were about. A collection of greasy dudes with tons of money and big guns, is what he had always thought. Men who did a miserable and risky business and took no prisoners. He thought of Pacino in *Scarface*. Yet seeing one of these characters up close could give you an entirely different impression than seeing some actor playing a scene.

Suddenly the smiling Cuban and the sweet-smelling room filled his heart with a ghostly fear. Bloodstained clothing and gunpowder smells. An image, he knew, that would have staying power.

His father would kill him. He had considered a hundred different ways to explain all this, and that was the way it always came out.

The Cuban looked gravely at him. "Are you all right?" he said.

"I'm fine." He winked at Luis: all is good.

An ice bucket, club soda, and tonic had been neatly arranged on a table. There were white linen napkins, some cheeses and fresh fruit. A bottle of light rum and one of vodka stood to one side. The motel room was not very large, just big enough for the table, a sofa, a bed, a stuffed chair, and a fake walnut cabinet with a television in it. Behind the table were large glass sliding doors that opened onto a balcony. It was a comfortable room for one person, and Luis seemed to be doing just fine.

The expression on Luis's face looked like a smile, but JoJo wasn't sure.

The Cuban's face was without a crease, and he was clean-shaven. He was wearing a pale blue guayabera in the pocket of which a gold pen was neatly clasped. He wore white trousers of a fine material that JoJo figured had to be silk. And he flashed jewelry. A gold chain necklace, gold Rolex. His skin was reddish-brown, and he had light brown hair that had a curl to it. About five ten or eleven, a hundred sixty pounds or so. Handsome. No not handsome, familiar, maybe that was it.

JoJo stared at him, thinking, I know what you look like when you do business. He thought about other men, dark and squinty-eyed, moving aside as Luis entered a room. He looked to JoJo like one sharp piece of work. JoJo drifted off a little, imagining Luis's people coming to him, grabbing his hand, patting his back. He could see the guy running his game, standing, arms folded, making sure everybody knew what was expected.

JoJo felt an immediate kinship and thought he understood what kind of man Luis really was. The guy certainly didn't look like an arch criminal or a tough guy, eyeing him with a soft, warm grin. The Cuban looked like a thinker. He moved slowly and seemed sure of himself. Right off he liked the guy. If anything the Cuban put JoJo in mind of his mother's brother Mario, and Mario had always seemed to JoJo to look more like a Latin singer than a shylock, whatever a shylock looked like. Luis, JoJo concluded, could just as easily have been born among the people of Cinisi as Havana. The guy looked f'n great. It made him think, this Luis is from a world I know something about.

"Have you had your dinner?" Luis asked.

"Uh-huh," trying to sound chipper.

"Are you sure? I can send for something."

Luis pulled a chair out from the table and sat.

"I'm sure," JoJo said. "To tell you the truth, I'd prefer you don't call out to anyone."

Luis laughed. "Drink?"

"Sure."

JoJo made himself comfortable on the sofa while Luis made the drinks. He placed the oversize attaché case on the floor between his legs.

Taking the vodka from Luis he said, *"Salud."* And it made him smile. It was, after all, the first time in his life that he spoke Spanish to a Spanish guy.

"What do you have in the bag?" Luis asked him.

"What was agreed upon. Two hundred and fifty K in fifties and hundreds."

"Joseph, you know that this money is not for me. It's for the friend in Miami who arranged this meeting."

JoJo smiled in approval, for Joseph Paradiso was a person of criminal status, an outlaw that understood the role of outlaw lawyers.

"Lawyers," JoJo told him, "always make money."

"Amen," Luis said. "Do you know this came as a surprise to me? I know a little something about you and your people. You've not done this business before."

JoJo debated whether to ask him how, how do you know this about me? But the guy's eyes told him that the man knew precisely what he was talking about. JoJo nodded his head. He felt cool and loose, he was on his game, an important man doing significant business.

Luis gazed up at the ceiling and thrust two hands in the air in the manner of someone about to surrender. He squinted at JoJo. "The last thing I need is trouble. You know what I mean?"

JoJo frowned for real. "Trouble? Later for trouble, nobody needs trouble."

Luis drank thoughtfully. He was inspecting JoJo, looking closely at him.

"Can I ask you something?" JoJo said.

"Of course."

"You have almost no accent at all. I don't know what I expected, but you're not it."

Luis put down his drink and slowly passed a hand across his mouth. "I don't know what you expected my friend, but I'm what you got." He smiled and nodded his head. His hands were firmly planted on his kneecaps. He took a deep breath, then started in. "I've lived most of my life in the States. I came with my mother to New York in the early fifties. We lived on the Lower East Side with all the wops."

JoJo shifted in his seat.

"It was a tough time. My mother couldn't make it work, so we went back to Cuba. I took off in 'sixty-one." He snapped his fingers. "I didn't get along with the commies, so I came back; landed in Miami and stayed. I was a printer, then a salesman for a printing firm. I traveled all over Latin America, met a lot of important people."

He spoke like he was reading his lines, like he'd told this story maybe a hundred times before.

JoJo stared at him blankly. Shit, the guy's an American, all right. He shrugged and tried to smile.

Luis got up and poured himself another rum and returned to his chair.

He took a long steady drink, finishing off the glass. "What do you need?" he said evenly.

"Product, material. You know what I need," JoJo said.

"Goods, material is not the problem. I can get you all the goods you want. I can get you a mountain of stuff. Transportation is the problem, and transportation determines the price."

"Talk to me, I'm here to listen."

"Look, the people I deal with have tons of product, and they trust me completely. I'm sure I can set up a consignment deal for you."

"That would be great, you're a gentleman."

Luis nodded but didn't return the compliment. "Ten-five a key delivered to the Bahamas. Twelve to Miami, and fifteen-five to New York. One-hundred-key minimum." Luis, still watching JoJo, began to smile; he leaned toward him. "So, whachew dink, big man?" he said in a heavy accent.

"I think you can do better." JoJo stood and went to the table and poured himself another Absolut with tonic.

"You think?" Luis told him.

"I know."

Luis shrugged and sighed. "Oh, you don't think, you know."

JoJo raised an imploring hand. "Luis, don't take me for a fool. I'm nobody's fool."

The more he thought about the idea of this cocaine business, making the move with Luis and all, the more he liked it. The guy was straightforward, not complicated. He didn't talk from the side of his mouth in twists and turns and use words and facial expressions with double and triple meanings. Luis was not a Sicilian.

JoJo had had a few dealings with zips, mafiosi who were Sicilian-born and retained their ties to the old country. They kept you on your toes with their little looks and a certain kind of expression, a twinkle of the eyes that says, you're amateurish and slow and I can have you for lunch, you fool. Zips never let you know what they were thinking. Some were totally insane. Their lives were about killing people. A good reason to stay away from the business of heroin: to deal in heroin you had to deal with zips.

And then, as part of the same thought, he considered that this deal was good, beyond anything he had done before. The trouble was, the whole thing would depend on his father, on whether he would have enough time to explain the good of it before the old man went batshit and grabbed a small ax. Shit, if he put a first-rate deal together his father would have to go for it. Such thoughts put a strain on him, and JoJo began to sweat. This whole thing, when you got right down to it, depended on how much nerve he had, how much heart, was he up for it, could he go all the way, did he have the balls to pull this off?

JoJo could trace his family to the Sicilian seacoast town of Castellammare del Golfo. It was the hometown of many American mafiosi. It was said that men from this town, when under the gun, were savage and had hearts of granite.

"I want," JoJo told him, "the best deal you can offer."

Luis seemed very interested. He was leaning forward, his elbows on his knees, his chin on his fists. He seemed relaxed, as though everything would be just fine between them, a couple of *pisans* talking.

"You get me heroin," Luis said, confiding. "I'll get you coke. Three for one: three keys of coke for one of heroin. That's the best deal possible."

"I'm not in that business."

"I know. But that is only a matter of choice. You could get all you need."

JoJo took a deep breath, held it, and released it in a hoarse whisper, saying, "I don't do that business."

Luis leaned his head back and cast his eyes in JoJo's approximate direction. He looked insulted. "But I do."

JoJo shook his head good-humoredly. "I would really have to think about that."

Luis only stared at him.

JoJo finished his drink and sat back against the sofa. It seemed to him that he was moving light years away from the counsel of his father.

"Speak," Luis said.

JoJo lowered his voice. "Listen, ah, let me explain. The Paradisos have never been in the drug business. Unfortunately times and conditions have changed, so now we will make this cocaine move. It's necessary, and I guess it will be a good thing. However we will not move heroin. We have always believed that business to be an *infamita*. Do you understand when I say *infamita?*"

"Yes, of course I do. But that is bullshit, you and I both know it. So don't talk to me like that, it's insulting. The smart ones among you have been moving stuff for thirty years, more. You can call the drugs coke or heroin, it's the same shit. Don't fool yourself." Luis made a face of anguished disapproval that was interestingly Italian.

JoJo was surprised at the passion of the Cuban's answer. "We'll need another meeting," he said, watching Luis's eyes. The look in the Cuban's eyes gave him a funny feeling. He had seen that look before, he knew that look. Black eyes staring hard, looking into your heart. Eyes meant to turn your head.

Luis nodded. "We'll set another meet. Listen," he said, his voice lower, more serious. "I think there is something we should talk about. Something we could possibly share."

"Go on," JoJo told him.

"Well," Luis said. "This is not the kind of business where you go around in a blindfold."

"Meaning?"

"It's helpful to have friends with the police. They are everywhere, be clear on that. In this business you never know who you're dealing with."

"I talk to no one I don't know. Unless of course he comes highly recommended. Like you."

"Good, good. And you have a connection or two with the police, huh? You have influence, no? I mean with the courts and the police?"

Okay, JoJo told himself proudly, this so-called big-time dealer needs my help. He rubbed his chin against his shoulder and felt his body downshift; he relaxed. JoJo was being asked a favor. And that was good.

Luis's eyes crinkled, he stood up like he was shot out of the chair and said loudly, "It's Domingo, my son-in-law. He was arrested in New York City, in Jackson Heights. You know the place?"

JoJo nodded.

"The charge is false and he is being held without bail. I mean, I thought they must set bail; however, they didn't. Domingo did not kill anyone. I know that."

JoJo figured that right now he should clam up and let the guy talk.

Luis smiled at him. "You help Domingo, I will make you a king of cocaine."

For the first time Luis succeeded in astounding him. A for-real major player did not let personal considerations affect business. If there was one thing he'd learned, it was that personal feelings cannot interfere with business. In the business of their business, if you spent time and energy worrying over personal shit you'll be out of the game before you know it. On the other hand, the Paradisos had a much valued reputation for never letting a member or a friend down. Sure, he had connections with the police, and with the courthouse too. He was not about to share that with Luis, at least not yet he wouldn't. Christ, he hardly knew the guy. Yet he could see in Luis's eyes a burning need. The guy was in pain. And that was good, a card he could play.

"My daughter's pregnant, she needs her husband home."

"And where's that, where's home?"

"Spain, my daughter and Domingo live with me in Spain. I need bail set for Domingo, they set bail I'll do the rest."

Luis whispered something that JoJo missed.

"What's that?" JoJo slid forward on the sofa.

"I said if they set bail I'll have Domingo in Spain the same day."

JoJo was about to tell Luis that was exactly what the court figured, why they wouldn't set bail, but he caught himself and kept quiet.

Luis rolled his eyes and shook his head sadly, he looked away from JoJo. "At this moment there is nothing more important to me than to help Domingo. For my daughter, you understand?"

"Of course, it's natural."

They refilled their glasses and drank to JoJo's health and the health of the new relationship. JoJo stood up abruptly.

"I have to go," he told Luis. "I feel for your troubles, maybe I can help. We'll see."

They shook hands and promised to be in touch. JoJo left the room and drove back to his hotel with Bruno. In the morning they flew back, landing at Newark Airport. From the airport he telephoned Barry Cooper, the family attorney and courthouse fixer. It was Barry who through his brother in Miami had arranged the meeting with Luis.

JoJo told Barry to hang loose for the next day or so. Said that he might have a murder case for him in Queens. With a mild comic spin he asked Barry if he spoke Spanish. Barry said he spoke cash. JoJo said what else is new?

CHAPTER FIVE

It was the sort of cool, crystal clear morning you can get in Queens in early spring, the kind of morning that made Dante imagine fall, with a strong breeze coming off the Rockaway Beach breakers and a taste of the soiled waters of Jamaica Bay in the air. The kind of morning that brought him back to teenage days and nights spent on the Broad Channel bridge, fishing for striped bass and spring flounder, coming up with eels and spider crabs. Watching Jimmy crack up as JoJo tossed those ugly black crabs under the wheels of passing cars. Cold brews and Irish broads with long legs and blond hair, and clams on the half shell in Funzy's shack by the water.

To Dante those days seemed a hundred years gone. He wondered if the girls of Stella Morris still wriggled in the back seats of cars at the Pizza King, the way it was before, the way he would always remember it. He wondered if there was still a Stella Morris High School. Maybe they bolted the doors and closed it down, the way they shut down so many other good things in the f'n city. Nevertheless he would bet a year's pay that on a morning such as this, kids were fishing from the bridge. And there would be one, a wild one like JoJo, and he'd throw spider crabs at passing cars. In his mind's eye Dante saw JoJo, he remembered that JoJo had always been different. The guy had crazy reckless eyes, and he seemed to know about things other kids never perceived. Only JoJo never knew, not from day one, when enough was enough.

The night before, trying to sleep in his mother's house, Dante found that when he closed his eyes the dizziness returned, leaving him twisting and turning, haunted by thoughts of his failing marriage, his never-ending train of bills, his dwindling bank account. Birds were singing and the sun was climbing by the time he slipped through the surface of sleep.

He was shaken out of his dreams sometime around eight. Jimmy called to remind him that they had a ten o'clock meet, and that he'd better get a move on. He stood for a long time under the shower, his face turned up into the water, looking at the same goddamn blue-green water stains on the ceiling he'd looked at when he was twelve. Possibly this day would be the beginning of some good luck. Although he didn't see the prospect of much difference from the day before, and the day before that. Tonight he figured he'd call Judy again. Talk to her, see how the ground lay, maybe he'd go home.

Standing outside the bathroom door, his mother called out, "You're welcome here whenever you like. For as long as you like. But we both know where you belong. You got a family. Don't start this business of staying away."

"It's not my decision," Dante said foolishly. "Not my decision at all."

"An Italian girl, you should have married an Italian."

"Just like you, hah Ma?"

"You're father was different. He was a good Irishman."

A good Irishman, Dante thought. What makes a good Irishman? Motionless, looking in the mirror, tugging at his lip, he felt like crying. He could never shake thoughts of his father, never.

Now driving along Old South Road, making that left that brought them onto Cross Bay Boulevard, glancing at Jimmy riding shotgun, Dante could find no energy and little interest in work. Still, he realized that he had to get through the day. Except his neck was stiff, his stomach ached, and he felt a bit feverish. He felt as though there was no way he could cope with everything. Christ, he felt like shit. He considered that tomorrow should be better. For Dante O'Donnell, thoughts of tomorrow were always an improvement.

They drove along in silence for the ten minutes it took to find the Woodhaven Diner. He angle-parked against the wooden stockade fence, and he and Jimmy got out and started toward the diner. As they went, he took note of the number of new cars parked in the lot. Why had Jimmy decided to have breakfast here? Why meet Ray here? There were times Jimmy's mind had holes in it. The place was a wiseguy hangout, and Dante hated the damn joint.

In the vestibule there was a bank of three phones and a cigarette machine. A cardboard sign taped to two of the phones said OUT OF ORDER. They rang constantly and were answered by this beefy blond guy named Blackie. Blackie took sports bets and lent money. Late payments he collected with a baseball bat.

Dante was in a killer mood, he felt tight as a bowstring. Suddenly he had energy, that speedy energy you get from an unknown source of anger, from being sleepless.

Inside were men dressed in neighborhood high fashion, silk pants and Italian knit shirts and tassel-topped loafers of soft leather. Some wore sporty warm-up outfits of bright blue and green. To Dante they all, to a man, exuded a kind of contented aimlessness. A bunch of half-assed wiseguys and wannabes starting their day.

Ray Velasquez, looking a bit stooped and weary, sat waiting in the last booth, which looked out onto Woodhaven Boulevard, the parking lot, and the Cross Bay movie theater beyond. He was talking to a waitress, who smiled broadly, showing off her new capped teeth.

Dante nodded to Ray, gave him his good-morning grin and took a seat. Jimmy came behind him.

Every now and then the guy at the cash register sneaked nervous glances at them. Dante knew him, he knew that he knew him but couldn't place him. When they came into the diner he caught a glimpse of the guy's tattoo, a cat with evil green eyes on the back of his hand. The dude had jailhouse skin, the dull gray look of a street runner just home from doing time. Bad crooked teeth, a short guy with quick moves, tense and nervous. And when he watched him through the corner of his eye, Dante caught him grinning like some skinny-ass alley cat.

To the best of Dante's understanding they were to meet Ray, one of the department's top tech men, to discuss the investigation. Ray had installed the wire and bug on the Paradisos, and he would be the third member of the four-officer investigative team. Ray spoke better Italian than most of the rough English-speaking Italians they worked. Raised speaking Spanish, he was a man of some intellect and curiosity. He had studied Italian at the New School, bought himself some Italian language tapes, and watched Italian TV on cable. Ray trusted the department's Italian translators about as far as he could throw his police cruiser, so he translated all his own tapes. Having grown up in the drug-infected barrio of East Harlem, he hated mafiosi. He also hated the government and its phony war on drugs, judges, and particularly lawyers; also bail bondsmen, reporters, and certain members of the department. It was said that he was fond of Dante and Jimmy, but Dante was never sure.

The team's fourth member was Detective Kathy Gibbons. On this morning she had gone directly to the bug plant, a vacant apartment above a store and directly across the street from JoJo's social club on 101st Avenue.

The club was JoJo's base of operations, the place he met with friends and friends of friends, a place where he could do the business of his business. A place he had swept for bugs once a week.

Jimmy told him that Kathy had been scheduled to arrive at the plant around six A.M. She was there to monitor and take photos with a Nikon camera that had a two-hundred-millimeter lens with a 4X converted, a night scope, and a light enhancer. If there was one star out or one streetlamp lit, you could take shots that would show the smile lines on the faces of people coming and going from the club.

The Organized Crime Control Bureau's intelligence teams were generally made up of four or six officers. There were times special agents of the FBI and DEA joined the teams and worked together with the NYPD detectives in a loosely knit joint task force. Dante and Jimmy were the most experienced detectives in the bureau, and their boss, Inspector Arthur Martin, shared them with no one.

Two years ago the supervising agent in charge of the New York office of the FBI requested Dante and Jimmy's services for a long-term investigation of the five New York crime families. Inspector Martin told him they were tied up working Colombian drug rings in Jackson Heights.

When joint task forces were formed and detectives were sent off to work with the feds, Inspector Martin sent only his least productive officers. The best he kept near him, under his own command. The FBI agent didn't understand, but Inspector Martin, who met weekly with the police commissioner in order to detail his own productivity, knew exactly what he was doing.

The Woodhaven Diner was a Greek joint, and like most Greek diners it had mirrored walls and potted plants adorned with red ribbons, and homemade cakes and pies. Framed black-and-white photos of members of the Mets and Yankees, all signed, hung from the walls. And there were a few film stars; Pacino and Dustin Hoffman hung above the coffee machine. Behind the cash register was an oil painting of Athens, and on the counter a Little League trophy. On the wall above the booth where Dante, Jimmy, and Raymond sat was a painting on black velvet of Elvis in action. "Unchained Melody," by the Platters, played on the jukebox.

Dante asked Jimmy to check out the guy at the cash register, maybe they'd worked him. "We know that guy at the register, don't we?" Dante didn't like the guy looking at him, glancing sideways at him. Jimmy was busy with his coffee and didn't answer. He asked Ray if he had seen him before. Ray said sure you know him. He hasn't been around in a while, he's probably been upstate. Yeah, Dante said, but who is he? And why the fuck is he looking at me like that?

The man at the cash register's name was Michael Pappa. Mike was home one month after doing three years of a seven-to-ten hijacking bit, and his parole officer told him, he said, Mike, you owe us four. I hear you contact any of the old Basile crew, I'll see to it that you disappear off radar. I'll have you back in the slammer in a heartbeat, back to breaking rocks, back where you belong, playing house with your cellmate, a dude that looks like Mr. T on speed.

Mike Pappa had listened good, because when you got right down to it, he'd done nothing but hard time, counting the months, days, and hours until he could come up in front of the parole board. The first time up he caught a break, the first time up they sent him home. Home thirty days and he was careful, not that he was going to find Jesus and live a straight life, he was just careful.

Except the night before he was standing at the corner of Liberty and Woodhaven and wouldn't you know, Little Ralphie Basile swooped in and picked him up in that red BMW that he knew was sizzling. Little Ralph specialized in lifting BMWs. So they cruised around, with Ralphie telling him about a drop-dead easy hit at the airport. Ralphie was slick and kept them in the dark streets of Rockaway Beach, snorting a little coke off the dash. But Mike was unsteady this morning, and he felt like he was going to puke because there were three cops sitting in the diner's last booth, giving him those squinty-eyed cop looks that said we spied you last night, we saw you with Little Ralph and we're gonna drop a dime to your PO. And then we'll do a tap dance when they drag your ass back to the joint, where Mr. T can blow up your asshole.

Mike Pappa was a Greek and his uncle George owned the diner. George spoke English with a heavy accent, but he knew a cop when he saw one, and he told his nephew, kept telling him, "Michael, you see those guys back there, they're cops. I know they're cops because one's got a gun in his boot and another one's wearing handcuffs and the third one's ordered three cups of hot water using the same teabag what, two, three times. Only Greeks and cops are that cheap, and they don't look like no Greeks."

Mike Pappa was a man who they built jailhouses for. He couldn't do right for doing wrong, and he knew with all his heart and soul that the trio of cops at the back table were checking him out just as if they were in a blue-and-white and he'd jumped a stop sign.

Dante fixed his eyes on the guy. He still couldn't place him and it was about to make him nuts.

"Jimmy we know that curly-haired mook by the cash register from before, don't we?"

Jimmy said, "What?"

"I asked you who that guy is. It's driving me crazy. I can't get a make on him."

"That's Mike the Greek, for chrissake."

Ray said, "He's a hijacker. He runs with the Basile crew from South Brooklyn. They use the airport like a shopping center. Shooters too, a bad bunch. The guy's an authentic A-hole."

"Stop looking at him," Jimmy said. "You're making him nervous."

"Mike the Greek," Dante said. "An A-hole, right. I know the guy."

Glancing over at them, taking his time, making it clear that he had done a straight eight through the night, detective Raymond Velasquez said, "Screw the Greek. Will you guys pay attention here? I've been up all night checking the wire and bug. They're all set. The old man made one outgoing about midnight. Long-distance to Rhode Island."

Ray had a heavy white mustache, and his skin was dark brown. His army fatigue jacket looked worn around the elbows and he kept it zipped. He wore blue jeans and cowboy boots. His voice was a rumbling bass, and he had the slightest trace of an accent. His hair was thick and tightly curling, you could say kinky, and it was white as Mike the Greek's brand spanking new apron. Like Dante and Jimmy, he was considered an organized-crime-family expert. He specialized in the Renina and Biscoglia families, but he was familiar enough with the Paradisos that Dante and Jimmy thought he would be perfect to work JoJo.

Raymond Velasquez had decided many years before, during the time he was assigned to the Narcotics Bureau, that he was no criminal. He wanted to help boost the image of Puerto Rican cops, so he kept himself on the straight and narrow. He had prepared himself for an uncomplicated and frugal life, living as he did in a rent-controlled Bronx apartment. His wife of eighteen years was a high school special education teacher and a social worker. His check was the only money he wanted to bring home, and his woman was the only woman he wanted to put his legs around. Honesty would have profound effect on Raymond Velasquez's future, his destiny.

A week back, after a few pops at Monahan's, Dante told Jimmy, "An honest man can infect people with his decency if you spend enough time with him. People like Ray, their righteousness can really get you." Jimmy had answered him by saying anyone can fool you sometimes.

Detective Velasquez shook his head quickly. "You know we're supposed to monitor and minimize this thing. Not supposed to leave the machine on and alone. Get yourself in a jam with that crap. And that's the truth of it."

Dante, who was stretching and appeared to be sliding into sleep, sat up straight in the booth. He said, "Bates was right about you."

Dante's reference was to a captain named Jack Bates who had spread the word that Raymond Velasquez was a weak link. Bates had decided that Ray didn't have the heart to be a cop. The proof was that he married a liberal Jew broad who thought most cops were Nazis. Velasquez, he told anyone who'd sit and listen, would side with any nigger or spic over his brother officers. The guy was a union member, a troublemaker. The guy, for chrissake, spoke French. He was probably a commie mole in the department. Bates had gone beyond just telling one or two people, he advertised his feeling everywhere he went, to the point where Ray got himself a thirty-day suspension defending his honor: he broke the jaw of a homicide detective who accused him of being a coward. Ray had been driven almost to the point of resigning from the department. Then he found his calling.

Detective Raymond Velasquez had come to the NYPD twenty-four years earlier. Captain Bates snapped him up right from the academy and tossed him in the Narcotics Bureau undercover unit. In no time at all he became a star. He had come to the job during the days when to be a Puerto Rican with white hair and a mustache made you stand out among mostly tall, mostly white Irish and German cops. When he had told Dante about it, he said that he had been standing with his recruit class at the academy; in two days he would be assigned a Harlem precinct. Bates, who was then a sergeant in the Narcotics Division, put an arm around his shoulders and whispered, "Hey kiddo, I got a deal for you the likes of which you won't believe." Bates put him directly into undercover narco.

Raymond Velasquez from the time he was a kid running in the streets of East Harlem always wanted to be a cop. He wanted to wear that uniform and play with all the toys, the gun, the whistle, the stick, the car with the light that went round and round. He dreamed of going back to his old neighborhood and laying the wood to drug dealers' heads. As luck would have it, he was never to play with the toys after all. He was a career undercover cop who went around convincing people he was anything but a police officer.

In the Narcotics Division he spent his time buying dope from junkies, drugged-out people who once they sold you heroin were likely to turn merrily around and walk into light poles and buses. Wasted and sick people, a bunch of nobodys out in the sporting life trying to get by. All of them with habits that would kill a horse. No challenge, no contest for a slick undercover cop. In those days he could knock off forty-fifty street pushers a month. And they were almost always black or Hispanic.

Ray knew he was doing diddly-shit about the drug problem, and certainly he was not helping his people. He hated walking burnt-out streets with blown-up people buying dope. He hated the job of undercover narcotics cop. Time and time again he put in for a transfer.

But the NYPD does not transfer undercover narcotics cops who are making forty or fifty street buys a month. Finally he threatened to resign. Working on small-time sick people who on a good day couldn't find their hands and feet was not what he had become a policeman for. And Bates told him, he said, hey, you do what you do. You go out and make numbers. That's what we're about. And any cop that objects to that has got to have a screw loose. Or worse yet, be a goddamn social worker hiding in a cop's skin. A renegade, a traitor, a disgrace to the thin blue line.

Ray told Bates that across the years, coming up in East Harlem, he could see that drugs were destroying his people and he wanted to do something about it. He wanted to work the white guys, the big fat guys driving Mercedeses and Caddies. The guys that lived in big houses in Jersey and on Long Island. The organized-crime vermin who poisoned his own brother.

Bates told him then that the day they met, he knew Ray was a troublemaker.

In time Raymond was granted an interview with the Organized Crime Control Bureau. Told the interviewing officer that he spoke Italian, Spanish, and French. Told Inspector Martin that he wanted to put away the people that buried more Americans than all the wars America had been involved in. Told Martin that chasing small-time junkies was ridiculous, and if the department in all its wisdom kept him doing that, he would resign and probably write a book, tell the story of his police career in the pages of a book. Get Raul Julia to play him in the movie, go on Donahue and Oprah.

No, no don't resign, Inspector Martin told him. You'll come to me and work guineas. We'll take you off the street so you don't get killed by some crazed nigger, and you'll make big cases against fat white people. You'll make me famous.

Ray Velasquez was more near black than white; still, Inspector Martin's offer brought a smile.

Assigned to the OCCB, he taught himself to use cameras and lenses and night scopes, wiretaps and bugs. He became an expert locksmith, and he attended the FBI academy, their technical school, and graduated at the very top of his class. He was a wire man, the best in the business, loved to hear people talk in soft voices without emotion about murder, corruption, and drug dealing. Loved the idea that most of the people he was responsible for busting wore suits and went away to do time that would bring them home in a box, or in the next century. And he loved to work with Dante and Jimmy.

"Speaking of Bates," Dante said, "anybody hear what he's up to these days?"

Both Jimmy and Ray looked at him blankly.

"Christ, the guy's a private investigator. Has a big firm. He's making more money now helping bad guys then he ever stole as a cop. It's terrifying when you realize that crime pays," he said fervently.

"I'm afraid that the heroic age of the good guy has come to an end," said Ray.

Dante looked at the clock on the wall behind the coffee urns. Ten thirty. Dante said, "We left a message for Kathy that we'd be at the social club plant by eleven."

"You want an English muffin?" Ray said. He offered his breakfast to Jimmy. Jimmy declined.

"I'm going home," Raymond said. "I'll check the machine tonight. Now, one of you guys will be there, right?"

"I'll be there," Dante told him.

Mike the Greek turned to look as Dante did, giving Dante his full-faced silly grin, crooked teeth, oily black curly hair hanging over his blue Italian knit. Dante heard Ray say, "I never liked working with a woman."

"Why's that?" said Jimmy.

"I don't know, I suppose it's the way I was brought up. But Kathy's fine. A good worker, knows the job, keeps to herself. And the fact that she dates an FBI agent don't hurt."

"I thought she was gay," Jimmy said.

And Dante said, "Sure she's gay."

"I didn't say she was gay or straight, I said she is dating an FBI agent."

"A woman?" said Jimmy.

"Yeah."

Dante saw some guy in one of the booths near the door trying to get Mike the Greek's attention, calling, "Mike, hey Mike. You wanna do me a favor over here, this table's filthy."

Dante left the booth and went to the men's room. He was not at all sure about working with Kathy, the woman always trying to make you believe she was a hardass, telling tales of her days in uniform, saying yo all the time. Yo, I kicked some ass when I was in the bag, took shit from nobody. They shouldn't have asked for help on this one. Well, maybe Ray to do some of the surveillance and paperwork. But they shouldn't have asked for Kathy.

He washed his hands and face and stared into the mirror. Like looking at a photo of his father. Big Dan O'Donnell. He narrowed his eyes and put on his father's mean look. Wondered what that man thought when he put the gun to his head. Who was he? That son of a bitch, leaving me with a wounded mother and nightmares. Dante's own son was twelve. He hadn't seen him in a week. He'd called, spoken briefly to his wife. She didn't want him to come back home. Not yet anyway. When? he'd asked her. When can I come home? She hadn't answered, just sighed and hung up the phone.

He came back from the men's room and Ray was gone.

"We best get going," Jimmy said. "Lemme have the check."

"No," Dante said. "I'll take care of this, you get the big ones. Okay?"

At the cash register he paid the bill with the twenty he had borrowed from his mother. Mike Pappa took the money and presented him with change without flinching. Dante felt the necessity to say and maybe do something. Get a little adrenaline to flow, maybe clear his clogged head.

"Are there any real men in this joint?" Dante rattled off. "Any real Americans here, ya know, people with jobs?"

Standing in the doorway, Jimmy said, "Uh-oh."

"Nobody here but ghosts," Mike Pappa said. "You can't see the people here."

"I can see you giving me those bad looks from the side of your eye and I don't like it."

"What?"

"What? What? I'll tell ya what. You've been giving me the evil eye. What if I told you I could kick the ass off any guinea in this joint?"

Jimmy said, "Excuse me, don't you think it's time you came up with a new line?"

"I just told this greasy-haired creep that I could kick the ass off any *wop* guinea hardass in this joint. That's what I said."

"Take your friend out of here," Mike said to Jimmy.

"Hey, creep, I'm talking to you," Dante said. "Did you hear me?"

"I'm not sure you're big enough to talk like that," Mike the Greek told him.

Dante rested his hands on the glass top of the counter. "The way I see it," he said, "I get to say any fucking thing I want."

Mike turned to the men sitting in booths and those sitting at the counter, who were frowning at him.

"You're an entertaining sort of guy," Mike told Dante. *Entertaining* being his word for steaming pile of bullshit. "But you'd better be real tough, you talk that shit here."

Dante's eyes told Mike Pappa that the worst thing possible was happening. He had run into a crazy cop.

"Sport," Jimmy said, coming up behind Dante, "you're looking at the baddest dude in the valley. If I were you I'd give him his change and wish him a good day."

"I gave him his change," Mike said. "What am I supposed to be, scared of this guy?"

Jimmy looked at Mike, who stood on the other side of the counter with his feet apart, his hands on his hips. Jimmy looked at him and shook his head.

Dante reached over and put his hand on Jimmy's shoulder. "This schmuck looked at me when I came in here. He looked at me and smiled like he likes me."

Jimmy shrugged and pulled a pack of Marlboros from his breast pocket.

Dante leaned toward Mike, saying, "You like me? You a fag, maybe? The way you look at me I gotta figure you're a smart bastard or a fag."

"Whatayou, a nut?" Mike the Greek said. And Blackie with his thick neck and six-foot frame stood up in the booth where he was sitting.

"I only see two of you guys," Blackie said.

No one noticed that Ray Velasquez had come back in and was standing just inside the doorway. He stood with his arms folded. Ray said, "We got the biggest gang in the world. You wanna see how fast they get here?"

"I ain't looking for trouble," Mike said then.

Dante's eyes crinkled, and he suddenly turned on Blackie. "Take those goddamn signs off those phones. I see those signs on the phones again, I'm gonna lock your ass up for malicious mischief."

"Cops?" Blackie said. "They're fucking cops?"

"Whataya think," said Mike the Greek, "normal people talk like this?"

"So what's the problem over here," Blackie said. "You guys cops, okay. So whataya want, a hat or something?"

Dante fixed his eyes on Blackie as if he were forced to look at something not worth looking at. "What did you say?" he said.

"Ey, I'll buy you guys breakfast and I can keep the signs on the phones. Hah?"

Dante turned abruptly, walked outside to the vestibule, and tore the signs off the telephones. He looked at Ray Velasquez, who watched him from the doorway, his arms still folded.

"What is it?" Dante asked Ray.

Ray shaded his eyes with his hand. "Nothing," he said. "I was just trying to remember how many cups of coffee you drank."

Dante began cursing under his breath. An elderly couple entering the diner moved away from him. Jimmy came from inside the diner and hooked Dante by the arm, saying, "Snap out of it, pally. C'mon, we're gonna go to work, go to the plant, do a little business, nice nice."

Dante pulled his arm free and walked back into the diner. "Here we go," he heard Jimmy say.

A half dozen customers were hunched over their coffees at the counter. Blackie and Mike had hitched a ride out of town, they were nowhere to be seen. Dante turned to leave, but as he did he caught a glimpse of Mike peeking at him from the kitchen. Dante bared his teeth, giving off one hell of a hiss. He took an ashtray from off the counter and threw a high inside fastball at Mike's head.

"All right, enough of this shit," Jimmy said, flat and quick. He grabbed Dante by the shoulder and pulled him from the diner, walked him down the steps and kept going until they stood before the blue department Pontiac.

Jimmy slowly brought his palms together. "I pray," he said, "that whatever is eating at you has had its fill, and you've cleared your head."

"What the hell was that all about?" Ray said.

"They're bastards," Dante told them. "They're all screwups and bastards."

"These days," Ray said, "you can say that for anybody."

"A bunch of bums they build jailhouses for," Dante said. "A hat, the bum wants to give me twenty bucks so he can put a sign on a phone. Bastards."

Ray became preoccupied with his car keys. He was a man who preferred to do his job quietly, without trouble. He smiled and turned to Jimmy and said, "It's the caffeine and sugar. Keep your partner away from caffeine."

"It's nothing serious," Jimmy told him. "It happens all the time. Side effect of a low-grade IQ."

"Why don't you two guys screw off?" Dante said.

And Jimmy said, "Sure."

CHAPTER SIX

JoJo spent a leisurely Saturday morning at the Nestor Club, and for the first time in days he felt relieved. He was in every sense at home in his world, among his people, on his streets. Getting nods and smiles and handshakes from kids, from old women in black who crossed themselves and twisted handkerchiefs when they saw him. And neighborhood businesspeople, straight-world folks, made absurd gestures of friendship toward him. Some didn't love him, some did, and those that didn't kept their mouths shut. His people, those who had given themselves to him, knew that being within the family gave them an identity they could find nowhere else.

True he had enemies, true that even within the family there were some that would have loved to see him gone. True there were those who thought he had not earned his position of power. And there were city cops and federal agents trying to nail him to get him in their cross hairs. True, all true, but he had grown to love this life, and he would master it and settle for nothing less. Strutting his stuff on 101st Avenue in Queens made him feel alive. He was a man of growing respect, and among all of the people on the street and in the club, there was not one who doubted that he was special. JoJo realized this. And in keeping with his position as the underboss and heir apparent of the Paradiso family, he carried and conducted himself as a made man of honor, a gangster who could lead.

As such a man he had considerable power and latitude. And it was within that latitude, he rationalized, that his recent breach of his father's trust, his treason to the family, fell. By JoJo's lights a leader inspired devotion, was flamboyant, daring, and deadly, and he danced to tunes others simply never heard. A leader, he told himself, grabbed the world by the short hairs and shook.

It was eleven o'clock in the morning, and he stood on the corner of the street enjoying himself, looking at the people passing in front of the club with Bruno and Frankie F'n Furillo, Bruno's man, behind him. JoJo rolled his shoulders, put on the big smile. He was a tough guy, the head man, he was God. He could kill anyone he wanted to.

If he was to lead this family, and lead this family he would, he could not expect that everyone would love him. The truth was, it was only his father he cared about, only the Skipper's love had meaning. It had been his father's authority alone that he acknowledged, not the law, which he knew could be bought, or the rules of the straight world. Other people's laws and rules meant nothing to him. And so if he no longer took his father's word as hallowed law, who then was going to tell him what to do?

Standing on the corner feeling cool and loose, he suddenly experienced a brief surge of panic. He had not made a conscious decision to enter this criminal life. He did what his father had him do, and the Skipper had to know that someday he would be his own man. So now it was over, buried. He had broken away from his father. The only way the Skipper could stop him was to kill him.

A group of neighborhood boys moved along the sidewalk in front of the club, walking on their toes in a slightly forward lurch. They bobbed their heads in his direction, trying to catch his eye and calling his name, JoJo heard one of them say something about "That's him, the big man, the main guy."

He looked at them and smiled. He appeared to the boys to be the king of Queens, an important wiseguy. He was their idol.

Win or lose, JoJo had decided that he was not going to give in to his father. It was the time of his time. He'd convinced himself that top-flight results are the consequences of smart actions. Soon he would be in a position to do exactly as he chose, and that thought pleased him.

On this morning filled with spring ripeness, all the people passing in the street and all the hangout guys at the club seemed cheerful. Everyone had a smile for JoJo Paradiso. Even Frankie F'n Furillo seemed happy, feeling the beat of the street, giving guys passing and the ones that hung out funky little hand slaps.

Twice a month on Saturday morning JoJo sat in for his father and held court at a table in the Nestor Club. On this morning he sat drinking a pot of coffee and eating Italian bread stuffed with scrambled eggs. He sat and reviewed applications from three men who wanted to mob up the family. They were stiffs, three losers sponsored by Mario Madonna, an aggressive lieutenant in Bruno's crew. Bruno Greco sat across the table from JoJo, and JoJo locked in on him, held his eyes as Mario went through his song and dance. Mario had taken a chair and he sat hunched over, elbows on knees, pleading his case.

"I like to make money," Mario said. "We all wanna make money, right?"

Bruno nodded at JoJo, a smirk on his face as if he had read his mind.

"You proposed these mopes twice already," Bruno said.

"Ey," Mario said. "I could use these guys. So I'm throwing their names out again."

"*Stunatu,*" JoJo said.

"I'm not dopey," Mario pleaded. "I need new blood, and these guys, they're money makers, earners."

Mario was paunchy and slope-shouldered, he had close-cropped curly hair, you could say kinky, and large pointy ears. His hands were trembling, so he kept them out of sight.

"You don't listen," JoJo told him. "You refuse to take me seriously. These guys are wacked out. They do dope, they're always coked up."

Bruno nodded enthusiastically. "What does he gotta do? Write you a letter, for chrissake?"

JoJo watched Mario's slack mouth tighten. "It ain't easy finding recruits," he said.

JoJo dismissed him with a quick flip of his hand. "Beat it," he said. "Go and do yourself a favor and find some good people. People you could trust, people with some heart. Don't come to me with these shitheads."

Mario smiled, he stood up. "I figured I'd give them one more shot. I figured it couldn't hurt."

"You figured wrong," Bruno said. His eyes flicked toward the door.

Mario leaned on the table and gripped the sides so hard his knuckles went white.

"They'll go to the Ramminos. They'll hook up with those bastards," Mario said.

JoJo sipped his coffee. "Good," he said. "They deserve each other."

Mario turned and headed for the street.

"He keeps trying," Bruno said.

"Sure," JoJo told him, "but not hard enough."

————

Neighborhood people came to the club on the second Saturday in order to solicit help from JoJo for one reason or another. He gave advice and lent money and dispensed some informal justice within the neighborhood. Most of the requests were mundane, a few fairly serious.

Once seated at the table with his sandwich and coffee, word hit the street that JoJo Paradiso was ready to listen. A small crowd then collected and formed a line outside the club, waiting for an audience. Sitting in for his father this way, JoJo felt as though he were anointed, the new boss of the Paradiso family.

A middle-aged businessman with a mild clerklike appearance wanted to get his average son into an above-average law school. The man wore gold-rimmed eyeglasses, an expensive suit, and way too much cologne. "I'll see what I can do," JoJo told him.

"Yale," the man said. "We have family in New Haven, it would be nice."

JoJo took a drink of his coffee. "Why not Harvard?" JoJo asked him.

The man said, "To tell you the truth, Harvard would be very nice, but I don't think Johnny Boy, that's my son, Johnny Boy, I doubt he'd be able to cut it at Harvard."

"But Yale," JoJo said. "You figure Johnny Boy could get along at Yale."

The man shrugged.

"There are good law schools in Florida," JoJo said. "Would Johnny Boy mind going to Florida?"

"Oh no," the man told him. "He'll go wherever you think he should go."

JoJo thought about that, about a kid who called himself Johnny Boy and would go to any law school he suggested. Bruno took notes and never once looked at the man.

After the man left the club, Bruno asked JoJo, he said, "Whataya want to do for that guy?"

"I don't know," JoJo said. "Maybe Barry can send the kid's application to his brother in Florida."

As an irredeemably compromised attorney, Barry Cooper was as much a part of the family as any made man. Similar to cops that lose it and go over to the other side, become reflections of the people they police, lawyers too can become walking, talking counterparts of their clients. The man walked the walk and talked the talk, a sharpie, a man on the inside, a guy who had a piss-poor regard for his oath. A wiseguy. That image had found a home in his heart, and now JoJo possessed his soul.

Back when JoJo told him you're one of us, it sounded right, almost memorable, but thinking on it later, Barry had a real hard time seeing himself as evil, he had never thought of himself as a hoodlum, yet that's what he was. In the purest sense he was a member of the Paradiso family, a lawyer the Paradisos had taken for keeps. Barry didn't carry a gun, guns scared the hell out of him. Then again, he didn't need one, his pal JoJo Paradiso could put hundreds of guns at his disposal, and all JoJo asked in return was undying loyalty to the family.

Barry bought his clothes in the same shops JoJo did, had his hair done by the same barber, bought his Mercedes from the same dealer. He accepted gifts, a Rolex watch, a star-sapphire pinky ring, both of which he wore with a kind of pride that was cranked-up and seemed sincere, but the reality was another story. Wiseguy glamour had gotten under his skin when he was young and full of himself, and now, years later, when he looked at himself in the mirrored walls of his bathroom, the slick dude that looked back at him made him a little queasy. Barry recognized that he had very few options, one has a bitch of a time resigning from the Mafia, at least if one wants to remain upright one does.

"Barry ain't gonna be able to help this kid. I know Johnny Boy, the kid usta run bets for me, he's a dunce," Bruno said.

"Oh that's terrific," JoJo said. "So why did you make me waste my time with the kid's old man?"

"The guy owns a car leasing company. We use his cars once in a while."

"All right, send the kid's application to Barry. We need to help our friends."

"I'm tellin' you, the kid's a dunce. What kinda lawyer is he gonna make?"

JoJo reached across and pinched Bruno's cheek. "What, you don't know any stupid lawyers?"

"I'll send it."

"Who's next?"

A legit workingman wanted to get his son a union card in a carpenters local. JoJo told the man to see his brother-in-law, Nicky Napoli. Bruno scratched out a telephone number where Nicky could be reached and gave it to the man.

The man said, quiet like, with his head down, "My son's no genius.

But he's a good boy, a hard worker. He never gave me no trouble. There's no jobs for boys his age. Nothing for him to do but to hang out on corners. I worry for him, for his future."

"Nicky will send him someplace where he will learn a good trade," JoJo told him. "He'll learn how to hang sheetrock and how to plaster. It's hard work, but he'll earn ten, twenty dollars an hour, and double that on Saturdays. He'll make a life for himself."

"He's no genius," the man said again. "But he is respectful to his mother and me."

JoJo shrugged, frowning at the man. "Maybe he's a lot smarter than you think. You ever think that maybe he keeps his smart thoughts to himself, you ever think that?"

"Whatayacallit?" the man said. "Sensitive. That's what my boy is, he's sensitive."

"Tell him to call Nicky, Nicky likes sensitive kids," JoJo told him.

"Sensitive is good," Bruno said.

"Like you," JoJo said.

"Yes," the man said. "I've heard that Bruno is a very sensitive man." Bringing it from his heart with a wide smile.

"Yeah," Bruno said. "Who the fuck told you that?"

A housewife with an unmarried and very pregnant daughter came to the table. Bruno was sitting close to JoJo now, whispering, telling him not to forget that Lilo Santamaria was due to arrive at two. And there was Frankie F'n Furillo, he too had a problem.

The woman made a production of standing at the table surveying the room. She wanted support from the already married soon-to-be father of her daughter's expected baby.

"And the man?" JoJo asked her. "Who is he?" The woman told him her daughter worked at the telephone company. Explained to JoJo that the man that knocked up her daughter was her daughter's supervisor. An important man in the telephone company.

JoJo gave the woman his attorney's business card. "This man," JoJo said, "his name is Barry Cooper. He's a good lawyer. You go see him, there will be no charge to you."

The woman sat still and quiet and held the card in her hand for a long time. "I thought maybe you could send somebody to see him," she said finally.

"For what?" Bruno said.

"You know."

"What?" JoJo said. "What do you want us to do?"

"Ey," the woman said. "This man is fifty years old. He romanced my daughter with a wife at home. He needs a kick in the ass."

Bruno had a sleepy smile on his face. "How many bones you want broken?" he said. And JoJo thought here we go.

"I don't know. Maybe an arm, a leg. Whatever," the woman said.

"No, no wait," JoJo said. "I'll tell you what. How about I send a couple of people to hold this guy down and you can beat him with a bat? How's that?"

"I don't think so," the woman said. "You see I'm not very strong."

JoJo made a circle with his thumb and forefinger. "Take the card I gave you. Go and see the lawyer. His pen is better than a bat."

The woman stared at JoJo in disgust.

"You can't get justice anywhere anymore," she said. "This man had no class, no self-respect. He needs a beating."

JoJo turned to look at the line of people standing in the street.

"So," the woman said testily, "I'll go and see the lawyer."

"Good," JoJo said.

There were doctor bills and unpaid rent; people with courage and without means of support came to JoJo for help. This tradition started by his father had become a pleasant habit for JoJo and endeared him to scores of straight people who would then, of course, owe him favors. Like the use of safe telephones, appearances in courtrooms, clean cars and safe apartments.

It occurred to JoJo that his two o'clock meeting with the arrogant, posturing bigmouth Lilo Santamaria might turn out to be a real pain in the ass. Lilo was a family capo, a bit of a mental case, who, JoJo had learned, wanted to kill one of JoJo's favorite younger members. He intended to change Lilo's mind, get a haircut, and then drop by unannounced at his father's house. Then Frankie F'n Furillo sat down and dropped the bomb.

"I was waiting for the right time to tell you what happened here," Frankie said. "I think now's the time to do it."

Bruno poured himself a cup of coffee, and JoJo looked at Frankie straight on. "What's up," JoJo said.

"I hadda whack a guy."

JoJo stood up. He felt Bruno's hand touch his arm.

"Joseph . . ."

"It's all right. I'm going outside to get some air. C'mon you two, let's go for a walk." His tone was soft, intimate and coaxing. He said, "Fellas, let me put it another way," still in a soft tone. "Get the fuck outside and let's walk and talk."

On the street in front of the club JoJo slapped the face of Frankie F'n Furillo. "Since when you talk killing inside the club?"

"Jesus," said Frankie, "I f'n forgot. I'm sorry, JoJo, I totally f'n forgot. Being nervous and all."

JoJo put a hand on Frankie's arm, and they walked and Frankie talked.

"Ya see, I got this f'n money out. This f'n loan to this f'n guy from f'n Sheepshead Bay."

"Tell us why you killed him," Bruno said, and JoJo said, "Talk quietly, will ya?"

Frankie F'n Furillo told both JoJo and Bruno that he had a made a loan to a Russian in Sheepshead Bay. The man owned a private cab company, and he'd borrowed ten thousand, paying a thousand a week vigorish. He was three weeks behind, so the payments had gone to $1,250 per week, which made his interest debt $3,750, not counting principal. During the past week, Frankie told them, he drove to the cab company to pick up some money from the Russian, whose name was Uri. A degenerate gambler, Uri was in the middle of a high-stakes poker game.

"He was drunk and insulted me," Frankie said. "Insults that I took with a smile. I was there to pick up money, not to find trouble."

It was at this meeting that Uri told Frankie that he would give his wife to Frankie for one night if Frankie would chop a thousand from the bill. The offer gave Frankie a case of the chokes. "Ya see," Frankie said, "I had eyes for the woman. And some people knew it."

The woman knew it too, she smiled at Frankie whenever they happened to meet.

"You did it. You slept with the woman and lowered the bill," Bruno said, and JoJo said, "Let him tell it."

Yes, Frankie told them, he arranged to meet Uri's wife at the bar of the Golden Gate Motel. He got a room and they spent a few hours. She was, as Frankie laid it out, "f'n terrific."

A week later, the past Friday, Frankie returned to the cab company, and Uri was waiting. Drunk again, in the middle of another poker game, he took Frankie into his office, where a young girl sat waiting. Uri told Frankie that the girl was his daughter, and for two weeks' payment, $2,400, Frankie could have her too. Frankie told JoJo and Bruno that he f'n flipped out. He left the cab company and returned late that night with Cockeyed Paulie. They caught Uri closing the place, and Frankie ice-picked him while Paulie shot him. They left the body on the street in front of the cab company, made it look like a street robbery.

"If it was me, I'da killed the guy too," Bruno said.

After a few moments JoJo said, "Frankie, you did what you did and now it's done. You know you got the man's bill. You owe Bruno, what is it? fourteen, fifteen grand. I hope this woman is worth it."

"Oh she's f'n worth it, Joseph. This is a nice woman, a real lady. She cried when we did it."

JoJo draped his arm over Bruno's shoulders, and they walked off a few feet.

"Jesus Christ," Bruno said, "I don't know what to say to the guy. Do I punish him or what?"

"Cut the shit, okay?" JoJo said. "You want me to believe Frankie clipped this Uri without your nod."

"Well, I thought it would be good for you to hear the story right from Frankie."

"So what do you want me to do?"

"Nothing. I don't want you to do nothing."

"I don't plan to. This is your headache, Bruno. All this chitchat with me is a bunch of bullshit. It's after the fact, don't come to me after the fact. You get my meaning?"

"I'll tell you something," Bruno said. "All the things you got going these days, I make decisions on my own. I got to."

"You mean you make decisions about family business without my okay?"

"In certain areas. I mean your father trusted me to make decisions like this one."

"That cab company," JoJo said, "you got a piece of it, don't you?"

Bruno nodded.

"Amazing," JoJo said. "Whataya think, I'm a moron?"

It hung there in the street with cars and buses going by, and the day growing warmer. He heard Bruno say, "Don't worry about me. I'm with you back to back, to the end. Don't worry about me at all."

JoJo didn't answer him.

"Joseph, you get a check each month. The White Nights Cab Company. You get two grand a month from them."

"Four grand from now on," JoJo said.

"Three," Bruno said.

JoJo smiled.

An hour later at the table near the window, a fresh cup of coffee in his hand, JoJo sat waiting for Lilo Santamaria. This day was not going easily. And now there was Lilo. Bruno had warned him that Lilo would come simply as a show of respect, put on a little song and dance, shrug, smile and nod his head. He would listen to what JoJo had to say, then go out and whack the kid. The kid, Vinny Rapino, Bruno told JoJo, was counting back from ten and that was that. "Well I'm gonna give Lilo one word of advice," JoJo told Bruno. "I'm gonna tell him how much I like the kid."

"Good, good," Bruno said. "Won't mean nothing. Lilo's gonna take him out, with or without your nod."

To kill a made member was no easy thing. There were rules, and in the Paradiso family, rules were enforced. Vinny Rapino was an inducted member, a soldier in Lilo's crew, who often visited the Nestor Club with his boss. JoJo got a kick out of the kid, he made him laugh. The way he swaggered through the streets with aplomb and the sense of a movie star. A major ladies' man, Vinny Rapino was full of himself, oblivious of the fact that his bedroom jumping could get him killed.

"The kid's in the hunt," JoJo told Bruno, "he's got a dick like a tire iron, with about as much sense. But he's a good kid, a good earner. I like him, I don't want to see him hurt."

"He ain't careful," Bruno told him. "Nicky told me he clocked him with three broads one night at Lilo's gambling joint. I mean, the kid's engaged to Lilo's daughter. Every goodfella in the joint was warning him."

This was a personal thing, a matter of respect. As a captain with a crew of strong earners, Lilo could kill Little Vinny without JoJo's approval, it was in the rules. Still, JoJo knew that Lilo wanted to be stroked, the Neanderthal executioner would want reassurance.

For his part, Lilo understood that even for powerful capos like himself, it was less than wise to anger JoJo Paradiso. The family underboss had a bloody temper and an army of shooters led by Bruno and Karl Marx Syracusa. And there was the Dancer, Rudy Randazzo, with a crew of fifty soldiers all loyal to JoJo, and JoJo's brother-in-law, Nicodemo Napoli.

Nicky Black Napoli was the husband of Patricia Paradiso, JoJo's sister. The black man—JoJo referred to his brother-in-law as the black man—would have loved the opportunity to go to war for JoJo. He'd go to war all right, drop bodies all over town, but he'd be plotting his own treachery. Nicky wore black clothes, black slacks, jackets, and shirts. He thought of himself as a rising star; to JoJo he was irreversibly insufferable. The guy made him nuts. Maybe it was his clothes, the black Caddy he drove, or maybe it was the Cuban chick he kept in Jackson Heights. The guy was too slick. He was or he wasn't, depending on your definition of slick. But for reasons JoJo couldn't fathom, his sister loved the creep. JoJo had less use for Nicky Black then he did for Lilo, and for Lilo he had none. How Patricia hooked up with the mope was beyond him.

JoJo believed that this life was a deadly game. It was a pure bitch to stay ahead and keep tabs on all your enemies, the cops, the jerks in the family out doing their own thing, putting him in the jackpot time and again. Still, he played all games to win. And when you won, everything was fine, no need for explanations. He needed to stay sharp and surround himself with trusted friends.

To trust nobody didn't sound like too bad an idea. Be all eyes, his father had told him. All eyes and ears. It was probably the best advice he ever got. Nevertheless, in this business confidence was a strong suit, and JoJo had a truckload of it. Years earlier he had decided to go at this life with intensity. Settle for less, he told himself, you die of holes in some gutter, or worse yet, end up in jail for a century.

Lilo, JoJo knew, was a treacherous bastard, a man he believed would participate in a revolt. Like Tommy Yale, his other Brooklyn capo, Lilo had always wanted to move drugs. Both Yale's and Lilo's loyalty to the family hung by a slim thread. They were committed to the Skipper, but in their hearts neither had submitted to him. Still, they were smart enough to know that a showdown with JoJo would unleash the Skipper. It would be suicide to take on the entire family. The Skipper could, if he had to, tap the other families and put a thousand shooters in the street.

Lilo was good with figures. He knew he was outmanned, and to be outmanned was to be outgunned. He'd submit to JoJo as long as the Skipper was around. Without his father, Lilo believed, JoJo's strength would evaporate quickly, the family would fragment, and he could line up the other capos on his side. That is what Lilo believed, and so he was not about to love and serve JoJo. He would hang with the family for as long as the old man survived, not a moment longer.

JoJo had always liked Little Vinny, a handsome kid with a good mind. One hell of a hijacker, who had made his bones when he shot and killed a renegade kidnapper in Jersey. Vinny Rapino was soft-spoken, dressed well, a kid on the rise. He had the heart of a bear and was inducted before his twenty-fifth birthday. Well-thought-of goodfellas said that someday Vinny's dick would certainly get him killed.

As for Lilo, he had always been a little crazy, an old-time shooter who ran a gambling club and numbers bank on President Street in Brooklyn. He had a load of shylock money in the street, and his crew were heavy into counterfeiting. Lilo's crew also specialized in hijacking truckloads of televisions, furs, meat, and seafood. Lilo's numbers bank gave him access to the blacks of Bedford-Stuyvesant, the Puerto Ricans and Dominicans in Red Hook. The best avenues to move drugs in the city.

Lilo had money, his money made money. For Lilo there was money here there and everywhere. Still, there was never enough. Lilo would hear stories about the trailer loads of drug cash the Sicilians and Colombians were counting, and those stories would burn his ears like a forest fire. The prohibition imposed by JoJo and his father regarding drug dealing drove him loony, it made Lilo want to march into battle.

JoJo had sniffed out Lilo making overtures to the Rammino family a while back. It was no secret that Armond Rammino was an international dope dealer, and Lilo had had several meetings with him. Reason enough, JoJo pointed out, to put Lilo away. The Skipper would not go for it. Let him slide, the Skipper had said, Lilo's been loyal for many years and has earned a pass. That's one pass, JoJo made it clear, one pass is all he gets. I'll warn him, the Skipper had said, and JoJo told his father no warnings, Pop. Lilo sees the Ramminos again without permission, I'll take his head.

A man in his early fifties, Lilo was fair-skinned and had short red hair, a belly, and thick shoulders and forearms developed in younger days when he was a furniture mover. He had a perfectly round head on a bulging neck, and a temper second only to Bruno's. He was a Brooklyn-born Sicilian and years earlier had had strong ties to the old renegade Gallo crew. Lilo owned much of the Gallo spirit. But he had more money than Crazy Joey Gallo, and more men in the street than Larry Gallo. Unlike the brothers Gallo, Lilo figured he could stand a war with the family and probably survive. It was the probably that kept him in place. Someday, he figured, he'd strike at JoJo with crippling ferocity. Kill him and change the family name. Someday, he told his crime partner Tommy Yale, our day will come.

Lilo thought of JoJo as a bust-out guy, a man not unlike Joe Colombo, a mob boss who had received an entire family as a gift. A man who Lilo believed hadn't earned a thing except the bullet that found his head. For JoJo, Lilo meant nothing but trouble.

Lilo arrived at the club around two wearing a blue running suit and sucking on a cigar. Lilo favored imported Italian cigars. The rope-shaped black thing hung from the corner of his mouth, and a large paper shopping bag dangled from his hand. He seemed tense even as he said, "I got two silver-tip roast beefs here, one for you one for your father. Get one of the kids to put 'em in the refrigerator."

You smart bastard, JoJo thought, you got it figured out. Bring gifts, let people know the boss's pleasures are always on your mind. Be smooth and cool, deliver tribute with a smile. You slick piece of work, JoJo thought, slick guy. Anyone could deliver money. But food was a thoughtful gift, and the Skipper would appreciate it.

"C'mon," JoJo said, standing. "Let's get outta here. Let's go for a walk."

Lilo wiped his nose uneasily. He handed the bag he carried to Frankie F'n Furillo, cleared his throat, shrugged and looked unhappy.

"Okay," Lilo said. "You wanna walk and talk we'll walk and talk. But my mind's made up, and I hope I'm not here, with all respect Joseph, to catch pressure."

JoJo went to the door, to see that Lilo had not moved.

"Lilo," he said. "C'mon."

People met at the club to discuss deals and scores, the business of the family. But JoJo laid down a law that no important business conversations were to take place inside the walls of the club. Walls, JoJo told his people, have ears. You got business to do, then you walk and talk.

Two years earlier he had taken a hatchet to the wall phone. You need to make a call or you expect a call, you use the pay phones in the candy store on the corner.

Sonny the Hawk, a hang-around guy who had shot so much dope in his younger days that his brain was half dead, worked the candy store and took messages. The Hawk also made the coffee, sandwich, and beer runs for the never-ending card game in the club's back room. There was a fifty-cup coffee machine that no one used. JoJo once as a joke pointed out that a traitor could whack out the whole *borgata* with a few drops of poison pitched into the coffee maker. Half the crew stopped drinking coffee entirely, the other half sent out.

It was a Paradiso family custom to gather the capos once a week for dinner, and dinner was held at a different restaurant each week. An hour before dinner, the capos were told where they were to eat. The restaurant owner closed his place for their private party. Doors were locked and guards were posted. Although the family was welcomed in Manhattan, dinner meetings were held in Queens. And although members of different crews came to the club to hang out and play cards during the week, crew members from other families were not welcome and never came around unless invited.

Wiseguys from the club were courteous and friendly with neighbor-hood storeowners and residents. The most legitimate neighborhood people kept their antennas up for a strange car or face; the club was warned when any stranger hit the street. Sunday mornings and afternoons the club was closed; Sundays the families of the family came together for the Sunday meal. It was expected.

Lilo started after JoJo, then turned back angrily. "Frankie," he said, "you get a call for me, you come get me. I'm expecting a call."

Trying to sound tough now, JoJo thought, a no-nonsense hardass boss. The guy was a regular goddamn floor show, an actor.

JoJo figured that what he had to do was tell him, keep telling Lilo that he liked Vinny Rapino. Ask Lilo to take a minute to think, realize that whacking out a good earner for personal reasons made no sense.

Walking, Lilo had been saying, "Ey, the guy's in my crew and he insulted me. *Me* he insulted, and I'm gonna bury him."

"Vinny's a good boy," JoJo said. "What you wanna go and do this for, Lilo?"

"A good boy?" Lilo said. He looked at JoJo with sympathy.

People greeted JoJo as he walked with his arm around Lilo's shoulders. A group of teenagers huddled on the corner near the candy store. One of them was smoking a marijuana cigarette. "Swallow that," JoJo told him. Stony teenage faces softened when JoJo smiled. "Swallow it," he said to the boy. The boy's dark pockmarked face showed a shadow of weary amusement.

There was some quick movement and clutching of hands as JoJo moved among the group. "Swallow it," he said again. The boy with the marijuana shrugged and swallowed the joint and then stood there looking at JoJo. JoJo reached into his pocket and removed a twenty-dollar bill. He handed the twenty to the boy, whose face had gone a bit pale.

"Go ahead," he told him. "Go do yourself a favor and catch a movie. Take your buddies here. Be a big man."

"I can't be such a big man with a twenty," the kid told him and gave him a nice-boy smile.

"Oh is that right?"

"Excuse me, Mr. Paradiso, but there's seven of us. The movie is five bucks a head. Then there's the girlfriends and sodas and popcorn, maybe a pizza later. Know what I mean?"

"You don't drink soda. And you don't eat f'n popcorn. Who you kidding?"

"Ey," the kid said. "I gave it a shot."

For a long moment everyone was quiet. Then JoJo laughed, he laughed in the sunlight, throwing his head back, he laughed like a drunk or a madman.

"What am I gonna do, Lilo?" JoJo said. "The kid's got heart. Maybe we got us a recruit here."

"Take the twenty and go," Lilo told the kid.

The kid turned to JoJo and JoJo nodded his okay.

"You know," Lilo said, "you got these kids with you too. They'll do anything you want."

"Yeah, kids I can get to do what I want. But with my captains I got problems."

They walked past a *granita* peddler pushing a cart of shaved ice.

"You want an ice?" JoJo asked him.

"No," Lilo said. "I don't eat that stuff. It gets on my clothes."

Lilo had a ferocious reputation. He wasn't quite as bad as Bruno Greco but he was bad enough to rattle the knees of anyone he turned on. Walking, Lilo made the sign of the gun.

"This piece of shit Vinny insulted me and now he's gotta go."

"Why?" JoJo said.

"Why? Why?" Lilo shook his head in mock reproach. "Cause I wanna do it is why."

JoJo stood still and stared at him. Lilo laughed softly.

"C'mon," JoJo said.

"No c'mon. He's engaged to my daughter. They were gonna get married next month. I got the whole thing arranged. The Italian Gardens out on Northern Boulevard. Three hundred people, gonna cost me a fortune, this f'n thing. I got Jimmy Roselli, he's gonna sing 'My Buddy' and all."

"Jimmy Roselli? You kidding? My father loves Jimmy Roselli. How did you get him?"

"The man's my cousin Baldo's goombah. They're close. They do anything for each other. He was coming to the wedding. I mean, this is the ultimate insult."

"So you're gonna go and stalk this kid. This twenty-five-year-old kid, whose got—and you said it yourself—all kinds of promise. The kid's smart, he's the best hijacker you got."

"He ain't no kid Joseph. You know Vinny ain't no kid, he's a man, and I'm gonna kill him. And that's it."

"I got nothing to say?"

"Joseph, you're the under. You tell me no, I gotta think about it. But it's my crew, Joseph, and this is a personal matter."

JoJo glanced at Lilo and spoke to him in Italian. "I'm asking you as a personal favor to reconsider. Give this anger of yours time to settle," he said.

Lilo's eyebrows came together as if he were counting money. "We're talking about my daughter here, Joseph. You don't have children. Maybe this is hard for you to understand."

JoJo nodded emphatically. "When you're right, you're right. I have no children, but I think I can understand a father's pain. I'm only asking that you reconsider."

"Reconsider what?"

"Look," JoJo said. "What does Vinny bring in a month?"

"Ten, twelve grand."

"And what do I see out of that?"

"Twenty, twenty-five percent."

"That's twenty grand a year, for chrissake. The kid's twenty-five years old. He doesn't get hit by a bus or anything, say he does business another twenty-five, thirty years. You know how much cash that adds up to?"

Lilo stepped back and held out his arms. "A lot," he said. "I ain't stupid, I know it's a lot, but money ain't everything Joseph. This is a personal matter. A matter of respect."

"Jesus Christ Almighty. This ain't the old days. You don't go around killing people for bullshit. And this is bullshit Lilo, total bullshit."

"My daughter ain't bullshit, Joseph."

"C'mere," JoJo said. He slipped his arms through Lilo's and gave him a bear hug. "I know the kid hurt you. He hurt you bad, huh?"

Lilo shrugged. "There's ways of doing things, you know what I mean?"

During the course of running this show called the Paradiso family JoJo had had several insights. One insight was that the most vicious of men, men capable of performing brutal torture and murder, men who would go for your throat at the slightest insult, were also men whose hearts could be melted by a woman's smile, a song, or the touch of a child's hand. Men as treacherous and unpredictable as rabid dogs, men whose souls were fired by acts of indiscriminate violence, demented and dangerous men could be moved to tears by moronic lines of long-forgotten poetry. It was a nutty scene, this life, nutty; it was also all he knew.

JoJo and Lilo Santamaria walked in silence for some moments. JoJo watched as Lilo took the cigar out of his mouth. He held it up, examined it, then threw it away. He said quietly, "My daughter ain't stopped crying for a week. Her mother is going crazy."

He sounded simply like a father in pain, describing, with heartfelt sadness, his daughter's unhappiness and his wife's anger.

"The bastard," Lilo went on. "I spent forty grand redoing the house. They were gonna live with me. You gotta see this kitchen I built in the basement."

"Kids don't think sometimes," JoJo said.

"Do me a favor Joseph, stop calling the bastard a kid, will ya?"

JoJo turned his back to Lilo, he looked across the street and folded his arms.

"What if the kid sees this through?" JoJo declared. "What if Vinny changes his mind again and decides to marry your beautiful daughter."

Lilo Santamaria had been a street fighter all his life and he liked to think of himself as a man who could strike fear with a look. He had sprung from the Italian ghetto of South Brooklyn, had his own crew at twenty-five. He'd made his reputation during the Gallo-Profaci wars, having killed five rival gang members. Then he had mobbed up with the Paradiso family, turning on the Gallos and throwing in with the family, bringing his entire crew with him. JoJo had reminded his father on more than one occasion that Lilo, in his heart, was a traitor. His own brother, a longshoreman-turned-hit man, had an even bigger reputation for violence. Lilo and his brother Sonny had joined different sides in the Brooklyn wars. It was said that Lilo had arranged the ambush where Sonny and two other Gallo men had been shotgunned.

"If Vinny does the right thing, you'll let this pass?" JoJo said finally.

"He won't."

As seen from the apartment window across the street, they were two men having a cosy chat.

"And if he will?" said JoJo, speaking softly in English with a smiling complacency. "Maybe I can help."

"I figure he's taken his stand. And he'll go down because of it."

"But what if he cleans up his act and comes home to your daughter?"

Lilo shrugged his shoulders, he took another cigar from his pocket and lit up. He laughed as if at the very notion. "He said he fell in love with another woman. Another woman, can you believe that?" In Italian, Lilo went on, "Any man that can't take care of two women is no man in my eyes."

"Send him to me," JoJo said. "I need a driver. Send him here for a week, maybe two. I know Vinny, he sometimes gets confused. Maybe I can straighten him out. Then your daughter won't lose the man she loves, and I won't lose an earner."

"You want me to send him here? To you?"

"That's what I said."

Lilo took an immense draw on his cigar. He squeezed his eyes shut. "Okay," he said. "In one month he don't come home to my daughter, you waste him."

"Done," JoJo said.

"And his debts," Lilo said. "You kill him and pick up his debts. He owes me twenty-five grand."

"Whoa!" JoJo said with a huge grin. "I didn't know about the bill. He owes you money, he owes you money. His bills have nothing to do with me."

"It's in the rules," Lilo said. "You kill him you pick up his debt."

"For chrissake," JoJo said. "I don't want to kill him, you do."

"This mook"—Lilo pointed at him—"is a brain tumor. And tumors, you gotta remove 'em."

They walked and talked a bit more, JoJo pointing out how difficult and thankless fatherhood can be. He was waiting to calm down. He had been on the edge of threatening. The sight of some of his men standing on the sidewalk in front of the club filled him with dread. He was their boss, they counted on him to lead. Lilo's words about killing the man his only daughter loved had stayed with him. He thought of his own father, how he was betraying him.

"And Lilo," he said at last. "Not now, not this minute, but I want to hear from you in a few days. And what I want to hear is exactly how much coke you could move if you had all you needed."

Lilo flicked the cigar he'd just lit out into the street. It took several seconds before he calmed down enough to speak. He clapped his hands together, then brought them to JoJo's cheeks. "You're serious?"

JoJo stared at him and glanced around the street.

"It's about time," Lilo said.

"And," JoJo said, "I want you to arrange a meeting for me with Armond Rammino. I know you can do it. I don't want to talk about it. Just get it done."

Lilo was giving him his are-you-kidding-me? look. That flat mean smile. All the same, JoJo saw real shock there. The fence jumper caught on the top rail.

"I'll do what you ask. I'll arrange the meeting for you. I think I can do that."

Sure you can do it, you lowlife, JoJo said to himself. He stood in the middle of the sidewalk and stretched. "Christ, I'm tired," he said.

Lilo's eyes were vacant. He looked stunned, a little lost, and indeed, caught. Everybody's Judas.

"I'll send the kid to you," he said. "You want me to reach out for Armond, I'll do it. But what makes you think a meet like that will be easy for me to arrange?"

"Instinct," JoJo told him.

CHAPTER SEVEN

D ante had worked with Kathy Gibbons, the fourth member of the Paradiso investigative team, only twice. On each occasion he had walked away with different impressions: an uptown Manhattan wiseass, a good-looking woman with an evil streak, a witch, a hell of a cop. He figured that whatever he knew of her was not the whole truth, yet it was the way he saw her. Not being one to suffer over the varied weirdness of temporary partners, he had hardly a notion about Kathy Gibbons since their last joint assignment.

At the Nestor Club plant, Dante looked out the window for a while, then glanced over at Kathy.

She sat on a high bar stool in front of a window that looked out onto 101st Avenue, and she was snapping pictures in quick succession, using the Nikon like a sniper's rifle. From her seat she had a perfect view of the candy store on the corner and the club just beyond.

Kathy favored him with a quick impatient smile, then bent her head to the Nikon again. He stood watching her do her routine with the camera, wondering why he hadn't taken a closer look at her before. He liked her hair, the way it was gathered at the back of her head in a blond ponytail. And those jeans and the violet T-shirt, the way she filled them out wasn't too shabby. Noticing Kathy, Dante felt a certain sexual energy. It was like somebody had flipped on a switch in him. For months the intensity of his marriage bed had been zero. Still, the sudden tightening in his groin puzzled him. This woman was, after all, gay. And then as part of the same thought he wondered, How does anyone know for certain?

She wore a red handkerchief tied around her neck and stood about five four or five, weighed probably one twenty. A knockout if you were into athletic-looking broads. She's a real babe, he thought, a genuine babe for sure.

Dante said, "How you doing? See anything exciting?"

"It looks like a goddamn gym in Rome. I've never seen so much black hair and muscles. Mostly hair."

She closed up tight with the telephoto lens, all aglow with enthusiasm. "I got about a dozen shots of Joseph. Oh shit," she said. "He's giving one of those Sons of Italy kisses to this hideous little fat creep."

Jimmy took up a pair of binoculars and looked through the venetian blind. "That's Lilo Santamaria. C'mere Dante," he said, and handed Dante the binoculars. "That's Lilo ain't it? He's a made guy from Brooklyn, a capo."

"That's him," Dante said.

"Oh no!" Kathy cried. Giggling, she clicked away. "The fat guy is pounding his chest. He looks like a gorilla with a hat and a cigar."

"Lilo's wasted about twenty people, sweetie," Dante said, handing the binoculars back to Jimmy. "He's not such a funny guy."

"Oh this is gonna be fun," Kathy said. "Please don't call me sweetie."

"JoJo looks good," Jimmy said, turning to Dante, giving him his you-be-careful smile.

Kathy shot him a look.

"Sorry," he said.

"About what?"

"Calling you sweetie."

"Forget it." Turning back to her telephoto lens, she whispered, "JoJo Paradiso, the handsome prince of One-hundred-and-first Avenue. The guy's been here all morning, walks the street like he owns the world and it owes him a living."

Dante said, "In his world it does."

"Actually," she told them, "when I get up real close with this thing here, I see worry lines all over that good-looking face of his. How old's this guy?"

"Thirty-nine," Jimmy and Dante cross-fired.

"The bugs?" Jimmy said. "How they doing?"

"Room bugs," Kathy said. "They're never great, but we'll get enough."

The past night Ray Velasquez had entered the club simply by going down the alley to the club's side door. He threw a black sheet over himself, and with a penlight and his small box of tricks he picked the lock.

His systematic bugging of the Nestor took him precisely twelve minutes. In three minutes he was through the door. There was no alarm system; if there had been, it would have taken maybe an additional five. Once inside, he removed the baseboard outlet beneath the coffee machine and replaced it with what looked like an exact duplicate. Four minutes.

The heart of the outlet was a transmitter. On the partition that divided the main club room from the smaller back room he discovered a wall phone. The lines to the phone had been slashed; it appeared the job had been done with a hatchet. The wall was scarred. Though useless, the phone was intact. He removed the mouth piece and dropped in a transmitter. Two minutes. Ray figured that both bugs were detection proof. The baseboard outlet had its own power source, and the drop-in mouthpiece emitted such a weak signal that a sweeping device would never pick it up. Correction—almost never.

He moved to the bathroom and checked the window. It had been nailed shut. Above the window was one of those metal curtain rods, on which two flowery curtains were hung. Behind the rod he taped a drop bug. This particular bug was powered by a ten-volt battery that would need changing every ten days or so. Three minutes. A wiseguy, when he used this bathroom, would have no privacy. In the Nestor Club, the men of the Paradiso family would have their voices and their body functions monitored.

Ray stood in the bathroom doorway and stared at the circle of light thrown by his penlight. There were times, particularly when he was tired, when his entire life seemed to have been nothing but eavesdropping. Nevertheless he could not rid himself of the pure light-headed pleasure his work gave him. His dreams were not of shootouts and car chases, of medal days at headquarters with crowds and reporters. Ray Velasquez fantasized about calmly dropping his nets, then carefully bringing in the bad guys.

In a week, maybe two, he figured, the Paradisos would find one, even two of the bugs. They would never find them all. But wiseguy nature being what it is, after a listening device is discovered by these characters who fully expect to be listened to, a sense of invulnerability seeps in. You figure it? A real bunch of deep thinkers, when wiseguys believe they know what's going on, nothing can change their minds. That is why they get killed by smiling friends, why they get popped and go to the can for a decade or two.

It was Ray's own private rule of thumb, if you bug a place other than a family residence, you drop your equipment everywhere. The worst killer bastard had the right to a certain privacy in his own home; Ray stayed away from bedrooms and bathrooms. But in a Mafia social club it was any target of opportunity.

Above all else, Ray recognized that tape-recorded conversation, when used in a criminal prosecution, is made available to all defendants. Defendants invariably have the right to scrutinize the court-ordered recordings of their chitchat, and fewer things in life gave him more pleasure than sharing with these morons words used by their friends and associates. Especially when those words contained their most intimate descriptions of each other. In one memorable case a vicious killer, a soldier in the Renina family, described his capo as a "mook, a pansy, a baby-fucker who would be nowhere without his wife's connections."

When transcripts of bugged conversation were circulated, bodies with holes showed up soon after. There was not widespread joy when the Renina capo heard his soldier's flowery description. The guy became an MIA real quick.

The problem for the Paradiso investigating team was that each bug installed by Ray sent a separate signal to a specific receiver. Line sheets, transcripts, had to be maintained for each device. No small task; who knew better than Dante and Jimmy that wiseguys, all wiseguys, gab like hell. Their lives were spent in hours of meaningless conversation. In order to keep the line-sheet books thinner than the Manhattan telephone directory, they decided to use the designation "general nonpertinent conversation" for every conversation they did not want to transcribe. The law gave them considerable discretion as to what was and was not pertinent.

Their plant was a vacant three-room apartment above a carpet store. The kitchen had a gas stove and refrigerator, a Formica table and four chairs. On the table were three FM radios wired to tape recorders. The transmissions were not clear, they were broken and heavy with static, but conversation could be heard, and it was clear that as they'd expected, there would be plenty of it.

The room from which they would make their observations of the street, the Nestor Club, and the candy store had three double-hung windows. Kathy Gibbons had set the Nikon and tripod up in front of the center window. Venetian blinds hid them from street view. On either side of the tripod were barstools, and in the center of the otherwise empty room was a card table. On the table was a book of mug shots of every known Paradiso family member, friend, and associate. On the first page was Salvatore Paradiso; the shot was thirty years old. He'd been forty-three at the time. Beneath the father's picture was a mug shot of JoJo. There followed, in alphabetical order the various capos, members of their crews, associates, friends, and frequently used lawyers, bankers, and businesspeople of the straight world.

The various Mafia family books had been put together by Chief Inspector Martin, the commanding officer of the Organized Crime Control Bureau. Dante had gone with him the day he turned them over to the first deputy police commissioner.

A bit stunned and ashen, the commissioner asked them, "Do you recognize how huge a predicament we could find ourselves in if these books fell into the hands of a journalist? You have people in here who have never been arrested; well-known, well-respected and politically powerful people." Dante recalled the commissioner's saying, "Think about deadly career moves Inspector."

Inspector Martin was not a man easily intimidated. He spelled out his feelings quietly, with dignity.

"There are lots of smart people making considerable amounts of money off organized crime in this country," he'd told the commissioner. "Lawyers, bankers, politicians and yes, even a cop or two. But nobody asks these people the right questions. Wiseguys are the enemy of our people, and people that associate themselves and become friends with the enemy of my people become my enemy."

"You know what I think, Inspector?" the commissioner said. "I think you've become a bit of a weirdo zealot. My kind of guy."

Dante flashed on the way the inspector smiled, how he winked at him and grinned. He recalled thinking, so there's still hope.

Standing at the window, studying the street, he could hear Jimmy going through the pages of the Paradiso family book, accompanying himself with a low whistle. When Jimmy whistled, Dante knew he was uneasy.

Over the years Dante had come to realize that unlike himself, Jimmy had not divided the world into good and evil. For Jimmy Burns a huge gray area existed. "Society is totally corrupt," Jimmy once told him. "How else can you explain this country's drug and violence problem?" Sometimes it seemed to Dante that police work bored Jimmy. He certainly wasn't in the job for the money. His parents, Dante understood, had left him plenty. Jimmy Burns was a painfully honest man, of that Dante was certain. As for himself, he would not concede that a set of circumstances did not exist in which he'd take a shot and grab some money. Then again, there was the memory of his father, the bullet he put into his head. Dante had come to realize that thought, fantasy, and daydreams were not action, were not real. Possibly there was no such thing as the perfect set of circumstances.

To Dante, Jimmy Burns was a man of action, a legit tough guy in an age where tough cops were going out of style. Even though they had been close friends since childhood, he did believe that there was a dark place way down in Jimmy's center that he was not privy to. It was weird, he thought, after so many years he knew Jimmy so well, and truthfully he hardly knew him at all.

On this day again he was worried about money. With Jimmy he forced himself not to mention the subject, but it caused him considerable stomach pain. He had succeeded in meeting last month's bills by taking another pension loan and borrowing a few hundred from his mother. He was in hock to the world.

Judy had run up the MasterCard when they'd moved into the house, what with furniture and carpeting and a kitchen set from Macy's. They needed a second car, so he got himself an auto loan and picked up a late-model Nissan. It cost him five thousand, banks just love lending money to cops. His Sunoco card was three months past due, and he hadn't paid the insurance on the Nissan or his Chevy. Next payday he was expecting a second check for the overtime he'd worked Christmas and New Year's; nevertheless, standing at the window looking out on 101st Avenue, he figured he'd have to hit his mother for another loan.

"Are you two going to run over to the wiretap?" Kathy asked. "Or do you want me to?"

"We should ask for help," Jimmy said. "You could use a partner."

"I have three partners, we don't need anyone else," Kathy said with a faint smile.

"Mostly you'll be working alone," Dante told her.

"Steady days, it's not bad. And I like working alone. A loner, that's me."

"Ray will put in hours. You know Ray, we won't be able to keep him away when things start hopping," Jimmy said.

"And now that my wife kicked my ass out in the street, I'm gonna have plenty of time on my hands," said Dante.

Kathy sat with her hand shading her eyes, staring down at the street. "It'll pass," she said. "Ray told me she's done it before."

"Yeah? How the hell does he know? Who told him?"

"The inspector told him," Kathy said. "Somebody must have told the boss."

"Like who?"

"You did," Jimmy said. "You told him the other day. Maybe you don't remember you told him, but you did. You told him the whole goddamn story, I was standing right there."

"I just told you last night, for chrissake. I didn't know the other day she was going to put me out."

"What did I tell you last night?" Jimmy said. "Didn't I say you were drinking, you know when you drink you get these tiny lapses, these blackouts."

Kathy turned from the street and threw Dante a small neat smile.

"Are you nuts?" Dante said. "I'm not an alcoholic, I don't drink that much."

Jimmy lowered the binoculars and stared at Dante for a moment. He cleared his throat and resumed his surveillance of the street.

"Well," Dante said.

"I don't want to embarrass you in front of Kathy."

"It's okay," Kathy said. "Embarrass him."

"Go on, go on. I can take it, say what you gotta say."

"It was last week that Judy threw you out. But you crawled back three nights in a row, begged and pleaded, and she let you in. Last week, pally, you were on the shoot and going down. You told me. You told the boss in front of me."

"Yeah, so what's the point?" Dante asked pleasantly, taking over the Nikon from Kathy.

"Maybe the point is there is no point," Kathy said. "Most cops I know shouldn't be married anyway."

Dante grunted and shook his head. He was amazed that he had blanked totally on the conversation with the inspector. "You're right, Kathy," he said. "I've been saying for years that cops make the worst husbands."

"And wives, don't forget the women," she said.

"There is nothing in this here investigation we got going," Jimmy said, "that I'm sure of—Nothing, that is, except that you, Detective Gibbons, will not let us forget about women."

"You know a better subject, Jimmy?" Kathy said matter-of-factly, taking the Nikon back from Dante, clicking away at the characters in the street. "The way I see it, women are one of the few things in this life worth spending time thinking about."

"Is that the way you see it?" Dante said avoiding Kathy's eyes, looking down into the street.

"You can take that to the bank," she told him. Then, going on, no pause, "You know, Dante, you're looking good. You been working out? You look, I don't know. Sexy, sort of. Your hair looks great, your skin looks good, you don't have a gut and you got those big black bedroom eyes."

It gave him a lift to be admired. He glanced at Kathy briefly, then turned away. "You making a pass at me?"

"It's spring," she said. "I'm feeling romantic, I like waking up in someone's arms."

"Don't we all," Jimmy said.

Dante said, "Excuse me, but can I ask you a very personal question?"

"You talking to me?" Kathy said.

"I got no personal questions to ask Jimmy that I don't already know the answers to."

"Don't bet on it, partner," Jimmy said.

Dante shrugged. "Kathy, I want to ask you a personal question."

Jimmy turned a hard stare on him. Then he took a quick look around. "Do we have a phone in here yet?"

"The one on the kitchen wall is turned on," Kathy said. "How personal?"

Jimmy gave them a sad smile, wagged his head, and went off to the kitchen.

"Very," Dante said.

"Uh, sure, I guess so. Why not?"

"Are you seeing anyone? I mean do you have a boyfriend?"

She looked at him admiringly, a slow smile on her lips. "On-and-off to the first, and no to the second. Does that help?"

"You sometimes see someone," he said, putting a hand on hers for emphasis. "But you don't have a boyfriend. I got that right?"

"Like everyone else in the office you're dying to know if I'm gay."

"Sure."

"Well, different than the others you have the nerve to just come out and ask. I like that." She nodded knowingly.

"You're not going to tell me, are you?" Dante said.

Kathy swallowed and under his stare slowly shook her head.

"Is that no, you're not gay? Or is that no, you're not going to tell me?"

Kathy turned to look at him directly, she reached across to him and placed her hand between his legs. Kathy gave him a quick little squeeze, making him jump back and spin around, surprising the hell out of him, frightening him a bit. "Whoa!" he said. "Easy, easy there girl."

"I bet you think I'd love to have one of those."

"Ey Dante," Jimmy called out, "are you through? Can we get going now? I want to run over to the wiretap. The boss is going to be there, he wants to talk to us."

"I'm coming, I'm coming," Dante said.

"Oooooh," Kathy said, "how nice for you."

"Go on," Dante said, holding out his hand, and Kathy slapped it, saying, "You're all right Dante, you're okay."

Dante knew right then that he would take a shot and try to get into this woman's pants. But now was not the time to pursue it.

"Oh yeah, Kathy," Jimmy said, "our boy here is a regular prince."

CHAPTER EIGHT

It was not until seven that night that JoJo arrived at his father's house. He parked in the driveway and got out, he could not recall a more beautiful evening. True it was warm, a bit too warm for June, but he hated the cold. Florida was comfortable, it was hot. Good and hot.

All JoJo really wanted to do was get his mind in order, he felt as though he were operating in midair. You're into too many things. Doing this and that, spreading yourself thin, JoJo thought. "Yeah, and why's that?" he said aloud. "Because all this business must be done—it's as simple as that." Lately, JoJo found himself talking aloud to himself. Standing there, he continued to think about life and how it could be lived, if you just went about it and lived it. He looked up at his father's house, at Monty Montana, his father's driver and bodyguard, standing alongside the Jaguar in his opaque sunglasses. His father loved that car, the forest green Jag with its saddle leather seats.

It was a general truth that wiseguys on Salvatore Paradiso's level could live as they pleased. He was a wealthy man by most standards. Even so, he chose to live modestly. There were no estates, no country houses, no yachts, airplanes, or world travel. There were, in fact, very few vacations. Sure the old man had money, there was plenty of cash, cash for expensive clothing. He had a dozen suits, about fifty Italian knit shirts, and twenty pairs of shoes. There were a couple of luxury cars, the Jaguar and black Mercedes with tinted windows. The Mercedes was JoJo's favorite. The cars were leased through his brother John's construction company and had Rhode Island registration. Officially JoJo was employed as a business representative for Paradiso Construction. He had a declared income of seventy-five thousand a year and not a clue of how much he actually earned. John Paradiso took care of the family books, the family money laundering, the family fortune.

Salvatore Paradiso owned one diamond ring, a gold bracelet, and a Tiffany watch, all gifts from his wife and his daughter Patricia. He ate at home, so no expensive restaurant bills, and he never gambled. Fact was, Salvatore Paradiso was a carbon copy, a replica of all the old-time mafiosi who believed firmly in the fundamental rule that you spent time cementing loyalties and keeping as low a profile as possible. That was the *via veccica,* the old way, the smart way. He vacationed only in his own house in Boca Raton. The man hated to travel, when travel became necessary for business he sent JoJo. Suspicious and shy outside the neighborhood, he was acutely aware of all his shortcomings, his lack of education, his inability to carry on much of a conversation with anyone who wasn't mob connected. And so he stayed at home, his home was as safe as anywhere and more comfortable than most places. At home he was king, ruler, the Don.

Before JoJo entered the house he spoke briefly to Monty Montana. Monty was waiting, he told JoJo, to run Lina home. JoJo was surprised to hear that Lina Santangelo, his father's housekeeper and cook, was still around at seven o'clock. That foxy old lady had an eye for his father; JoJo knew it and smiled at the thought.

"You wanna hear some crazy shit? You go in the kitchen," Monty told him, "go on and listen to your father trying to explain to Rosalina how he wants his meals cooked. He goes, I want it this way, and she goes, I know what I'm doing, leave me alone. I mean it's a kick to hear 'em."

Monty was a Vietnam vet, paratrooper, a Special Forces guy who entered the army when he was seventeen. A tough neighborhood kid looking to learn something and travel the world and find some adventure. In ten years of military service, Monty learned how to kill people and little else. There was nothing for him when he came home, zip for a guy like Monty, but he was smart, quiet, and kept himself together. He could sit still as an oak for ten, twelve hours at a time, it blew JoJo's mind the way Monty could sit still. And he'd kill you in a heartbeat. JoJo spoke to him soon after Monty was recruited by Bruno, he asked Monty if he could kill someone. And Monty told him, the truth is you never know until the moment comes.

But could you? JoJo had persisted. And Monty told him, sure, it doesn't bother me a bit."

JoJo entered the house with his own key and sauntered into the kitchen. He smiled as he greeted his father and Lina. His father, he supposed, would most likely be angry. He had not contacted the Skipper in two days. JoJo's smile widened as his father told him how painful it was to try and teach this Neapolitan woman to cook. Lina took JoJo's hands in hers and they stood with their fingers twined; her wide-eyed expression made him laugh.

"Call Nancy," his father said.

"Later," JoJo told him. He went to the kitchen table and set down the bag containing the two silver-tip roast beefs Lilo had given him. He set the bag down where his father could see it. Lina nodded soberly.

"She hasn't heard from you in a month," his father said. There was a long pause. His father turned his fixed vacant smile on him, a smile that was built on a thousand years of suspicion.

"She gets her envelope every week," JoJo said. "That's all she wants, all she's ever wanted."

His father went to the table and peeked inside the bag. He reached in and felt around. "Meat from Lilo?" he said.

JoJo nodded.

"Call Nancy. People who care about you should know where you are."

"Later," JoJo said again, and went to the refrigerator and took out a beer. He sat down at the kitchen table, lit a cigarette, and smoked lazily, watching Rosalina Santangelo take cooking instructions from his father.

JoJo had been separated from Nancy for five years. Not divorced, just separated. They would divorce when his father died, not before. He called her once, sometimes twice a month, sent her a thousand dollars a week in hundreds. If Nancy wanted more she'd ask. She did, often, she asked and JoJo would send whatever she needed, but the deal was a thousand a week. Nothing on paper, just the deal between them.

Rosalina Santangelo, who everyone called Lina, had been married to an old-time family soldier whose name was Red. Red Santangelo had three months earlier returned from a family business trip to Rhode Island suffering from stomach cramps. And he was complaining of chills, he told Lina that he felt cold, colder than he'd ever been. His stomach, he told her, was killing him. Probably the crappy Rhode Island deep-fried clam cakes he ate. Red undressed and got into their bed. Sometime after midnight he rolled from the bed, and before Red Santangelo hit the floor he was dead.

Sixty-five years old, never a day sick in his life, a little chill, a small stomachache, and bang, he was a goner. Red Santangelo left their house with the undertaker, leaving behind a metal box containing all their savings, exactly ten thousand dollars in hundreds. People came to his wake and gave Lina envelopes with money folded inside. The men who came whispered and nodded their heads. Red may have been too young to die, but considering his life, a massive heart attack in bed with his wife was a gift, some said, from God.

The Skipper had come to Red's wake dressed in his black suit. The mourners moved back and forth past Red's box. When the Don entered the room, everything stopped. Lina Santangelo stood when the Don approached her, she had short bowed legs and huge breasts. When the Don kissed her cheek she began to cry, she had not cried before. Hearing Lina wail, the paid mourners joined in. JoJo remembered it as being quite a circus. When the Don whispered to her that after a proper period of mourning she should come to his house and cook his meals, and for that service he would pay her three hundred dollars a week, Lina stopped crying and had a smile for her Don.

Red Santangelo had been a trusted soldier for thirty years. He and Lina and the Skipper were friends from the old days, and the Skipper valued them both. Though somewhat short and a bit round, Lina Santangelo was not an unattractive woman. And knowing that the Don had been a widower for nearly five years gave her a certain amount of hope.

She waited for the spirit of Red to leave her house. It took two months.

Monty Montana picked Lina up in the blue Mercedes with tinted windows at six A.M. each day and returned her home usually by two. As it turned out, there was a small problem with Lina's cooking. She was a Neapolitan who could work magic with heavy sauces, which she called gravy and *ragu.* She cooked with pancetta, cured bacon, and much olive oil and *lardo,* fatback and salt pork. She made her own sausages, loved to eat and cook with prosciutto and other kinds of salami, cured pork. She used rendered lard, *strutto,* in place of butter for baking and for deep-frying. The Skipper, whose arteries were as clogged as the Long Island Expressway on a Friday night, ate none of these foods.

Lina and the Skipper would argue together, soft arguments meant to inform. The Skipper told her he was a Sicilian, ate mostly seafood, wanted light oil and white wines for cooking. He loved vegetables, rabe, escarole, spinach, zucchini, green beans and mushrooms, fennel, and of course eggplant. Lina reminded him that Sicilians fried their eggs in olive oil.

Sicilians, she told him, cook like Arabs and are famous for their heavy dishes.

Not me, he told her. I got a bad heart, what you wanna do, blow up my heart too the way you exploded your husband's? Ey, she told him. What you wanna do, live forever?

There was no loss of respect between Lina and the Skipper, she was an old-school woman who understood her place in the world she had chosen to live in. She had, after all, spent her life in the arms of a Mafia soldier.

Born in a small mountain village outside of Naples, she had emigrated to America at the age of five.

"In Italy," she once told the Skipper, "women would be strangled by men." Lina would open her eyes wide and put her hands around her throat, sometimes she'd hang her tongue out. She could twist up her face and make her mouth and nose come together. Lina Santangelo, for as long as the Skipper had known her, and he'd known her for thirty years, always made him laugh. And Salvatore Paradiso loved to smell cooking smells and laugh.

"Now listen," he told her. "You wanna listen or are you going to keep turning your head? First you take the mussels, put them in a colander and wash them. They have little pieces of seaweed in the crack and sometimes a tiny sea shell attached to the body."

Lina turned to JoJo. "Because he is a man he thinks he knows everything," she said.

Her cheerfulness as she said it caused Salvatore to forget his teaching for a moment and laugh.

"C'mon," he said. "You gonna listen?"

"Go on," she told him.

"You wash that off, it takes a minute. Then you set them aside. You slice an onion, you mince some garlic, I like garlic so for me you put in a little more."

Lina looked from the paper the Skipper was writing on to the Skipper and then at JoJo. "I'm cooking for forty years," she said. "He's gonna tell *me* about garlic?"

"Then," the Skipper went on, "you slice a red pepper. Chop some parsley, no basil. Basil is too strong for this sauce, so you don't use basil. You put basil in your daughter's womb when she was pregnant, I remember that. I know you wanna use basil, you put basil in everything, but not in a mussel sauce, okay? Then in a good heavy pot you put in a couple of drops of olive oil, and for me a sliver of margarine. I don't want butter, and I don't want too much olive oil, okay? If you need more liquid you add a little white wine. Now you sauté the onions the garlic the red pepper the parsley. Add about a half cup of white wine. Drop in the mussels put on the pot lid and let that cook for about another ten minutes. When you see steam coming from the pot you check it, see if the mussels are open. You transfer the mussels to the colander, open them, and remove the meat. You put the meat back in the pot and add some imported tomato, *without—* are you paying attention?—basil. You cook that another twenty minutes, you make your pasta, imported linguine or angel hair. I like 'em both al dente. Pour over the sauce and that's it."

"And that's it?" Lina said.

"That's it."

"No basil?"

"None."

The woman shivered with disgust.

"Now, tomorrow is Sunday. Tomorrow I'm having a few dozen mussels brought fresh from Sheepshead Bay. I want my pasta with the mussels and maybe a side dish of escarole, a nice loaf of fresh bread and that's it, *fini.*"

"I was going to make you spaghetti al vesuvio, and a roast chicken with potatoes."

"Too much food, I don't want it. And you're not going to make me spaghetti named after a volcano."

Lina suddenly threw her hips into motion. "Too much food," she said. "No chicken and potatoes. Just a little black mussels and tomato, a little stringy escarole."

Lina had black hair streaked with gray as long as your arm and wore it piled on her head. She wore a black dress so severe and dull that is appeared to have been made in the last century. She had wide hips that, JoJo had noticed, she liked to move, and she moved well. And with the motion of her hips her huge breasts swayed this way and that.

All this movement was not lost on Salvatore Paradiso, who was less concerned with moving hips and swaying breasts than he was with getting a good meal of mussels and pasta.

"So are you going to come tomorrow or what?" Salvatore said.

"Come? Come? Ey, I haven't come in twenty years."

"Ey," Salvatore said. "I don't like that kind of talk. You're a respectable woman, why do you talk like that?"

"Talk is easy, Don Paradiso. Talk, talk, talk. I'm not dead, you know. My husband Red, he is the dead one, not me."

"Do me a favor," Salvatore said. "Don't call me Don Paradiso, it sounds silly." He poured her a glass of wine from an open bottle that stood on the kitchen counter. "Here," he said. "Take a glass of wine with me, and then I'll have Monty bring you home."

Over his beer, JoJo watched her flirt with his father. Her presence made him feel relieved; he had not decided if he were going to tell the Skipper of his meeting with the Cuban. Through the class on mussel sauce, the thought grew on JoJo that his cocaine move was the right thing. It was time for him to take charge of this family.

Watching his father, JoJo tried to measure the image the man left on family members, and his father himself. His father, he knew, could be as easygoing as anyone. A pure pleasure to be around. He could also be a wild tiger. His height and steel blue eyes caught everyone's attention, and his bearing, the way he moved, inspired a great deal of respect. But lately Dante had noticed there was something gentle about the man. It was a quality he saw in no one else in this business, a quality, he thought, that could make the Skipper careless and get him killed.

The conversation between Lina and the Skipper was so comical that JoJo found himself caught up in it, and he smiled at Lina like a loving son. His own mother had been dead five years, and all at once he understood the feeling that played in his chest. It was a yearning for that laugh, that great smile, that wonderful voice. He could see a remote but similar smile on the face of Lina Santangelo. His mother, however, had been far more beautiful. Carolina Paradiso was a great beauty, many said she had a face that put you in mind of Sophia Loren.

"I'll be here in the morning, do your laundry and make your mussels," Lina was telling his father. "My needs will always be subordinate to yours."

"The hell you talking about?" Salvatore said. "Subordinate, where you hear that word?"

"The woman libbers," she said, "use it all the time."

"What are you trying to tell me?" Salvatore said.

"Tomorrow is Sunday. The third Sunday of the month. On the third Sunday, I like to visit my son in Staten Island."

"So go visit your son. I'll make my own mussels. Maybe you should stay on Staten Island. Move in with your son, live in the basement. He said he was going to finish it for you, so maybe you should go there and live."

Salvatore Paradiso sipped his wine while Lina bent her head and read the cooking instructions on the pad in front of her.

"I hate his wife," she said, "the woman got fingernails out to here. Watching TV all day. To tell you the truth, I'm not nuts about my son, either. Thank you, but no thank you. I'm gonna stay in my own house in Queens."

"Do what you want."

"Tomorrow morning." She smirked, not looking up. "Nine o'clock sharp. I am in your kitchen."

"Good."

"And when I finish up here, you can have Monty drive me in the big car to Staten Island. I come out of the back seat of that car, everybody on that Staten Island block goes dumb. They drop their mouths like this." Lina stood up straight, shoulders pushed back, hands on her hips. She opened her mouth and held it open for a long time.

Two hours later, still sitting at the kitchen table, talking with his father about Lilo, Tommy Yale, Frankie F'n Furillo, and the kid Vinny Rapino, JoJo came to realize that there was no way he would tell him about the Cuban. Why bring trouble on himself? Soon, yes, he would have to tell him soon, but not now, not tonight. Tonight was just too soon.

His father had given Lina the bag with the two silver-tipped roast beefs. And before she left, the Skipper had kissed her twice, once on the cheek then once again on the forehead.

The telephone rang, Nicky Black calling to tell his father-in-law that he would be by the following day, and then JoJo's brother John called just to say hi. His father asked JoJo if Nicky was still seeing the woman in Jackson Heights. JoJo nodded his head but said nothing. His father nodded too, in heavy but silent disapproval. Once JoJo had asked his father if he should put an end to Nicky's love affair, and his father had told him that someday he might have to hurt Nicky a little in order to teach him a lot. But he would decide when, there was no rush. When JoJo told his father about Frankie Furillo's hit on the Russian, Salvatore Paradiso sat with his hands folded in front of him on the table and listened carefully, staring at JoJo with his old Sicilian eyes in a way that made JoJo bend his head.

When JoJo thought about himself he couldn't understand himself. One minute he was defiant on the subject, he felt in control and gave himself credit for taking charge. But he was shooting crap and he knew it. And everywhere he looked he saw those goddamn snake eyes. When he tried to explain Frankie F'n Furillo's hit, there came from his father more silence and deep nasal breathing.

CHAPTER NINE

Three days had gone by.

Jimmy stood behind a tripod at the surveillance plant, looking down at the entrance of JoJo's club. It was partway through the morning, and it appeared that the club was in for a busy day. A steady stream of gang members had been entering and leaving. Through the hidden microphones there came sounds, bits and pieces of delicate wiseguy conversation. Dante, in the plant's kitchen, made coffee, as across the street the dim minds spoke.

"Ey Frankie, it's unbelievable, ya know that guy, what's-his-name from over there? Over on First, that guy? Looo, Louie, ya know that guy? Well anyway I think he's a faggot." And the answer: "No, he's no faggot, he's just a moron."

"Yeah, well he walks like a real faggot."

"Ah yes," Dante said, listening, pursing his lips and nodding. "Words of wisdom from the nation's criminal threat. La Cosa Nostra. What a bunch of mutts."

Jimmy and Dante had come on duty at six that morning, and around seven, seven thirty, Jimmy's beeper began to pop. It was Inspector Martin, he knew that, and he wanted to duck the boss for as long as possible. It was the end of the month, his paperwork was due, he was behind a week with his dailies and three months late on his expenses.

"Can't we get these cameras to go on automatic?" Jimmy asked. He hunched over the Nikon and screwed down the 4X converter, his muscular arms wrapped around the tripod. Kathy Gibbons sat across from him, her own camera clicking away. Dante was fixing the coffee when at around ten o'clock Ray came through the door, the New York *Post* folded under his arm, a bag of bagels in his hand.

Ray told Jimmy that Inspector Martin wanted to talk to him. "Call him," Ray said. "The man's been beeping you for an hour. He called my house at six this morning, told me he couldn't reach you."

Dante asked Ray what was up. Ray said he didn't know what it was about.

"I know what he wants," Jimmy said. "He wants my dailies and expenses."

Dante turned to look at Jimmy across the room, who was at last satisfied that the camera he was shooting worked the way he wanted. Jimmy met Dante's questioning eyes, shrugged, and bent again to the camera. Dante offered Ray a cup of coffee.

"You going to call the boss, Jimmy?" Dante said. "Or do you want me to?"

Jimmy nodded in reply, then answered the question in Dante's eyes. "He is going to ask us to meet him for lunch. Dante," he said, "there are two things that could ruin my day. One would be to take a bullet in the teeth and the second would be to have lunch with the boss."

Dante didn't respond, turning his back on Jimmy. Kathy came into the kitchen with her cup and he poured her some coffee.

Jimmy left the tripod and came and snatched up the wall phone in the kitchen, his annoyance obvious. Dante sipped his coffee, wondering what was important enough to get the boss to make such an early call. He was getting nervous, deciding he'd ask Kathy Gibbons to go to dinner. Watching her stare at him as she drank, feeling all knotted inside. He could taste it already, the rejection. Kathy wheeled around and walked into the surveillance room. What a great butt, Dante thought. That woman has a fine ass. Ray joined her and began taking photos of the street action. Ray, as was his way, was extremely serious, checking f-stops and film speed, making a judgment about the available light and so on. All the people in and around the Nestor Club were serious too, scheming, plotting and planning. Wiseguys plotted and planned all the time. Their days and nights were filled with a never-ending series of meaningless sitdowns and meetings.

Get up, dress, go to the club pick up Tony. Then drive over to the Greek's for breakfast with Vinny and Joe. Bacon eggs and chitchat. Then drive into Brooklyn meet Louie for coffee and more chitchat. Then it's lunch back in Queens with Willie and Tom, see what's up. And so it goes into the night, sometimes right through the night. Here there and everywhere, chitchatting all the way.

"The inspector says it's confirmed. There's an informant with the Paradisos," Jimmy said.

Dante shrugged. "It don't matter," he said. "Why should that affect us?"

"It doesn't. We're just getting started. What the feds do or don't do means nothing to us."

Dante watched Jimmy glance at him, only a glance. He handed Jimmy a cup of coffee, watched him drinking it as though he didn't really want any coffee. For a moment it seemed to Dante that a chill ran through his partner. He thought of the meeting with Inspector Martin at the telephone plant the past Saturday; he had thought of that meeting every day since. The inspector standing there smiling, saying this Paradiso case can turn out to be a big one all right. Something is stirring among the families. The FBI think maybe a war.

For New York's mafiosi it was that time of year. Oil the pistols, work out the kinks and shake loose the rust. Time to thin the ranks, a time for handkerchiefs and handcuffs. And look out if *Godfather I, II,* or *III* hit cable TV. Mobsters ended up sprawled all over the streets when those movies played.

It seemed that petty jealousies flared up in springtime. Clan splinter factions reached for some power and prestige. Any reason, real or imagined, sent rival gangsters to war.

New York mobsters had no sense of place or history, no love of the ancient, poor, and tired land that had spawned the *contadini* who were their parents and grandparents. They were American gangsters, very few even spoke the language of their forefathers. But they loved the idea of the Mafia, the concept of heritage, sensing in some way that they belonged to something special and secret. They just weren't sure exactly what it was.

In response to gang warfare, the federal government and local district attorneys made a push each spring against the five New York families. We are getting better, Inspector Martin had told Dante and Jimmy. The FBI, for example, have informants everywhere. One, he believed, was real close to Joseph Paradiso.

The feds trusted Inspector Martin, told him just about everything they were doing with the crime families. The inspector, in turn, told the FBI as little as possible. Inspector Martin had no interest in holding back information, he just did not want to let the feds in on everything he did. Sometimes the inspector felt as though he were cheating, not doing right by the feds. Sometimes, but not often. He was a man who got himself a masters, then a Ph.D. from the John Jay School of Criminal Justice. A classic cop, an Irishman born in the North Bronx, the inspector was tough as nails, hard-core honest, Catholic up to here, and politically about as far right as a sane man could get. By all who knew him, Inspector Martin was thought to be an extraordinarly fine man. Except when he drank. When he drank, Arthur Martin if you crossed him would put a heel on your throat. The problem was that when he was drinking, if your smile had a crooked turn to it you crossed him. He'd run his hands through his hair, and wise people, those that knew him, would leave the room, the building, the state.

There was a time in his youth when friends thought the inspector would end up a priest. That thought went south when he met and married a neighborhood girl, had seven kids, all boys. A few years back his oldest son was coming home on spring break from Boston College. He was riding a Honda road bike, a big one, and should have been seen by the driver of the eighteen-wheeler that crushed him. It seemed the inspector had handled it well, falling back on his religion and all. And he did have six other children.

Dante knew better. The man spun out of control, jumped into a bottle of Jack Daniel's and stayed for a while. More than a few nights Dante held him, held him close. Dante's thoughts at the time were that no one cries with pain like an Irishman. The inspector loved that boy. He loved him just a bit more than he loved Dante O'Donnell. And Dante guessed he liked the inspector as much as he liked anyone other than Jimmy: not much. The truth of it was, Dante could get close to no one after his father put that gun to his head. Everybody, he figured, was really out for themselves. Then again, there was his wife Judy and his son Danny. He didn't like to imagine what life would be like without them.

Dante stood in the kitchen listening to Jimmy talk for a time, mostly about the federal informant. If they could get access to him, if the feds would share their CI they could do some real business here. Dante nodded his head once or twice, his mood turning sour with Jimmy standing there talking crap, silliness.

"Whataya dreamin'," he said to Jimmy. "Since when does the FBI share a confidential informant?"

"Maybe," Jimmy said, "with the right approach, ask to compare notes. Something like that." Jimmy tapped his teeth with his index finger. "We should think of some way to have the inspector approach the feds," he said.

Dante was conscious of a motor running; the refrigerator motor was the only sound he heard. And he had this odd feeling of nervousness. It was odd because there was no reason for it. Who cared what the feds were doing? They do their thing and we do ours, he thought.

"It's a puzzle," Jimmy said.

"What is?"

"How we get access to the informant, whataya think?"

Dante looked at Jimmy and Jimmy returned that look in a peculiar way. "It's stupid to worry about what the feds are up to," Jimmy said finally.

"You fooled me," Dante told him. "I thought that was just what you were doing."

Jimmy smiled, and his smile stretched slowly all the way across his face. That handsome face. It was the kind of smile Jimmy had shown him since they were kids, the kind of smile that made Dante wish he could smile back the same way. JoJo too, he remembered, had that kind of smile.

"Hey." Jimmy's voice went low and confidential. "Who am I kiddin', I know the feds don't share. And the truth is we don't need 'em. It's me and you, big guy. Who's better than us?"

Dante looked at him but let it go.

It came to Dante that he hated JoJo Paradiso, always had. *Hated* was a bit harsh. He didn't *hate* the guy. Didn't respect him. That was it, he had no respect for JoJo Paradiso. The guy was a screwup. Always looking for the easy way out. Jimmy liked him. Always had. There rose in him an old familiar feeling, and he remembered it as jealousy. He had always been jealous of Jimmy and JoJo's friendship, their intimacy. Their shared, for lack of a better word, weirdness. He considered the fact that boys and men become friends for different reasons. It's human nature. He was careful not to dwell on human nature too long. He pushed all thoughts of human nature out of his mind, afraid of where they might lead.

Kathy called out, "C'mere you two. Take a look at this guy. This is the second day he's here, the second day he's driving the son."

Going to the window, Dante lit a cigarette and squinted through the smoke. He saw the black Mercedes parked in front of the candy store. First two men in suits walked out of the club and stood alongside the car. Then JoJo exited the car from the passenger's side, checked the street, and moved toward the club, waving as he went to Sonny the Hawk. The driver, wearing a navy blue windbreaker, followed him.

"Whew," Kathy said, looking though the telephoto lens, taking a dozen shots. "That's one good-looking guy."

"Don't know him," Dante said.

"I ain't never seen him," said Jimmy.

"I have," Ray said. "But I can't remember his name. He's a real slick piece of work, looks like a movie actor."

The reels on the tape recorders had been spinning all morning. Dante and Ray went into the kitchen and listened. The men inside the club were making sandwiches, they ate and Dante listened to the small talk, wanting to hear a name called, a name he hadn't heard before. The talk was soft. A voice he was familiar with asked for a beer. Then someone else laughed. Dante listened without really hearing. There was nothing much to hear: sandwiches being eaten, someone asked if anyone was going to Atlantic City over the weekend, then asked for the Brooklyn number. The voice sounding antsy now, a voice Dante hadn't heard before. He touched Ray's arm. Ray nodded.

"Anyone got the *News* or the *Post?*" the voice said. "I need the number."

"Vinny," JoJo's voice called out, "you'll get the number later, first tell 'em about the wedding. G'head, tell 'em. They'll get a kick out of it."

"Nah, they don't wanna hear it."

Ray went over to the table and opened the Paradiso family mug book, went quickly through the pages. "Vinny Rapino," he said. Sounding like a prosecutor or a clerk in court.

"I heard of the guy," Dante said under his breath.

"Tell it," JoJo said.

"I tol' it."

"Mr. JoJo," a voice that Dante recognized as belonging to Sonny the Hawk called out. "You got a call."

"We have to be on that line," Dante said. "We need to be on that candy store phone."

"It's a public phone," Ray said. "It's a total bitch trying to get a judge to sign for a public phone."

"We need it," Dante said.

"Can we get it?" Jimmy asked.

And Kathy said, "Our boy's leaving the club, going into the candy store."

"Ray," Jimmy said, "why don't we give it a shot? All they can say is no."

"You going to do the paperwork? You're talking two, three days of paperwork to draw up the applications. And the chances are slim and none a judge will go for it," Ray said.

"Maybe if we had a judge on the payroll like these wiseguys do, we'd get whatever we needed," Jimmy said. He threw Dante a warm smile and Dante gave him a nod.

Suddenly everyone in the clubroom was laughing, and the laughter bounced through the FM radios, getting Dante's attention, getting both Ray's and Dante's attention.

"I never said marriage," Vinny's voice said. "All I said was baby I think I love ya. I mean I was fucking her at the time. You say things when you got a woman's feet in the air. I mean, I do. Next thing I know her father is rebuilding the basement. I'm gonna live in Lilo's basement? Can you believe that shit."

"I can believe it." Bruno Greco's voice said.

"Bruno, with all respect," Vinny said, "I ain't living in nobody's basement. I ain't living nowhere with a woman that got a mustache and muscles bigger than mine. I'd ask you to whack me out before I did that, for chrissake."

The room became quiet. For a moment they listened to the hum of the reels making a full revolution.

Bruno's voice could be heard close to the telephone bug. "Don't go asking for things you don't want," Bruno said.

"Jesus Christ," Ray said. "That's one bad ass, that Bruno Greco. He'll cut your heart out and drink your blood. That's one bad dude, man."

Dante drained his cup of coffee and poured himself another, this time without sugar and cream, wanting the full blast of caffeine.

"Fucking Bruno Greco," Dante snorted, "been around for years. How come nobody has wrapped that jerk in a carpet yet?"

"You know how many battles that man's been in?" Jimmy asked him. "From the Gallo wars to the revolution in the Renina family last year, the guy's been shot at, stabbed, hit by a truck. Once I heard they had him alone in a room with three stone killers out for his blood. He came out with a couple of scratches, and the Reninas had three less soldiers. They say if the Nazis had him on their side in the last war we'd all be speaking German."

"Yeah?" Dante said. "Who said that? Where you hear all this shit?"

"Common knowledge, buddy of mine," Jimmy said. "It's common knowledge."

Dante made a face. "Bullshit. Whataya do, partner, make this shit up as you go along? I'll tell ya, Jimmy, a few weeks from now I'm gonna go in that club and grab that guinea bastard by the ear. And I'm gonna say, 'Come with me mister tough guy Bruno Greco.' Screw him. I'll just start off by grabbing his ear. Then I'll drag him up to the Bronx and let crazy Freddie

Miller get in his face for a while. We'll see how bad ol' Bruno Greco is, I grab him by the ear and Freddie gets up in his face. We'll see how tough he is. Screw him."

"Yeah, well, he's a for-real tough guy," Jimmy said.

"Screw you too," Dante said angrily. "That's the problem with most people around these jerks, they believe their publicity."

"Is that the problem?" Ray Velasquez said.

"Yeah, you bet your ass," Dante muttered, feeling as if he'd said maybe a tad too much.

Kathy got down from her barstool and came and stood next to Dante. She said, soft and quiet, "They're a bunch of kids that never grew up. A bunch of uneducated dead-end kids going nowhere, except maybe jail and the cemetery."

"Tell 'em, Kathy," Dante said. "You're the only one in here with some brains. And," he told her, "if you're real smart, you'll go to dinner with me tonight."

"Look out," Jimmy said. "My partner's making a move."

"Sure," Kathy said. "As long as you don't try to pick up the check and take payment later."

"I doubt that will be a problem," Jimmy said.

"We're on," said Dante.

Jimmy looked both amused and annoyed as Dante put his arm around Kathy's shoulders and walked her off to the kitchen, making dinner plans, throwing his other hand behind him as he went, giving Jimmy the one-finger salute.

––––––––

That night, it was around ten o'clock.

JoJo left his house, he had Vinny with him, he told Vinny to square the block when they were sure there was no tail, he told Vinny to go into Rockaway. Vinny Rapino tromped the Mercedes and drove JoJo over the Cross Bay Bridge, then over the Broad Channel Bridge into Rockaway Beach.

On Beach Channel Drive at the corner of 110th Street they sat in the car and waited. It amazed JoJo that Vinny always looked so good, brand-new fresh-showered good, with his shirt tucked into his neatly creased pants, his shoes always shined, his face clean-shaven. He was about five eleven, one hundred fifty pounds, to be that good-looking, JoJo thought, is dangerous.

When it was exactly ten thirty, JoJo went to a phone booth and dialed a number.

The phone rang once and his police friend answered, saying, "How ya been?"

"As compared to what?" JoJo asked him.

"I got news and it's all bad," his police friend said.

"Why don't you let me decide how bad it is?"

"Your father's phone is tapped. There are bugs all over the Nestor, and the feds got a stool pigeon so close to you he's in your underwear."

"Things are that good, huh?" JoJo said.

"It's bad buddy, real bad. What are you going to do?"

"What would you do?"

"Me, I'd probably kill somebody."

"Well if you ain't nothing else, buddy of mine, you certainly are original."

A tall thin guy in a camouflage jacket turned the corner and walked past JoJo with his hands in his pockets. Vinny jumped from the car and the guy looked at him, surprised. And JoJo knew that if he gave Vinny Rapino a nod he'd shoot the guy. JoJo stared at Vinny, held his eyes for a long moment, Vinny Rapino puckered his lips and gave him a slow nod.

"Well, what are you going to do?" his police friend said again.

"You know," JoJo said into the telephone, "sometimes I think I can see things where everyone else is blind. Sometimes I'm very weird. I had a feeling something strange was coming down. I did, I had this funny feeling."

The guy in the camouflage jacket wrapped his arms around himself as if he were freezing and walked off. The guy walked with a side-to-side bowlegged step, his hands buried deep in his pockets. Could be a cop, JoJo thought, probably not, probably a drunk out for a stroll, but maybe a cop. Who knows, who cares. What a pain in the ass, is what he thought.

Back in the Mercedes, JoJo said, "What was with that guy in the jacket?" Not waiting for an answer he asked Vinny if he'd ever been to Rhode Island.

"That's near Maine, ain't it?"

"Closer to Boston."

"Whoa," Vinny said. "I got a broad in Boston, one of those American bitches with straight blond hair, she'd knock your socks off." He stepped on the Mercedes, went a block and swung a quick U-turn. A nice move, but there wasn't another car on the street. "I love driving this car," he said.

"Get me back to my father's," JoJo told him. "And stop driving like a nut job. You're carrying a pistol, ain't ya?"

"Yeah sure."

"Well we don't need to get stopped and pinched for no gun. So drive, get me there quick, but be careful."

Vinny smiled, embarrassed, then he said, talking real fast now, "The guy in the jacket was a strange dude, man. You think maybe he was a cop or something?"

JoJo did a bad job of coming on surprised. "A cop?" he said. "Why would a cop want to check me out?"

A saints-preserve-us look crossed Vinny's face. "No reason at all," he said. "Nothing I can think of. Boss," he said, "this broad I got in Boston, her name is Annie Sheldon, a real beauty of an American girl. I'm telling you boss, she'll knock your socks off. Lives right in Boston."

"Well there's a lot of things I need right now Vinny," JoJo told him. "Getting my socks knocked off is not one of them."

Vinny Rapino nodded his head, and JoJo told him, "You'll drop me for a minute at my father's. I'll only be a minute, when I come out you'll go and find Ninety-five and then head north. We're outta here. I need someplace to go and think, rest up a bit, I'm beat."

Vinny shrugged in a way that meant, of course you are.

CHAPTER TEN

Later that night several people had alarming experiences. First there was JoJo, later it was Dante, and still later, in the early morning hours, sometime near sunrise, with sea gulls from Jamaica Bay circling in a pale gray-pink sky, Kathy Gibbons's reasoning and control went south.

JoJo had fully intended to return immediately to his father's house, tell the old man not to use the phones and to think about taking a short vacation. Forget think, he was going to tell him it was time for a trip to his place in Florida. Tell him, you're leaving town, Pop. It was smart to skip out now and then, keep enemies and cops guessing. He rehearsed, had a little conversation with himself, fought down the nervous stomach. Pop, we got a stool pigeon among us. Like a f'n cancer, there's a rat in the gut of this family. It made him nuts, the thought of it. Repeat the conversation he'd had with his police friend, figure who else had to be told, and that was that. But when he crossed the bridge back into Broad Channel he got this urge and told Vinny to pull over in front of Chaplin's, feeling a sudden flush of anxiety, telling himself he needed a minute to think this through. He told Vinny to wait in the car.

The restaurant had a brand-new oyster-house sort of look, spider plants and palms in the window seats, copper kettles hanging from the ceiling, captain's chairs around heavy maple tables, oars mounted on walls of unfinished brick, and salty gray wooden plank paneling. The spot put JoJo in mind of travel, sailing wide seas. Adventure, leaving it all behind. There were prints of ocean liners, schooners, and double- and triple-masted sailing ships. He took a chair at a table in the rear, making sure his back was to the wall. An electric ceiling fan turned slowly over his head. JoJo had always loved the sea. Sure you do, his father told him, it's in your genes. JoJo's great grandfather was a seaman who had sailed to China and Japan, a Sicilian adventurer who sailed the South Seas.

A middle-aged couple was at the bar, and two women with very short hair sat smoking long black cigarettes at a table near the door. One of the women was wearing a blue slicker and sweat pants and new tennis shoes, she was drinking a beer. Her friend wore an aqua jacket and faded jeans, a pink button-down shirt covered what JoJo considered to be no breasts. The no-breasted woman droned on, telling her friend that she hated New York, hated the city and her brother. JoJo thought of them as being part of the Brie and Chablis set. People he had not once in his life spoken to. He knew nothing of people like that, understood not a thing about them. People like that lived in another dimension, a place as alien to him as the moons of Saturn. Lying on the floor between the two women was a backpack.

A black guy stood at the far end of the bar wearing checkered trousers, a leather jacket, and a black leather cap. No one in the place seemed to know anyone else, and that pleased him.

A waitress with short black hair parted in the center of her head came to his table and delivered to him a basket of Eagle nuts and pretzels. She asked if he'd care for a drink. JoJo told her that was exactly what he wanted. She said what flavor? And JoJo said an Absolut martini straight up with some ice on the side. She was small and thin, maybe twenty-five, nice-looking in her black jeans and some sort of white cotton vest with hand-stitched red flowers over her breasts. She probably couldn't bribe a wino with the tips she made in this place, he thought.

He'd need to reach out for Bruno and his brother-in-law, Nicky Black. Pull their coats, tell them to lay still for a while. And the others, all the others. He banged his fist lightly on the table in frustration. Who do you tell? Talk to somebody and you could be talking to a rat. He tried to force himself to relax. Maybe, he thought, just Bruno, let Bruno decide who to tell.

Watching the waitress walk off, JoJo experienced a sizzling buzz of disappointment. He hadn't been with a woman, Christ, he couldn't remember when. He could barely work up the inspiration to flirt lately. JoJo fought down the twitches, thinking about this life of his. A great f'n life: money, broads, big times. A ton of laughs. What a crock of shit. The girl returned with his drink and walked off again. He took the first sharp sip of his martini. Big-time bad guy, he thought. What a crock. He gulped the martini, he was sick of everybody bringing him puzzles and problems. He thought about his police friend and wondered if he should reach out for him again. Who is this stool pigeon, this rat beside me? The bum is next to me. He talks to me. Who is it? JoJo was momentarily overwhelmed by the feeling that he was in some strange and bottomless trick bag.

Spooked by the mystery of who the informant could be, JoJo sat at his table for an hour. He had three martinis. He heard the woman in the blue slicker say, "Sounds like zen to me." She had a round head, chubby cheeks, and bedroom eyes, and that real short haircut, like a male model in one of those hairdresser's magazines. She smoked nonstop.

Impulsively he went to the telephone on the wall and dialed his police friend. "Are you nuts?" his friend said. "Where are you calling me from?"

JoJo touched his forehead to the phone. "Look," he said, "I'm sorry, don't get tense. I'm calling from a pay phone at Chaplin's."

His friend's voice came back, quiet and soft and personal. "Listen, just be careful. I don't know what to tell you."

"I know, I know. There's nothing more you can tell me huh? Who is this rat bastard? Is he some small-time shithead or one of my people? How close is he to me?"

"The FBI's got him. He's not small-time. I don't know who he is. Buddy," his friend said, careful not to use a name, "I don't like this, I don't like you calling me like this. It ain't safe."

JoJo didn't care about safe right now. He felt a mixture of panic and anger, and then there was some relief when his friend said, "Ey, I ain't gonna let you get hurt. You know that. I'm on the lookout, I'll watch your back as good as I can. But I can't know everything that's going down, so be careful."

JoJo rubbed his forehead. Get going, leave it alone.

"Ey," he said, "I'm sorry about the call."

"Hey, I'm sorry you felt you hadda make it."

Suddenly, JoJo felt very tired, he bent his head and shrugged. "See you around the neighborhood," he said.

"You just be careful, all right?"

"Thanks," JoJo said.

"Don't thank me. You never gotta thank me. You know that."

"Yeah, well, thanks anyway."

Hang up hang up hang *up*. He suddenly felt miserable, crazed, more crazed than usual, his concentration torn apart by anger and fear. He stood with his back against the wall, the receiver in his hand. It was the most frightening sensation he had ever felt. He just could not hang up the god-damn telephone.

He saw them come through the door, recognized the guy immediately, then quickly looked away. The woman leading like she knew where she was going. He couldn't help himself, he turned and looked right at them, the phone still glued to his hand. Bright lights were going off in JoJo's head; he hated to be taken by surprise. He felt as though he were in an airplane and was veering off into a mountain. His hand, his hand was frozen to the receiver.

The woman turned toward him, smiled briefly, a nervous smile. JoJo turned slightly toward the wall, took the receiver and hung it up. His throat constricted, but he forced a grin. Ignore them, he thought, go back and drop a twenty on the table and leave. Starting back to his table, reaching into his pocket, he again glanced at the couple. How dumb, man, how stupid. He turned away and scanned the room for his waitress. He flashed on snake eyes, that bastard snake eyes, that sinking feeling in his gut getting deeper now. He turned back and Dante was staring at him as if he were a goddamn mirage. Snake eyes.

It must have been showing in his face because Dante's tone when he approached was soft and personal.

"Hey JoJo, how you been? You look f'n great. You always looked f'n great." A major smile from Dante. The woman stood wide-eyed, like, holy shit.

"I'm fine Dante," he said. "You don't look bad yourself."

They spoke for five minutes, he shook hands with Dante and the woman too. The woman, he noted, had one hell of a hard grip. Her name was Kathy. Dante was married, he knew that. He'd married Judy what's-her-name from Richmond Hill.

JoJo felt frightened and didn't know why. He collected himself and thought, What in the hell's the big deal. He latched on to the last few seconds of what Dante was saying. Dante sounded like some guy in a movie or something, talking about when they were kids. He was nervous too. JoJo cut him short by grabbing his hand.

"Man," Dante said, "it's great seeing you. We should get together. I'll get Jimmy and we'll go out for a brew or something."

What a big pile of bullshit. "Yeah, yeah, yeah," JoJo said. "Anytime."

"Where can I reach you?"

"I'm at the club."

"Same place, huh?"

"Yeah, I'm in that place so often I could be a mirror there."

"I'll stop by."

"Listen," JoJo said. "I know the guy what owns this joint. Whataya say you two let me buy you dinner?" He turned to find the waitress and felt Dante grab his elbow. JoJo looked into Dante's eyes. "It's just dinner," he said. He felt unsteady, unsure of what to say. They had been standing almost nose to nose; Dante stepped back. He folded his arms, and to JoJo he seemed unnatural. But still the old Dante, tough as stone, a quiet circus going off in his head. You never knew what the boy or the man was thinking. JoJo purposely nodded his head, as if that was a sign of his deep understanding of Dante's loony mind.

"You're still a cop, huh, buddy?" JoJo said.

"Sure am."

"Ey, we're old friends. I can buy you dinner. I won't tell anybody," JoJo said casually, mainly to ease the mood, which was starting to get dark.

"Thanks for the thought, pally," Dante said. "But I'll pass this time. Next time out, we'll go to an expensive joint in the city."

He was trying to sound soft and friendly.

"Fine by me."

"Nice to meet you," Kathy said. She sounded very polite.

"You a cop too?" JoJo asked.

"My life's a secret," she said with a wide grin.

"Mine too," JoJo said. They all gave a short, preoccupied chuckle. "At least I hope it is," JoJo whispered, shooting for a real laugh now. "Whoa, listen," he said. "I gotta get going. It was great seeing you, Dante. And Kathy, it was interesting meeting someone with a secret life." Her face had a quiet, dreamy look, composed. JoJo turned, he wanted out the door. He felt a horrible sliding sensation.

Kathy called after him, "That's a nice ride you got out there."

"Borrowed," JoJo called back.

Dante was waving for the waitress.

Sonofabitch, JoJo thought, the broad knows my car. Sonofabitch.

———————

Dante sat with his hands clasped in his lap, staring at the restaurant door. Next to him Kathy was giving him the stare, sipping a Virgin Mary. Kathy was a problem drinker and that fact was unknown to Dante. Her drinking problem was known to a select few in the department. Inspector Martin knew, and he could care less as long as she stayed on the wagon. He liked to take a drink himself and understood, at least he thought he did. What he did not know and would never have understood was that she once had a raging cocaine problem as well. No one knew that.

Leaning back, Dante lit a cigarette and clasped his hands over his stomach. "What a break," he said. "I can't believe we ran into the guy."

"Stop looking at the door," Kathy said. "Lighten up, I don't think he's coming back."

"What a break. I haven't run into the guy in ten years. What a goddamn break," Dante said. "He looked nervous, didn't he?"

She answered him by putting her hand over his. "You're right," she said. "He was pale as a ghost. But he did seem to like you. He did."

"The Ghost of Christmas past," said Dante. He laughed and shook his head.

Kathy buttered a rye bread roll, it was hard, more than a little stale, saying, "You knew him, huh?"

"Knew him? Yeah we knew him. Me and Jimmy and JoJo Paradiso grew up together," Dante said.

"You're kidding."

Dante didn't seem to hear.

"He looked nervous and pale, I never saw JoJo pale, that man's scared of something. It's the why and wherefore, that's the thing. Why was he so rattled to see me? It's the life, I guess. In his life death can come through the door anytime. I suppose when you're surprised by someone unexpected coming through a door—"

"I didn't know if he had the Mercedes with him," she said. "I didn't see it in the street. I thought I'd zing him. Let him know that I know his car. A good zinger for the slick bastard."

Dante looked at her for a minute, then finished his beer. "Listen, Kathy," he said. "He was on the phone when we came in." He scanned the restaurant. "That wall phone, he was on it."

"Yeah, he was."

Dante put his glass down.

"If he made an outgoing, do you think we could find out what number he called?"

"Got me, I don't know anything about that stuff. We can ask Ray. He'll know. We'll take the number off the phone and make a note of the time. What was it, eleven, eleven oh five?"

Dante took a pen out of his shirt pocket and wrote *between 11 and 11:05* in his pad, then drew a series of exclamation points. He felt dead calm now.

The waitress returned and they ordered more drinks, a Beck's dark for Dante and Kathy her Virgin Mary. Dante asked for a swordfish steak and salad, Kathy the broiled chicken and spring potatoes.

———

When JoJo returned to his father's house he found the old man asleep. He sat on the edge of his father's bed, woke him, and recounted his telephone conversation with his police friend, telling his father it was time for a vacation. "The thing is," he said, "I don't know who else to tell. This rat can be anybody. I'm telling you," he went on before his father could protest, "it could be anybody. Who can we trust? I don't think it's smart to call the usual people together. This bastard might be in a spot right near us."

"In a perfect world, my son," his father told him, "we could give 'em all lie detector tests." He smiled.

What is he, JoJo thought, a babe in the woods? Does he really think this is funny? Speechless, JoJo gave a little shrug.

"C'mon, Joseph," the Skipper said more softly now, as if someone might be eavesdropping. "You don't think it's Bruno, Nicky Black, or the dwarf. It couldn't be the Dancer. He didn't say who?"

"He just said the guy's a major guy. The feds don't fool with some low-rent shit."

"A major guy? What the hell does that mean? How come you look so pale?"

JoJo shrugged, looking around. "Me pale? I ain't pale, Pop. I'm pissed, but I ain't pale."

"C'mere," his father said. He put his arm around JoJo's neck and pulled him in close. "I ain't gonna bite you. C'mere." He tightened his arm around JoJo's neck and kissed his cheek. His beard was rough and his breath a little stale. There rose in JoJo such a feeling of warmth and affection he was near tears. "Don't let this shit get to you," his father said. "What are they gonna do? Put some wannabe in front of the grand jury, let him run his mouth a little. They can't hurt us. The world around us is the world that protects us. Stop worrying."

"You'll go to Florida, Pop. You'll take Monty and maybe one of the others and go."

"I'll go. Sure I'll go. I'll take Monty and I'll take Lina too. You know, that woman has never been out of New York City since she landed here."

"Good. You'll take whoever you want, go to Boca, enjoy yourself, Pop. You could use a vacation."

His father rocked his head from side to side. "I've been feeling a little tense, you know, tight," he said. "A week or two in Florida may be just the thing. And you, what are you going to do?"

"I'm gonna go to John's."

His father gave him a dip of the head. "That's a great idea. Go and see your brother. Tell him hello for me."

"Yeah." JoJo grinned. "If you want me, use John's beeper."

"You'll find out who this traitor is. Remember a few years back how we drew out Philly Rags? Remember how we did that? Use your head, do something like we did with Philly."

JoJo nodded to himself, feeling vaguely confident now, wanting to get going. "You're right Pop. If there's any justice, I'll nail this rat bastard."

"Is there any? You think there's some justice somewhere JoJo?"

"Yeah, sure there is. When there's serious money involved, you can always find justice."

His father gave him another hug, JoJo's neck going all pins and needles from the pressure.

"You be careful," his father told him. "You're the best there is. The best I got."

————

As they drove toward Manhattan, Dante tried to imagine asking Kathy about this gay business. Was she or wasn't she? But he couldn't even work up the courage to choose the words he'd use. I'm ah, curious about this gay stuff. I'm ah, curious. . . . You wouldn't believe what I was told about you, hah-hah. Forget it, is what he thought, just let it slide.

Dante had a small beer buzz on. He fantasized about really breaking loose, getting ripped, loaded, stoned. He wondered what Jimmy was up to. He wondered what Kathy looked like under her clothes. She was a solid-looking woman with wide shoulders and great breasts, her thighs looked muscled and strong in her jeans, and she had one of those heart-shaped riding-high butts that you see a whole lot of in Harlem. A turkey ass, a substantial woman. Solid, was the word.

They parked on the street just off First Avenue on Fifty-fourth Street. Sheridan's was supposed to be a pretty good place to drink. It was set up like an Irish pub. Dark wood bar and prints of the old country; copper kettles and small farm tools hung from a beamed ceiling. Two bartenders in white shirts, a small color television over the bar in the corner near the door.

It was near one o'clock and the place was packed. There were no stools available, so he and Kathy stood at a chest-high oak divider, on which they put their drinks, the house gin for him over ice, club soda for Kathy. They stood facing, she with her back to the door. Behind him there were three women seated at the bar with frozen smiles, pretending to watch the television with a certain amount of intensity. The set was on without sound. Dante could not tell what show was on, one of those cable talk shows; a man sitting on a sofa listened politely as some shaved-skull weirdo in leather ranted on soundlessly.

"Am I going to drink alone all night or what?" Dante said.

"I'm drinking," Kathy said. Her eyes darted around the room. She looked in his face, stared straight at him, then looked past him, behind him to the bar.

"The hell you looking at?" He turned and saw only a barroom full of people, maybe fifteen guys and eight women.

Kathy shook her head and smiled.

A tall thin girl walked in wearing one of those body stockings under a loose green sweater. Guys around her suddenly gave her room. Kathy frowned, she seemed as though she was pulling into herself.

On the ride into the city they'd talked cop talk and laughed nonstop. They took apart straitlaced Ray and Inspector Martin; Dante told her of his years with Jimmy, how they were close as brothers. Good cop talk, how everyone else was a schmuck saying stupid things, how the world outside their world was chock full of people that pissed them off. They had laughed and elbowed each other. Before they walked into Sheridan's they slapped palms, let's go get 'em. Now Kathy seemed as though she were coming down, getting serious.

"You see that woman?" she said to him.

"The one in the sweater, that one?"

"Uh-huh."

"You know, I've been wondering all night what to say to you, so I'm just going to say it." She squinted at Dante as if to read the silly smile that had found its way to his face and set up shop. Dante looked away. Kathy dropped her arm across his shoulders, and when he turned to look at her she locked in on him.

"That woman," she said, "that woman in the bodysuit. Well you see . . ."

She mumbled something, and Dante winced seriously.

"What did you say?" he asked.

"I said, that's one fine-looking woman. And to tell you the truth, I'd rather have her legs wrapped around me than yours."

That was it, Dante headed for the men's room.

Vinny Rapino drove the Mercedes ten miles above the speed limit, and so it was close to two o'clock when they turned off the interstate onto a road that would bring them into the town of Narragansett in Rhode Island.

JoJo had slept most of the way listening to Sinatra tapes, remembering a glorious night in Fort Lauderdale when he had front row tickets for a Liza Minnelli–Sinatra concert. Now he was awake, giving Vinny directions to his brother's house. Listening to Vinny moan and marvel about his life, how little mistakes can jam you up.

"I get a call from Lilo, right?" Vinny said. "Now, I've been out all night, I mean all night. I had maybe an hour sleep when the phone rings."

JoJo stared out the window, not really hearing Vinny. It was a two-lane country road; there were no lights, and the road curved lazily. There was a house here and there, some farmland, and roadside stands that advertised local corn and fresh eggs, and one that announced LOBSTERS.

"You know," Vinny said, "I ain't no freeloader. I earn, and I handle things myself. Anyway, I get this call, it was maybe six o'clock in the morning. The guy tells me Lilo told him to call. I say yeah, he says he's going to Atlantic City with a couple of people, could I arrange for a few women to meet him at the Sands. I says, whataya think I am, a f'n pimp? He says, what's this? This some kind of joke? I says I ain't no pimp, who are you? He says you're an asshole. Now I don't take that from nobody. I tell him the only reason I'm talking to him this time of day is because he mentioned a name. Ya know, he mentioned Lilo."

Interested now, JoJo asked Vinny, "Who was he?"

"Who was he? It was Tony Conti, the *consigliere* of the Ramminos. A big f'n guy. Whew, how was I supposed to know that? Let me say it backwards: now, how was I supposed to know who I was talking to. The guy never told me."

JoJo began to laugh. "So what did you say to the guy?"

"I told him I'd give him a number. He says what number? I says a phone number of a chick in Atlantic City that will straighten him out. He says, I don't want no number you asshole I want three broads. I says I'll give you my whole fucking book, take it to bed and have an orgy you pain in the ass. And then I hang up on the guy."

JoJo was laughing so hard he began to cough, he coughed and gagged and coughed some more. Vinny turned and squinted at him. "Joseph," he said, "you smoke too much, you know that?"

JoJo kept on laughing and coughing, thinking as he gagged that Vinny had spoken to a man as high up in a family as you can get, and he'd spoken to him as if he were a nobody. He called the guy a pain in the ass. And then—he couldn't believe it—he hung up on him. Vinny was a lunatic, he had a death wish.

"In my mind, Joseph," Vinny said, "I really didn't believe that I'd done anything wrong. When Lilo told me who the man was, I apologized."

"Yeah," JoJo said. "And what did Lilo say?"

"I'm sorry, Joseph," Vinny said. "But in all due respect, you don't know Lilo like I do. He can be, ya know, a little nuts. Anyway, he don't accept my apology too well, because he chases me with a f'n bat when I told him."

JoJo almost fell off his seat he was laughing so hard—then suddenly he stopped.

"What in the hell is Lilo doing entertaining the *consigliere* of the Ramminos, I'd like to know," JoJo said.

Little Vinny Rapino shrugged. "Beats me," he said.

JoJo nodded his head, he nodded and gave a small laugh. "Lilo's a creep," he said.

Vinny didn't answer. Lilo was his boss, his capo. He just looked over at JoJo like he didn't know what to say.

They turned down Ocean Road, which ran along a palisade over-looking Narragansett Bay. JoJo told Vinny to look for the fourth driveway on the left; when they came to it, the electric gate swung open. Mushroom lamps lit the drive and there were lights on in the house.

"*Marrone,*" Vinny said. "This is some f'n castle." He looked very impressed.

———

At just before one o'clock, Dante left the men's room in Sheridan's Pub and walked across the floor through a crowd of singles shopping, he supposed, for women and men they had had or hoped to have and of course could never have.

He had a weird feeling of comfort, knowing for sure that Kathy was gay. He didn't know why exactly, just a feeling. Maybe he and Kathy would become good friends. He chuckled to himself, seeing Kathy at the bar talking to the woman in the green sweater and bodysuit. Dante stood outside the crowd for a minute, watching Kathy try to score. The men and women crowded at the bar smelled of deodorant, powder, and perfume. To Dante they all looked like they were trying to find a break from sorrow and loneliness. The good feeling he had earlier was taking a dive. He thought about Judy, Danny, Jimmy and f'n JoJo. He imagined himself making love to Kathy. Balling the hell out of her, to be precise. She'd drop women in no time flat. Screw a baby into her, turn her into something different from what she was.

Around him men were making moves on the women like sharks in a feeding frenzy. Using lines even *he* had heard before. The women, it seemed to him, listened politely.

"It's my first time here. I usually like to sit at the piano bar in the Drake, thought maybe tonight I'd just make the rounds."

Their ineptness and stupidity made him feel better.

Some guy with a white sweater tied around his neck was hitting on a woman with cantaloupe-size tits.

"I'm thinking about maybe taking a trip this summer to France. Ever been there, ever been to Paris, France? Last summer two buddies of mine, they play for the Jets. Well anyway we took a place out in the Hamptons. One of them called this morning begging me to room up this summer. Ever been out there, out to the Hamptons?"

Small wonder, Dante thought, nobody ever gets laid.

Kathy's eyes, as he watched her, darted around the bar. When she saw him, she smiled. The woman in the green sweater turned and began to watch the soundless television.

Kathy moved away from the bar carrying a drink. She elbowed her way through the crowd.

"You know," Kathy said to him, "I've been standing here fifteen minutes wondering where in the hell you went."

"You figure it's hard to get laid in here," Dante side-mouthed.

Kathy gave him a shot on the arm like, will you lighten up? His spirits rose. It could turn into a good night.

They walked across the street to the Mayfair. Kathy seemed to know half the people in the place. Dante had another vodka and tonic, Kathy drank a stinger. They left and stomped uptown five blocks. The streets were thick with well-dressed people cruising bars.

They stopped at a small Mexican restaurant and bar because Kathy said she needed a drink. The place was called Tio Javier's; there was music, a strolling guitar player, a small quiet crowd and a good long oak bar.

The bartender was a young man of about twenty-five or -six with a long blond ponytail. He was wearing sunglasses and a white shirt. Dante and Kathy found seats at the bar as the bartender served a woman wearing a flowered shirt and sickly green shorts. She had a mountainous ass and . thighs as wide around as a healthy maple.

Dante pointed at her with his chin. "That woman catches you looking at her she'll wet her panties," he said.

"It's amazing how dumb and mean some men can be," Kathy said. She sounded defensive.

"Kidding, kidding," Dante said. He wanted to tell her he wasn't kidding, but he chickened out.

Kathy asked the bartender for another stinger. Then she turned to Dante and gave him a slow smile. "You kid too much. So," she said. "Who are you, Dante O'Donnell?"

Suddenly Dante felt very tired. He wasn't going to score with Kathy, he knew that. So why hang around and get drunk with her? And getting drunk, it seemed to him, was exactly what Kathy was up to. At that moment he felt as though he might as well go home and get a good night's sleep.

"Who are you, Dante?" she said again. "C'mon, tell me what kind of man you are."

"The way I see it, Kathy, I'm just a normal man in an abnormal situation."

"What does that mean?"

"I dunno," he said. He squinted around the bar.

"C'mon," she said, sounding a bit tough now. "Give me a sense of your core beliefs."

"I don't have any. Listen," he said, "let's get out of this joint and go downtown. I know a spot in Little Italy where normal wiseguys hang out. It may be a bit boring to you. Then again, maybe you'll like it."

Kathy sat there staring at her drink for a long time. Dante touched the back of her head. "C'mon," he said, his tone as soft as personal as he knew how to make it. "Let's go."

She gave one nod, got up from the barstool, and downed that drink she had like magic. Zap, it was gone.

They headed downtown, jumping on the FDR at Sixty-second Street. Dante felt up now, game for whatever lay ahead, but he also felt angry. He did want this woman.

After five minutes of totally meaningless conversation she turned her head away from him, opened the window, then turned back to him and told him that the pleasure and triumph and hell of her life was drink. She said she was an alcoholic, and that she had not had a drink in three years. Tonight was a first, a first in three years.

They passed under the Fifty-ninth Street Bridge where a brown car was in flames on the curb. The acrid smell of burning rubber drifted in curls and then in waves into their car.

"You know that wasn't true what I just told you, don't you?" she said.

"How would I know if it were true or not? Anyway," Dante said, "I'm sorry if I made you drink."

"No," Kathy said. "I don't think you made me drink. Nobody makes anyone drink or do drugs. I've been taking a drink lately. Not often, just once in a while."

It was around Fourteenth Street that she seemed to get hyper. She was talking a mile a minute about her early days as a cop, all the bullshit that Dante did not want to hear.

"When I first came on the job, they put me in TPF. I figured I'd caught a real break. I mean, there were plenty of rookies that would have loved to work there."

Dante had worked the Tactical Patrol Force, and Jimmy too. An old friend of his father's headed up the unit at the time and arranged the assignment for both of them. But that was way before Kathy was there, probably before she was out of high school.

As she spoke, Dante figured that maybe he should answer her, join in the conversation. But the woman was speed-rapping, making him nuts. He nodded his head as she went on. Nodded and smiled.

"I had this captain, Captain Cantrell. You know him?"

Dante nodded, and that wigged him out. He'd never heard of the guy.

"Anyway he holds this meeting with my squad. Tells us he's going to send a decoy with backups into Central Park. He comes on like John f'n Wayne. At night, he says, they're beating the crap out of women in the park. At the time, I'm thinking, so what's new? For chrissake, they kill people there. I want muggers, he says. No bullshit pansy collars, dickie wavers or anything like that. I want muggers. Assault and robbery of women is what we're looking for. Anything but A and R collars, forget it. Gibbons, he says, you're going to do it for us. We'll back you, you won't be alone.

"If anyone could make an A and R in the park, I figure it's me. You know what I mean?"

Dante nodded. He was starting to feel embarrassed. He hated hearing people's war stories.

"Anyway, we staked out a high-incidence bench right off the One-hundred-and-tenth Street entrance. The location was a class-A perfect mugging spot. There was some but not too much light. Easy access to Central Park West, and the subway on the corner. There were trees, old oaks and maples with underbrush. Dim light along the trail. So I headed for the bench trailed by three backups, big guys, strong guys. I'm wearing these three-inch pumps, carrying a pocketbook."

Dante twisted his shoulders and neck, he was feeling tight and tense, there seemed to be something wrong with his back. He smiled at her.

"You see, Dante," she went on, "I was anxious but ready. I know that half-a-hump skel predators hit quick without warning. I knew that." She squinted at him.

Dante nodded.

"The park was deserted. My backups hid with these baseball bats behind some trees near the bench."

Dante started feeling sleepy, a panicky sleepy. Kathy wasn't going to rest. Tomorrow, he thought, tomorrow I'll sleep late.

"Anyway, I'm sitting like a statue and the longer I sat the more scared I got. I could feel myself tremble."

Dante could make out the lights of the Brooklyn Bridge off in the distance. The harbor and the Manhattan skyline were bright with reflected city light. His spirits were hitting rock bottom; he had a real yearning for more alcohol. Then he yawned.

Kathy frowned. "Am I starting to bore you?"

"Hey, no. No!" Was she kidding? he thought. He wanted to talk about lovemaking. He had this feeling, this urge to unbutton those jeans of hers. Through his drowsiness he needed to know if a gay woman might, just maybe, sleep with a man once in a while. He'd met a ton of cops that loved to bullshit, but a gabber like Kathy he'd never seen or heard before.

" 'Cause if I'm boring you, you should let me know."

"Kathy," he said. "You do a whole lot of things to me. But what you don't do is bore me."

"Good," she said. "Because there is a point to this story."

"A point, hah?" He glanced at her.

"I'm sitting for an hour on this bench when I hear voices in the darkness along the trail."

Okay, he thought, there are worse things than cop stories. Dante pinched the back of his hand and got a terrific spasm at the base of his neck. He was now driving along Grand Street, heading for Mott and Hester, that warm glow in his gut getting stronger now.

"I see three of them standing with their arms folded, these baseball caps on their heads, ten feet from where I'm sitting. They're standing just outside the circle of light from the streetlamp. They were young, and let me tell you they looked strong. Take the bag, I thought, snatch the f'n bag and go. The tallest of the three walked toward me, stopped, turned and walked back to join his friends. You see Dante, these creeps never just take a bag and run. I'm out of the academy one month and I'd already learned the lesson that all cops everywhere know: street skel half-a-humps get off on hurting. Sure they wanted the money, and they'd take it, but what they really wanted, what they got off on were screams of fear, and causing pain. Man I'd seen them whoop and holler and jump in the air after they hurt people bad. They scared me to death."

Dante found a spot just across from Ferrara's cafe on Grand Street and parked. He latched on to the last few sentences of what Kathy was saying. She sounded like some kind of rookie. He was trying to figure some way, any way to cut her short.

"Whatcha doin in the park, lady? It's late man, this place is dangerous. That's what one of these creeps said to me. I had my off-duty in my coat pocket, and let me tell you, that gun felt good in my hand. To sit still and be cool, to play victim, it was hard, harder than anything I'd ever done—hey look." Kathy slapped the dashboard.

Dante looked through the windshield at the quiet, late night street. He turned his head back to Kathy, then back to the street, like watching a tennis match.

"This creep comes back, and he starts to yell at me. You sneaky little bitch! he yells. You got money in that bag and that money is mine. He comes right up to me, man I could smell his breath. The guy's got a f'n straightedge razor in his hand. I believe, he says, we'll have us a lesson tonight about the right way to treat big O Man, he was smiling at me. His street name was O Man. I found that out later. What a f'n name, O Man. Dante," she said, "you ever feel physical terror, I mean terror so bad you could puke?"

Dante rubbed his wrist across his forehead, discovering that his arm had gone numb. He nodded.

"You're a victim, when terror grabs your heart like that you're a victim, and that's that."

"What happened?" Dante said.

"I shot him. Bam. One shot in the chest is all it took. Bam in the chest, he dropped like a rock."

"Good," Dante said. "You killed him?"

"He'll never be deader."

"Kathy," he said, "for god's sakes, you think there's a chance that I'll get laid tonight?"

Gripping his shoulders with trembling hands she said to him, "The point of this story is that I'm nobody's victim. Nobody's. Far as you getting laid, not a shot in a million. Well." She took his face in her hands. "Well, if I could just have a drink first, I could lay there and if I don't have to listen to you or look at you, I'll lay there pretend I'm dead. Think you'll like that?"

Dante opened the car door and went out into the nighttime street. He glanced at Kathy, who stood on the sidewalk now, and took a package of cigarettes from his pocket and lit one up. He hadn't finished his first long pull on the butt when he looked across the roof of the car at her, and she was smiling, a child's smile, gently, with infinite tenderness.

CHAPTER ELEVEN

At breakfast John Paradiso talked and JoJo listened. He smiled once in a while. Last night late, in the same bright white kitchen with floor-to-ceiling windows that looked out on Narragansett Bay, Goat Island, and Jamestown beyond, he had listened to John talk about the family construction company, about dealing with the unions, state inspectors, finding work. JoJo had smiled a lot because he could feel what his brother was feeling and wondered what living outside the family combat and street business would be like, what it would feel like to leave it all behind and join his brother in business, move to Rhode Island, sail the bay, fish for yellow fin tuna and striped bass, play golf and tennis. This morning he smiled to be polite, not feeling a thing other than a small anger, listening to John describe how tough his life was, his daily problems with the business, with his wife and daughters, both of whom were at boarding school. JoJo nodding thinking, Those poor fucking kids.

John said, "After Mom died, the old man never came to see me. What did he expect me to do? I couldn't leave the business and fly down to the city every week. Get involved in his business when I know so little about it? I'm responsible for the money; I take care of it as well as anyone could. I'm not a street guy, not like you or Nicky Black. Hell no, I stay here and take care of the really important things. The family's investments, your money, Pop's money."

JoJo nodded in admiration to show that he understood as John told him about the old man's refusal to retire, his attitude about the real business of the family, his bad heart. John sounded like he really cared. JoJo doubted it, but his brother did it well, the caring-good-son-and-brother sound.

John said, "I talk to Barry Cooper all the time. He wanted to come up and see you, but he's very busy." He paused. "He has a busy practice. A lawyer, you know. Has a hectic schedule. He tells me that you're constantly giving him these small assignments. Getting neighborhoods kids into law school, setting up people with family court lawyers and so on."

Listening, nodding, it occurred to JoJo that John was spending more time talking to the family lawyer than he was. John was pouring him coffee from the Italian coffee maker he'd bought in Rome the past Christmas. His brother had poise, style, was a sharp guy with investments and all. What else? He tended to talk about family business with Barry too much. But that wasn't so bad. Barry had some good ideas.

John brought him to the top floor of the house, his study, almost bare save for a large curved sofa, a telescope on a tripod through which John watched sailboats heading for the western passage, a small round table with four chairs. The walls were mostly of glass. John Paradiso's house was surrounded by three acres of trees and gardens, planted first by some long-dead sea captain's wife, added to and embellished by John. The air was impregnated with aromas that JoJo had never smelled before. In every room of the twenty-room house there were Persian rugs, massive sofas, and high-backed carved mahogany chairs. The house, with its beamed ceilings, was rugged, far more masculine than feminine; JoJo, ever since the first time he saw it, remembered the rooms as smelling of woodsmoke. He liked that, loved that smell of burning wood and the salt sea air that came through the open windows.

John had brought him to the study. "I've made you and Pop rich, you know that, don't you?" he said. "You and Pop are wealthy."

John was shorter than JoJo, with delicate features like his mother's. He was thin, with a smooth, hairless face. John Paradiso could shave once a week and no one would notice. His hands were small and as smooth as his face.

"I like having money," JoJo said. "But that's never been a problem with us, has it?"

"You don't remember the hard times. JoJo, it always was the same with you, you have a selective memory." He hesitated, giving JoJo a serious look. "Why did you come? You're bringing me some bad news, right? I mean, you're always welcome, even when you bring one of your people.

I've asked you not to bring any of those guys here. They make Penny nervous."

Penny was John's wife, a woman he met one summer on Cape Cod. The American girl, is what his father called her. A woman whose family was Scotch, Irish, German, with some English thrown in. A woman that made JoJo scratch his head. A nonperson, in JoJo's mind.

"JoJo," he said, "why not give up the life? Convince Pop to retire and you move up here. Come and work with me, if you like. The truth is, you don't have to work at all. Christ, what are you, thirty-nine, forty? You could retire yourself if you wanted."

"Work for you?"

"Work with me. If you want to, that is."

"I don't know anything about it."

"Neither do most people that run big businesses. You know people, how to handle people. That's all it takes." John looked at him over the rim of his coffee cup. "What's going on? Something's going on, I can feel it."

"You tell Barry to get his ass up here. You tell him I want to see him. I don't want to hear he's busy. I better not hear he's too busy to see me."

"Listen, I'll call him. Sure, you want I'll call him. I'll call him right now."

"Tell him to take the first flight out. Tell him I'm pissed, that's all. Tell him to get here."

"Jesus Christ," John said, staring out the window, out at the sea, his expression changing as he tightened up. He seemed to grin. "But why are you so angry? You make me nervous when you get so mad."

"Boy, you're really funny John." JoJo stood and went to the telescope. "This whole setup. You're dumber now than when you were a kid, and when you were a kid you were stupid."

"JoJo?"

"Screw you. Where do you think this all comes from? From your shit-ass construction company maybe? You'd better realize it man, realize where all this comes from. You don't talk to Barry Cooper about me and what I tell him to do or don't do. You don't listen to his crap. You know how much money we made for that man last year? Call him now and tell him to get here."

———

It was a little before five in the morning when Dante and Kathy got out of the elevator in Kathy's apartment building and walked down the musty hallway to apartment 14H. Kathy fought with her keys for about a minute before finding the right one. "I'm not sleeping on any sofa," Dante said as she unlocked the door.

She didn't answer, just walked into the apartment and left the door open for him. He moved a few steps into the room and raised his voice. "Please don't make me sleep on the sofa. I'll behave myself. I promise, I won't touch you."

She stared at him, and her mouth got funny, a funny ugly grin. Dante's brain was screaming, Dummy, how stupid you sound.

"Uh-huh," Kathy grunted without suggesting where he would sleep.

He was impressed with the apartment, a large L-shaped studio with plenty of windows, which meant good light during the day. Dante hated dark places. The apartment was in a Rego Park high rise overlooking Queens Boulevard. The convertible sofa was open, and it took up a good deal of space. On the wall over the open sofa hung a lithograph of two rednecks holding shotguns; one wore a cap with I LOVE YOU EL PASO on it. In script, on the bottom of the print were the words *They'll take our guns when they pry them from our cold dead hands.* It was done by some guy named Robertson. Dante liked it, he liked it a lot. There was a VCR on top of a TV, and a bowl of yellow apples on a small round table. A wall unit was covered with framed family photos, one a wedding photo that was, Dante's best guess, fifty years old. There were books by Danielle Steel, Jackie Collins, three by Le Carré, two by Wambaugh, and Robert Daley's *Target Blue.* On the night-stand was a Jeffrey Archer and a paperback anthology of modern American poems.

In the bathroom, looking at his tired reflection in the mirror, Dante decided that at least he would go through the motions. Give her one more chance to appreciate the quality of his lovemaking. What a nightmare. He should have gone home.

But where was home? His mother's house? Dante was startled by the thought that at that moment he had no home.

Every day since the night Judy put him out he had this crazed feeling of I'm not going back, I'm going to die in the street and I'll never see my son again.

Riding from Manhattan to Queens he played with this fantasy that he'd come into Kathy's apartment and she'd tell him it was all a joke, I was pulling your leg, I pull everybody's leg, I'm not gay you jerk. And sweetie I love sex, and I need to have some wild head-to-toe sex with you. He felt as though he hadn't made the good move yet. But it was coming, he experienced an intangible something, something good and strong. For a moment he had a sensation that he was disoriented, and he started to turn in circles in the tiny bathroom, he was horny as a toad and crazed and figured maybe his penis would split his pants. This could be good, it could be bad it could be a nightmare. It was in fact a life experience, an adventure.

Dante walked out of the bathroom, ran his fingers through his hair feeling cool and loose, if there was room he would have done a little soft shoe. To hell with Judy. And his son Danny? He could see him on his days off. Christ, half the cops he knew were divorced. He was going to get himself a real New York woman. Leave the crabgrass and Little League and bills behind, join the city scene. Find a pub to hang out in, a place where everyone called his name. Watch Sunday football with good buddies and drink tap beer.

He thanked God for his father's good looks. He stalked into the living room—bedroom like a burglar. There was a night-light beneath the end table. When he heard the sound he felt like dying. After a moment of nonblink paralysis the thought crossed his mind that he'd spent too much time in the goddamn bathroom with its bright blue toilet seat. He grabbed at himself and stared at the digital on the end table. Five thirty, of course she would be asleep. Anyone would be at five thirty in the morning. But that sound, that dull heavy sound, Christ, that was a man's snore. He found his way onto the edge of the bed and took off his clothes down to his shorts. In a slow arc he brought his legs up and around and under the covers.

She was wearing some kind of sweat pants and a T-shirt, at least it felt like a T-shirt. He pressed his belly into the small of her back and she grunted with annoyance but didn't budge, wake up, nothing. Sighing deeply, he placed his hands on her shoulders and gently pulled her. He felt like yelling, Hey, hey you up?

"Kathy?" he said in a normal speaking voice. She quickly raised her face from her pillow and turned toward him. "Dante, I want you to answer this question," she said. "If you were asleep and Jimmy Burns crawled into bed with you and tried to shove his dick in your butt, how would you feel?"

He rolled over onto his back and stared at the ceiling. Oh great move, he thought, what a terrific way to close out the night.

Sometime around seven, seven thirty, Kathy rolled onto her side and started to rub his back. He rolled over fast as a shot.

"Turn back the other way, dummy," she said.

And so he did and moved away from her, playing hard to get. She moved closer to him and rubbed his back some more. He began to drift off into sleep, he heard her yawn and felt a thumb in his shoulder blades.

She threw a leg across his hip and continued to massage him, and that felt great, down to his lower back around his hips. He felt guilty and apologetic. Dante gave one hell of a deep sigh and fell through the surface of sleep.

———

Vinny Rapino left Narragansett sometime around noon, taking the old Boston Neck Road, and made a left onto 138, heading for Route 4 past all the construction and onto I-95 north toward Providence. In fifteen minutes he saw the sign for Green Airport and zipped off. In less than a half hour from the time he left John's house, he was parking the Mercedes in the short-term lot. It seemed to him that this Rhode Island was a jerkwater place, for chrissake you could bomb through the whole state in forty-five minutes. And the friends, JoJo told him, the goodfellas from up here ran their entire operation out of a laundry from someplace they called the Hill. A bunch of cowboys, is what Vinny thought.

As he walked through the terminal he was looking for a short thin Jewish guy in a gray three-piece suit. The place was crowded but there he was next to the shoeshine stand, gold watch flashing, pinky ring winking.

"Barry?" Vinny said.

"It's me."

"Got any bags?"

"Why?"

He's got those uh-oh eyes. Oofa, Vinny thought, this guy's got a problem. Vinny was still not too clear on what he was doing with JoJo in the first place. A loan, Lilo told him, I'm gonna lend you out for a while. Fine by him, JoJo was a classy guy, top flight, a f'n prince compared to that numbnuts Lilo. But he figured his pulling out of the marriage with Sofia, Lilo's daughter, was at the heart of the matter. Goddamn Lilo didn't trust his left fingers, figured they were scheming on his right hand. The guy was pure one-hundred-percent gimme. But Lilo loved Sofia, and Vinny had screwed her, screwed the only person that mad dog loved. Jesus, that wasn't smart. A pussy collar, that's what he had, a pussy collar. So he'd have to pay. Hang out with JoJo a while, be relegated to a driver and bodyguard. So what, he'd figure some way to turn a buck and maybe even get laid. Yeah, even in Rhode Island.

"If you don't have any baggage, I got the car right out front, we can go."

"No, I don't have any baggage. I don't expect to be here long enough to need any baggage. You know something I don't, kid?"

In the car on the way back, Barry asked questions and Vinny shrugged. This guy was an outsider, and Vinny would not speak to him about anything other than the weather, which was perfect.

"Where are you from, Vinny?"

"The city."

"You like this place? How would you like to live up here?"

Shrug.

"I could never live here. There isn't anything here. Where do you go to eat here?"

Shrug.

"John look good? How's he been feeling? You know, he has a little heart trouble, like his father. He has to exercise and watch what he eats. Sure he plays golf, but hell, he rides around in a cart. And the stress, the man's got a ton of stress in that construction business."

Two shrugs.

"Ah, excuse me Vinny. But you don't have a whole lot to say, do you?"

"Ey, I just drive the car."

Barry took a Wash 'N' Wipe out of his briefcase and wiped his face. "What I need," he said, "is a week in Bermuda. We all need our vacations. Vacation time is important. Unwind, chill out. A time to gather our thoughts. Right Vinny?"

Vinny thought about Rhode Island, Lilo, and Sofia.

"Right Vinny?"

"You better believe it."

Therapy, Barry thought. What these guys need, what all these wiseguys need is some serious encounter therapy, lots of free associating. They're all so goddamn remote. He wondered if he was in trouble. If I am, there is always a way to square it. Rule one, there is always a way to save your skin, just act in good faith. Be sly, be careful, and if at all possible act in good faith. Of course, when you're dealing with very nasty people rule one goes out the window, the part about good faith. If you don't want to see yourself die for no good or valid reason, when you're dealing with nasty people bullshit your way through, and keep an escape hatch open.

They were driving slowly along Ocean Road, the sky was all brightness and blue; trees were thick with leaves, and there were flower gardens of crocus and tulips. The place seemed pretty much the same as Barry remembered, but he remembered it in winter, bare trees and wind-whipped rain. Abruptly they were driving between mansions on the left and merely very expensive homes on the right; the lawns were spacious, and on the bay side of the road the homes were set deep in. Ocean Road was a boundary between average well-to-do and serious bucks. John Paradiso lived on the serious-bucks side. From his back porch you could watch the sun rise over water once sailed by Norsemen to a land they called Vinland; Verrazano anchored in the waters now called Newport Harbor.

JoJo and his brother stood watching as Vinny parked the Mercedes. They were dressed curiously alike, both in white shorts with blue cotton shirts, tennis shoes, and socks. Barry stared at them through the windshield and then he smiled. They returned his stare without greeting.

Vinny turned off the engine and looked at Barry.

―――――――――

Dante finished off an English muffin and ordered pancakes and Virginia ham, content to wait with his second cup of coffee, believing he felt as bad as he'd ever felt in his life. Drowsy and anxious after a miserable couple of hours sleep, completely exhausted.

He got up at nine. Kathy was still sleeping. He slipped out of the apartment and went to the Lock and Key coffee shop to call Jimmy at the social club plant. He was expected to be at the plant by noon.

Dante was still buzzing a little from the massage Kathy'd given him, how it felt in his back and neck and hips. Horny and lonely, he wondered how Judy and Danny were spending their morning and thought for the first time in a long time that maybe, just maybe he was in the wrong line of work.

Ray answered the phone and told him Jimmy was sitting at the kitchen table transcribing club conversation from the night before. "Tell Jimmy I'll take over for him later." Dante rubbed his eyes and tried to get his thoughts together. He was talking about a whole lot of work. Transcribing dumb-ass conversations between a bunch of stone-headed gunslingers. Keep him and Jimmy busy all day, five or six hours at any rate.

"Ray," he said, "why don't you come and meet me for breakfast?"

"Sure," Ray said. "I'll have something to eat. Why not? I'll be right there. Listen," he said. "Do you know if Kathy is coming in today?"

"Nope. I guess so. Why not?"

"Nobody's heard from her. She with you last night?"

"With me? Why would she be with me?" Dante did not know, in all honesty, why the hell he lied.

"What are you doing, going mental on me?" Ray said. "She left with you. Hello? Dante you left here with Kathy last night."

"We had dinner together." Dante felt sleepy again. He didn't know what to say. He was feeling shitty and depressed, physically whipped, and a little bit like wanting a drink. That, he considered, could be a growing problem. Christ, it wasn't even eleven o'clock. A Saturday morning in June.

He sat in the last booth in the Lock and Key, a coffee shop across from the Queens Courthouse. A place where cops, lawyers, victims, and moron defendants shared breakfast space. Ray came in as the waitress poured Dante his fourth cup of coffee. He took a seat, yawning into his hand.

"I didn't sleep at all last night," he said. "Both my kids got a virus or something."

"Me neither, I feel like shit."

"Where were you?"

"Never mind."

Ray ordered eggs over easy with ham. His expression was noticeably sour. "A big night, huh?"

"No big night, I just didn't sleep well. Ray, let me ask you something. Me and Kathy grabbed something to eat last night at Chaplin's. You know the place?"

"Sure, yeah. Why? You and Kathy, huh?"

"Just dinner. Anyway, we ran into JoJo Paradiso."

"What?"

"We ran into JoJo. It freaked me out, the guy was in the joint." Dante was almost shouting.

"That's a hell of a thing. He say anything to you?"

"Yeah, sure, I know the guy. You know I know the guy. Anyway, he was on the pay phone when we walked into the place. We got the number of the phone there. Ray, can we find out who he was calling, what number he dialed?"

"How do you know he made the call? He may have been getting a call there."

"I don't know if he made the call. But say he did, could we get the number?"

"If it was a toll call, we can get the number. You got the time the call was made?"

"Not the exact time, but close enough."

"A toll call we can get. If it was local, forget it. Give me the time and number, I'll call my connection at telephone security. Maybe I'll need an administrative subpoena or something. I'll take care of it."

"It could be important."

The waitress came by to pour them more coffee. Dante was rubbing his face. Ray said, "I've done the paperwork for a pen register on the pay phone in the candy store near the club."

"That's great," Dante said, nodding in approval.

A pen register does not record conversations, but it will register all the phone numbers dialed out from the phone. A great device for intelligence, and much easier to get a court's approval than an eavesdropping device. A damn good idea. Something they should have done earlier.

"We should have put that phone up earlier," Dante said.

"Well we'll have it now," Ray said. "So tell me, where you end up, huh? I mean last night, where did you sleep?"

"In the arms of a stranger, my friend. In the loving arms of one strange woman."

"Kathy?"

Dante ran the edge of his pinky around the edge of his coffee cup.

"Man, I hope you didn't ruin a significant friendship with sex," Ray said with false brightness. There was silence for a long, long twenty seconds. "Why don't you just go home buddy? You've been away long enough."

"I dunno," Dante said. "I don't feel like I can. I mean, I never hear from her. If I didn't call, we wouldn't speak at all."

"Do you want to go back or what?"

Dante was squirming so much he felt like a snake.

Ray said, "All you talk about is how much you miss your son, and how lonely you are, and how your life is with your family. Is that all bullshit or what?"

"No! No! I mean it, but . . ."

He did not feel he could tell Ray, the guy sitting across from him all smiles and sincere, the story of his life, even if he wanted to. He said, "I meant what I said, I do miss my family. I just don't know what to do."

"Look," Ray told him, "you can't live like your partner. Jimmy's been a loner all his life. You can't live like he does. I mean, does he have anybody in his life? Excuse me, Dante," Ray said, "I know how tight you two are. But you gotta admit, the guy's strange."

"Yeah, you're right, he's strange," Dante said. He tried to think of something to add and was saved when Ray's beeper went off. His own beeper was where it always was, in the trunk of his car. He watched Ray go to the pay phone, unhurried but very efficient. He decided that he would go and just show up at his house. What the hell would Judy do? Call the cops on him? He wondered about Jimmy, just how strange was he anyway? He wondered if he was forgetting on purpose just how weird his lifelong friend was.

Ray came back, asked the waitress for another cup of coffee, and said, barely moving his mouth, "That was Jimmy, he said he thinks JoJo's gone, and the old man too. He thinks they both left town."

"How the hell he know that?" Dante glanced over his shoulder at the coffee shop. It was getting crowded, a noisy cop crowd coming in for breakfast or early lunch, their voices filling the place. A young black woman in uniform went to the jukebox and put on some upbeat music.

"Jimmy said it's all over the tapes. The jerks are trying to be cool and all, talking in codes, dumb shits. But it's all over the tapes, he said. Jimmy thinks they've skipped."

Dante wondered if running into JoJo last night drew a tip or something. He didn't know what to think.

Ray said, "Don't look around, but Freddie Miller just came out of the men's room. Sitting down now, two booths over."

"Freddie?" Dante turned and looked. "I don't see him."

"Two booths over, how can you miss him? Don't look man, don't look at the guy. He makes me nuts. I hate the racist son of a bitch."

"C'mon," Dante said, "Freddie's not such a bad guy."

He saw the back, as wide across as a compact car, shoulders slumped. "Freddie," he called out. "How you doing, buddy?"

Freddie turned from his two stacks of pancakes and raised a fist.

"Thanks a lot," Ray said. "The big bastard is coming over here now."

Freddie joined them and did a little something with his eyebrows. "Hey," he said. "How you guys doing?"

Ray said, "Freddie, I heard about that dick print bullshit. Is that true or what?"

"Dick print?" Dante said. "What's a dick print?"

"Tell him, Freddie."

"No, no. Wait, wait," Freddie said. "I got a joke, you guys hear the one about the Jew and the pizza?"

"My wife's Jewish," Ray said. "My kids're half Jewish, I don't think I want to hear your joke."

But when Freddie was cranked up like this from coffee or whatever, it was impossible to shut him down. "Sure you do," he said. "What's the difference between a pizza and a Jew."

Ray took a deep breath and made a kind of face.

"A pizza don't scream when you stick it in an oven."

Dante said, "Tell that joke to Jimmy Burns, why don't ya? He'll hit you with a bat, you big dope."

Freddie shrugged. "It's a joke."

"So what's with this dick print business," Dante said. "Another one of your screwball schemes, hah?"

"G'head," Ray said, "tell him. Wait'll you hear this. Then tell me if this nut job doesn't need a rubber room."

"Naw, it ain't no big deal." Freddie sounded sincere.

"Will you tell the goddamn story?" Dante shouted. Then he said to the room. "Ain't this some shit?"

"I guess you heard that they got a whole lot of child abusers up in the Bronx. I guess you guys know that?"

"That's a national problem, a f'n national disgrace is what it is," said Ray.

"Yeah, but it's worse in the Bronx. Anyway, me and the squad commander came up with this idea. I mean I came up with it and the lieutenant, well he went along."

"I met that guy, he's loose in the head," Dante said. "Ray, me, and Jimmy met this lieutenant." His voice went low and confidential. "The guy is a total space shot."

"A good black guy," Freddie said. "There ain't many, but he's one."

"I know the guy," Ray said. "They've tried to commit him more than once. A perfect boss for Freddie here."

Freddie extended his arms like an airplane and held his pose. "Ray," he said, "child abuse in that precinct has taken a nosedive, and I believe I'm responsible."

"What'd you do?" said Dante.

"I take dick prints."

"What?"

"A guy gets busted for abusing a kid, they bring him to me and I print his dick. I tell the jerkoff that dicks leave prints just like fingers. I sit at this old wooden desk, the kind that has a printing board, you know the type. Anyway I sit at the desk, the perp stands next to me. I do the paperwork on the collar and then I tell him to drop his pants. Tell him I need to print his dick to see if his dick print matches up with other prints we've taken from various asses and mouths of victims. Anyway, these jerkoffs do it. They all do it, Dante, they drop their pants and I take ahold of their dicks and roll 'em just like a thumb or something across a print card. Then I take ahold of the guy's dick and give it a whack with a slapper I keep in the top drawer. A good ten-ounce slapper. Man, you wanna be there when these guys jump around, it's a sight to see. They jump and holler and f'n moonwalk all over the squad room. It's something to see, man."

Dante was staring, his jaw slack.

"And what do you know," Freddie said, his big mouth curling into a grin. "Child abuse collars have dropped off in the precinct. You know, an infant will suck anything you put into its crib. You guys know that? An infant will suck on anything. I had one of those, some piece of crap walked into his girlfriend's baby's room and—"

"Oh Christ," Ray said. "I've heard enough. Shut the hell up, Freddie."

"Well you don't wanna hear it, but it's true."

Ray said, "Well goddammit Dante, say something."

"Son of a bitch," Dante said.

CHAPTER TWELVE

L ate in the afternoon as the Mercedes found the crest of the Jamestown Bridge, Barry Cooper found himself riding in the passenger's seat gazing at the bay. The glint of reflected sunlight forced him to shade his eyes. On his right, though some distance off, the bay met the Atlantic. The sun was high and intense, the ocean a cold dark blue fading to dull aqua near shore. The sea seemed rough, with whitecaps and heavy swells. Block Island was out there somewhere, and Paris too. Barry Cooper had been to Block Island once and Paris twice. He had fallen in love with both places. And on this afternoon, with JoJo in the back seat of the Mercedes and dull-headed Vinny driving, Barry would have happily given five years of his life to be in either place, to be any place other than where he was.

From somewhere came the smell of burning asphalt, as though the very road they drove upon was afire. He kept thinking of lines from a book, a novel, or maybe it was poetry he'd read some years back: *People are watching you. Always. Evil people who wish you bad things are watching. You are not among friends.*

Immediately after Barry had arrived at John's house from the airport, John excused himself, said he was needed at the office. JoJo walked him out to the car, and Barry watched through the window as JoJo discussed something with John, speaking enthusiastically and at some length. John, it seemed to him, was pouting. It took him a moment to understand that he was seeing a performance. JoJo was making it clear he was the boss. As far as Barry was concerned there had never been a doubt. It was JoJo that directed him to the guest room and told him to change into more comfortable clothing. For a moment it crossed Barry's mind to protest. He could tell JoJo that he had business in New York City, that he had to take a deposition or some such thing. He did not know what was going on. What a screwed-up position he was in, how much at the mercy of events beyond his control.

In the guest room Barry found a warm-up suit, a sweatshirt, and sneakers. "Put on the sneakers," JoJo told him. "You'll need sneakers where we're going." He appeared to be in fairly good spirits and he seemed rested, but Barry was not certain of either impression. He was anxious, and it was difficult, impossible really, to get a straight answer from JoJo as to why he had made this trip. Why couldn't they meet at the usual place in the city?

"I came here for a break, I need a rest. But we have to chat," JoJo told him. That was it, no further explanation.

After Barry had dressed, JoJo told him they were going for a ride. The mere sound of that sentence gave him the trots.

At the foot of the Jamestown Bridge, Barry took note of all the heavy construction machinery, gigantic backhoes and dozers. Workers milled about. He saw a man in bib overalls and a blue bandana carrying a shovel. The thought crossed his mind that John Paradiso should have a piece of this contract.

At the intersection Vinny made a right. Gradually the country changed; the road ran through low rolling hills, bordered on either side by thick woods. Obscure and seemingly deserted dirt roads cut it at quarter-mile intervals. Further on there was pastureland, a Friends meetinghouse, a neat salty shack that advertised native lobsters.

Pretty, Barry thought. But what in the hell was he doing here?

It didn't just happen that JoJo had John call and tell him to appear, no ifs, ands, or buts. Things just didn't happen with JoJo. He made them happen. He made everything happen with this family. The old man was a goner, out of the box now. And John was John. JoJo was the boss, period. Still, Barry knew he was special. That wasn't just his point of view, it was JoJo's too, JoJo felt that Barry was special. There were a whole lot of special people in JoJo's life. But just because JoJo considered Barry special didn't mean he wouldn't have Bruno take a bat to his head if he thought Barry had turned on him.

But his ties to JoJo were old and strong. They had met ten years earlier, when Barry was employed as an assistant prosecutor at the Brooklyn district attorney's office. JoJo had reached him through another corrupt attorney who had an office on Court Street. The man was small and thin and in his seventies; he wore a business suit every day of his life. An uncle of a minor lieutenant in Bruno's crew, he had been loyal to the family, but he was growing old and had a habit of too much small talk with strangers. In any event, he had arranged a sitdown with Barry.

At that meeting JoJo delivered ten thousand dollars to Barry. And Barry, for his part, delivered a promise of future help. You should have heard Barry on the subject of being a wiseguy, of being part of the action. When Barry left the prosecutor's office and went into business on his own, JoJo asked what would be an appropriate retainer for him if he and his friends were Barry's only clients. Barry shrugged, and JoJo offered him a hundred grand. Barry asked for a hundred and fifty and JoJo told him you're a good guy. I trust you, I'll give you two hundred and fifty. Barry said shit! and JoJo told him worry about nothing; I like you.

JoJo liked him, he did. He thought of him as ambitious and brave, which could make him dangerous. Still, he was charming, and loyal—JoJo had tested him more than once. And most important, he was smart, smarter than anyone JoJo had ever met, except the old man. He knew how the cops and courthouse worked. He knew which detectives business could be done with. He knew judges and politicians, and he had a brother who was a successful bigtime attorney in south Florida. A place where it seemed money grew on orange trees. So dangerous ambition had to be measured against connections and loyalty. But he was a Jew. The smartest and toughest man I ever met, his father told him, was Meyer Lansky. He had more brains and more balls than any wiseguy I ever knew.

And so it was that Barry Cooper became the family attorney. And so it remained. His current retainer was one million dollars, half tax free in cash, the other half through John's construction company.

The sign for Beavertail points to a fine paved road that leads to a lighthouse. The road wound a bit through scrub pine and thick beach-rose bushes, and suddenly they came upon the lighthouse and a parking lot.

From the back seat JoJo put a friendly hand on Barry's shoulder. Barry almost jumped through the roof of the car.

"C'mon Barry," JoJo said. "Let's take a walk. Vinny," he said, "we'll be right back."

Somehow reassured that he was not here to be killed, Barry walked along a path; JoJo came behind him, walking carefully. There was a stiff ocean wind. Barry went straight to the edge of a cliff and stood looking out across the ocean.

"Why couldn't we meet in the city?" Barry said. "This place is beautiful, but why here?"

JoJo breathed deeply and looked out to sea.

"You're making me nervous," Barry said. "What's going on?"

JoJo kept looking out to sea. There was the sound of a bell buoy, and scores of lobster traps, their blue and yellow and green markers bobbing in a truly rough sea. A fishing trawler and sailboats were strung along the horizon.

"There are some good things happening, but there are also problems. Some bad problems," JoJo said.

"Your problems are mine," Barry told him.

JoJo laughed and so did he.

"C'mon," Barry said. "What is it? How did the Florida trip go?"

"Good," JoJo said. "It went even better than I thought."

"You're going to do it, then? You'll make that move?"

"Maybe." JoJo smiled, thinking Barry had no business asking that question. Shifting gears, speaking quickly now, he told Barry about the Cuban's son-in-law, asked him to look into the arrest, see if there was anything they could do. Then he said, slow and easy, wanting the words to sink in, turning to see Barry's reaction, "I got a call. I got a stool pigeon right next to me."

Barry seemed amused. "Who told you that?"

JoJo didn't answer.

"Can I tell you something?" Barry's voice was soft and solicitous. "He would have to be right next to you to hurt you."

"You think so?" JoJo asked sharply.

"It's my understanding that you only talk to your captains, right? I mean, you don't discuss business with just anybody."

"I talk to all kinds of people every day. What are you talking about?"

"Joseph, if they have some character ready to testify in front of a grand jury, and if that somebody is someone that knows your business, knows you and can back up that testimony, you could have a very serious problem."

"I know that."

"And your father too."

"I know, I know."

"Listen," Barry said. "Maybe your information is off. Maybe this connection of yours is just talking, looking for a payday."

JoJo shook his head. Man, would he love to believe that, but he knew better.

"Listen Barry, this Cuban. He wants me to get him heroin. He wants to trade heroin for cocaine. Even though this is not my business, I know this is a top-flight deal. We could earn here. There's a ton of money in that shit."

"And the money doesn't know where it came from. Money is money is money. Right?"

"Sure."

"Can you do it? Keep it quiet, keep it away from your father?"

Frowning, JoJo closed his eyes. "I can sure as hell try. Tomorrow I'll have fifty kilos of the stuff parked inside a rented car in Manhattan."

This was a lie. A test, the first of several he would give trusted friends. "You know the garage," he said. "The one where I park my car when I come to your office."

"Joseph, you're standing here telling me that you have one hundred pounds of heroin stashed in a car?"

JoJo put his hand on Barry's shoulder. "That's what I said, ain't it?"

"Then you have it, you have the goods, you can pull this off?" A faint caution entered Barry's eyes.

"I'm asking you this because I want your advice, my friend: do you think I should go ahead with this move or what?"

"I'm not about to tell you what you should or should not do, Joseph. I can tell you how exposed you've made yourself, and that's about all I can tell you."

"Ey, listen to me. I'm asking you what do you think. Your brother vouched for this guy, am I right?"

Barry looked over his shoulder. "Michael has done business with the man for years," he said, his voice low. "He assures me he is authentic. The man is international, has connections in Columbia, Spain, and Mexico."

JoJo nodded thoughtfully. He eased away from Barry. His lawyer had been drawing closer, and he smelled of sweat. Tense sweat.

"Big is good. Big is important. But can the man be trusted?"

Barry held up his hand. "Jesus, Joseph, what do you want me to say? My brother has confidence in the fellow. Michael's my blood, what do you want me to say?"

"Tell me I can trust him, that's what I want you to say."

"Trust him." Barry tilted his head back. "If I say you can trust him, then of course I believe you can."

"Believe?" JoJo said in a very showy concentration.

Barry exhaled heavily, then spoke in a somewhat depressed manner. "You have to trust *me,* Joseph. I mean what else is there?"

"Barry, I can see you're nervous, and I can't figure what you're nervous about. If there is some kind of riddle here, tell me. Now listen to me, we've been together a while now, I know you. So when you're tense, I've got to ask myself why. Why is my friend and lawyer nervous? You don't have money problems. How could you have money problems? As far as I know, everything at home is okay. So I have to think it's something else. I have to think that my friend has a dilemma he don't want to share with me. I have to think—"

"No problems, I don't have any problems." Barry cut him off. "The truth is I'm very pleased." His eyes were wide and there was a great smile on his face, and his voice rose almost to a shout.

"Everything's fine, then? You're happy with me, with our arrangement?"

"Happy as a man can be." Barry's voice went light and airy, but there was a slight shakiness there too. He glanced quickly at JoJo and then went back to watching the sea, the turbulent waters bursting over the boulders below, the sailboats and fishing trawlers off on the horizon.

"Joseph?"

JoJo didn't hear his name. He was debating with himself, should he believe this guy or what?

"All right, listen," JoJo said. "I ain't gonna repeat this. Do me a favor, in the future don't talk to John about matters that are between you and me. You've been telling my brother things that are none of his business. Don't do it."

Barry was stunned. "I'm not sure I know what you mean, but I assure you—"

JoJo jabbed a finger into the center of Barry's chest. "You talk to him about the construction company business and that's it."

Barry shrugged.

"What's the matter now?" JoJo asked.

"Forget it."

"No, go ahead."

"Forget it, I understand."

"Yeah, but you're touchy as hell and it's making me nuts. What is it?"

Barry said, almost pleading now, "Put yourself in my place, Joseph. I get a call to come to Rhode Island. No explanation, nothing. I don't know what's going on. I'm in a haze." Barry seemed to rise within himself, showing some strength now. "I'm told get up here, you want to see me and it has to be like, now. What am I made of, steel? You bet your ass I worry when I get a call like that."

JoJo saw the honesty in Barry's eyes and lost his uneasiness.

Barry was fine. No problem there. Still, he would test him.

They stood and talked for another twenty minutes, JoJo telling Barry to make sure he reached out for somebody that could help Luis's son-in-law, Barry telling him that it would cost big. JoJo saying whatever. Barry getting stronger as they went on, flexing a bit, telling JoJo that the cocaine move was heads-up, reminding him to stay as far away from the product as possible, acting cool now, one of the boys. On the ride back to John's house, JoJo drifted off into his own world in the back seat of the Mercedes, wading through memories in search of images of the people around him, images that would somehow give him an indication as to who the informant could be. Behind the wheel, Vinny would glance in the rearview at JoJo and then from JoJo over to Barry, whose eyes wandered from the country road to the salt marsh and ponds and bird sanctuary off to the right.

JoJo could not think of anyone who would turn on him, not like that, be a rat. He recollected the time three years back when he and Bruno ran a test on these three soldiers in Bruno's crew. One of the three, they were confident, had flipped to the cops.

Bruno took each soldier aside, sat down with each one of them and told them one after the other that he was setting up a high-roller heavy-money crap game. Bruno gave them each an address and told each one to keep it under his hat.

Except there was no game. The locations were apartments of straight-world friends. And later, when the cops hit one of the apartments, coming with sledgehammers and a crew of twenty, shattering the door of a legitimate sanitation worker's home, Bruno figured he had the rat pinned.

And it came to JoJo, making him feel both better and worse, that this current stool pigeon too must surface; sooner or later he'd know the traitor. It was only a matter of time. Then it hit him, the way three years back Bruno had made the guy confess.

His name was Philip Raneri, but everybody called him Philly Rags. JoJo told Rags that he was going to take Bruno to dinner, asked Rags if he would drive them to this seafood joint on City Island. He sat in the front seat of Rags's new Buick, and Bruno sat behind Rags. JoJo remembered how miserable the night was. Rainy and windy, an awful chill in the air, traffic was light and nobody was out, a real loser of a night.

Riding to the restaurant Bruno talked on and on about what they were going to do to the rat when they nailed him. Hanging tight, unsmiling, Rags drove, listening as Bruno whispered as if he were sitting in church. His words, the way he spoke them even made JoJo tense up.

"How you feeling today?" Bruno whispered in Rags's ear from his spot in the back of the car. It was more like a warning than a question. At the time it occurred to JoJo that Bruno's voice, his breath in Philly Rags's ear acted like a truth serum. "You know, I'm gonna take a piece of you. A big piece, if you don't tell me the truth."

"About what, about what boss?"

"GRRRrrrrrrr," Bruno growled. Just like that—"GRRRrrrrrrr."

Philly Rags began quivering, a good and evil sign. A good sign for Bruno, he knew he had the right guy. A bad portent for Rags. He couldn't think clearly, didn't know what to say.

"Christ, if I did something you want to talk to me about, tell me."

He turned to JoJo, his hand grabbing for his groin as if he had to pee. JoJo thinking, Guilty . . .

Sitting in the Mercedes now, Sinatra on the tape deck, Vinny humming and Barry sitting back with his arms folded, JoJo remembered the way Rags pulled into the vacant parking lot, the way his eyes became huge when he realized that the restaurant was closed.

Even at that moment, three years later, he recalled the way Philly's mouth tightened, the way his gaze swung back and forth between Bruno and JoJo. How he began to run down his crime partners, saying they couldn't be trusted, how he reminded JoJo and Bruno of all his good works, his devotion to the family. The way his eyes focused on the empty parking lot. How he stared off into the distance when he got out of the car and then ran off a few steps, instantly regretting his strategy. The way he fell to his knees, the way he begged, the way he lost all control and wet himself. JoJo remembered it all, watching the poor guy, a good kid the cops turned into a stool pigeon, watching him beg and groan, hearing him again crying like a baby. Maybe beginning to understand Philly Rags for the first time. Remembering the way he cried out, "I had no choice, no where to go."

"Go ahead you fuckers," he said finally. "Set me free, I'm tired of all this shit and I don't give a damn." And JoJo remembered the way Bruno spit on the ground after he shot him, spit on the ground next to where Philly Rags's body lay twitching, the heels of his feet kicking and drumming the ground he lay on.

Since their arrival back at John's house, JoJo had been quietly sitting alone on the rear deck, drinking from a bottle of wine, looking out to sea. The fact that there seemed to be a decision involved did not put Barry's heart to rest, he was frightened out of his skin and wanted to get the hell out of there, out of Rhode Island, he wanted to be back in New York City, back where he felt safe. Around JoJo, as far as he could tell, everyone was nervous.

Vinny and John were in the kitchen making pasta and lobsters, Vinny explaining to John that he was a city guy and that if John was happy living here among fishermen and small-town people, he considered it likely that John was losing his mind. John looked over at Vinny and smiled. It struck Barry that in some curious way John was frightened of Vinny, and the significance of that fear was lost on him. John was, after all, JoJo's older brother and should have no concern over a small-time hood like Vinny.

It was five o'clock, Barry would catch the seven o'clock flight out of Providence back to LaGuardia. He had been drinking wine and felt a little stoned, though not stoned enough. These people frightened him. He'd had no idea, when he hooked up with them ten long years ago, just how terrified he could get. JoJo and these people lived in another time, another century, in a part of the world that put him in mind of Mexico, a dark and mysterious place, unforgiving and menacing. A place he didn't like to visit, forget living there. He had found that to be with wiseguys was to live with them, and that was fine if you didn't count the dread-filled days and the sleepless nights ablaze with dreams of the worst sort. Giving himself to the Paradisos was not the brightest thing he'd ever done.

When the platter of pasta and lobsters was brought out everyone regarded it with silent respect. JoJo poured each of them a glass of wine. Barry put his arm around John and felt him trembling.

"Good food," JoJo said. "Good wine, good friends."

"Salute," said Vinny.

And John toasted their health and prosperity.

JoJo smiled.

"To friends," said Barry. "Those that are present and those that are not here to enjoy this feast. To all our friends."

Later that night, sometime around nine o'clock, JoJo told Vinny to come out on the back deck. He gave him a halfhearted hug.

"Tell me, Vinny," he said, "what do you think of Barry?"

Vinny looked at him, about to answer, but then caught himself and clammed up.

"I asked you a question."

"He's your guy boss, what do you want me to say?"

"Ey, c'mon. Just tell me what you think of him."

"He's a f'n lawyer, a thief in his heart. I guess he's okay."

"Would you trust him?"

"Me? Trust a lawyer? Forget about it."

"Tomorrow, Vinny, you're going to slide back to the city and run this guy down." He gave Vinny the business card of the man that had come to him at the Nestor asking help for his son, the mild-mannered fellow who wanted to get his son into law school. "This guy owns a car leasing company. You'll get a car from him, and in the trunk of that car I want you to put twenty five-pound bags of flour. Put them in a suitcase."

"Flour?" Vinny said.

"Then I want you to take that car and park it in this garage." He handed Vinny a slip of paper. On the paper was the address of a parking garage across the street from Barry Cooper's law office.

"After you park the car I want you to go unannounced to Barry's office."

Vinny nodded.

JoJo held up a finger. "Unannounced, that means you just go up to his office without calling or anything."

Vinny stared at JoJo for a second, then said, "I understand."

"Good, good. When you get to his office, offer to take him to lunch or something. I want you to run me down. Badmouth me."

"I don't think he'll believe me, boss."

"Vinny, I want you to do exactly what I tell you. Don't question me, okay?"

Vinny nodded.

"When I say run me down, I want you to come on strong. Yell about having to drive around with a f'n trunkload of junk. Tell him you're talking about life imprisonment here. Say you think I've gone nutty. I don't care what you say. Just convince him that you're scared."

Vinny stuck a cigarette in his mouth to mask a smile.

"You follow this Vinny? Can you do what I tell you?"

Vinny gathered himself. "It don't sound too complicated, boss."

JoJo grinned and turned away; he looked up at the night sky.

Vinny was thinking, Well, maybe the guy really has flipped his f'n wig. "Does it matter what kind of flour I put in the bags?" he asked.

"Do you think it does?"

"Nope."

"Then why ask such a stupid f'n question? You're not stupid, Vinny. Don't play dumb with me, it's annoying."

"I'm sorry boss. Can I ask you something?"

"G'head."

"When I'm done, can I make a stop?"

"When you're done you'll go to the club and pick up my brother-in-law and Bruno, they'll be waiting. Pick them up and bring them here. Whataya mean, a stop?"

"I mean before I pick up the fellas, can I make a stop. You know, a stop."

"Vinny, you got no time to get laid. You got things to do. Stop thinking about banging all these broads, you got business to do."

"Wooooooo Joseph, but you gotta see this one. I got this one in Queens, twenty-two years old."

JoJo stood with his arms folded now, staring at Vinny and rocking on his heels. Vinny smiled.

"You keep this shit up I'll go to your wake. You hear me, stay away from the broads for a while."

Vinny said, "Come on, Joseph, Jesus Christ," a little panic edging into his voice, JoJo giving him that forty-yard stare. "You're not serious, are you?"

"About as serious as a hatchet in the head, you dumbo. Don't you understand that you got a hot-blooded little wop with a big gun very pissed at you."

Vinny felt that old familiar feeling, that great restlessness between his thighs, and was instantly depressed.

"Lilo will get over it. This is no big deal. It's just a wedding that ain't gonna be, is all."

JoJo said this was the kind of thing he was talking about. Nobody listened to him. You talk to hear yourself talk. It wasn't the lame cops or wacky feds or the creep stool pigeon that were going to do him in, it was his own people causing his problems. A cement-head like Vinny who thought with his dick, there was no way to protect yourself from cement-heads.

Vinny listened to him, fascinated. He thought of clarifying one point: he was no cement-head. He did what he was told, kept quiet, and had balls the size of a bull's. But JoJo kept talking, and later, when Vinny thought about it again, he decided that the top guys like JoJo and Lilo got off on stroking stacks of money, enjoyed that money smell a whole lot more than a pair of good strong woman's legs draped over their shoulders. Fine for them, they figure they got something going, but they got nothing going. What the hell good is cash if you don't enjoy yourself? If you can't find the time to drop your head between the legs of some sweet, sweet woman, what was this all about? And Lilo, that pathological nut case, trying to stick him in a basement with his daughter. Man's gotta be nuts. Sofia was all right, but he sure as hell wasn't going to live in some basement like a dog with her. F'n wacky Lilo, you couldn't figure that guy, just because he wanted to bed down with a broad now and then the guy wanted to kill him. Screwball, hard-on Lilo. That was him.

Vinny remembered Lilo from the time when he was a kid coming up in South Brooklyn. Lilo's brother Sonny and Lilo himself were South Brooklyn legends. They kept a lion in the basement of their house. You could walk down President Street and smell that lion from a block away. You owed them money, say, and you were late with a payment, you got to play tag with the f'n lion. Those two lumps did shit you wouldn't believe. At Sonny's wake, when they laid him out all nice with tons of flowers, Lilo went nuts. And him, the phony bastard, the one that set Sonny up. The bum set up his own brother to be shotgunned. Sonny, he howled, whadiddey dotaya? There's gonna be blood on the moon, Sonny. That crazy bastard, and he the one that arranged the ambush. Lilo, with his small eyes and pointy nose. Vinny hated people with small eyes and pointy noses. They looked like rats.

Sometime in the future Vinny would remember that he forgot to remember that you had to be prepared for a nut job like Lilo.

CHAPTER THIRTEEN

That entire afternoon Dante, Ray, Kathy, and Jimmy transcribed tapes and listened to the ramblings of the wiseguys at the club. It was a radiant day and warm, the kind that made you think about nothing but good. All over Queens people were opening windows, trying to catch some of the fresh spring breeze. In front of the club three men sat on vinyl kitchen chairs, passersby smiled at the men as they gingerly walked past. An urbane effort which wiseguy nature resisted. There came from them not one smile.

Inside the club conversations were short, and the wiseguys sounded concerned. Nobody seemed to know where JoJo was. Even Bruno Greco was baffled, asking Nicky Black and the crazy killer dwarf Karl Marx Syracusa it they'd seen or heard from JoJo. They all were running around like a bunch of drugged sheep, pursuing each other to the corner candy store, using the pay phones, clicking their gadgets that allowed them to place calls without paying. Their faces were cemented with furious determination. A group of four stood on the sidewalk in front of the candy store. One, Dante knew, was Frankie F'n Furillo, he looked apprehensive in his aviator glasses, shaking his head, looking around as if he were being set up. Dante watched all of them and took note of the uneasy looks on their faces; he nodded, thinking, something's wrong, someone's missing, someone important is an MIA.

He had returned from breakfast with Ray to find Kathy and Jimmy transcribing, Jimmy making a big show of following him with his eyes when he came into the surveillance apartment, a half-amused smirk on his face like he knew something. Dante went to the windows overlooking the street; he'd been watching the street action for about fifteen minutes when Jimmy joined him.

"Something's going down. I don't know what, but something's not right," Jimmy said.

"Did you check the house? Is the old man at home? Is his car around? How about the phone? Anything on the wiretap?"

"They're gone Dante, they're both gone," Jimmy said, sounding slightly winded.

Jimmy took a pair of binoculars and scanned the street. "Nicky Black showed up about an hour ago, Bruno's been here all morning, and the dwarf's inside the club. It looks like most of the crew is here, but no JoJo and no old man."

"Well the old man stays away from the club."

"Right, but his house is empty. There's no car, no bodyguard. I rang the phone and no one answered."

"We should be on JoJo from dawn to midnight," Kathy called from the kitchen. "We should go round the clock on him."

"We don't have enough people to cover what we're doing," Jimmy said. "I guess we could ask for some help." Jimmy waited for a response. Nothing. He turned from the window and went back to the kitchen, leaving Dante standing alone, puzzled that Jimmy had not asked about last night.

Dante wondered what he might say, feeling a flash of pleasure now recalling that great massage. He eased himself up onto the barstool and continued to watch the street. In his mind's eye he saw Kathy in her T-shirt, no bra, the woman's good strong legs, the sofa bed in her apartment, and pictured what she would be like naked, wanting to see her above him, riding him. Then thought, what the hell you doing? and tried to figure what Kathy had said to Jimmy. Flashing on the past night, out on the town, running into good ol' JoJo, getting loaded and ending up in Kathy's bed. Wondering what in the hell was going on with JoJo. The guy was always here at the club, every day by eleven.

Dante sat locked in on the street, feeling a little stiff and a bit cranky. Maybe JoJo had been out too. The guy always liked to party. Dante was thinking that JoJo had not seemed in a party mood when he saw him last night. He wondered just what Jimmy did in his off hours, they never talked about that, about the way Jimmy spent his off time. A friendship could disappear on you if you didn't talk. Right then he was thinking about Jimmy and nothing else.

Ray and Kathy were staring at him. Ray said, "We're going to run over to the wiretap. Then I'm going to check that phone number you gave me."

"What number?" Jimmy said.

"We ran into JoJo last night," Kathy said. "Me and Dante did, dude was making a call from Chaplin's. We figure the number he called could be important."

"You ran into JoJo?" Jimmy laughed as if he knew what must have happened when Dante and JoJo met.

"Very weird. To tell you the truth, Jimmy, the guy hasn't changed much. Put on a little weight is all. Anyway, he was on the phone, and I figure what do we lose if we check out the number he called?"

Jimmy hunched his shoulders, staring silently out the window at a group of JoJo's men in the street. "You're right, what can we lose?"

Five minutes later Jimmy and Dante were standing alone at the windows, Jimmy moving like he had to go to the toilet. Kathy and Ray had left for the wiretap plant.

"Christ, I hate working with a woman, I really do," Jimmy said.

"You didn't have a problem before."

Jimmy stared at the ceiling, took a deep breath. "I don't know, she bugs me. And Ray too. With his fucking good-guy routine. We should have worked this case alone."

"This case? Are you kidding? What's going on with you? How the hell could we have worked this case by ourselves?" Dante said it more as an announcement than a question.

Jimmy shrugged.

"Do me a favor, will ya? Don't shrug at me. You got a bug up your ass, tell me about it. Don't shrug."

"Wake up, will ya?" Jimmy said. "We got us a no-win case here. The more I see of it the more I got to figure it's bound to give us grief."

"Wrong," Dante said. "The good news is we're gonna stop being passive here. We're going out, we're gonna go out and get on some people."

"Like who?"

"Lilo Santamaria, for one. We're gonna get on that guy and see what he's up to."

"We are, hah?"

"You got a problem with that?"

"No problem. I'm ready, let's go do it. Let's do something. I don't give a damn, anything's better than hanging around watching these jerks down here."

Dante felt a sudden unexplainable gust of anxiety, he didn't feel right. Something was wrong but he wouldn't even try to guess at what it was.

"So what did you do last night?" Dante tried to sound casual.

"I did what I always do: went home, sent out for dinner, and watched a little TV. Why?"

"It's curiosity," Dante said. "Nothing more than that."

"And you? A night out with Kathy, ey? How did that go?"

"I had a bit of a rocky night." He went on for about ten minutes, detailing the previous night's experiences, throwing in Kathy's war story. "Anyhow," he said finally, "we wind up at her apartment and I'm sort of freaking out, wanting to get laid and all, and she telling me she's gay. The woman's gay, Jimmy, still I figure, well, ya know . . ." Dante trailed off, furious at himself for telling Jimmy each detail of his night out, furious at himself for betraying Kathy's confidence. Crazy with himself for his never-ending attempts to gain Jimmy's esteem and maybe earn a bit of amazement. It was just that Jimmy always kept him off balance. He would give up all there was in him, all his secrets, every shadow in his mind and heart, all his fears, which numbered in the thousands, all his hopes and dreams. And Jimmy, as was his way from the time they were kids playing stickball on the street, gave up squat.

"I've been thinking," Dante said.

"Oh shit. Now we got real trouble."

With a mock-angry look on his face, Dante grumbled, "Shut up. We have to get out in the street, you know. Out there."

"Yeah, and do what?"

"Let's get on the dwarf, or Bruno. How about Nicky Black? How about Lilo, he sits on his ass in that coffee shop in Brooklyn. Let's get on him."

Jimmy shrugged again. "She's really gay, hah?"

"Yeah, yeah, I think so."

"Think?"

"I guess so. Who cares, it's her business. She's a good worker, that's all I care about."

"You're nuts, you know that Dante? You were loose in the head when you were a kid, and you're still a nut job."

"What are you talking about?"

"Never mind."

"Let me explain something so you understand," Dante said. He turned, nodding toward the street below. "I don't care about Kathy's sex life. What I care about is this f'n case. I wanted this case. This case, buddy of mine, was my idea. Now we're in it and we're going to see it through. It is not, no matter what I tell myself, just another case. I want JoJo real bad and that's the truth of it. But I need your help. You're my partner, my best friend. And the way things are shaking out in this circus I call my life, you may be my only friend."

"Christ, is that your father coming out of you or what?"

"Whataya mean by that?"

"All that Irish blarney. My best friend, the only friend I got in this cruel, cruel world. Give me a break."

"Hey Jimmy, this ain't no bullshit."

"I'm a New York City police detective. I should know the truth from the lie when I hear it. We're in this case, what, a week, a week and a half? This case is the best excuse you can come up with for not going home. It's not the case, it's not JoJo, it's not you wanting to prove something, it's you not wanting to go home. Just do me a favor, and stop bullshitting me, okay?"

Dante nodded, feeling humiliated now, trying to figure a way to bail himself out. Jimmy continued to talk, and the sounds he made had a bitter edge to them. Dante felt a stab of resentment listening to Jimmy, his head bobbing in polite acknowledgment. Jimmy was wrong, he was right; Dante wondered if his partner had him nailed. But then he dismissed it out of hand. It's JoJo, he thought, it's that no-good bastard he wanted. See that oily smile of his disappear when he told him you're busted, asshole.

"If you want out of this case, we'll get out," Dante said.

Jimmy squinted as if in pain. "Who said I wanted to shit-can the case? Are you listening to me or what? I'm telling you not to use this job to straighten out your personal life. People do it, ya know, they do it all the time, use the job as an excuse not to deal with all their personal shit."

"Why are you so pissed? It's weird how ticked off you're getting lately."

"C'mon, hey. Look at me. Do I sound pissed? You're missing the point. You don't have to agree with me, but this is how I see it."

Jimmy kept talking. Dante lost interest and began pacing, his mind busy with the next move they should make to nail JoJo. He sneaked a peek through the venetian blinds.

"I just don't see where this case if going," Jimmy said. "You know it's possible that JoJo is just hanging out doing nothing. Maybe we got him in the slow season."

"You're kidding me, right?" Dante said. Then he said, slow and easy,

"Jimmy, see if you can hear anything. I just saw Bruno run into the club. He looks like he's about to go into orbit."

The voice of Bruno Greco, the most powerful capo of the Paradiso clan, came over the radio. "I want everybody outta here," the *consigliere* said.

Jimmy went dark, he turned his head and stretched.

"Turn it up," Dante said.

"Whataya, deaf?"

"Turn the goddamn thing up, will ya Jimmy?"

Dante stared down into the street, listening intently. Behind him the reel-to-reel turned quietly.

"Nicky," Bruno said, talking to Nicky Black, JoJo's brother-in-law, "don't you have to go over to that place? Your new construction site? Didn't you tell me you have to be there by four?"

"Wha? Huh?" Nicky Black said, "Oh, yeah, yeah. Good you reminded me. I'll see ya later Bruno, I better get going."

Then it was the dwarf and Frankie F'n Furillo making lame excuses to leave the club. Then Bruno again, "I want all these f'n morons outta here, the club's closed. I'm gonna get the joint painted, this place is turning into a dump."

"Maybe we should just torch the joint," one of the hang-around guys said in a high twitter.

"What are you, nuts?" said another voice, a more frightened one. "That's against the law, you jerk. Now beat it, the place is closed."

His nose through the blinds, his hand up against the windowframe, Dante stared down into the street and muttered like a mantra, "What's up, what's up, what's up?" He turned and gave Jimmy a brief, blank stare. "What time is it, three, four o'clock?"

"It's four."

"Put in the log that we were burnt at four o'clock on June the tenth."

"Excuse me?"

"We can take these bugs out of the oven. They're done."

"What are you saying?"

"I'm saying that some rat bastard burnt us. What are you, deaf and blind? These guys are jumping ship, getting out of the club like their asses are on fire. We've been burnt, buddy of mine."

"You don't know that."

Jimmy sought Dante's eyes and was startled to see the amount of anger in them. He hesitated to say anything, fearing what he might say.

"Dante," Jimmy said, "you can't be sure."

Dante stood with his hands on his hips, making a show of staring into the street. There was nothing left for him to do at the surveillance plant, or anywhere else in New York City at the moment, and he was getting buggy with his thoughts. He found himself grinning and walked real slow out of the apartment. It was as if he were unaware of Jimmy's presence, that Jimmy was behind him. In the police cruiser, he said to Jimmy, "I'm going home, out to the Island. I want to see my kid."

He watched Jimmy's bright blue eyes fix briefly on his. Maybe there was nothing to it, nothing to the crazy thoughts banging around his head.

Jimmy, driving, stared at the road again, expressionless except for a pulsing in his jaw. "This case is a killer, we need a break," he said. "Go home, maybe Judy will take you back in, no questions. That's what you want, that's what you need." He looked at Dante, who nodded and gazed back.

Dante said, "I'll be across from Lilo's joint in the morning around eleven, eleven thirty. I'll see you there."

"Sure."

"Good, that's good. Because I'm telling you, buddy of mine, I'm going to nail these bastards, I'm gonna nail 'em good, and when I find out who burnt us, I'll kick his ass all over Queens."

Dante walked from the cruiser to his car, he walked with his head down in a funky hardass bad mood. He was getting sick of this case, of thinking about JoJo, of thinking about Jimmy and Kathy. Everybody was out to screw with his head. He thought about Judy and his son Danny, wondered if he should call first before he headed out. The hell with it, he'd drive home, just show up and blow Judy away with some warmth and tenderness.

Not that he felt sentimental about her. At that moment he had a fondness for no one. Not Judy, she hadn't picked up the phone in days. She didn't want him home, he didn't want to go home, staying away was starting to feel like a routine, and that he knew did not exactly bode well for the marriage. The thing was, he had no idea how she was feeling about their future. The last time they spoke about their marriage was about five weeks ago. Judy looked angry and hurt at the same time. She began to sulk on a Friday night and didn't stop until he left for work Monday morning. Judy was a world-class sulker, her shoulders would fall into a permanent hunch and she'd glare at him for days, not talking, just moving around the house in that killer mood, looking for a showdown.

Now, standing on the street, he felt something coming for sure. Bad vibes were in the air. He figured that the best thing to do was to go home and make some promises. Kiss and hug Judy and maybe feel better about this life of his. Bust his hump making that two-hour drive out to the sticks, go through the motions of being the suburban husband and father so that at some point in the future he would be able to tell himself that at least he tried.

The seventy-mile move out to no-man's-land was not such a bright move. Jimmy was absolutely right on that score. But the sad fact was that he realized it too late. He liked to think about how good things were with Judy when they were good. In the old days, when he lived in Glendale, he could be home in twenty minutes, be home and in the sack with Judy wrapped around him in a half hour. Life was easier in Glendale, they had a six-room attached house on a street with other city workers. But Judy was getting more scared all the time, the neighborhood was changing. One night the past January she heard gunshots and that was it.

Dante sighed, gazed dreamily around the old neighborhood and shook his head with regret. Then he began to think about Jimmy and freaked. His buddy acting all jumpy from the minute they began the case. Sure he'd acted jumpy before, plenty of times. But this was a different type of jumpiness. It frightened him, this jumpy and peculiar act Jimmy was into. Standing on the corner of Pitken Avenue and Eighty-fifth Street, Dante thought over the situation. He suddenly felt as though his life was turning into one great burlesque show. He was in debt to the world. His marriage sucked, there was no marriage. He was doing his job under false pretenses, and his best friend, a guy he would give an arm for, seemed to be living on one of the moons of Saturn. And the greatest, the topper, the premium move of the past week, he'd found a woman that really turned him on, more than Judy, more than any woman he had met in a very long time, and she was a lesbian alcoholic. Way to go Dante, he thought, way to go.

As he searched his pockets for his car keys, Jimmy pulled alongside in the cruiser.

"Are you okay?"

"Great," Dante said. "I'm doing great, just f'n great."

"You need me, I'll be home, give me a call. I'm there for you buddy."

Dante raised his hand, not knowing what to say, making a show of nodding his head. "See ya," he said.

Driving to Long Island, Dante was clinging to the sincerity in Jimmy's tone. But a deadness was spreading through his body. Something very strange was going on with Jimmy, and he wasn't a part of it. It was the being cut out part that really bugged him. He wanted to partake in Jimmy's life the way Jimmy shared his, that was all he wanted. The guy was so f'n uptight and tense lately that he had to believe it was something to do with JoJo, with the case and with JoJo.

Dante had never shaken the childlike dread of losing his best friend. Sometimes he felt sorry for himself, felt like he was ten years old and unable to deal with life without his buddy. What if there was more to it? What if Jimmy's recent eerie behavior was more convoluted than he thought? What if he actually had gone over to JoJo? That was not possible. That, he thought, wasn't feasible, it would be agony. Christ, he was far more likely to make a move and grab some money than Jimmy was. At least he liked to think that he could do it, be a knockaround guy and grab some bread. Yeah, yeah. Find himself neck deep in shit, like his old man. Driving with the windows open, the air from the open window cooling him, Dante said aloud, "Buddy, you weren't born to be a thief and that's the gospel truth."

He suddenly felt profoundly relaxed because he had said something honest, and for a time he felt comfortable. But then he thought, What if the sun doesn't shine tomorrow, what if the bubble pops and you find out Jimmy did go over to JoJo? He hated to think about that likelihood, that would be a howling nightmare. His father liked to say there was nobody you couldn't get to. Even the Pope had his price. Someone's price could be as uncomplicated as friendship, a sick compulsion to be needed, coveted, and loved. Big Dan O'Donnell was one cynical bastard, he loved to point to senators and congressmen; judges, mayors, vice presidents for chrissake have been nailed with their hands out.

During the time of his father's time in the department, everybody was in the game. They all had their hands out. His father could call all his bosses by their first names because he did the "right thing" by them. And the right thing for his father and a whole lot of others in the days of the pad was an envelope filled with cash, delivered at the end of the month. Thank God times had changed. He could never deal with that crap. People handing him envelopes, people buying his shield. A bunch of crap.

Jesus, his father was crazy! When the Internal Affairs Division wiretapped him, after a bunch of them forgot their own days out in the street folding money, they heard a ton of conversations with captains and inspectors and chief inspectors, forget the patrolmen, sergeants, and lieutenants and other detectives his father had taken care of for years. The IAD investigators with their earphones and notepads couldn't believe what they had. They could have brought down the entire top brass of the department. Transcribers wouldn't transcribe it; instead they reached out and grabbed his father and told Big Dan he was going to go down, and he was going to go down big-time. And he'd better go down alone.

Driving now in light traffic on the Long Island Expressway, Dante flashed on the night it happened. It was around Christmas. He remembered snowflakes and songs about wise men. He was nineteen, slow-dancing with Mary Marlucci to "I Saw Mommy Kissing Santa Claus," it was at Gloria Goodman's party. Jimmy came in, he remembered the look on his face, how pale he was. Jimmy grabbed hold of his shoulder and whispered, "C'mon, we got to go. I need to talk to you."

Back at his house that night, his sister asleep in the room next to his, his mother propped up on pillows in the bedroom she shared with Big Dan, staring at *The Tonight Show*. He remembered leaning against the headboard of the king-size bed, Jimmy quiet, standing out in the hallway. His mother just lay there, her hands crossed to her shoulders like she was shielding her breasts from the world. A gilt-framed picture of his father on her lap. He recalled thinking there's no light in her eyes, she looked bewildered and enraged but there was no sadness there.

She nodded toward the photograph on her lap, a grimace on her face like she had read his mind. "Your father never said good-bye," was all she said.

He remembered going back to the living room, the way he sat on the sofa till morning, Jimmy sitting next to him, patting his shoulder and rubbing his neck like you'd stroke a cat or a dog or something. He remembered the way Jimmy said sometime around seven o'clock in the morning, "I'm gonna call JoJo. I bet he can find out what happened."

Driving now, with some down-home earsplitting country music coming from the radio, he thought of his father as a scuz and a coward and he missed him like crazy. He wanted to shriek like Hamlet, "I need you, you bastard, I need you now and Christ I miss you, you big son of a bitch."

He was maybe three, four miles from home when his beeper went off. Before he had left Queens he had taken it from the trunk of his car and placed it on the seat next to him. The beeper sounded again and Dante checked it, saw the wiretap plant telephone number blinking up at him.

Looking out at the passing highway, he thought, I'll call when I get home. Then the beeper went off again and he decided to jump off at the next exit and call. He figured it was probably Kathy. Then again maybe it was Ray, maybe something was up.

When he dialed the number he felt something powerful click inside him. When the phone rang and Kathy answered, he felt both solid and composed.

"What's up?" he said. Dante pressed the flat of his hand against his stomach and made little circles.

"Maybe you'd better come back to the city."

"Well what's up?"

"I don't know what's up. Ray made a call to telephone security and I'm telling you he looked like death."

"So, what was it?"

"He didn't say. He didn't say a goddamn thing, except that he had to go and see someone. Then he left me here alone."

"Anything on the wiretap? Anything going on?"

"Nothing Dante, they're dead. The last call was an outgoing to Rhode Island. Just a ring then a hangup. C'mon back, will ya, something's going down here and I don't know what it is."

He stood and listened and wondered how to play this.

"I'm practically home. I'm f'n tired Kathy. Where the hell is Ray?"

"I don't know. He didn't tell me. I don't like this Dante. I don't like this at all. I don't work like this."

Dante stooped to pick up a twenty-five-cent piece that stood shining near his foot. "It's probably nothing, Kathy."

"No, no, no. This is not nothing, this is something. I know it is."

"You know shit, Kathy. Stop being so goddamn female, stop worrying about every little thing. Where is Jimmy? Did you try him at home?"

Kathy said nothing for a long moment. Dante sniffed.

"I'll call Jimmy," she said. She sounded far away.

"All right. Lookit, I'll head back. Say I meet you at the surveillance plant in about, I don't know, an hour and a half, two hours. Anyway, I'll meet you there."

"You going to stop at home?"

"What for?"

"Maybe you should stop and get some coffee. You sound wasted."

"I'll just get in the car and come on back." Dante tried to sound neutral, as if the whole idea of driving one hundred forty miles round trip was reasonable. But the notion of turning around and driving back to Queens nauseated him.

"Look, it's up to you. But I think you should come on back. Why the hell you live way out there anyway?"

Between the trepidation in Kathy's voice and his own dread of having to face Judy, Dante figured he'd just climb back into his car and wheel back to Queens. He took a deep breath in order to find some energy. Discovering nothing but fatigue, he said, "Kathy, you're right to be worried, but I think everything's okay. I'm gonna go home and get some rest, then I'll call you. In the meantime, I'll beep Ray, see if I can get in touch with Jimmy. That's the best I can do. I'm zoned out, I need a rest. I won't do you or anyone else any good the way I'm feeling."

"Call me later," she mumbled.

———

JoJo walked into the living room where John sat with his feet up on the coffee table, eating a sandwich and watching the late news on TV. He seemed small and alone, but mostly he appeared lonely, a little lost in his big house. This made JoJo mad. John's wife Penny was off visiting the girls at their Vermont boarding school. John was traipsing around the house in a funk, making his own meals, fixing his bed, acting like a nineties sort of guy, sharing the load. To make a long story short, John was acting like an American husband. When JoJo flashed on John's wife, he pictured his father giving him that knowing head bob, side-mouthing, "American girl."

Years back, when John met, fell in love with, and then made plans to marry Penny, the Skipper instructed JoJo to speak to him. JoJo's father did not want to appear to be interfering with his elder son's love life. But of course he would. He left it to JoJo to express his frustration. And JoJo did as he was instructed. He pointed out to John that Penny was from a different world, truly an outsider. It was not simply that she was not an Italian; she was not Jewish or even Irish. She was, as the Skipper put it, some kind of an American. Whatever that was. People like that could create conflict within the family, he told him. They don't understand any of our customs, our relationships, they know diddly about the value of belonging and loyalty. Penny is a likable person but don't you think you should find yourself a good, stand-up Italian girl.

John was in love with his American girl, with her straight blond hair and round blue eyes, her tits like buttons and stick legs. And for the first and last time in his life, he stood up to his younger brother, and to the not so unseen pressure from his father.

"I'm going to marry her," he told JoJo. "Listen to me, I love Penny. You convince Pop that I'm not making a mistake. You're my brother, support me for a change."

"Whatever you want, brother, whatever pleases you. But you'll see, you're gonna be eating sandwiches for supper and you'll have to make your own bed. But if that's what you want, be my guest."

Now, standing in John's living room some seventeen years later, JoJo felt his nerves tighten. At any other time he would point out that Penny had left the house without preparing food. She could have roasted a chicken, for chrissake, or made a platter of lasagna, something, anything John could have slid into the microwave. He was annoyed and ready to say something, to point out to John what a loser move it was to marry that woman. He had just enough wine in him to make it sound casual, but then he figured, why make John uneasy. The guy seemed shaky enough since JoJo had been there. And the truth was, since their marriage, John had been able to keep Penny almost completely out of the life of the family. JoJo couldn't remember the last time he saw her, or the kids for that matter. Not that he missed any of them. Just like their old lady, the kids gave him the creeps, with their little blond heads and silly-ass grins, saying gosh and gee and isn't that sweet. Goofy kids.

"I need to go out," JoJo said, "I've got to make a few calls."

John watched JoJo standing there with his hands in his pockets. He seemed calm, not as agitated as he was earlier.

"Use my office, why don't you. Or the phone in the kitchen. There's no one here, JoJo, be comfortable." John seemed reluctant to look at his brother. He kept glancing about the room as if he were expecting someone. "Where's Vinny?" he said finally.

"He's watching TV in the guest room. Vinny is going to leave early tomorrow morning. Listen," JoJo told him, "I don't want to use these phones. Is there a pay phone nearby?"

"Geez, I don't know. What do you mean you don't want to use the phones here?"

JoJo shook his head, smiling as if John just didn't get it.

"You think my phones could be tapped?" His words came out in a tiny moan.

"Why, you doing something against the law?"

John shrugged, looking away.

JoJo wasn't about to tell John all his troubles. Say he laid it out, even told him about the drug move, the fed informant, say. Christ, John could wind up with a stroke or something. An image of John spilling out family secrets to Penny came into his head, and he shook it off. Even John's not that stupid.

He told his brother only those things that concerned him and that was it. Generally they spoke about the movement of cash. When the family was rolling and things were good, he would send three hundred thousand a month to Rhode Island, cash packed in boxes, bags, and suitcases, delivered to John's construction company office by van. But during the past year or so, with business being off, he was lucky to ship one hundred G's a month.

"Excuse me," John said, sliding forward on the sofa he was sitting on. "I asked if you think my phone's tapped."

"Your phone's not tapped, John. I just feel better on a public phone. *Capisc?*"

John smiled and shook his head as if it was JoJo who just didn't get it.

"What's so funny?"

Turning away, John mumbled something that JoJo couldn't pick up.

"C'mon," JoJo said. "Where's the nearest pay phone?"

"JoJo, if there's some bad shit coming down, I want to know about it. I want to help if I can."

"Yeah, how you wanna help? You gonna pick up a pistol, maybe blow somebody up or something? Keep your mind on your own business John, let me worry about the small shit, will ya?"

John shook his head impatiently. "You'd be surprised what I could do. What I'm capable of getting done if I feel threatened."

"Yeah, John, you're a regular f'n killer, you are. I go down here on the main road or what? For the phone, where do I go?"

"Go out of the driveway and make a right. There's a gas station down by Heffie's, the ice cream joint. There's a phone there."

John followed him out to the Mercedes parked in the driveway. "You'd be surprised," John said again as JoJo prepared to leave. "I bet you'd be amazed at what my capabilities are." John spoke so low that JoJo had difficulty understanding just what he was saying.

"Look," JoJo said, "I love ya, brother. I know you're a little dopey, but I love ya anyway. I think I'd even love ya if you weren't my brother."

Driving, JoJo thought about John. His brother had always been that way: quiet; withdrawn and emotional at the same time. He could be a hard guy and give you a look that made you think, made you shut up and think he had something important to say. Still, John was no fighter. He worried about his wife and kids too much. If John knew half the shit that JoJo had to do to keep the family going, the guy would come apart. He'd have the trots for a year. JoJo momentarily thought about that himself, all the horrors he had to do to keep the family afloat, to support this life, to stay alive.

———

Bruno Greco, Nicky Black, the dwarf, and a few of the others had beepers. JoJo would not call them directly. Whenever he needed to reach out to his people he would phone a contact, a family member, a friend, whatever. For Bruno it was his sister. JoJo dialed the number and when Laura Greco answered he said, "Hi, howyadoin?" He gave her the number of the public phone and waited. Ten minutes later he was talking to his *consigliere*.

"The kid Vinny will come and get you tomorrow. Get a hold of Nicky and bring him along."

"I cleared the club out," Bruno told him. "When I seen that you and your father were both in the wind, I cleaned the club."

"Good, good. See anybody around? Any cops or anything?"

"I didn't see nobody. They supposed to be here or what?"

"Could be. I'll see ya tomorrow, huh?"

"Later."

Then he dialed the newsstand on the corner across from Lilo's club. He told the kid Fat Ronnie to go over to Lilo's club, giving him the number of the pay phone.

As he waited for the call back from Lilo, he wondered if Lilo had made contact with Armond Rammino, the heroin importer, and as part of that same thought he went over again in his head this drug move. It may not be the smartest move to go ahead with this now. He nodded in agreement with himself. But he had no choice, he was in this up to here and he had to see it through. This goddamn romantic illusion his father had about running a family these days without the drug business was bullshit. Still, he had to consider the informant, the bastard could be anyone. He'd show himself, they always do. He shook his head trying to get rid of the thought that the rat could be anyone.

He didn't know what to make of Lilo. The guy set up his own brother to be killed, and something about that story chilled him to the bones. He'd kill Vinny, no doubt about it. Lilo was a screwball and that was the end of it. Spending these past few days with the kid made him realize that Vinny would have to be dragged screaming and kicking back to Lilo's daughter. That problem was a major pain in the ass. No way was he going to marry that girl. That wasn't going to happen. It was feasible he could persuade Lilo to let Vinny be, overlook the kid and let Vinny stay with JoJo. Ooofa, this Vinny thing was going to make him nuts. Along with all the other stupidity, the informant and all, he had to spend time worrying over lover boy.

The phone rang. JoJo answered and Lilo said, "Hey, what's up?"

"I want you to make that move we discussed. Go see that guy, see if we can set up a sitdown."

"It's been done."

JoJo laughed by reflex.

"I figured you wanted it done. So I took care of it. Just tell me the time and place, he'll be there. He's happy to talk to you Joseph. You know he likes you."

JoJo hesitated for a moment, thinking what else to say, when Lilo added, "This is the best thing we could possibly do. This will turn everything around."

"Outside the city," JoJo said.

"Whoa. I doubt that. The guy never leaves Brooklyn."

"He knows what's involved, he'll come. I'll tell you when and where. I'll get word to you tomorrow or the next day."

"The man's doing you a favor over here. He don't need the money, Joseph."

They fell into silence, JoJo thinking, what bullshit, this is some mountain of crap. "Tell him if he wants to meet me he's got to come to me. I ain't coming into the city for a while."

"Geez, I don't know, Joseph."

Incensed now, JoJo asked in Italian, "Explain to me Lilo, who in the fuck side you on?" He said it like his father would, deep-voiced and deliberate.

In Italian, Lilo said quickly, "Yours, yours, I'm just trying to do the right thing here."

There wasn't a wiseguy worth the name who could not figure out when he was being threatened. And Lilo was one hell of a wiseguy. He withdrew into himself and came on all polite and pleasant and obliging.

"Ey," he said. "I'll do whatever you ask. Whatever it is, I'm yours, you know that. What is it you want me to do?"

"Tell your friend that I'm ready to do some great things. Tell him it's time we sat and had a chat. Tell him I'm ready to make him a very rich man."

"Yes, yes, yes, of course, Joseph." Lilo's voice was still very courteous and formal. "The man is not my friend. I know him, sure I know him, we're shoulder to shoulder here in Brooklyn. But he is not my friend, Joseph."

JoJo felt flushed with relief. He was using his head, wondering where to take Lilo now. The guy was a renegade, he was sure of that. But how and what and where was a puzzle to him. He was wondering how to play this out when Lilo hastily announced that his daughter Sophia was doing just fine.

Lilo described some character that his daughter apparently had met through a legit business friend. He owned the Golden Rooster, a restaurant in Sheepshead Bay, an actual restaurant, not one of those mussel-and-clam joints on Emmons Avenue. A genuine restaurant with a chef and waiters, the bartender, he said, wears a jacket and tie. Suddenly he no longer was concerned with Vinny, all is fine and dandy.

JoJo felt himself sinking like a stone. Lilo was lying, the creep had something going. But what, what? His puzzlement became rage, and JoJo was furious at himself, real unhappy that he hadn't reacted to his first impulse back when he'd recognized that a revolt was in the air and this bastard was a part of it. He should have banged out Lilo, and Tommy Yale too. Maybe he still would.

"I'm glad for your daughter," he said. "I'm delighted for your wife, your daughter, and you too Lilo. I'm happy for all of you."

"Yeah, yeah. I appreciate it Joseph. I guess you can tell Vinny that he is out of danger. Life's too short for all that anger. Ey Joseph? Ain't that the truth?"

JoJo sighed and rested his head against the telephone. He was feeling shitty and depressed and a little bit in trouble. But mostly he was feeling a growing anger. He stuck a cigarette in his mouth and stared out over the dead Rhode Island intersection. It looked like a neutron bomb had hit the place. Zilch living here, no one around, nothing moving, a quiet peacefulness. A sanctuary, a favorable place to hang low.

In his mind's eye he saw Lilo standing in those work boots of his, lying about this and that, sneering at him from the other end of the line. He tried to picture what the guy's scheme was.

"It's true Lilo, you're right. Anger does no one any good. Do me a favor pal, arrange this sitdown for me. I'll send Bruno to see you in a couple of days, he'll have the sitdown spot and time. Okay?"

"Sure thing."

JoJo hung up and made three more calls. He placed a call to Miami, a number he had been given to reach Luis, the Cuban dealer. A woman answered in heavily accented English and gave him a phone number in Spain. She pointed out that because of the time difference, he should telephone Luis the following day. Then she told him that Luis was eager to hear from him. He hung up the phone, stared at his fingernails a second, then picked up the receiver and tapped out the number.

Two rings and an answering machine picked up. JoJo never voluntarily made a recording. He tapped out the number of his police friend. It was near midnight, the phone rang maybe nine times, no answer. "F'n cops," he said aloud, "are never around when you need 'em."

CHAPTER FOURTEEN

Ray Velasquez sat parked in his Jeep for almost two hours, window up then down for a while while he smoked nonstop, something he hadn't done in about ten years. He sat and listened to the Yankee game, then, bored, flipped to some classic rock, felt the onrush of old memories at "Hey Jude," shook that and discovered an easy-listening station and kept it there.

The guy's an ace, he kept telling himself, regarded as one of the finest intelligence men on the job. And a friend, a staunch friend, a hell of a guy, a damn good man and they don't come around often, valuable men don't. He put his head back against the headrest and closed his eyes. There had been nothing in his police career that made him feel as crazed and as blind with visions of what might lay ahead for him and Jimmy, and for Dante too, if what he assumed was true. At that moment he felt tortured, sensing in a frightful way that a shitstorm was just around the corner. He shut the radio off and sat in silence, looking out at the busy street as if the silence in the car would deliver an answer. Except there was no answer.

Ray took another cigarette from the pack in his shirt pocket, lit it, and let it hang from the corner of his mouth. What was it that he knew for certain? Jimmy Burns, his friend for ten years, got a call from f'n Joseph Paradiso. And the following day their wires go dead. Christ there's a lot of doubt here, too many questions. Ray Velasquez was not used to being this shaky. It could be a coincidence. Except that in his experiences, coincidences didn't happen. His entire police career he went by three unbreakable rules: never turn your back on a prisoner, always give a cop the benefit of the doubt, and only work with people you can place your faith and trust in. He thought that over. He thought it over and then nodded his head. He trusted Jimmy Burns, and that was it, there ain't no more. Still, he'd been around long enough to know that it was not unheard of. You set aside all this brother cop bullshit and realize that everybody was really out for themselves. Not Jimmy, not Jimmy Burns. He refused to believe it, that Jimmy could turn on him, turn on him and Dante and Kathy too. They were partners for chrissake.

Unlike most police officers, when Ray was bewildered and felt lost, he spoke to no one other than his wife. The woman was bright and perceptive and understood the street. She could see things cops missed, being a social worker and all. He had phoned Sarah earlier and played out his problem, played it all out for her. She didn't hesitate. "Honey," she said. "You like this man. You've always accepted and trusted him. I don't think you should do anything, tell anyone until you first give him the opportunity to explain. You would want the same consideration for yourself. I mean, you don't have too many pals in the department. You like Jimmy Burns. I'm sure he has a reasonable explanation."

"So you agree, I should talk to him?"

"Of course. How could it hurt?"

And so it was a little past eight o'clock when Ray Velasquez got out of his car in front of 250 East Eightieth Street near First Avenue. A lone doorman stood under the awning of the white brick apartment building smoking a cigarette, staring at him.

"You'd better move that car before seven in the morning or they'll tow it," he said.

"I don't plan on being here that long," Ray said.

"You've been squatting here two hours, I ain't never seen anybody do that."

Ray didn't answer, he went through the lobby to the elevator, rang for it, and waited.

"You can't go up till I ring," the doorman said. "Who is it you want to see?"

"I'm expected."

"What apartment?"

"I'm expected, I told you."

"Yeah, that's fine. I need to know what apartment you're going to?"

"Ten C."

The elevator arrived; the door opened and Ray got in. From the corner of his eye he spotted the doorman actually running to the house phone and he heard him mutter, "Screwball pain in the ass."

He took the elevator to the tenth floor.

"That you Ray?" Jimmy Burns's voice came muffled through the apartment door.

"It's me," Ray said, and after a moment, heard the door lock rattle.

"What's up?"

"Can I come in?"

Jimmy motioned Ray in through the door, and he followed him down the hall. They passed the kitchen and then the bedroom and Ray heard Jimmy sniff once or twice. "I've got to get this joint cleaned," Jimmy said so quietly that Ray supposed he was talking to himself. "I've been waiting two hours, you called me two hours ago, said you'd be right here. What's going on?"

Ray shrugged.

The living room was a large and pleasant space. There was a piano standing under one of the tall windows. The windows were open slightly and the sharp sound of traffic from First Avenue drifted in. This was a special apartment, Ray thought, some serious bucks here. They sat on a sofa, half facing each other, half facing the piano.

"So whataya think?" Jimmy said.

"This is a hell of a joint. One hell of a joint for a cop."

"Yeah, it's a nice place. I've been here twelve years, it's rent-stabilized. I pay eight fifty a month. It may go co-op, then I'll have a problem."

Ray studied Jimmy maybe for the first time since he'd known him, and he had known him for years. Decided he looked like the actor Paul Newman. Only he had more hair, but the eyes, he had Newman's blue eyes. He and Dante had been a team for years, were friends, he understood, since they were little kids. Another reason to give Jimmy the benefit of the doubt. Ray didn't have anybody like that in his life. Almost nobody did.

"What kind of problem you talking about?" Ray said.

"Whataya mean?"

"With the apartment? What kind of problem could you have?" Ray was about to ask more about the apartment but stopped when Jimmy's phone rang. His answering machine handled the call.

"They voted," Jimmy said. "About fifty-five percent of the people here decided to have the building go co-op. In a year or so, I'm going to have to decide if I want to buy in or what."

"You got that kind of bread, Jimmy?"

"Oh yeah. My folks left me some money."

"No shit. Good for you."

"It makes life easier. Would you like some coffee or tea? I could send out for a pizza or something."

Ray tried to relax, but nothing made him more tense than trying to relax. "Thanks, but I'm not hungry."

"Actually," Jimmy said, "I'd like a beer, how about it?"

"Yeah, a beer would be great." Ray's heart was going bump bump bump. He felt as though his chest would explode. "You mind if I have a smoke?"

"Are you kidding? Smoke, g'head. Knock yourself out. I smoke myself once in a while. I'll go and get you a beer."

Ray began wondering if he could take much more, because Jimmy didn't seem a bit troubled. And the guy had to know that he had checked out that phone call. Christ, he told him he was going to search it out. Told him, and Dante and Kathy too. Maybe he was taking this too seriously. Maybe there was nothing to it. Maybe Jimmy got calls from wiseguys all the time, maybe he got calls from the people he was working all the time? Right. And maybe Mother Teresa watches Madonna videos in her off time. What kind of crazy shit is this? Jesus how do I ask the man? He almost got up and left then, but he didn't, and it was a shame he didn't. Considering that the decision changed the course of his life.

Less than five minutes later, as Ray sat on Jimmy's sofa drinking a Beck's dark from the bottle, some kind of classical music coming from the stereo, Jimmy, softly and with unmistakable clarity, began to talk.

"You checked the number JoJo called from Chaplin's, that right?"

"Yeah, I did." Ray was relieved to hear him say something about it. Delighted it was Jimmy who finally broached the subject.

"And what did you find out?"

"You know what I found out."

"I know you checked the number JoJo called and it came back to me. But I don't know what you found out."

"The hell you talking about?"

All Ray's instincts, all his experience told him that he was sliding into something diseased and clouded and menacing. It served him right, he should have gone straight to IAD with this. The internal affairs people should deal with this one. But he could never do that, it wasn't in his nature to squeal on a friend.

Jimmy let him get whatever he could out of a grin, saying, "Let's see what you know. You know he called me from the restaurant, but you don't know what we talked about, why he called. Do you know that me and Dante know JoJo since we were kids? You know that?"

"I grew up with half the drug dealers in East Harlem, my f'n cousin is a major guy on the West Side. I don't talk to them, and I don't talk to my f'n cousin. So don't give me this crap we've been friends for years. It ain't gonna work with me."

Jimmy laughed in an uneasy way. "You sure you don't want something to eat?"

Ray's mouth tightened, and he shook his head. "My wife's waiting dinner for me."

"It's damn near nine o'clock. How long will she wait?"

"Till I get there." Ray got up from the sofa and began to pace. "There are some things I want to get straight."

"I won't tell you shit before you make me a promise."

"If I can."

"You won't run to IAD with this, and you're not going to breathe a word to Dante. You and I can straighten this out. I'll tell you what you need to know."

"That's good," Ray said. Then he tried to tell Jimmy something, tried to get to the thing he wanted to say, but it was beyond his reach.

Jimmy frowned and bent his head. Gazing at the floor, he said, "I'll do whatever you want me to do—within reason, that is. I'll ask for a transfer if that's what you want, but you must promise you'll keep this just between us."

Ray raised his right hand. "No problem."

Ray took his measure: the red Polo shirt, clean and crisp, it looked brand new; the pleated corduroy slacks, the expensive kind, the soft kind with the heavy cord, and a brown real leather belt; the sleek gold ID bracelet on one wrist and the Seiko with its leather band on the other. Ray thinking, Goddamn, I look like a bum next to this guy.

"So," Jimmy said. "Run them out. You ask, I'll answer."

Ray shrugged. "Joseph Paradiso called your phone here," he said. "He called you here and spoke for fifteen minutes." He paused. "The guy's a f'n made man. He's a member of the f'n Mafia."

"I know him all my life."

"Yeah, yeah, I know that. But we're working him. I'm very disturbed, more than a little scared, this is bad shit, buddy. Anyone else came up with this, you'd be in front of a grand jury in a heartbeat. And we'd be standing right next to you. Your ass would be grass, if it was the feds or a DA's tap. You know how lucky you are Jimmy?"

"But it wasn't the feds and it wasn't a DA's tap, it was a friend of mine, a guy I know for ten years that came up with this. And human nature being what it is, I'm sure my friend will let me spell it out."

"It's a funny thing about human nature. I'll tell you what I think of human nature," Ray said. But he didn't. He looked around the room, spotless, the drapes on the windows imported. The TV and stereo, the furniture, most of which looked to him antique. "I'm asking you to tell me what business you got with this guy. I'm telling you that I want to hear the truth. I promise I won't go anywhere with it, I couldn't put you in the jackpot, I just couldn't do that. But I want to know the truth."

Jimmy looked at him, and Ray tried to imagine what he was thinking, what he was up to. Jimmy shook his head, and seeing that, Ray nodded. They stared at each other, having a discussion without words.

"Money," Ray said, still nodding, getting a little angry now. "You're on with this guy, he's paying you?"

"He never paid me a nickel for as long as I've known him."

"You talk to him all the time?"

"I talk to him a lot."

"About police business, about his business and about police business?"

"Never."

Ray had the passing thought that once you start lying it's impossible to keep yourself straight. "What do you two guys got in common then?" he asked. "I mean you have pretty different life-styles. I mean what the hell can you be talking about?"

Jimmy got up off the sofa, and Ray sat down again. Now it was Jimmy's turn to pace. And Ray suddenly sensed that he was being carefully thought about. He didn't like that, didn't like to have someone make a judgment about him and him not knowing what the conclusion was.

Ray sat still, Jimmy was a few steps from him now and Ray studied his face, watching his expressions change. They were truly a contrast, Jimmy taller but Ray with a much better build, looking like a much tougher guy. Jimmy had a gentle, soft face, but his eyes, those blue eyes were icy now, and shrewd and mean. A side of Jimmy Burns Ray had never seen before. He determined, he wished, he tried to make himself believe it was his imagination, all these demons running around in his head making Jimmy Burns, good old Jimmy, a bad guy. What was he, going nuts or something? The guy's my buddy. Ray Velasquez was beginning to feel real damn low.

Suddenly he had a sense that this could be it, thought for just a fleeting second about what he would do if Jimmy pulled a gun. Then he thought, The guy has no gun on him, for chrissake. Whataya thinking?

"Do you know anything about Dante's father?" Jimmy's voice was almost a whisper.

"I know he was on the job, got jammed up, so they say, and killed himself."

"That's true and that's not true. There's a whole lot more to it."

Ray sat perfectly still and allowed Jimmy to stare at him, permitted Jimmy to go on with the story.

"We were kids—well, we weren't such kids, we were nineteen. Me, Dante, and JoJo are the same age, born the same year, three months apart. Dante's father, Dan O'Donnell, was the bagman for the old Public Morals Division. As the story goes, the DA's squad made a homicide case against a guy named Willie Morales, one of your people. Morales was a three-time loser, and this was a guaranteed life bit he was facing. Between me and you, the creep would have never gotten life, but he figured he would. Or they convinced him that he would, I don't know. Anyway, he flips. Gives up all the shit about the pads and all, Dante's father and all—nothing these DA guys didn't know, mind you, but now they got it official, with Morales's lawyer present, they got to do something. Plus, plus there were these news-paper stories showing up once a week about corruption, the same old shit that goes on every five years in this job. They had to make a move of some kind.

"They set up on Dan O'Donnell's phone. They tap his phone at work and at home, zoom in on him real good, come up with a ton of shit, all kinds of names, amounts, locations, big-time people involved, top brass and all. You know, Ray, I was just thinking of how life is a funny thing," Jimmy said absently. "Me and Dante were probably all over that tap, Christ we usta talk on the phone all the time."

Ray saw Jimmy's lips twitch, and his face cloud. He wished that he hadn't stopped by, wished that he hadn't got himself involved in this crap at all. Jimmy was a good guy, and Dante, the poor bastard, must have had it pretty tough.

"The pad in those days," Jimmy said, "went right to headquarters, to the courthouse and to City Hall. So they grab Dante's father, throw him in front of the grand jury, him asking what the hell you doing to me? Them telling him you'd better take this like a man, take this weight and do the time. They tell him you got two choices here, you go to jail, take all the weight and we'll take care of your family, or you can kill yourself. You certainly are not going to cooperate with the investigation and knock over the whole freaking department."

Ray looked at Jimmy as if for verification, and Jimmy nodded.

"What they don't know," Jimmy said, "is that Dan O'Donnell is as tight as piano wire. They don't know a whole lot of things. Like the fact that Dan O'Donnell has a second life. He's got a woman and a kid in the Bronx, keeps an apartment there and it's there that he keeps his records, his pickup book, and his cash. Nobody knows how much money he had, but he had plenty. Okay, so meanwhile this is turning into a huge circus, there's talk of an ongoing grand jury investigation, people start coming around telling him to stand up, to take the weight and all. This guy's going nuts for real, his life's coming apart and"—Jimmy narrowed his eyes—"he's led this double life a long time, and no one knows about it, about the woman and the kid. And so he cracks. Now he just don't go off somewhere and blow himself away. Not Dan O'Donnell. He cruises up to the Bronx, and the way they tell it, he shoots the woman, and then the kid. Then he gets his records and his money and burns them in the center of the living room floor. Starts a little fire and burns everything. Then he sucks on his gun."

Out of nowhere Ray flashed on his own death. Lying in a big parlor in his blue police suit, the massive odor of flowers, his wife sobbing, his kids dazed and confused, his friends, all two of them, walking to the casket and gawking at him. He was fearful, afraid of dying and being stretched out in a box, of people standing around saying what a shame, what a terrible shame, he was so young, so full of life, had so much to live for.

Jimmy finished his beer and said, "Sal Paradiso, JoJo's father, he gets a call. Don't ask me how, I don't know. Probably somebody in the apartment building, the super or the landlord, somebody called some wiseguy who got in touch with the old man. I don't know. JoJo with two of his people went up the Bronx and carried Dante's father out of the place, then cleaned the joint up. They put Dan O'Donnell in his car and drove him over to Queens to the bird sanctuary. Then they called the police. Right after they called the cops, JoJo phoned me."

Jimmy closed his eyes and crossed his hands on his chest. "I'm telling you the truth, Dante don't know a thing about this." He opened his eyes, breathing in deeply. "And I don't want him to ever know. Now, the city never gave his father an inspector's funeral with horses and motorcycles, you don't get that when you're a suicide. But every cop in the city came to his wake. You had to see the goddamn thing, bagpipes, flags, the whole nine yards. What do you think the department's response would have been if word leaked out that Dan O'Donnell's death was a murder-suicide? I'll tell you what they would have done, they would have marked him for shit. And the press? Those lowlifes, I don't have to tell you what they would have done with that story. The bottom line was, Dante's mother was able to apply for his father's pension, and she got it."

Jimmy Burns looked at Ray, waiting, and Ray was not at all sure what Jimmy was waiting for.

"We owe JoJo Paradiso, big-time. Me and Dante both, but Dante don't know it." Jimmy took a breather and Ray went into the kitchen and poured two more beers.

Drinking the beer now, Jimmy went on. "I was the one that told Dante about his father. I stayed with him that night. Stayed with him throughout the wake and funeral. As bad as it was, it would have been a f'n nightmare if the truth were known. Only family and close friends probably would have showed up. And the pension, you can forget that. Dante would have never recovered. He owes JoJo, he certainly does. And me? JoJo gave me my friend. Dante may be a bit of a wacko, but nothing like he would have been had things gone differently."

Ray could not bring himself to say what he was thinking. He had been sitting here for a half hour listening, and he could have sworn that Jimmy was about to give it up. Maybe he was wrong, absolutely he was wrong.

Jimmy, on the sofa, stretched and let his head hang, his chin pointing toward the ceiling. "Sure," he said, "we stay in touch, me and JoJo, he sometimes tells me his problems and I tell him mine. But we never discuss business, not his, not mine. And there's no money involved, never has been and never will be."

Ray nodded his head.

"Well aren't you going to say anything?" Jimmy said, staring at him.

"One hell of a story."

"Calm down. Don't go all agog on me now."

"Well, I mean," he said, trying to be convincing, "it's some story. Could be a f'n movie. 'The Life and Death of Big Dan O'Donnell.' The hell you want me to say?"

"I don't know if I want you to say anything."

"Like hell you don't. You want me to say that I'm touched by JoJo Paradiso and his old man, the way they reached out to help some poor, demented cop's family. They did that for no reason than they got these great big warm hearts. Is that what you want me to believe?"

Jimmy smiled, saying, "C'mon, c'mon."

"No, I get it," Ray said. "The Paradisos stopped Dante from turning into a social outcast and alcoholic and they gave you a buddy for life. Man, that is something, ain't it? Forget the poor woman and kid that this nut job killed."

Jimmy stopped smiling, and the look he threw at Ray froze Ray's heart.

"Look," Ray said in a measured tone, "I'm not going to do anything, or say anything, certainly not to Dante. I'll tell him and Kathy that I couldn't get a make on the phone. I'll say it was a local call, you can't get a make on those. As far as the department goes, you know I would never drop a dime on you. So it's a dead issue. Forget it, it's forgotten."

"I owe you one," Jimmy said with an apologetic smile.

"You don't owe me anything. I think you're screwed up, I think you know you're screwed up, so maybe you owe yourself something, pally, but you don't owe me a thing. You've been a good friend to me. And that's all there is to it."

Having said it, he threw Jimmy an anxious glance. Jimmy seemed to be smiling, but you could never be sure with the guy.

"If you have more questions I'll answer them," Jimmy said.

"You've already impressed me, save it for the next guy. I believe your story, it's probably true, it sure as hell sounds true enough. Remember, Jimmy, I'm not a new kid on the block. I've got to figure there's more to this than I want to think about."

Ray got up and went over to the piano, which was an upright and quite beautiful. He caught a glint, a flash of something in Jimmy's eyes. He stood still and sullen, he wanted to go, leave, get home to his wife and kids. A little breath of fresh air.

"I'm off this case," Ray said. "I'm off this case and I'm off this team. I'll keep what you told me to myself. You've got nothing to fear from me, but I'm outta here."

Jimmy said, "Fair enough. At least I know where you stand."

Ray thinking it would be crazy and careless to take this guy for granted.

Later, when he was driving home, Detective Raymond Velasquez snorted with contempt. "I loved you once. Then you betrayed me. You'll never get an opportunity to do it again."

Earlier that night, the remains of a six-pack on the seat next to him, Dante O'Donnell decided that he could not cross the street and enter the house. He lacked the courage to take that walk. The hike from the car to that house required more nerve than he was able to marshal. And so he sat, lost and exhausted, feeling that his life was taking a nosedive into the toilet.

It was his house after all, his wife and son inside that house, his marriage. Marriages were going down the tubes all around him, and he never wanted that for him and Judy. He always figured they'd end up walking the beach in Florida, maybe no longer lovers but at least friends, having hung together for the years it took to find old age. Only right now there were things eating at him and he couldn't shake them. And so he sat.

Around eight, eight thirty, a Suffolk County police cruiser pulled alongside his car. "Excuse me," the cop said, a little smartass for Dante's taste. "You have a problem or something?" He told the cop he lived across the street and the cop asked for some ID. He flashed his tin, and the cop nodded and smiled like he understood. It was nine o'clock when he got out of the car and made that walk, knocked on the front door cool as you please.

"What do you want?" Judy said. There was no smile on her face.

Angry now for no reason he could comprehend, he said, "I came to pick up some clothes."

"You know you made yourself the butt of the neighbors' jokes, sitting across the street like that?"

She stood clad in the hot pink terry-cloth robe that disgusted him, the one that emphasized the fifteen pounds she'd gained in the past two years.

"Who called the cops?"

"I didn't," she said.

"Can I come in?" he said softly, wanting to avoid a fight.

"Hell no. You're not coming in here. I've packed some things for you. I've got them upstairs, you wait here, I'll go get them."

"Where's Danny?"

"Like you care? He's at a sleepover."

"At whose house?"

"You got some goddamn nerve. You're gone for a week—more. You call once or twice, now you come home to pick up some clothes and ask for your son. You got some nerve, you jerk."

"Look," he said. "I've been working."

"Oh please."

"I need to use the bathroom, let me come in a minute. Don't push me Judy, I'm tired and pissed, don't push."

Judy finally consented, and the woman he married with her bright pink robe and white slippers allowed him into his house. She then turned and went to their bedroom and returned with a suitcase. Dante went off to the first-floor bathroom to pee and take a look at himself.

In the bathroom now, looking at his father's face in the mirror, Dante heard the phone. It rang and rang, stopped, then began ringing again. He heard Judy answer it, heard her say, "Hold on, I'll get him."

It was Kathy, she wanted to know if he had reached Jimmy or Ray. She needed to know what his plans were.

He heard her speaking the words and felt the tightening in his gut, thought for a second about Kathy's hard tanned thighs, and those buns of hers. When he considered her he got hard. Another thing about his marriage, with Judy lately, he was Mr. Softie. Not always, but more than he liked to think about. Sometimes his whole body ached trying to understand just what was happening. He thought for a moment that maybe he'd buy Kathy a stuffed animal, then thought what in the hell you thinking, dumbo?

Judy sat on the kitchen chair, drinking coffee, lifting her cup with both her hands as if she were going to smell it, staring at him. She leaned toward him, trying to hear his conversation with Kathy, nodding the way she always nodded when she wanted him to know that she understood what was happening, when she knew nothing of what was going on.

"I didn't reach anybody," he told Kathy.

"What are you going to do?"

"I don't know."

"Well, c'mon back. You can stay here."

"Good. That's good."

It was quite a moment whan Dante, standing in the foyer holding his suitcase, looked back at Judy. It seemed to him that she was reasoning a way to sabotage his life but couldn't figure just what to do.

"Who was that woman?"

"My partner."

Dante was anxious to go. When Kathy said you can stay here, his hopes shot through the ceiling. He really had a thing going for Kathy and wouldn't lie to himself about that.

"Go," Judy said. "Get in your car and go. I could care less." Judy stood there, her hands on her hips, biting her lower lip. "I don't want you here."

This he knew was not true, and it tugged at him. It made him feel like shit.

"I gotta go, I'll see ya later," he mumbled.

"Good," she said.

"Gotta go." He felt like a caged tiger.

"So go already, who's stopping you. Go, go, go."

"I'll call when I get the chance. We're working a big case, the feds are involved, and the DA's office. The biggest job I've ever had."

Judy was biting her nails.

"I'll be home tomorrow. Probably, I'll be home tomorrow." Lies, lies, and more lies.

"Don't call, you don't have to call."

"C'mon."

"Take your stuff and go," she told him. "I'm kissing you off, Dante. I've had you up to here. You're going to hear from my lawyer. You will, you'll see. You know," she said, "you're just like your father."

"Nice, nice, that's pleasant of you to say that," he said.

Judy drew herself up, put her hands on her hips, and nodded her head. She looked hurt and furious at the same time. All he felt, besides ten years old, was a burning need to get going.

———

Late that night, about two in the morning, the telephone rang in the Paradiso house on Ocean Road in Narragansett. JoJo answered it, telling himself it's a lead-pipe cinch that this is a hot call, watch what you say, watch what you say.

"What're you doing?" his police friend said.

"Talking to you on my brother's phone, goddammit."

"It's okay, it's okay."

"If you say so. What's up? What time is it anyway?"

"Late." A long pause, then, "I have a gigantic problem."

"You do, or we do?"

"That's a good question. I'd say the problem is mine."

"There is no problem you could have that I can't fix."

Another pause. "I thought a whole lot about this," his friend said finally. "Thought about it and thought about it, I don't think I have any choice."

"When there is no choice, then there is no problem."

"When can I see you?"

"That bad, huh?"

"Worse."

"Think you can find Rhode Island?"

———

At the precise moment that JoJo hung up the guest room telephone, Detective Raymond Velasquez rolled over in his bed on Fordham Road in the North Bronx and threw his arm across his sleeping wife, waking her.

Sarah said, "Are you all right?"

"No I'm not."

Ray touched her breast, and Sarah stretched her arms and legs toward the four corners of the bed. "You want to play?"

He'd awakened her from a sound sleep and now, a moment later, her eyes were beaming. Ray marveled. It made him happy. She was lithesome and graceful, even in her half sleep. She turned to him and put her arms around his waist and rested her head against his shoulder.

"This life," he said, "I'm just now starting to figure how it works. Either you have it or you don't."

"Have what, baby?"

"Harmony, tranquillity, satisfaction."

"And do you have it?"

"I did."

She reached for the string of his pajama bottoms, and struggled with the tie for a moment. Ray helped and her hand went inside, sliding along his hip, across his stomach to find his penis. It was soft in her hand. "I am going to find for you all the tranquillity you'll need to get through this night," she said, her lips now even with his pubic hair.

"It may be too late," Ray said. And he felt again, the fires in his chest, all that he'd been feeling from the moment he'd left Jimmy's apartment, fiery arrows of fear.

Jimmy Burns glanced at the digital on the nightstand. Three o'clock. He lay dead awake, his fingers laced behind his head, staring at a spot on the bedroom ceiling of his eighteen-hundred-dollar-a-month apartment. The guy can't believe I pay eight fifty a month for this place. Ray's bright, a thinker. I got a problem here, he thought, a real f'n headache.

He turned on the night table lamp, got out of bed, went into the kitchen, made himself a drink and took it to the window. He felt frightened and weary. He stared out the window at the city street below and watched a succession of cabs make their way along First Avenue.

Raymond, you're giving me no options here at all. You're screwing down real hard on me, Ray. Giving me no alternative. Feeling a chill at the back of his neck, Jimmy stood before the window, nodding and grimacing. He tried to imagine how he'd explain it to JoJo, he'd have to choose the words carefully. Spell out to JoJo precisely what he had in mind. There could be no confusion here, he'd lay it out, make it crystal clear. He wanted Raymond gone, out of his life. He did not want him hurt. "Fuck," Jimmy growled, still spooked by the look in Ray's eyes, the anger there.

And at 3:00 A.M., Dante O'Donnell asked Kathy Gibbons the following questions:

"Why did you tell me to come and sleep here?

"How can you know without trying?

"Tell me, is this a forever kind of thing? I mean, is there any chance that tomorrow morning when you wake up, maybe then? How about it? Do I have any shot here at all?"

At about 3:02 Kathy gave the following answers:

"I was trying to be friendly.

"Believe me, I know.

"It's possible. Then again, it's possible that the sun will blow up."

He looked at her as though he wanted her dead. "You know," he said. "When we finally do it, it's gonna be a grudge hump, I'm gonna get even with you."

"Roll over," she said. "I'll massage your back."

"Massage this," he said.

"No," she said. "You stroke that, I'll rub your back."

Back in Narragansett, JoJo slept like a slab of granite.

Little Vinny Rapino tensed his stomach and went for the record. He filled his left, then his right hand with Vaseline Intensive Care lotion. His head teeming with visions of the ladies in his life, he masturbated for the third time that night. When he was about to come he flashed on his sixth-grade homeroom teacher, and the fact that she was a Dominican nun and had one of those born-terrified faces made it all the better.

John Paradiso too had difficulty sleeping; at three forty-five he made himself a glass of hot milk laced with honey and sprinkled with cinnamon.

In South Brooklyn, on the corner of Fourth Avenue and Union Street, four junkies from Red Hook sat in a car waiting for their connection. They'd been waiting since midnight. The night was warm; clouds hid the stars. A few blocks west at Carroll and Court Street a car thief checked a parked BMW. According to a sticker pasted on the driver's window, the car had an alarm system. And oh-oh, it was real. Damn. He peeped across the street, and there it was, an oil blue motherf'n diamond. Jesus, he thought, Jesus Christ, a score, a Lexus. He yipped like a dog. Alarm or no, he was going to pluck that ride.

The car thief sniffed, then pinched his nose. Then he made a beeline for the Lexus. He focused on the car and didn't keep an eye on the street; he'd always been like that, see the target and go for it, a straight-on kind of guy, as drawn to direct paths as handcuffs are to wrists. He'd been busted sixteen times, spent a total of eighteen months at Rikers. He was twenty-three years old and his name was Bobby Watkins, in the street they called him Black Robbie.

Robbie took one turn around the car. Revved as he was, his heart banging around his chest, he never heard them.

"Lookit that guy," Lilo Santamaria said to his crime partner Tommy Yale.

"He's checking your car. Can you believe it?"

They stood on the corner, clearly lit by a streetlamp's white spill. Lilo touched his forehead as a mother might check a feverish child.

Robbie licked his dry lips, the wheels were beautiful, total class, he'd get thirty-five hundred easy in Jersey for this car.

Lilo said, "You got your pistol?"

"What're you nuts? Let's just chase him."

"Give me your fuckin' pistol."

They walked fast, two men on a mission. Robbie heard nothing. Other boosters, street thieves had been telling him for years, a thief's gotta listen, gotta look and listen, otherwise you end up in the slammer. No one ever said he'd end up dead. It was only a car, for Christ's sake. A beautiful car, sure, real expensive, absolutely. Still only a car, man, just f'n wheels.

Yale and Lilo were six feet from him when Yale handed Lilo the 9-millimeter S&W.

Robbie bobbed his head automatically, distracted finally by the sound behind him: metal sliding on metal.

"Having fun, nigger?" Lilo said, and nodded his head to prompt a response.

Robbie turned to look at them, a dreamy half-smile on his face. He didn't know what to think, that he'd take a cap in the ass, maybe. He stood up straight and crossed his arms just so. Not so fast that he'd spook them, hoping like crazy that they were cops.

Lilo said, "I make my living stealing, asshole, but I know who I steal from."

Tommy said, "We know who we steal from, asshole."

Lilo said, "Shut up." Then he said, soft and easy, "You're a dead man."

Robbie looked at the gun, saw that it was genuine and thought oh shit. "Your car hah? Nice wheels, I was just lookin'. Those real leather seats? Tough to clean I bet."

Lilo stared at Robbie like he was an extraterrestrial, his eyes got big, real big, and his cheeks puffed up. Tommy Yale who knew Lilo for twenty-five years, spent seven of those years with him at Greenhaven Prison, knew that look.

"Lilo," he said. "It's late, give this jerk a kick in the ass and let's chase him."

Black Robbie was dead, he knew he was dead because he looked in the f'n nut's eyes and saw his finish. Those glazed eyes, man, and those nose holes drawn out from the effort to breathe, each breath coming with an animal grunt. Oh shit, he'd found one, he'd caught a section eight, a real f'n nut job. Robbie'd seen that look before, plenty of times. Some kind of animal, some kind of hunter animal.

Lilo gave him a head-to-toe look.

Robbie leaned back against the car and crossed his legs, trying to be cool. The guy standing with the nut shot Robbie a quick, nervous look. Robbie instinctively turning his chin into his shoulder, said, "You guys cops?"

"You should be so f'n lucky," Lilo said.

For a moment no one spoke, the three of them stood on the street as if waiting for a bus.

"Get on your knees. Get on your knees, nigger. Gonna steal my car, huh? Gonna take something that's mine? All right man, we'll see what you can take, how good you can take something that's mine."

Robbie thinking of some way, any way to get his terrified ass out of there.

"Ey Lilo, Lilo." Tommy Yale put out a placating hand. "Whataya say we go hah? It's getting real late, kick him, Lilo, kick him in the face and let's go, man."

Lilo said, "Shut up."

"Fellas, I'm real sorry. But you got me wrong, I'm out walking I see this beautiful car here, a f'n Lexus is a beautiful car. I just wanna take a look-see."

"Your knees brother."

Robbie shook his head, then dropped to his knees. "Whatcha gonna do man? C'mon it's a f'n car. Whatcha gonna do?"

Lilo let out a yelp and kicked him, Lilo strong as a bear, kicked him hard, so unmercifully that Robbie was lifted off his knees and slammed against the car.

Figuring this is for real, real, Robbie tried begging. "Please mister"— he did one hell of a job, Robbie was a master street actor—"I'm sorry, I'm sorry," snot coming out, screaming, "don't kill me, please don't kill me!"

"I ain't gonna kill ya," Lilo said.

Robbie thinking thank God.

Lilo said, "He is." He handed Tommy Yale the 9-millimeter, saying, "Shoot this motherfucker."

Robbie started crying again.

"Are you crazy? I ain't gonna shoot this guy." Tommy walked off a few steps. Robbie thinking it's now or never, he jumped to his feet and was in the wind so fast he could have run circles around Carl Lewis.

Tommy Yale stood still and watched him go, thinking wow, can this kid go or what? Then he turned and sought out Lilo's eyes, and Tommy was startled to see that the man was laughing, laughing so hard tears ran.

"C'mon," Lilo said, "let's go get some bacon and eggs."

"You're crazy, you know that? You're f'n nuts, man."

"Yeah, maybe. But I'll tell ya this, next time I tell ya t' shoot some piece of shit, you don't do it, I'm gonna shoot you."

CHAPTER FIFTEEN

When Dante awoke Wednesday morning, the apartment was empty, Kathy had already left to meet Ray at the social club plant. He lay on his stomach with the gentle sound of a Bach sonata and the fragrance of freshly brewed coffee filling the apartment.

Dante rolled out of bed, padded across the room to the stereo, flipped to AM, and found Imus. Now move it, he told himself. He put his suitcase on the bed and opened it, took out clean underwear, a shirt, sweater, and socks, and went into the bathroom. Then, for no good reason, he locked the door. Two nights back-to-back in Kathy's bed. What we need here, he told himself, is a little dose of reality. On the one hand he was trying to figure why the hell he spent so much time with a woman who made it crystal clear where he stood, and where he stood was not the place he wanted to be. On the other hand where he wanted to be was a riddle.

Dante put some water on his face and brushed his teeth and felt better. But only for a moment. He felt a sudden onrush of loneliness; then again, he liked being alone, in spite of this deserted feeling. Boy, you are loony. Leaning on the bathroom sink, he studied his face in the mirror. He was having a hard time getting rolling. He took a deep breath, swallowed, then stood erect. Holding his forehead, he laughed at his reflection. "The woman's gay, you jerk." Whoa, it was ten o'clock he was to meet Jimmy at eleven. He jumped into the shower.

Jimmy had been sitting in his car for close to an hour when Dante showed up carrying a brown paper bag. Dante took his seat and looked over at him. Jimmy sat reading the *Post,* his annoyance obvious.

Dante shook the bag. "Bagels," he said. "Bagels and coffee."

Jimmy turned his head in Dante's direction, then went back to reading.

As if picking up his partner's thoughts, Dante checked the headlines. 10 SLAIN IN 11 HOURS.

"This city's a pit," Jimmy said, "a f'n hole. We should nuke this place and start over." He threw the newspaper into the back seat and stretched. "I'm reading this stuff and I'm thinking—"

"Bagels," Dante said, "I've got bagels and coffee, whatayasay?"

Jimmy gave him a bewildered look. "You know what I'm thinking? I'm thinking wiseguys don't kill cabdrivers, mothers in front of their children, gas station attendants. Ten people in eleven hours, can you believe that shit?"

Dante shrugged in a way that meant, I don't understand.

"That's organized crime," Jimmy said. "When people talk about organized crime, that's what they mean, that's what they're afraid of. Indifferent, unconscious mayhem."

"Your coffee is going to get cold," Dante said. "Lilo show yet?"

"Lilo's with Tommy Yale in the coffee shop on the corner."

Jimmy started up the car and they did a slow turn around the block, trying to find a safe place to squat, a place where they could check the street action and not be spotted. Jimmy parked behind a house painter's van. They sat there for as long as it took to finish their coffee and then made another turn, parking a block further down the street, in front of a bakery that served espresso.

Jimmy said, "You seem like you're in a good mood."

"I'm fine."

"You were a half hour late."

"I know, I know. I couldn't get started."

"Did you go home last night?"

"Drove out, spoke to Judy, then drove back. A great freakin' experience."

"You look fine."

"I feel good."

"You weren't fine yesterday. Yesterday you were ready to kill somebody. Yesterday you figured someone sold us out and you were ready to kill them. What happened to change your mind?" Jimmy leaned against his window.

Dante couldn't imagine how to answer a question like that. "Nothing happened," he said.

"Well you're a different guy today."

"You think so?"

Jimmy shrugged. "Maybe you found a little sunshine in your life."

"Don't count on it. There's our guy."

It was time for his afternoon stroll, and Lilo walked slowly up President Street, then down it, then back up again, with Tommy Yale at his side. Everyone on the street looked at them, they stopped here and there and made meaningless small talk with the street's residents. Two kids were playing catch; Lilo took their ball and kicked it into traffic.

"This guy's a hard-core psycho," Dante said.

"You'll get no argument from me. Whataya wanna do? We can't just sit here."

Dante figured that Jimmy was right, they had better move the car, can't just sit. Word would hit the street as soon as they were spotted, and they were bound to be spotted in a matter of minutes, seconds maybe.

Sitting with Jimmy, doing what they had been doing so well for the past thirteen years, watching bad guys, Dante felt as though his mind were smoothing out all that was wrinkled. Nice, nice. Satisfied and cheerful, he decided that Jimmy made him feel good, terrific in fact. He was connected, healthy and happy. He guessed he was not the kind of person that could get along without his best buddy. He loved Jimmy, he did, even though the guy's making excuses for wiseguys was getting old. Sometimes, Dante thought, Jimmy thinks with his ass. Wiseguys don't kill gas station attendants, or rob and kill cabdrivers—right, they're too busy figuring ways to drop a mountain of junk on people.

Looking at Jimmy now, watching how he stared out the window of the car biting his thumbnail, Dante thought, the guy hasn't changed in twenty-five years, not a bit older, always off on his own planet. He wanted to say hey Jimmy, ever check out newborn heroin- or crack-addicted babies? Ever ask yourself who brings that shit into this country? Ol' Jimmy thinking with his ass again. Dante felt a strange dizziness come over him: here with Jimmy, drinking coffee, eating a bagel, watching Lilo hanging out, checking the spots where the wiseguys hung their hats. Just him and his best buddy doing their thing. He never felt so solid, so close to anyone as he did to Jimmy Burns.

"Shit," Jimmy said, "holy shit, look at this."

He was looking down the street at a Mercedes that had turned into the block. "That's JoJo's car, oh yeah," Jimmy said, "that's his all right."

Dante ducked down trying to see and not be seen.

Jimmy made a face, then smiled, and it seemed to Dante it was the first time he'd seen his buddy smile in days.

Dante said, "Freaking JoJo? Is that him?"

Jimmy looked across at Dante, then back out at the street. He held up his palm. "Wait," he said. "That's not JoJo." He sounded relieved. "It's that kid, what's his name? Rapino. Vinny Rapino, driving JoJo's car. Ain't this a bitch?"

"Let me get back to my car."

"What for?"

"You got a radio?"

"That's right, and so do you. What do you want to do?"

"We'll set up on the Mercedes. We'll tail this kid and see what he's up to. Man, it's JoJo's car, sooner or later he'll be in it. Whataya say, a little tail job, me and you, how about it buddy?"

"Fine."

———

Eight o'clock that morning, somewhere near Old Saybrook, driving the Mercedes south on I-95 at about seventy-five miles an hour, Vinny Rapino thought for a moment about the family rules. He thought about how strong and well respected Lilo was in the street. How well he got along with the guys in his own crew. Tommy Yale, Joey, Carmine the Actor, Toto, those guys. He thought and thought and thought that all he wanted was to stay pals with those guys. Now, here's the thing. What he was doing now, running around for JoJo, maybe he would get all those guys pissed at him. Maybe they would figure, the kid Vinny's a fence jumper.

Vinny's spirits sagged when he thought of how people would talk about him. How they just might make plans about him. He knew that JoJo didn't care for Lilo that much; he had seen enough in the past few days to convince him that JoJo was making some kind of move, and he'd bet Lilo was involved. The truth was, Lilo and JoJo hated each other. In fact, he was sure that his little stint here with JoJo would lose him some respect in Lilo's eyes. G'head, Lilo had told him, g'head and hang out with the jerkoff a week or so. But remember where you belong. Jerkoff? You don't call the head man a jerkoff—unless, of course, you got plans of your own.

Vinny shuddered, envisioning Lilo making plans, his game face on. Suddenly he felt devoured by fear. Lilo was gonna go for it, he was gonna take his shot. Driving, Vinny felt rubber-legged. Where would that leave him? Say Lilo took his shot at JoJo, where would he be? Sitting on the bull's-eye, that's where he'd be, a f'n target. He took some comfort in the predictability of nut job Lilo.

Driving, smoking, drinking coffee from a plastic container, extra light with six sugars, listening to some good Frankie Valli, he figured he'd better play it safe and ease up to Lilo. Then he would do what JoJo had asked him to and then make himself scarce. Vinny complimented himself for having such sharp thoughts, at least for a moment he did. Then he thought about the predicament he was in with Lilo, and his apprehension returned like a barbed ache, like an almost forgotten plea. Sophia, Lilo's daughter; in his heart Lilo had to understand, the guy was always cheating on his wife, taking his girlfriend here and there. F'n Lilo should practice what he preached.

Remember where you belong, Lilo had said. Screw with Lilo, he told himself, he'll cut your tongue out, cut your dick off and stick it in your ear. Jesus, he wanted no trouble with Lilo, the guy was a mad hatter. Killing his own; it was a fact of life in his crew. Vinnie wasn't scared of anything else, not the cops, not doing time, but Christ, your tongue ripped out and your dick in your ass. *Marrone,* he was scared of Lilo, and that, he told himself, was a wise thing to be.

Vinny left the highway just north of New Haven and phoned the coffee shop where Lilo hung out. Lilo sounded weird on the phone, like he was putting on an act for someone, he sounded like a big brother or something. Vinnie hated to think this, but Lilo sounded too friendly. That wasn't Lilo. It made Vinny wonder.

"Why'nt you come down here? I'm dying to see ya, kid. Why'nt ya take the ride?"

"Sure," was all Vinny said.

"Pass by here," said Lilo.

He asked Vinny how he was, was he feeling okay. He asked how their friend was doing, meaning JoJo. Asked if he needed anything. Fine, fine, Vinny told him, everything is good. When Vinny told him he'd stop by before he ran his errands, Lilo seemed relieved. Whatever you think is best, Lilo told him. That was definitely not the Lilo he knew.

On the East River Drive an hour and a half later, the stereo now blasting Jay and the Americans, Vinny considered family rules again and wondered if he was breaking them. "Whataya, kiddin,' " he said aloud. "You work for Lilo, not JoJo." Sure JoJo was the boss of bosses, but Vinny was in Lilo's crew, and it was to Lilo he had to answer, not JoJo. It was in the rules. So what was he doing the past few days scheming with JoJo? Getting involved in some sort of scam with the Jew lawyer. It was hard sometimes to admit his mistakes, but he had to take it as a sign that he was coming up, getting wiser. And in this business you got wise or you got dead. Who was stronger, Lilo or JoJo? JoJo for sure. Who would kill him faster? No question there, it was Lilo. And when you figured it the way you're supposed to figure it, according to the rules and all, it was to Lilo that he was connected and it was to Lilo that he must be loyal. JoJo understood that, of course he did. Christ, JoJo's father made the rules, of course JoJo would understand.

Frankly Vinny Rapino was scared to death, had no idea what to do. He wished he had a little coke, maybe some pot or something, anything to take the edge off. He didn't want to get sloppy or anything, just a little something to clear his head. Do all that JoJo asked and be loyal to Lilo, that was not easy. Ey, he told himself, do what you think is right, you can't do wrong if you keep doing what you think is the right thing. This business, he told himself, can drive you crazy, and not the kind of crazy he liked to be drove, either.

────────

Setting up in his car, Dante parked on the opposite side of the street from Jimmy and one block behind him and observed the busy street. He tried, but there was no way he could see Lilo, or Tommy Yale or the kid Rapino. Just too far away, with a line of cars, a couple of big-ass trucks, and a blue van parked and double-parked in front of him. However, Jimmy had an unobstructed view of Lilo's café and a radio to keep him apprised of what was going down.

As Vinny got out of the car, he waved an arm in the air. Lilo clapped his hands and spread his arms in greeting like a courtly priest.

Jimmy's car stood on the street in front of the bakery; above the bakery were apartments. In the third-floor apartment, a woman whose name was Filomena DiBuono sat at the window. Filomena or her husband Ralph constantly were on duty at the window. Street sentinels, lookouts. She had a telephone near her perch and the number of the coffee shop in her head. Filomena scrutinized suspicious cars parked or passing slowly in the street, took plate numbers and phoned the coffee shop with anything she thought Lilo would want to hear.

Filomena often thought of how stimulating and rewarding her world was. For her time and effort Lilo paid her and Ralph's rent. She didn't see Jimmy's car beneath her, or Dante, who was a block away. She did see Tommy Yale and Lilo standing with Benny Bats, the three of them so close together on the sidewalk they pushed against each other with every word and gesture. When she saw Vinny Rapino pull over in the Mercedes and park at the curb, Filomena crossed herself and took his plate number.

———

"Blue one," Dante said into his radio, "anything yet?"

"Scrub the code," Jimmy said. "We're on a closed channel, buddy. Nothing yet, they're standing on the street bullshitting is all. When our guy moves, I'll call ya."

"Don't forget me."

"I wish I could."

Dante changed channels and called in to his office base radio, asked to be patched to the radio at the surveillance plant. Ray answered, saying, "Where the hell are you guys?"

"We're set up on Lilo's café in Brooklyn. The kid Rapino is here in JoJo's car. We figure we'll stay on him till he leads us to JoJo."

"Jimmy with you?"

"Who do you think, Batman?"

Kathy came on saying, "Hey, how are you?"

"Fine, fine, I'm just great."

"What are you doing later? Got any plans?"

"I thought maybe some surgery, surgery would be good this afternoon. We're working, Kathy, me and Jimmy. We're out here chasing bad guys."

"Oh boy," Kathy said. "I'm impressed."

"Good. I'll give you a call later. Although I can't conceive why I will, but I will."

"Call me."

"Yeah. Why?"

"Shut up and call me. Listen," she said, "Ray just went into the kitchen." She was whispering, making it real hard for Dante to hear. "The guy seems a little spaced."

"Who?"

"Ray, that's who. Ray our partner."

"That's not spacey Kathy, that's Puerto Rican."

"The hell you talking about?"

"It's Ray's way to be spacey, it's him. I'll call you later."

He clicked off, wondering what the hell was bugging Ray. Then Jimmy's voice came back, telling him the four mopes have moved from the street into the café, asking "What do you want to do?"

"Sit tight brother, sit tight and wait. We're gonna nail these guys."

"Yeah, for what?"

"Mopery, treason, pissing me off. We'll figure something."

Dante sat back and watched the street. The business of the business of the intelligence cop was to sit and watch, sit, watch, and record. The truth was he loved this part of the job. Lying in the grass like a leopard, keeping an eye out. He looked around, imagined seeing people in the windows. Then he actually saw a few. Watching them, seeing them, the phenomenon of being a seer. Check 'em out, check 'em all out, the people breathing, eating, drinking, moving, hearts beating; people walking around, plotting, planning, scheming, figuring they're alone with their plots and schemes, not knowing he was there watching. It was a kick. Wiretaps and bugs were the greatest, brought you home, inside them. Thirty days on a wiretap you knew what made them sad or happy. In this case, this Paradiso thing, maybe the wires were burnt. Then again, maybe not. In any event, no matter what anyone else thought, he figured the case was at halftime and the third quarter was about to start. Dante, he told himself, there's college, there's education, there's book learning, and there's wisdom. You got wisdom.

On the radio Jimmy said, "The kid's leaving. Saddle up, he's heading for his car. Let's do it, buddy."

———————

A half hour earlier, a little wobbly on his feet, and cold despite the warm day, Vinny got out of the car and walked into the waiting arms of Lilo. Tommy Yale and Benny Bats the zip smuggler looked at him with easygoing interest. Benny smuggled zips, Sicilians, into the States. And he was a slugger in Lilo's crew, a hit man, a shooter, a strong-arm guy. A person whose sheer presence scared hell out of Vinny.

They talked for a while on the street, Lilo telling Vinny how good he looked, rested or something. Benny smiled at him like he wanted to take him to bed.

"Where you been staying?" Lilo said.

"In the sticks, Rhode Island. Talk about dead."

"The brother's?"

"One hell of a house."

"Those people got money."

"They sure do."

"See," Lilo said to Tommy Yale, "I know what's going on. Guys like you and Benny and the kid here are oblivious to everything. Not me; I know what's going on."

Tommy Yale's eyebrows rose. "I ain't oblivious."

Benny pursed his lips and nodded his head as if to say, well, maybe.

"He sent you on a few errands, huh?" Lilo said. "Trying to make a boob out of you, is he?"

Vinny shrugged.

"C'mere," Lilo said. "Let's go inside and chat. We'll have us a little coffee and chat a bit."

Tommy Yale nodded as if it didn't matter. Benny Bats said, "I need a coffee."

Lilo threw his arm around Vinny's shoulders and led him toward the café saying, "He's been treating you with respect and courtesy?"

Vinny didn't answer.

"Ey," Lilo said, "you're one of mine. He'd better treat you good. He don't treat one of mine right I tell him to go fuck himself, we roll it up and go to war."

"Sure, sure," Vinny said, trying to think, trying to figure what Lilo was up to.

Inside the café four of Lilo's crew, Ralph, Punchy, Joey T, and Tommy the Saint, were sitting at a table in the corner playing gin. Vinny hated gin rummy, he was bad at it. It was boring, all card playing sucked, he was a craps man, loved to toss those dice.

They sat at a table against the wall under a photo of Pope John and ordered coffee. Then Lilo said something that made Vinny freeze.

"I've been waiting for you. I've been waiting, to put it mildly, to chat with you."

"Well you know, Lilo," Vinny said, "a lot of things came at me. Things from that guy about this and that."

He didn't use JoJo's name, didn't have to.

"The guy," Lilo said, "likes to flatter himself. He thinks maybe he's dealing with a fool."

Two of the four guys playing cards went and stood by the door, the other two came and stood behind Lilo and Benny Bats. Tommy Yale went to the counter and poured himself more coffee.

Vinny could not have been more alarmed, but he had to hook on to whatever calm was left in him. He figured he had one shot here, he had to lay it on, lay it on thick and hope for a miracle.

He said, "I know I did no wrong. I just tried to do the right thing over here. I'm told what to do and I do it. I ain't no captain, I'm just a soldier doing what I'm told."

Lilo said, "You know, sometimes a kid will sulk when his father embraces another kid. You know what I mean Vinny?"

Vinny shrugged, he had no idea what Lilo was talking about. Lilo regularly confused the hell out of him.

Going on, no pause, Lilo said, "Jealousy is a funny thing, you know I'm the jealous type."

He knew that Lilo liked to blabber, the guy was a big talker. But in their business, the less said the better. So often, Lilo the talker spoke in half sentences and his own nutty code. Say he thought cops were around, he'd say, "The sun is strong today." And if you made a remark, said something to him that he didn't like or didn't agree with, he'd say, "Who is this woman asleep beside me?" People said it was his Sicilian roots. Vinny thought it was f'n weird, period. He folded his hands in front of him and bent his head.

"You know," Lilo said, "not for nothing Vinny, but Sophia's been asking about you. What's going on?"

He shrugged, looking down at his hands. "If I said I'm sorry a thousand times, would you believe me?" Vinny said, still not looking up.

"You, sorry? What do you have to be sorry about? It's me who should apologize. I upset you, pissed you off or something. I know how I can be sometimes. But whatever I did, I'm making it clear right now, I apologize." Lilo looked around the café when he said this.

"Whatever happened, happened," Vinny said, "I'm as much to blame as anybody." He then went on for a long time about how he had to grow up and mature, particularly when it came to dealing with the ladies. And Sofia was a lady, his voice following his mind, which was now on automatic pilot. He figured shit, I got this guy in my pocket. He took out his cigarettes and put one in his mouth, leaning toward Lilo, and Lilo lit it. He then went on about how he couldn't sleep, how he got this awful f'n pain in his gut thinking he'd hurt a real lady, not meaning to, mind you, just his dumb way. How he hoped more than anything, more than hitting the number or anything else, how he hoped he could make it up to her.

Lilo didn't answer. Benny Bats lit a cigarette of his own and excused himself, said he had to go to the john. He walked off a few steps, turned and tiptoed back, to stand behind Vinny. Quickly and quietly, Benny took a section of clothesline from his jacket pocket.

Tommy Yale poured about a half pound of sugar into his coffee. He took a long sip and then watched Vinny with an amused, frozen grin.

Vinny heard a long, deep nasal inhale. At first he thought someone behind him was doing some heavy lifting. He turned toward the sound, then all his composure and sanity hitched a ride out of town.

In the next fraction of a second Vinny Rapino was lying flat on his back kicking his feet, staring at the ceiling, the clothesline in a noose around his neck. Trying like hell to get the words *Get the fuck away from me* out of his mouth.

Benny held the end of the rope and Lilo stood over Vinny, a .25 Beretta in his hand, rubbing his face like he had caught a stone in the eye.

"You piece of shit," he said. "You no good rat bastard, this is how you die."

"No, no, no, wait boss," Vinny croaked hoarsely, figuring he'd better come up with one hell of a last-minute plea bargain, "Will ya wait goddammit!"

His own coolness surprised him, he would have guessed that when his time came he would be scared shitless and screaming with terror. Instead he studied the wack job in his work boots and blue running suit, wondering what the hell was going on behind those nutty eyes. He didn't cry, didn't beg for mercy, he'd seen that kind of move and knew that begging and pleading didn't work anyway. He thought that he didn't know what to think, listening for something and sneaking glances at nutso Lilo, hoping for some sign that maybe the man was not as nuts as he seemed, because if he heard or saw something maybe, just maybe he had a shot here.

"Wait?" Lilo said, "You want me to wait?" and he gave the sign to Benny Bats. "Hold it, Benny, don't kill him yet."

Lilo looked at the asshole kid on the floor and all he hoped was that he'd cry and moan. Lilo loved to hear crying and moaning.

Benny Bats raised his eyebrows in wonder and looked at Lilo, then at Vinny, then back at Lilo.

"I came to you because I wanna do the right thing," Vinny hurried on. "I got something to tell you. You should hear me out."

Suddenly Lilo's crazed expression vanished. He stared at him, a phony, pleasant look.

"You got your last shot, I'm waiting."

Vinny lay there stonelike, the rope dangling around his neck. He lay there staring at Lilo. Things were not going the way he'd hoped. How could he have forgotten how deranged and degenerate Lilo was. A moment ago he supposed he'd catch a beating, get busted up. So what, he'd been busted up before, he could take it. A week or two he'd be fine. But these bums were looking to kill him, f'n kill him. He had to figure a way out of this, a way to walk out of here.

"What are you thinking about?" Lilo shrieked.

Possibly Lilo had no intention of killing him. Maybe he just wanted to scare him a little, more than a little, he wanted to scare the piss out of him. Score one for nutso. Vinny's Brioni slacks were wet to the knees.

"Talk, you peon prick," said Lilo, all-powerfully.

"Can I get up?" It came out irate and low.

"Stay there," Lilo said.

"Just stay put," Benny Bats said.

Lilo spun on Benny and slapped his face, saying, "Don't you talk when I'm thinking."

Vinny didn't know what to say next.

"You better say something smart," Lilo said.

"These errands, those jobs I gotta run for JoJo Paradiso, I came here to tell you about 'em." Vinny winked at Lilo, gave him his best smile. "I work for you, you don't wanna do this to me. I'm with you."

Lilo spread out his eyes in a stare.

After a long pause, Lilo said, "So tell me. What's with these errands you gotta run?"

Vinny smoothed his hair with both hands. He hated to have to think fast, especially when he was on his back talking with Lilo and his messenger boy Tommy Yale, not to mention the lord high executioner, Benny Bats.

"I'm told, get a suitcase, go and rent a car. And you tell me if this don't blow you away—JoJo tells me to put twenty five-pound bags of flour in the suitcase, drop it in the trunk of the car. I'm supposed to take the car and park it in a midtown garage."

Screw these guys, screw all of 'em, JoJo included. He was going to slip through this jackpot in one piece, and if it took telling Lilo about JoJo's plans, then that's what it took. If he got out from under all this heat it would be see-ya time. He'd go to Florida, Africa, anyplace to be away from these lunatic jerkoffs. Tell the screwy bastard everything, about Barry Cooper, the whole thing. How he was to tell the lawyer about the parked rental car. Only Lilo would not allow him to finish. He couldn't picture that he'd walk out of the café in one piece and he couldn't imagine that he wouldn't; he never would have believed for a second Lilo's reaction.

Tommy Yale looked at Lilo, they stared at each other.

Tommy said, "That son of a bitch, that rat bastard. He's gonna run a game on Armond Rammino. He's gonna beat Armond Rammino. He's trying to get us all killed."

Lilo smiled. Vinny hadn't seen him this happy in years.

"You're beautiful kid, you're f'n beautiful." He helped Vinny off the floor and then with practiced grace kissed his cheeks, first his left then his right. The guy was weirdness itself.

"I told you you'd wanna hear this," Vinny said.

Lilo, his hands on his hips, his head back, his eyes on the ceiling of the café, walked in small circles. What, Vinny wondered, is this guy seeing now? The thought threw him into a sudden panic.

Lilo clapped his hands, and at the sound Vinny jumped.

"He's done it for me," Lilo said. "The moron has made life easy for me."

Vinny took the rope from around his neck and looked around the café. No one else moved, they all stood and watched Lilo, watched the nut job do a little dance. Hitler in Paris.

Lilo went behind the counter and poured himself a Johnnie Walker Black. He left the bottle on the counter took his glass and sat down at the table again.

"You're gonna leave here Vinny. You're gonna go and do everything JoJo asked," he said quietly. "But you're gonna call me here. You're gonna tell me every move you make. JoJo is out of control. Now's the time, Tommy, this is our time."

Vinny waited.

Lilo stood up again and began pacing. It was as if he were hearing voices, several, and didn't know which one to listen to.

"What kind of fucking move is that?" Tommy Yale said, "What kind of sick diseased brain does the man have? Don't JoJo know who he's playing with here?"

The mailman came to the door, tried it, found it locked. He peered in for a second, saw Punchy and Tommy the Saint standing guard, turned and left.

"Maybe we should unlock the door," Benny Bats said.

Lilo was not listening. "Go on Vinny, go and do what you were told to do. But you call me every four hours."

Vinny waited. "You telling me to go back to Rhode Island?"

"Of course, you do what you've been told."

Lilo let Vinny think for a moment how he was going to deal with JoJo. "Bruno, the Dwarf, Nicky Black—JoJo tell you anything about those guys?" Lilo asked him. "You got any messages for them or anything?"

"No message, I go and pick 'em up, then bring 'em to Rhode Island."

"Jesus Christ, I can't believe this mutt JoJo is giving me this shot. He's setting himself up for me."

There was a long silence in the café.

"When Armond hears what he's up to he'll kill him," Tommy Yale said finally. "You can't fool with a man like that."

Lilo made a face. "You think so?" he said.

Tommy shrugged. "Armond hates him, hates the old man too. They've always been the opposition." He paused, looking at Lilo. "Armond just needs an alibi that will stand up with the others to waste the whole family."

What others? Vinny thought. What're they talking about? The other bosses? The other family heads? Ooofa, this is turning into some very grim shit. A trip to Africa was looking healthier all the time.

"Lookit," Lilo said. "You'd better get going. Do just what JoJo instructed, and make sure you call me. You've done righteous kid, you've made my year."

———

Vinny finally got loose of Lilo about noon, and driving from Brooklyn toward Queens, he thought about Lilo, understanding that his capo was going to stage a bloody mutiny. *Overthrow:* the word came down on him in a hurry, and Vinny experienced a wave of powerless misery that made his head whirl. He drove at high speed, swearing to himself that he was going to have no part in this. He was gonna be AWOL for this crap, and that was for sure.

Just before he jumped off the Belt Parkway at Cross Bay Boulevard, he resolved to tell JoJo what had taken place with Lilo. When he made that right that brought him into Howard Beach, he modified his plan. As he pulled into the lot of the rental car agency, Vinny tried to imagine telling JoJo about his encounter with Lilo, but he couldn't even work up the nerve to choose the words he'd use. And he could feel his terror waiting to snare him; it had been there all day, fading in and out, and by now he'd almost become used to it. Still, he'd see these errands through, check the situation out, and then split.

He pulled up in front of the rental agency and parked.

Vinny Rapino slammed the heel of his hand against his forehead. You're a regular coulda-woulda-shoulda specialist, you dumbo—JoJo was right, you're a dumbo, stopping by to see Lilo, trying to back yourself up. Phenomenal job, Vinny, he told himself. You did great, you probably started a war. Then he glanced at himself in the rearview, pinched his bottom lip, jacked Sinatra out of the tape deck, and decided that hell, man, he was still alive, still kicking, and that had to count for something.

———

Dante had grown up in Queens, and even on his worst day he couldn't lose a tail there. He knew all the streets, avenues, and boulevards like the back of his hand, nothing was unfriendly to him in Queens. Shadowing the Mercedes and this guy Rapino into the neighborhood where he was born and raised was easy. The guy drove without imagination, speeding up now and again but never checking the rearview, like the day was his, like he hadn't a care in the world.

CHAPTER SIXTEEN

Dante and Jimmy followed Vinny to the rental car agency, observed him leave the car and take a suitcase from the trunk. Watched him enter the agency door and then come out fifteen minutes later. Vinny squinted in the sun, looking around the parking lot. He held the suitcase under his arm and went to the rear of a white Chrysler Le Baron.

"Yo, Jimmy," Dante said into the radio. "He's carrying a suitcase and it's empty. He just threw it into the trunk of the Chrysler."

"I ain't blind, Dante. Whataya figure, he's changing cars, ain't he?"

Dante watched him, thinking, what the hell is this jerk up to?

"He's taking the Chrysler, Jimmy, you stay with him. I'll fall back."

Vinny pulled out onto the avenue and went past Jimmy's parked car. Jimmy waited until traffic got between him and the Chrysler and then took off. Dante followed.

"Come on," Dante said into the radio. "Get up on him, I don't want to lose this guy."

"I'm there," Jimmy said. "I'm with him."

Vinny drove out onto Woodhaven Boulevard, and Dante watched the traffic build around him. Jimmy was on Vinny's right, a cab and a van between him and the Chrysler, Dante right behind Jimmy. At Woodhaven and Liberty Avenue, Vinny jumped a light. Jimmy stopped. Dante couldn't believe it, he veered around Jimmy's car and shot through the intersection, and traffic light on dead red.

"C'mon, c'mon, c'mon," Dante said into the radio.

"What c'mon? I'm stuck. Stay with him, I'll catch up."

To Dante, Jimmy was trying to sound thoughtful, as if to stop at a traffic light when you're on a hot tail was reasonable.

"Just make sure you do," Dante growled, giving Jimmy a double click of the radio. There was only one car between him and the Chrysler now, a gypsy cab. "You coming?" he called back. And Jimmy said, "On my way."

Vinny made a left off of Woodhaven onto Metropolitan Avenue, went down about ten blocks or so and parked in front of a small pizza parlor with dingy red curtains and a sign that said WE DELIVER FULL MEALS. Vinny was on the sidewalk now, and it seemed to Dante that he looked around for effect.

Jimmy said, "That's him parked in front of the pizza joint."

"Right," said Dante. He could see Jimmy inside his car parked in the lot of a Mobil station about a block away. He said, "Stay right where you are. I'm across the street from him, this guy ain't looking. You stay put, okay?"

Vinny went to the trunk of the Le Baron, took out the suitcase, and strode through the door of the restaurant.

"He went into the pizza joint carrying the empty suitcase," Dante told Jimmy.

"How do you know it's empty?"

"He tossed it from hand to hand, and he's been carrying it under his arm, for chrissake."

Fifteen minutes later Dante clocked Vinny as he walked from the pizza parlor to the Chrysler, his upper body twisted, using both hands now to carry the suitcase, bouncing it against his leg.

He said, "He's out now, going back to the car, that suitcase is loaded man."

"How do you know?"

"How do I know, how do I know? Ey, take my word for it, all right? This guy just picked up something, and whatever it is, it weighs a ton."

"Wanna jump him?"

"I was just thinking the same thing."

"It could be nothing," Jimmy said.

"I'll tell you what it ain't, it ain't ten pizza pies with extra cheese and onions."

"Let's jump him," Jimmy said.

Almost a minute passed. "He put the suitcase in the trunk. Whataya say we let him slide a while, stay with him, see what he's up to?" Dante thinking, I'll stay with you till Christmas you slick son of a bitch.

"You call it," Jimmy said.

Rapino looked shaky now, turning, looking up and then down the street, taking in the view that was every picture ever taken of an Italian neighborhood, with salumerias, pastry shops, pork stores, cafés, and a travel agency advertising the wonder of Rome, Florence, and Venice.

"Let's just not lose him," Dante said.

An elderly woman all in black walked slowly down the street; she looked at Dante seated in his car, turned and looked away. These neighborhood Italian women were a breed apart, separating themselves from the reality of their men's lives, thinking of their men as the Don Quixotes of the underworld doing their godfather routines. What was with these people?

His own grandparents came from some poverty-stricken town south of Naples. He'd heard that they'd skipped out the first chance they had, arriving in the States in their early twenties. He never met them, both of them died of diphtheria in the space of one week before his mother was ten. A poor people's disease, his mother told him, her parents died of poverty. She had no other family, consequently she was raised in foster homes and as a child he listened endlessly to stories of anguish and bitterness, stories about his mother's own upbringing, about her having been set adrift alone in this world to fend for herself. She left little doubt that she had been eager to marry, to find someone to whom she could give love and be loved by, someone who would provide her the family she needed.

At seventeen she met and married his father and immediately disassociated herself from any of her Italian roots. Big Dan would not have it any other way. So his mother settled into a life with a man who was a racist and a bigot, a man who never had a good word to say in regard to dagos, wops, his words for Italians. As a result, there was zilch in his life that was Italian besides Dante, his grandfather's name, a name his mother insisted on and was allowed to give him only after tremendous battles with big Dan.

The name was a curious fit. He was no Italian, never felt like one, whatever being an Italian felt like. However, lately a strange curiosity was growing in him. No, not strange, really weird. When he was alone a song like "Sorrento" could break his heart. He'd take out a photograph of his grandparents, throw Pavarotti on the stereo, and would get such a melancholy pang that he thought he was losing it. Yeah, it was funny. Then his father's face would float like a cloud around his head and all affinity for things Italian vanished. Hell man, it was his destiny to become the dutiful only son of one hard Irishman, a man born to be a cop, a man that built him body and soul to be a reflection of himself, to reflect his tastes and advertise his toughness, to reaffirm his talent to drink and womanize and find trouble. Good old Da.

"Hey Dante," Jimmy's voice said over the radio, "what about the Mercedes?"

"You're reading my mind," Dante said.

He picked up the radio and patched himself to the surveillance plant, hoping to get Ray and getting Kathy. Pushing thoughts of his father, his mother, his life out of his overloaded head, he gave Kathy the name and address of the rental car agency where Vinny had dropped the Mercedes. Told her to go and set up on the car, asked her to tell Ray to stay put at the plant.

Kathy said, "Ray's gone."

"Whataya mean gone?"

"Gone, he left, said 'bye, I'm off this case."

"Are you kidding me?"

They were following the Chrysler now onto the Long Island Express-way heading east, through miles of traffic, of cars pushing along bumper to bumper, New York rush hour. People heading for home, out to the burbs to their frame development houses, an evening of crabgrass and Little League and decent small lives. Dante thinking, that is exactly where you should be heading, buddy, a normal decent life. Then thinking, ey, you tried, it just didn't seem possible to make that work. He felt a sudden swell of hope-lessness come over him, a drowning feeling, as if he'd just fallen overboard and was being swept away in an icy silver sea. The stuff of his life kept flashing by and those thoughts didn't make him happy, didn't make him happy at all. Caught between the sudden gust of anxiety and the irritation of wondering what the hell was going on with their partner Ray, Dante wanted to push it. So he radioed to Jimmy, asked him straight out if he knew what the hell was wrong with Ray?

Jimmy said, "I couldn't even guess."

Driving point now, three cars behind the Chrysler, Jimmy said, "Ra-pino's going on to the Grand Central, heading for the city."

Dante said, "I just called in to Kathy, told her to set up on the Mercedes. And listen to this, Ray left."

"Whataya mean, left?"

"He told Kathy he quit, he's finished, he's off this case. No reason, no explanation. He was calm, Kathy said."

"Hmm."

"That's all you gotta say?"

"What am I supposed to say?"

"Look, I'm starting to freak out with this guy. I'm thinking the guy's flipping out or something. He's been real strange lately."

"Strange is what Ray is," Jimmy said.

Dante maneuvered his car so that he was alongside Jimmy, there were a bunch of cars now between them and the Chrysler. He briefly caught Jimmy's eye and sensed that Jimmy was as baffled by Ray as he was. Jimmy took his hands off his steering wheel and shrugged, you got me.

Dante pointed to the Chrysler, Rapino was speeding up, stepping on it, jumping lane to lane, he was off and running.

They tailed the Chrysler over the Triborough, through the toll plaza and onto the FDR going downtown. He got off at Fifty-fourth Street, shot up to First Avenue, hung a left to Fifty-seventh and headed crosstown.

Dante remained on his tail, wondering why Ray had jumped ship, then remembering that Ray didn't like working with a woman too much. He presumably had had it with Kathy, always alone with her and so on. Maybe it was just an impulse, and he'd wind up coming back to the team. When you had to work ten, twelve hours a day with a partner, it was a pure bitch if you didn't get along. Dante figured he'd better run Ray down, get him to come on back. Christ, they needed him, Ray knew that, how essential he was. Goddamn macho Puerto Rican, can't work with a woman. What kind of crap was that?

Vinny drove up Fifty-seventh Street to a garage between Fifth and Sixth. Dante stopped and parked at the curb just before he got to the garage entrance. Jimmy eased to the curb beyond the garage's ramp on the same side of the street.

Dante turned off the ignition and sat there waiting. What if Rapino swapped cars again and came out the other exit on Fifty-eighth Street? He'd tailed guys like that before, sharp guys who'd have a second and third car waiting. Conceivably this guy Rapino was real slick. And he thought hey Mr. Slick, what's in that suitcase? Drugs? The Paradisos were not into drugs. It looked like it weighed a ton. Granted Rapino was no Superman, still that bag looked heavy as hell. Their information down through the years was that the Paradiso family steered clear of the drug business, but that didn't necessarily make it so. And if it wasn't drugs? What then? Money? Whooooa, if there was money in that bag, we're talking see-ya money. He shook his head hard as if to clear it.

Dante began planning what he'd do if he had all the cash he needed. Travel to Rome, Venice, Florence, the town where his grandparents were born. Find a garret someplace in Paris and write the memoirs of Big Dan O'Donnell, his father's story, the story of the Irish mafia in the NYPD.

Dante was momentarily distracted by a skinny elderly woman looking at him through the windshield. She wore granny glasses and a scowl on her face, and she carried two shopping bags filled with God knew what. On her feet were one red and one black sneaker, over her shoulders like a cape was an olive green man's raincoat that was maybe four sizes too large for her. She pointed to a no-standing sign and spit. Dante ran his hand over his mouth and sighed through his nose. He looked past the woman to the parking garage entrance and shit, here came Vinny Rapino, walking straight at him. The woman strolled over to Dante's car and banged her fist on the roof. Unnerved, he turned away. The woman whacked the car again.

Dante opened the driver's window and called out, "Do I know you lady?"

"You stupid jerk, can't you read? You can't park here."

Rapino was maybe twenty feet from him now, standing at the curb, watching the heavy stream of traffic, looking for an opening so he could cross the street. When the woman shouted, he turned his head.

"Dumb jerk, you can't park here." Bang! she pounded once again on the roof. Dante could see that she was very drunk. Giving up, he rolled up the window and radioed Jimmy.

"You gonna go on foot or do you want me to?" he asked.

"I'll go," Jimmy said.

"I'll keep an eye out for the Chrysler, if it leaves, I'm going with it."

"Good, good. Maybe we should call for some help."

"Not yet, let's wait and see."

Dante scanned the street, all the people walking fast, good-looking people, exquisitely dressed. Probably the best-dressed and finest-looking people in New York in motion along Fifty-seventh Street heading for Fifth Avenue. His eyes came to rest on the bag lady, who walked around now to the passenger-side window, one arm outstretched, pointing at the street sign. Suddenly she dropped to one knee like a priest at the altar, grabbed the front of her coat, and pitched forward, smashing her face on the sidewalk, flopping around like a salmon on the beach, kicking her feet and letting loose a scream that scared the hell out of everyone within fifty feet.

People walking by stopped, but only Dante went over to her. The woman was making a disgusted hissing sound, shaking her head, confused.

"Take it easy, stay calm," Dante said. "I'll get help for you."

He sounded the way he always did when he played cop, like an adult reassuring a small child. He touched her shoulder and cocked his head, trying to come on playful and charming. "You're gonna be fine," he said.

"Oh yeah?" the woman said. "Whataya wanna bet?"

Her voice was tight and hoarse. Dante crouched down next to her. "What's your name? Where do you live."

The woman mouthed, *Leave me alone, please. Leave me the fuck alone.* She looked knotted-up and crazy, a shrill laugh coming from her now. Dante went to his car and called the intelligence office base and asked the detective on duty to patch him into Midtown South, told the operator at the precinct to send a car and ambulance to Fifty-seventh and Fifth, front of 775 Fifty-seventh Street.

The woman gazed at the people passing, looking from one face to another, then zeroed in on Dante as he crouched down by her again, hesitating as if she knew him from somewhere but wasn't sure just where. She said, "You're a cop? I know you, you sing on the stage." Then she pulled a straightedge razor from her bag and swung wildly. Dante jerked back like he'd been punched in the face, springing to his feet. He spun around and grabbed his cheek. Everyone who had been standing there screamed and ran off, the woman now sitting in a perfectly normal position with a perplexed scowl on her face, just sitting there as if in deep thought, the razor in her hand.

Not until he heard the sirens coming did Dante straighten up. He glanced around, still holding his cheek, wondering if his face was still there. He saw Jimmy standing behind him, his mouth wide open as if he'd been shot in the stomach, staring at him with those big blue eyes of his, looking wild and pumped and terrified.

"She cut you? Did that bitch cut you?"

"No, no she missed. Christ, it was close."

"The hell you doing kneeling down next to a psycho, where's your head?"

He watched the woman stagger toward the ambulance, a uniformed cop on either arm, and wondered where the razor went, who the woman was, why'd she want to cut him, kill him. He heard Jimmy talking, saying, "Why you holding your cheek?" too lost in his own head to answer.

"You see Rapino leave?" Jimmy asked him. "Huh? I lost him in the building, you see him leave?" Dante heard the sirens and whoopers, then somebody laughing, then again, "You see him leave? I lost him." Jimmy was coming back at him despite his silence, talking slow and easy as if Dante were ten years old. "I followed him inside that office building there. Saw him get on an elevator and then I lost him. I waited in the lobby, never saw him come down. I figured you'd spot him if he got past me. How'd you get involved in this street shit? What were you thinking? Dante, you okay?" He felt Jimmy grab his arm, yell into his ear, "Hello, anyone home? Hey straighten out for a second. Yo, buddy, you all right?"

"That bitch tried to kill me. I just wanted to help her and she tried to cut my face off."

Jimmy put out a pacifying hand, took a hold of Dante's shoulder. "Easy, easy buddy. You're all right, you're fine."

"That miserable bitch could have ended it for me right here," Dante snapped. He put his hands out like he wanted to strangle someone. "That wacky bitch."

Then his beeper went off.

Dante got back in his car and used his cellular to call. He got Kathy, she was in Queens, parked up the street from the rental car agency. He told her to wait there. "Sit tight, we lost Rapino. If he shows, get on him and stay in touch."

"Are you coming out here?"

"Me or Jimmy, one of us will be there."

"You come."

"Me or Jimmy, I told you. One of us will be there soon."

"Look I'm not trying to lay anything heavy on you but I want to see you, okay?"

"Oh yeah?" Dante said with false brightness. He didn't know what else to say.

"Actually I've been feeling shitty."

"What's the problem?"

"I dunno."

"Something with the case, with work, with what?"

"Yeah, I guess—no. I don't know."

"Kathy, I'm on a cellular phone here. What's going on?"

Silence. "I just feel deserted," she said.

"The hell you talking about?"

"Lonely, I feel lonely."

A long silence, maybe thirty seconds of stillness.

"Look, in twenty minutes, a half hour depending on traffic, either me or Jimmy will be with you. Just sit tight, one of us will be there."

"You," she said. "You be here."

"I'll try."

Dante got off the phone thinking that he didn't want to think about that conversation, which made him start thinking about Ray and why the guy hated to work with women.

Striding into the garage with Jimmy at his side, he grabbed ahold of the garage manager. Dante figured the guy was the manager because he was wearing a gray workman's outfit with *Manager* stenciled over his breast pocket. A young guy, maybe twenty-five, shoulder-length hair and nervous eyes, wearing a frown and holding a clipboard. Dante showed him his shield, saying, "You mind if we just take a look around? I want to show my partner that black BMW you got downstairs."

"Which one?"

"The black one."

"There's about ten black ones downstairs."

Jimmy went to the stairway that led to the underground garage, "We'll know it when we see it," he said. Dante followed him.

The manager stood still and sullen, not wanting to let them pass but lacking the heart to interfere.

The Chrysler was on the third level, parked by its lonesome at the far end. Dante tried the doors, found them locked. He squatted down next to the right front tire, took out his knife, and jabbed. Jimmy did the left rear and then the taillight, so they could recognize the car easily if they had to follow it at night. "Twenty bucks an hour to park your car, come back and find two f'n flats and your taillight busted, can you believe that?" Dante said. "What a city."

They returned to the main floor and walked past the manager, Jimmy throwing the guy a sweeping gesture of farewell.

Dante got into his car and phoned his office while Jimmy leaned in the open door, his hands folded on the roof. He kept one eye on the garage entrance while Dante ran down the day's action to Inspector Martin.

After he brought the inspector up to speed, Dante said, "Boss, somebody should sit on this car. There could be something here."

"Let me tell you," Inspector Martin said, "there could be anything in that suitcase."

Dante leaned back against the seat and nodded in agreement. "You're right," he said.

"Hell, you remember about five years ago, we found body parts of that Rammino capo in three different suitcases."

"Whataya think? A warrant maybe?"

"I don't think you got enough for a warrant. Why don't we just sit on it?" The inspector told him he'd send a team over to give them a hand.

"By the way," the inspector said, "your partner Velasquez put in for two weeks off. Said his wife and both kids came down with a virus or something. I couldn't say no, couldn't turn the guy down, we owe him six months lost time as it is. If he wants the time I've got to give it to him. If you need any additional help with this case, let me know. I've got people sitting over here doing crossword puzzles. You need someone, tell me."

"Yeah, yeah, maybe. I don't know, we'll see. If we need any help I'll let you know."

"You okay, Dante?"

"Great, why you ask?"

"I dunno, I heard maybe you're having some trouble at home."

"Who told you that?"

"You did."

"I was drunk."

"You need any help you let me know, all right?"

"Sure boss, I'll let you know."

Jimmy lit a cigarette. "I hate to bring this up, but where is Rapino?"

Dante and Jimmy exchanged glances. Dante gave a quick shake of his head. "How'd you lose him?" he said, drawing only a shrug from Jimmy.

"Tell ya what, Dante said, "Whyn't you hang tight here till the team from the office shows. I'll cruise out to Queens and team up with Kathy. We'll stay with the Mercedes."

"And after the team shows up?"

"Reach out for us, we'll be with the Mercedes, wherever it goes, we'll be with it."

"Ey," Jimmy said, "What if there's a half million in the suitcase of that rental?"

Dante held a finger to his lips. "Shh. I don't want to think about that." He had thought about the possibilities of that suitcase and told himself forget it. Jimmy mentioning it was a bit strange, but there was a whole lot about Jimmy Burns that was eerie lately.

Jimmy dropped into a squat next to Dante's open car door. "Look," he said, "I got some personal shit to take care of. Whataya say, when the team shows, I take a few hours, then I'll reach out for you?"

"Jimmy, it's only me, you, and Kathy." Dante stared at him, feeling the elevated moan of his nerves. Wondering, not wanting to, wonder what was on Jimmy's mind.

"Dante," Jimmy said, "I got some real serious personal stuff I've got to take care of."

"Yeah? Like what?"

Jimmy stood up. "Ey, what do I have to do, tell you every single thing that's going on in my life? It's personal, it has to do with this woman I've been seeing. Her mother's in the hospital, she's dying. I promised I'd go with her to visit her mother, okay?"

"Then go."

"Christ."

"You gotta do what you gotta do when you gotta do it," Dante said out loud to Jimmy, hearing the hollowness of it, amazed that he had never heard about this woman before.

"I gotta go," Jimmy said. "I'll wait for the team to show, then I've got to go. I won't be long, a few hours is all."

Dante nodded, watching him, feeling a bit frantic and a little lost.

"Ey, how many times have I covered for you?" Jimmy came back at him. "I ain't gonna be gone long. I'll stay in touch."

"Fine," Dante said.

A hour and a half later he was driving behind the Mercedes, having picked it up at the Nestor Club. Kathy had put it over the air that Rapino had returned in a cab and went right to the Mercedes, she was following him from the rental car agency. She got on Rapino and stayed with him until he reached the Nestor Club, then found a place where she could park and keep an eye out. Dante was waiting when she arrived.

They parked at opposite ends of the block, speaking by radio, and watched Vinny Rapino jump from the car and scoot across the street to the Nestor Club in one big hurry. He came out five minutes later with Bruno Greco and JoJo's brother-in-law in tow. Dante slouched down in his seat and turned away, watching the trio out of the corner of his eye as they drove off, making a flashy U-turn in front of Kathy in her blue T-bird. Then he and Kathy picked up the tail.

For Barry Cooper this life he'd chosen was like a parody of sanity, much as Robin, his wife, with her produce-on-demand, give-me show-me buy-me bring-me imperatives, was a parody of wifeliness. Robin spent as he made; he hadn't thought it possible, she showed him how.

Between his born-to-shop wife and his insane brother, Barry found himself up to here in a monstrous fix; in effect, life as he knew it was vaporizing. And now, as he sat at The Oyster Bar of the Plaza Hotel and sipped Campari and soda, one of JoJo's favorites, he believed with all his heart and soul that all had turned to shit.

To pull off what he originally planned required imagination and chutz-pah, and Barry, six months into the deal he'd made with the feds, began to suspect that he lacked an adequate amount of either. This cooperation deal was a bit much, this was life-altering in the most dramatic sense. This was shoot the moon.

True, if he were to believe the government agents, he and he alone could save himself and Michael from a thousand-year jail term. And a fine, let's not forget the fine, a fine that resembled the national debt of Poland. He prayed that Michael, sleazy bastard that he was, appreciated all that he had done.

In any event, when the government agents came to him and made their proposal, he thought he understood all the ramifications. He would be through with the practice of law; he could live with that, he had no practice to speak of, no clients other than the Paradiso clan. His marriage would be *fini*, over, done, history—that would break his heart, he loved the woman. But Robin would simply not do the Witness Protection Program bit. Then again, when you compare the loss of love to fifty years of making little rocks out of big ones, the choice seemed somewhat less painful. And, of course, he would be forced to relocate in another state; he had decided right off, forget another city. Another state—he would have to leave the country, for chrissake. Granted the one positive was significant—okay, monumental. Still the negatives had to be dealt with, and at this point, sitting at the bar, his head in his hands, he hadn't the foggiest idea how he was going to pull this off.

The FBI, he didn't know what to make of them. Sometimes as understanding and as concerned as he could possibly have hoped, especially during the initial meetings. When he asked about the new identity, would it stand up, could he get a passport and travel to wherever he wanted in the entire world? Oh they came on all reassuring and positive. He could go where he liked. Yes, yes, even that island off the coast of Thailand. And by the way, the agent in charge said, we have a resident agent in Bangkok who would be more than delighted to assist you with whatever you require.

It was certainly true that the Bureau agents and the U.S. attorney did little to conceal their mutual hatred of Michael. Screwing around with those South American drug lords for years, and Barry suspected that his brother was involved with a corrupt Mexican government official or two. The drug involvement didn't seem to bother the agents all that much, is was the anti-American government official that really burned their asses.

The main thing was, of course, Joseph and Salvatore Paradiso. If he could offer them up, he and his brother would slide. The question Barry would have asked Michael, had they been left alone long enough for him to ask a question, was how come you told them we could land the Paradisos, and more than that, how come when you were nabbed you gave up your own brother? What, Barry asked himself, had he done to deserve this?

When he had met the agents who would be his contacts and was told just what was expected, Barry felt as though he had already been left for dead. Though when he heard them out he saw for a fleeting moment a chance to leave behind this wretched life he was leading. He would just have to set up Joseph Paradiso. Pity. Barry sort of liked him. However, he liked Michael more, and truth was, his own ass needed protection, thanks to his brother.

So now he sat at the Oyster Bar preparing to embark on a bender, having just placed a call to the New York office of the FBI to tell his contact that Vincent Rapino had that very afternoon confirmed what Joseph Paradiso had told Barry in confidence the day before. There was in fact one hundred pounds of heroin parked in a rented Chrysler in the garage across from his office. The FBI couldn't miss this one. He put it right under their nose.

Barry felt sick. Oh how miserable he felt, sitting at the bar, watching an emaciated man just like himself behind the bar pouring martinis for a pair of British businessmen. The bartender and the businessmen didn't notice Barry, didn't realize for a second that they were in the presence of the man that was about to topple a major Mafia family. He was suffering with shame, nauseous with fear. He was sick with anger at his brother Michael. But mostly it was fear.

Then he thought about the one positive, the million and a half deposited in a numbered Swiss account. That money put there for Barry by Michael. What a fine brother he could be. Soon, he told himself, there will be palm trees, warm sands, and no place to get pasta within five thousand miles. All he had to do was survive this. Sure it was his own opinion, but Barry Cooper thought if he could keep his wits about him, he would be just fine.

CHAPTER SEVENTEEN

JoJo stood at the water's edge behind his brother's house, watching three old-timers down the beach standing knee-deep in water, quietly casting into the surf. He had been standing here for a half hour, collecting his thoughts, and had seen them catch one fish between them. Not a whole lot for all that work, but still they seemed at peace with their world, a condition he envied, to say the least.

JoJo had intended to stay in the house, throw caution to the wind and make a few calls, but he grew antsy and walked down to the water. He wondered how Vinny made out with Barry Cooper, how Lilo made out with Armond Rammino. He didn't for one minute think that Lilo would straighten up and do the right thing. Even so, he could tell the guy was hot over the drug move—the shithead always wanted more money.

After Vinny left he drove out to the pay phone in John's car and placed a call to Spain, anxious to get Luis going, praying he could reach him. He got the Cuban right off and was shocked out of his socks when the guy told him soft and easy that he'd be in the States tomorrow. Simple, he'd fly into Boston, rent a car, and meet him in Providence. Just like that.

Walking along the beach now he tossed stones into the water and watched sea birds swoop. When John found him he was lifting a rock the size of a football, figured he'd pitch it in the water and frighten the fish off, see if he could get a rise out of the fishermen.

"You got a call," John said. "I think it was your cop friend. If he called you here the phone can't be tapped, right?"

"You think?"

John patted his lips with his thumbnail, wrapping his other arm around him. "Christ," he said, "he's a cop, right? He wouldn't call on a tapped phone."

JoJo was about to express the opinion that John was an absolute simpleton, but before he could get the words out, John threw his arms around his brother and gave him a hug.

"You're probably right," JoJo said, figuring, simpleton, right, but still a brother. "You sure it was him?"

"I haven't heard his voice in a long time, but I remember it. It was him, wasn't it? Anyway, he said he'd call back in twenty minutes. It was him, huh?"

"Who?"

"Your cop friend, what's-his-name."

"You tell me."

"I can't remember."

"Good."

An hour later, carrying in his head the number Jimmy Burns gave him when he'd called back, JoJo stood in the sunlight at his favorite pay phone. He felt rubber-legged thinking of all the crap that was coming down, one problem after the other. Now, Jimmy—what the hell did he have going?

The number Jimmy had given him was in code, a code that would be no big deal to crack if someone was interested. You subtracted each digit from ten: Jimmy says 555–5444, he wants JoJo to call 555–5666.

"Whataya doin'?" JoJo said.

"Talking to you is what I'm doing, but earlier I was following your car around, watching Vinny switch to a rental and following that."

"What?"

"Yeah, that's right, following the Mercedes with kid Rapino driving. You know I'm working on this case with Dante and all, it's been nuts." A long pause then, "What the hell is Rapino up to? Pally, we saw him carry a suitcase loaded with something, throw it into the trunk of the rental, and park the car in a garage in midtown. What's going on?"

JoJo bit his lower lip, cast his eyes skyward, thinking about what to say, how to say it. He shook his head in confusion. He wasn't about to tell Jimmy all his business.

"What's going on is my concern"—JoJo reminding himself that no matter what, Jimmy was a cop, questioning whether his buddy could be going through some kind of guilt trip. Jimmy with a conscience could cause them both no end of grief.

Jimmy said, "Your business?"

"Yeah, my business, it ain't nothing for you to be thinking about. It ain't nothing at all, is what it is." Jimmy didn't answer and JoJo went on. "Is this the big-time problem you were telling me about last night?"

"No, no that f'n headache, that f'n headache we need to talk about immediately. There's this cop, this cop friend of mine. He knows you called me from Chaplin's the other night. Remember buddy, remember when you called my apartment? Dante saw you make that call, and he had it checked out."

"Dante checked it out?"

"No, not Dante, another guy, this guy I work with."

"He told Dante?"

"No, he won't tell Dante, he gave me his word. I trust him. His word's good with me."

"You gave him some money?"

"Ray wouldn't take money. If I offered Ray money he'd freak out."

JoJo ran his finger around the lock of the telephone coin box. When he was a kid he could pop these things in no time flat. There was silence on both ends.

"He'd freak out if you offered him money and you trust this jerk?" JoJo said at last.

"Yeah, I do."

"I want you to get up here. Get up here as soon as you can, okay?"

"Yeah, yeah I want to, but you see the thing is, Dante and this woman we work with are following the Mercedes. Where's that freak'n' car heading anyway?"

"Here, it's coming here. Hey buddy, what in the hell is going on?" His eyes focused on two teenage girls getting out of a red Jeep ragtop. More silence and deep nasal breathing. "What's going on pal? I don't like this."

"I want to get up and see you, but I certainly don't want to bump into the other two. If you get my meaning."

"Look, you work it out. You can reach me at the other number, my brother's place. But I want to see you."

"I think we have to discuss this other problem."

"Another one?" It seemed to JoJo that the question stumped and embarrassed Jimmy.

"Ray. That problem, the problem we got with Ray."

"For chrissake, who the hell is Ray?"

"He's the guy that checked your number."

"Yeah, yeah okay. So tell me, go on, what the hell are you waiting for? Tell me, will ya?"

"I'm a little nervous, pally, I don't want no misunderstanding here."

"Hey, screw off, will ya man? You got something to tell me you tell me. What do you think I'm gonna do? I'm not stupid. C'mon now, what is it?"

"Ya see, this guy we work with, this guy Ray. I figure he's got this thing figured out."

"What thing?"

"Between you and me."

"What?" Don't panic, JoJo told himself.

"Well, he knows you called me and we spoke for fifteen minutes."

"We're old friends, for chrissake."

"Right, that's what I told him. But ya see—"

"What's his name? Ray what?"

"Christ, I hate talking on a phone."

"Ey, I'm on a pay phone. Where are you?"

"A safe phone."

Years ago Jimmy had told him there was no such thing, no telephone was safe. And he'd believed him then just the way he believed him now. But his head was f'n busting, he wanted this call over and done with.

"His name is Ray Velasquez, a real good guy. He works in our office. Lives up in the Bronx, has a wife and a couple of kids. A good guy."

JoJo thinking, I've seen a mob of good guys go down for a lot less reason.

"If he's such a good guy, why can't you talk to him? Put a few bucks on his table, tell him to get himself a new TV or something."

"He's not like that."

"All right, fine, so what do you want me to do?"

"I can't have him working in my office. This is one smart guy, he knows something's not right here. If he gets transferred, you know, time will go by and he'll get into other things."

"Buddy, what do you want me to do?"

"I figured with the people you know, you can, you know, have him moved, transferred. I mean the guy's a super guy, but I don't want to go down in flames because of him."

"What am I for chrissake, the personnel director of the police department? How am I gonna get him transferred?"

"How about your lawyer friend? He's an ex-DA, got all kinds of pull in the department. Somebody like that, they can reach people, have him moved somewhere he can't do no harm. Christ, I don't know."

"Give me his name again." JoJo took a pad and pen from his pocket.

"Raymond Velasquez."

"Where's he live?"

"In the Bronx."

"I need his address," JoJo said.

Jimmy gave him Ray's address and his social security and badge numbers, gave them to him like he was reading it from a pad.

"Okay, fine, fine. I'll see what I can do. Tell me something—don't bullshit me, okay? How big a problem can this guy make for you?"

"If he had a mind to he could fry my ass."

"And you tell me this is a friend of yours?"

"Hey, the guy can't help the way he is. Ray's a superstraight guy is all."

"What's he drive?"

"What do you need that for?"

"C'mon Jimmy, stop fucking around. I got a million things to do. Tell me what this fucking guy drives, I need to know all I can about the man. You want my help here, don't ya?"

"Transferred out of my office, out of my life. Nothing else." There was a long pause before Jimmy said, "He drives a red Jeep."

JoJo flashed on the two teenage girls in the red ragtop and smirked. He wanted to ask Jimmy to be more specific. What time did he leave for work, what time did he get home? Did this guy hang out somewhere, did he have a girlfriend? So he wouldn't take a dollar, maybe he ran around a little. Everybody does that. He wanted as much information as he could get, then figured he had enough with the home address and the car. A red Jeep, who could miss that?

"And JoJo," Jimmy said, "and now I'm saying the truth—"

"Why, before you weren't telling me the truth?"

"You know what I mean. I don't want anything to happen to Ray, he's a friend, a real good guy with a nice family."

Hey, I don't give a fuck, is what he wanted to say. What he did say was, "Jimmy, what do you take me for? I'm not in the business of whacking out cops. You think I'm deranged?"

"No, no, I just want to make sure you understand what I'm asking. Get Ray transferred, get him out of my life."

Speaking as softly as he could, JoJo said, "I understand you Jimmy, don't worry. I'll take care of it, it's done."

JoJo hung up the telephone and stared at his shoes, his guts grinding. Jimmy's goddamn story so f'n familiar, what did the guy expect him to do? He ran all that crap about this and that, this guy Ray is straight as an arrow, a real good guy, a family man. Well who the hell isn't a family man? The creep was probably a bastard with no sense of humor, out mocking people who were trying to make a living, taking people's liberty away, out to screw the world because he didn't have the heart to take what he needed to survive in this bitch of a life. Some guy that would rather take some scrawny-ass paycheck than make a real life for himself. JoJo headed for the car, thinking about Jimmy, about this character Ray, he figured he'd use the Dwarf, have the Dwarf take care of this character Ray Velasquez. Before getting into his brother's car he yawned, stretching, going up on tiptoe, arms high. He glanced at the pad he carried. Tomorrow he would meet the Cuban again, tonight, Bruno and Nicky. F'n Dante O'Donnell and that broad cop following Vinny. What else? Damn, *damn*—what else could be going on that he didn't know?

He decided he'd stop at this Willows joint he passed on the way to the phone booth, he'd stop there and get himself some fish. John told him they had notable fish and chips at this Willows place. Christ, he was in Rhode Island, he should eat some fish and chips, and maybe a beer would be good. He liked this place, this Rhode Island, the way the sun came up around here was pretty, made everything seem tranquil and soft, the sun coming up over the bay, nice.

Dante drove briskly north on I-95 tailing the Mercedes, Kathy doing well to keep up in her T-Bird, telling him for the third time, "We're heading out of our jurisdiction, out of the damn state, it's time to let somebody know what we're doing." It was four o'clock in the afternoon.

When they left Westchester and crossed the Connecticut border he'd radioed the office and, unable to reach Inspector Martin, left a message with a detective by the name of Michael Sweeney, one of the clerical people, telling the guy they were in close pursuit and out of the state.

"Where you going?" Sweeney asked.

"No way to tell exactly," Dante told him. "I think Rhode Island maybe."

"This character you're following, he heads for Canada you'd better call back."

"Where's the boss?"

"Down at the Federal building, got a call and shot out of here like he was riding a rocket."

"Leave a message for him," Dante told Sweeney. "Tell him I'll reach back to him later. Got any idea what he has going with the feds?"

"Naw, he's probably going downtown to have a few pops, I don't figure he'll be back today. I could beep him for you if you want."

"Yeah—no, I'll beep him myself later."

"Ey, you know you need permission to be out of state, you know that don't ya?"

"Close pursuit, buddy. I could follow these guys to the moon if I had to."

Dante slipped into the left lane, got right on the Mercedes's tail, then passed, going to the center lane and back, stepping on it, doing eighty to get by Rapino. Kathy fell in behind the Mercedes. Dante congratulated himself on the move, they had Rapino boxed now, getting high on the camaraderie of the tail, talking to Kathy over the radio. Gradually the pure joy of the chase retreated into absolute concentration, he was convinced that whatever was going down he could handle it, him and Kathy together.

Just north of New Haven, the three cars riding the highway abreast of each other now, Dante looked across at Kathy; she was licking her lips, pop-eyed with excitement. She swung from the right lane, fell in behind him then neatly pulled in behind the Mercedes, Dante fell back. A perfect leapfrog move, the woman was good. Watching Kathy do her stuff he was suddenly swept by a wave of anxiety: he wanted Jimmy to be here with him. On a job like this they hadn't been apart in what, ten years? Their job, sharing this life took precedence over all else. That's the way it was, the way he thought it always would be. Jimmy's recent behavior came back to him like a sharp pain, the excitement of the tail completely evaporating. His buddy, the man closer to him than the brother he never had, was in some deep shit, he knew it, and knowing that, the horrors settled in. When they passed Mystic Seaport and crossed the Rhode Island border he picked up the radio.

"Kathy," he said, "our first out-of-state trip together."

"That's right Dante, for Bogie it was Paris, for us there will always be Rhode Island."

"Play it again, babes."

"Ey, I'm looking forward to playing it for the first time."

"I'm waiting with bated breath. Whoa, hold it, hold it . . . Heads up, what's this now?" The Mercedes slowed and signaled just as they came off the highway, and Vinny pulled over and stopped at a MacDonald's. He got out of the car and went toward a phone booth, turning back and calling out to one of the passengers. Vinny looked as though he were in a hurry;

Dante figured the guy must be calling ahead, telling whomever he was nearby.

Dante and Kathy watched as Vinny Rapino made two phone calls. Hung up, did a little turn-and-spin move, then casually jogged back to the car. Dante was close enough to catch the look on Rapino's face; the guy looked terror-stricken.

————

After his fish and chips, JoJo left the Willows and drove back to his pay phone. He had made up his mind, Jimmy giving him no choice. Like his father, his buddy gave him no options, and the fact that he felt that there were no alternatives cleared his head and steadied his hand.

He wasn't too worried about taking out a cop. Like with dealing in drugs, times and prohibitions had changed, you did what you did to survive and worried about consequences later. He tried three numbers, reaching out for the Dwarf, found him at his girlfriend's apartment, gave Karl the number of the pay phone, and waited for the call back.

"Where you at?"

"In Rhode Island, at my brother's."

"You all right?"

"F'n great is what I am, just f'n terrific. Listen," he told the dwarf, "I've got a piece of work for you." He gave Karl Marx Syracusa the information Jimmy had given him: the cop Ray Velasquez's address, the description of his car, all that was needed.

The dwarf said, "All right, fine."

"He's a cop," JoJo said.

"All right, fine," the dwarf said in Italian.

————

Sitting in Aldo's, an Italian restaurant in Foley Square across the street from the Federal Building, looking into the brown eyes of Frank Russo, the assistant supervising agent in charge of the New York office of the FBI, and sipping an Absolut martini on the rocks, no olive, Inspector Arthur Martin wished three things. He wished that Frank didn't feel it necessary to point out that he himself didn't drink during office hours. He wished that his friend and colleague had better sense than to stare at him with those stony eyes when *he* drank. And he wished he didn't believe what Frank was telling him.

Frank detailed the required hedges. "We" don't know anything for sure and "we" can't be positive until "we" move further on in the investigation. However, "we" have a hombre—Frank liked to use the word *hombre* when he discussed his top agents—one of our best undercover agents, not an informer mind you, an experienced Bureau agent, real close to the Paradisos, and I pray to God the guy's safe.

He lowered his voice as if he were giving up something he had no right to, which, of course, the inspector knew he was. "We" flipped one of Joseph Paradiso's top people and he's been working with us. This character is in the hopper real deep, I can't tell you who he is, but he sits in on most of the family deals. Arthur, he recently told us that Joseph has a cop on the payroll. You very well may have a leak in your office. Joseph Paradiso has been warned—at least, we've been told he's been warned—that he is the target of an investigation.

Feeling a little bite from the martini, Inspector Martin had to force himself to make eye contact with Russo. "Frank," he said, "I hate to break this to you, but you already told me about the informant. I didn't know about the agent, but the informant I knew about."

Frank Russo got a look of slow enchantment on his face. "I did?"

"You know you did."

Frank scratched at the tip of his nose, nodding.

"What makes you think that the leak is in my office? Why not yours?"

Frank spread his hands and smiled. "How did I know you were going to ask that very question? Our source said a cop, he didn't say agent."

Inspector Martin smiled back. "C'mon, cop, agent, same thing as far as these jerks are concerned."

"Okay, a good point. But answer me this; you are working the Paradisos right?"

"Maybe."

"Okay, you have a wiretap on the old man and a bug at the Nestor?"

Inspector Martin went very still.

"Look, I'm taking a hell of a chance, bypassing your internal affairs people, my own chain of command, and a bunch of other bureaucratic horseshit to sit here with you. I'm not even here, right? And do you know why I'm sticking my neck out?"

After a long pause Inspector Martin grunted.

Frank realigned himself in his chair and raised a hand to indicate a shift in focus. "Because you're a good cop, my friend, and I like good cops. You got a turncoat, I want you to be the one to find him."

Frank winked and the inspector nodded. He was beginning to feel sick.

"I nail the guy out from under you, you may as well throw in your retirement papers and head for a dog track in Fort Lauderdale."

Inspector Martin exhaled and rubbed the back of his head. This guy was right.

"Now here's the thing, are you ready for the thing?" Russo asked.

"Keep talking."

"The Paradisos stashed a car in a garage on Fifty-seventh Street. We don't know where they got it, but we understand there's maybe a hundred pounds of drugs in that car."

"So why don't you take it down?"

"I'm letting you do the honors."

"Frank, you hear the story about the three dope-sniffing dogs?" Going on without waiting for an answer, Inspector Martin said, "There were these three narco-trained sniffing hounds, one a New York City police dog, one a New York State police dog, and one a FBI dog. They take these three dogs out into the country and test them. They stash some dope and let the dogs loose one at a time. First the NYPD dog goes off and starts sniffing around this big old tree, he goes round and round, then he starts digging in the dirt like you wouldn't believe, and bingo, up pops a bag of dope. Then they send out the state police dog, he bounds right off to this huge boulder, goes at it like hell, beneath the boulder is another bag of dope. Now it's the FBI's turn. Out prances their dog, he quietly goes round and round. First to the tree and then to the boulder, he circles like some kind of f'n lion down for the kill. The dog circles and circles, then jumps the NYPD dog and the state police dog and fucks them both."

Frank took a long breath. "That's not so funny, Arthur."

"Because you lack a sense of humor."

"For the life of me I don't find anything funny in what I'm telling you. Arthur, I'm trying to do you a favor."

"Why me?"

"Because when I came to this town five years ago everybody told me stay away from the locals, the cops in New York are a bunch of sharks. Then I met you. You didn't bullshit me, you didn't play with me, you didn't glad-hand me and run that typical we'll-work-together bullshit and then never come through. You talked to me straight, you helped me. I never once asked for a favor that didn't happen. Sure I know you hold back, I'm not stupid Arthur. You do hold back some things." Frank raised his hands in exasperation. "You hold some things back because you're good at what you do and you're loyal to your own department. I respect loyalty. It's maybe the only thing I really do respect. You're one of the most decent people I've ever met in this business, and I don't want to see a great career go all to shit because of some bum that works for you."

"I handpick every man and woman that works for me, I have no bums."

"Have it your way. But if I were you, I'd get a warrant for that car in a heartbeat. And I'd start to look real close at my detectives."

"You know, Frank," Inspector Martin said, "in many ways you're special. But still you're a typical FBI agent, you bore the shit out of me. There's nothing solid here. You haven't told me one specific thing about any of my detectives."

The inspector looked at Frank as if for verification, and Frank nodded.

"Okay, you think I have a leak in my office because information about a wire and bug is in the street," Martin went on. "Let me tell you, my friend, wiretaps go through a lot of hands: there's court stenographers, judges' clerks, judges themselves, assistant DAs, telephone company security people. I can keep going. All sorts of people can get access to confidential information; that is not too confidential, if you know what I mean."

Frank tilted his head. "Arthur," he said gently, "our source said a cop, a detective."

Frank was starting to get under the inspector's skin a little, and the feeling was anything but good. In fact, for the inspector this was turning into a bitch of a day, he felt shabby and genuinely miserable about the stories he'd heard. Truth was, he figured Frank might be right on target, and the target was a man he loved like a son. A man with all sorts of money and family problems, the son of a father who too was one hell of a guy, but who turned out to be a thief in his heart. The thought that Dante O'Donnell was some kind of dirty pounded him. The inspector winced, the word *dirty* came to his lips halfhearted and faint, as if it wasn't worth the breath it took to say.

———

Dante cruised along a country road, driving slowly, the Mercedes making the choice for him. He announced to the radio and himself the obvious: "Give them some room, Kathy."

The three cars traveled at a sedate pace for the better part of an hour, passing through farmland; a sign advertised German shepherd pups and fresh eggs. They proceeded by the University of Rhode Island, the Mercedes at a crawl. Dante opened his window and tasted the air, fresh and clean, smelling of freshly cut fields. Further on Rapino slowed to a stop at a traffic light, then hung a right and picked up speed. Now the air through the open window brought a scent both friendly and familiar: they were near the sea.

"Will you look at these houses, Dante," Kathy said dreamily over the radio. "I don't know where we are exactly, but you can bet it's not the Bronx."

The houses were far apart, with well-kept lawns and gardens, and it seemed to Dante that they all had tennis courts. The sea air was unrestrained here and clean, unlike in his contaminated and polluted Jamaica Bay, where the blue crabs, flounder, and clam beds were a long time gone. Rapino turned into a driveway and Dante knew two things for certain: from the back door of that house you would have a short walk to the ocean, and JoJo was here.

The smell of ocean air triggered a memory from when he was a kid maybe eleven years old. He and Jimmy and JoJo would ride their bikes to the Broad Channel bridge at night. They would wait for the tide to go out and then, using flashlights and a long pole with a net attached, they'd fish blue crabs from the pilings near the bridge. At times they stayed on that bridge until the sun came up, filling a bushel basket with glossy blue and white crabs, which they carried back to JoJo's house. JoJo's mother applauded them, and they would bow. He and Jimmy would make it back later in the day for a meal of steamed crabs and pasta and fresh-baked bread. JoJo's mother had a way of looking him up and down and repeating his name over and over. She'd pronounce his name in a way he had never heard before or since.

"Don-tee," she'd say smiling. "A grand name." She'd stare at him, saying, "You are built for pleasure, and for fighting, but you are named for learning and to teach. I hope in your life it's the pleasure that you find."

Dante parked his car across the street from the driveway, remembering, and smiled.

Over the air Kathy said, "Okay, now what?"

She pulled her T-Bird right up behind him and got out with a little bounce and skip. But instead of walking directly to his car, she made a detour to the driveway the Mercedes had gone down. She stood hunched over for a minute, her hands on her hips, staring. The driveway was curved and lined with shrubs and ornamental trees; the house itself was hidden from view. Mushroom lamps were lit. They stood in two long rows, covered in spots with ground ivy.

"Get on back to your car," Dante called out.

Kathy turned her head, "C'mere, take a look at this joint, will ya?"

"Get back in the car, he's here, I know he's here. If JoJo spots you or me, we've taken a hell of a trip for nothing."

Dante wanted to set up away from the driveway, away from the house. He hadn't felt comfortable stopping in front of the house to begin with, and when he spotted the headlights coming up the driveway toward them, he had a real oh-shit moment. Kathy had spotted the headlights too and was back in her car; they both pulled off in a rush. The Mercedes made a left out of the driveway and headed in the opposite direction. Dante gave it a couple of beats, then hung a quick U.

Kathy following called over the air, "I love this."

"Yeah, well, stay behind me. Could be our guy in the car now, we don't want him to spot us."

They moved along Ocean Road in light traffic, one car, a green MG, between them and the Mercedes. The MG turned into a side road and soon there was no one in their lane but the Mercedes, Dante's blue unmarked department Ford, and Kathy's T-Bird.

They tailed the Mercedes to the parking lot of a restaurant called the Coast Guard House, a small, exquisite stone castle of a place with a veranda that overlooked the ocean.

Dante had been on duty now for nearly fourteen hours, still he was keyed up and filled with a dizzying energy. He watched JoJo pop out of the passenger seat as Bruno Greco and Nicky Black Napoli got out of the back. Vinny Rapino stayed behind the wheel of the parked car. Nicky Black walked ahead, followed closely by Bruno. Nicky held the door open for Bruno and JoJo, who was dressed in a jacket and tie and walked slowly behind. There was a rightness in the way the three men moved toward the restaurant, a sort of wiseguy symmetry. As Dante watched, all his longing to nail these guys for something, anything, came clawing back at him. He had a sense that the time was drawing near, they didn't know it yet but these twerps were hang-gliding in his tornado, the clock was clanging, he meant to chain them all and drag them through the street. An easy sort of peace settled over him. Part of him felt like a priest, another part like an executioner—then again, wasn't it Ray that said that the priest and the executioner have always been soul mates.

Dante sat back in his car wondering what JoJo was up to here in Rhode Island. He knew that John, JoJo's brother, lived up here; it was probably John's house they had just left, the guy living like a king on wiseguy money. He drifted off for a moment, thinking, I can't stay with this tail forever. Possibly JoJo was just hanging loose up here. Except his father was gone too, and the wires were dead. Something had happened, JoJo wouldn't have Bruno Greco and Nicky Black here if something wasn't going down. And what about that f'n suitcase? He was resigned to the fact that he was here and was going to stay with it, stay with JoJo till the guy made a move.

Dante was intrigued by what might come out of this surveillance. He hated this job with a deep abiding love, and he'd do it right, always had. That, he knew, was what distinguished him from Jimmy, the love of the job. He'd hunt JoJo down like a wild animal, it was his way; sooner or later he'd hit paydirt. With wiseguys, with all wiseguys, you watch them long enough you're bound to trip over something. Beginning now to imagine himself standing next to JoJo in a courtroom, the guy in his thousand-dollar suit, his hands in cuffs. I'm going to put the hat on all these guys, drop chains on all these Mafia morons. Then we'll see who is the heavyweight champion, JoJo, me or you?

Dante found himself grinning, thinking of Jimmy sitting in the back of the courtroom watching. Thoughts of Jimmy brought a knot of fear to his stomach, and it began to lock on him, he gave himself a moment to calm down. What the hell was it with him, Jimmy, and JoJo? Whatever it was, it wasn't healthy, he knew that. He was no dummy. Only what was it exactly? He could probably give a shrink a year's worth of couch time and still not find out, feeling the ripple of it run through him now.

Dante had spent the last few hours trying to get Jimmy out of his head, keeping busy with the tail and all. He was ninety-nine and nine tenths sure that Jimmy had something to do with the wires going dead. And the odd thing was, he was less angry then he was envious. Dante let that lie there in his head and almost gagged on the thought. Like some kind of fag caught up in a love triangle.

Surprised by the weirdness of his own thoughts, Dante told himself to calm down. But Christ, he knew that if he didn't see or speak to Jimmy every day he almost fell apart. Like when they were kids; when they were teenagers his life was a never-ending game of trying to impress Jimmy. And lately the phone bills for the calls from his house on Long Island to Jimmy's apartment were ridiculous. Some sort of misguided sense of love or hero worship, anyway it sure as hell wasn't good. He shook his head, amazed at how screwed up his life was. Then his beeper went off.

Inspector Martin calling from his home.

Dante lit a cigarette, realizing that it had been hours since he'd last checked in with the office. He imagined laying it out for his boss, trying to defend a trip to Rhode Island, his personal interest in this particular case, getting have-you-lost-it looks in return. He chewed on it for a minute, figuring that it would be better to call the inspector now than to wait until later. But his cellular was acting up, maybe it was the rarified atmosphere of Rhode Island; in any event his car phone was as unusable as the wild thoughts banging around in his head.

The only phone booth he could see was in the restaurant parking lot, and Rapino was sitting in the Mercedes and he didn't want the slick piece of work to spot him.

The inspector wanted to talk to him, his beeper going off again. Shit, he was parked in a perfect spot, a block from the restaurant, the restaurant's door and the parking lot in plain view.

Dante radioed Kathy. In a self-conscious whisper he asked her to do him a favor and see if she could find a pay phone and call for him. "Tell the inspector that we're on JoJo and I don't want to leave. He's been in a situation like this a thousand times himself, he'll understand."

Looking up and down the quiet evening boulevard, he watched Kathy make a quick U and drive off. He smiled and shook his head. F'n Rhode Island, what a kick. Jimmy, where the hell are you? He felt a mixture of fear and anger. Jimmy Burns, with his goofy thoughts and strange ideas about loyalty and friendship, his solitary life, alone in that apartment of his, up to his neck in women and never in love, walking around town in a cloud, defending JoJo Paradiso, for chrissake. Dante flipped his cigarette out the window. He experienced a sizzling buzz of disappointment, not having his best friend and partner with him bugged him like crazy.

CHAPTER EIGHTEEN

It was about seven thirty when Ray Velasquez pushed the loaded cart from the A&P to his Jeep. He was incensed, muttering over and over, "Seventy-five bucks and no meat." No meat, a half week's worth of groceries, milk and eggs, some canned goods, bread and vegetables, four boxes of pasta and tomato sauce, cheeses, those damn cheeses all imported, stuff Sarah couldn't live without. Imported pasta, why imported pasta? Because there is no comparison, she'd said, it's just better. And fruit, fruit cost a mint, grapes and oranges, apples and tangerines, she had to have tangerines and pears. No sweets, no candy for their kids, the girls teeth will cost a lot more to fix than the fruit does to buy. Sarah all the time making sense. And Listerine, mouthwash, he couldn't believe how much mouthwash cost, and forget cranberry juice, not the store brand, the name brand, it was just better. Yeah it was better, sure it tasted superior to the store brand but it cost as much as a bottle of decent French wine, who's kidding who here? Razor blades, now they really are a killer. You want to talk about razor blades, they're like a buck each. Seventy-five dollars gone in a flash, and no meat.

Not that they ate much meat anyway, not with Sarah getting on him with that red-meat-will-kill-you jazz. Loading the bags of groceries into the back of the Jeep, Ray tried to think back on the last time he had a sirloin steak topped with mushrooms and onions, a baked potato sour cream and chives and a good Beck's dark beer, heaven itself. At his sister's house? At his mother's? Or maybe Sarah broke down and made him one? Not that he could remember. Shit, if he wanted a steak that badly he certainly could grab one while working. But you know how much that costs? A righteous steak dinner in an average steak house, we're not talking Peter Lugar's either, just an average place somewhere in the city. It'd be thirty bucks, no doubt about it, thirty bucks easy. Hell he should go for it, a steak dinner, he was eating so much chicken lately he was about to sprout wings.

On the way back to his apartment with the groceries, Ray realized how close he'd come to telling Jimmy Burns what he thought of his bullshit story about Dante's father, JoJo, all that crap. But the man was a guy he had respected and was concerned about. Only how can a guy like Jimmy have anything to do with trash like Joseph Paradiso? Sarah told him, when she sat him down and spoke to him, she told him that the way she saw it, Jimmy was probably doing it out of a sense of friendship and loyalty. But shit, that wasn't good enough. Somebody ought to pull Jimmy's coat. Dante should have, years ago. Somebody should tell somebody about Jimmy Burns, do it for Jimmy's own sake. But here it was again, the dilemma: how do you burn a friend, how do you do it and live with yourself?

And then it came to him, just like that: tell the guy to throw his papers in. Tell him to retire. He had fifteen years in the job, he could get out on a vested-interest pension. At least, Ray thought Jimmy had fifteen years in.

But maybe it would be best to call Dante, tell him the whole goddamn story about his father and all, the whole thing. Christ it was what, twenty years ago? That was it, go right to the source, ask Dante for help. Dante would screw it up, probably go out and get himself bombed for a week or two and kill somebody. Dante could be outrageous. He recalled the day at the Woodhaven Diner, the day Dante went batshit and tried to brain the Greek with an ashtray because he thought the Greek threw him a dirty look.

It would be better to call Inspector Martin. Tomorrow, he told himself, he'd call the inspector and have a sitdown. The man was dynamite, the best, he loved Dante like a son and was a big fan of Jimmy's. Ray couldn't imagine that the inspector would not hear him out in confidence.

Parking the Jeep, Ray did a little preparation, aimed a few discerning, meaningful sentences, coming from the heart, at the bags of groceries, hit home with the inspector, easy does it, no big thing, lay this package in the inspector's lap.

He was carrying three sacks of groceries when he first spotted the two guys walking toward him, they were walking in the gutter, and shit, if they weren't white guys he'd drop the bags and go for his piece, because the way they were coming, for chrissake they looked f'n serious. Two young guys in zippered leather jackets, heavy jackets for this warm night. Oh shit, he said to himself as they turned toward him, wanting to drop the bags and go for his ankle holster, then thought, whataya thinking, you ain't dropping seventy-five dollars' worth of groceries for a pair of guys out walking. Ray was a good twenty feet from his Jeep and maybe ten feet from the pair in the street when they drew guns and started firing at him.

First it was the fright, then the impact and agony of being hit, so sharp and unyielding that Ray howled, seeing flares of light behind his eyelids. The bags of groceries flew into the air, and whatever alertness he still possessed was drawn to the grating burning in the center of his chest. More shots, and Ray felt himself being lifted; he shouted, hearing his own voice inside his head, twelve bullets hitting him in a steady deluge, Ray seeing a corkscrew in his head go from light red to strobes of yellow-green to blazing blue, then nothing but a cosmos of jet black spinning to an infinite point of blazing white.

———————

Vinny Rapino sat behind the wheel of the Mercedes looking out at a tranquil ocean that reflected the lights of the restaurant. He had called Lilo's café earlier and spoken to Lilo's man Punchy, Punchy telling him, hey babe, the man wants to know what you're doing, where you're going, what those people are up to? Vinny asking where was Lilo? Punchy telling him it's none of his business. Punchy known for being an idiot and a slugger like Benny Bats. Vinny told him he'd picked up Bruno Greco and Nicky Black, that he was in Rhode Island, would probably pick up JoJo and bring them all to some restaurant called the Coast Guard House. He figured he'd likely bring them there because Bruno kept talking about the place, saying he loved the fish and chips at the Coast Guard House and liked to sit by a window and look out at the ocean.

Punchy said Yeah, I know the place. Vinny thinking, Yeah? How? Punchy asking what time you figure you'll make it to the restaurant? Vinny was mesmerized, everything charging up into his head, telling Punchy how the hell am I supposed to know? I'm driving where and when they tell me, I got nothing to do with the plans here.

Punchy said, "Shit, they go someplace else you gotta find a way to call me."

"Hey," Vinny said, "hey! Goddamm it, what's going on here?"

"You through? You through?" Punchy said. "You do what you're told, where you come off asking questions?"

Vinny wondered what he had done to get himself into this trick bag. This was a hit, pure and simple, he could see it, feel it coming. What a damn sneaky business this was. And what was worse, he was in the bull's-eye, a f'n target was what he was. For a moment he wondered if it was safe to tell JoJo about his meeting with Lilo, forget that because JoJo could go batty and have Bruno put a bullet up his ass. He'd told Punchy that he'd stay in touch, all the time figuring the best way to take a quick hike out of town. He didn't know where to take it, what to do, so now he sat three hours later wondering if Lilo had already gone to war, bringing Tommy Yale, insane Benny Bats, and a bunch of the others, probably Ralphie, Tommy the Saint, Joey T, all the shooters—all that muscle, shit—if they were going to show here.

He tried to decide: should he get in the wind or hang loose and pick a side when the shooting started. Looking up and down the empty Narragansett boulevard, Vinny was quivering in his two-hundred-dollar tassel-topped loafers. He reached under the seat and touched the butt end of his pistol and felt a little better, not much, just a little. Picking up the gun, feeling the weight of it in his hand, he wondered if he was going to get any older, thinking, what the fuck are you doing here?

———

Only minutes after Kathy had returned from calling the inspector, Dante sat staring at the restaurant's door, at the parking lot, at the Mercedes with Rapino still behind the wheel, and weighed his choices against the clock. Screw it, he thought. Lighting his next to last cigarette, he asked Kathy to run it by him again.

"He said right now, not an hour from now, not tomorrow morning, not fucking Thanksgiving. Now."

"Did he sound as though he meant it?"

"You're kidding me, right? Hey Dante, I never heard the man use foul language before. He never curses, at least in front of me he never curses. He said, 'Right fucking now.' "

Kathy talked and Dante listened, he nodded his head once in a while with barely concealed weariness, trying to hold it together. This woman and her chatter. He glanced at her, the wide face, button nose, no makeup at all, full full lips and thick eyebrows, eyebrows that he figured maybe she should pluck at least once in a while, looking at her closely now, wondering again what it would be like to live with her full-time. She was so damn hyper, full of energy, the kind of woman you'd want to set up housekeeping with if you lived on the prairie or maybe in a deep forest, strong as a man but sexy too, boylike a little—correction, a lot. Yakking, always yakking, with those big blue eyes staring at him, he wondered just what she was thinking when she thought of him.

"The inspector wants to know what we're doing in Rhode Island. He wants to know where Jimmy is exactly," she said, sounding amused. "He said he never pages you, but when he does he expects to be called." Kathy was rapping on the dashboard. "I wanted to tell him about the cars I saw. I wanted to tell him about the suitcase and Rapino picking up Greco and Nicky Black, I wanted to explain what we were doing here, but he wouldn't let me."

"What did you want to tell him for?" Dante said, sounding only mildly concerned. "He already knows about the suitcase, I talked to him about the suitcase this afternoon."

Kathy reached for the pack of cigarettes. "I stopped smoking two years ago."

"That's good, because that's my last one. Put it back. Now tell me again about the cars."

"Goddammit." Kathy threw the pack back onto the dash in disgust. "And you ain't gonna call the inspector, right?"

"We could have front row seats to a Mafia war in about five minutes. I'll call him later. The cars, Kathy."

"Okay, I'm driving all over this town looking for a phone booth, right, and I'm noticing these cars with New York plates. Maybe four, five cars parked along the avenue two blocks from the restaurant. I'm thinking, no big deal, plenty of New Yorkers come up to Rhode Island in the summer, right? Except it ain't summer, Dante, it's spring."

"Where'd you see Lilo?"

"About two blocks from here, parked in his Lexus with three guys, I couldn't make out their faces. Lilo was in the driver's seat, there was someone next to him and two guys in the back seat. I pulled right up alongside his f'n car, stared him right in the face, the guy turned and looked at me. I got so tense that I smiled at him and the greasy bastard stuck out his tongue and wagged it at me. Greasy bastard."

Kathy let it hang, and Dante waited.

"I grabbed the numbers of two other cars with New York plates and ran them. One comes back to Frank Catalano, a Sheepshead Bay address—"

"Whoa! Catalano, Frank Catalano? You sure?"

Kathy's eyes got wide, gravely curious. "Why? What? Who is Catalano? Frank Catalano, that's how it came back."

"I'll tell you in a minute. Go on, what about the second car?"

"It came back to a Mary Ricci, a Third Street address in Brooklyn, the four-hundred block. That's South Brooklyn."

"Christ!"

"What? What? Jesus Christ, you're making me crazy, what's going on here?"

Dante looked around; for effect he rubbed his chin with his palm. "We stumbled into something here."

"Yeah, yeah, what, *what* did we stumble into?"

"Calm down, will you. Let me think a minute."

Thirty seconds passed.

Kathy said, "Tell me what you're thinking, or are you going to keep it a secret?" She gave Dante an optimistic smile. He looked into her eyes, then shit, his pager went off. He glanced down, saw the inspector's home number flashing up at him.

"I don't know who Mary Ricci is, but Benny Bats Ricci is Lilo's main slammer, his main hit man. A total maniac, a real f'n wild man." Dante sat with his hands clasped in his lap. "Okay, so you figure he's with Lilo, Lilo's out doing some hunting. The kicker is Catalano. Frank Catalano is a *caporegime* in the Rammino family. Lilo's bringing outside help here, I figure he's bolted to theRamminos."

Kathy looked distracted, more than a little anxious. She crossed her arms over her chest. "Was that page the inspector again?"

"Yeah, it's the inspector, I'll call him later."

"Later?"

"I'll call, don't worry, I'll call him."

Dante thought about Lilo and Benny Bats, two of the most feared people anywhere. And the bums deserved to be. A lot of wiseguys talked bad—he'd been listening to them on wiretaps and bugs, following them around for thirteen years, gonna kill this guy, gonna whack that guy, gonna clip that guy—but the real thing was scarce. Lilo and Benny Bats were the real thing. He was never able to figure guys like that, real f'n demons, between the two of them, if someone asked who was worse he'd call it a tie.

But Frank Catalano was a whole other thing, the guy was an important capo with the Rammino family, a drug dealing family, a family the Paradisos stayed clear of.

Kathy was smiling as if she had some great news, extending her hands out in front of her face. "This is no hit," she said. "There's not going to be any war here. What we got going is a meeting, a sitdown."

"Maybe."

"No, no, no—listen. You're gonna go and take out three guys in another state, would you bring your own car? I mean, Lilo Santamaria is one ugly, bad son of a bitch, but he ain't stupid."

"Right Kathy, right, that makes sense." Dante cocked his head as if he were teasing. "Now," he said, "do you want to take a wild guess and tell me why you think those two vans just pulled up and parked across the street."

Dante took his binoculars from under the seat and was able to see quite clearly two men in the front seat of the white van, and in the blue van parked directly behind the white, a driver and Benny Bats in the passenger seat.

"Oh Dante, man, c'mon. You're kidding me aren't you?"

"No I'm not kidding. Benny Bats is a passenger in that blue van. I can't place the others."

"Shit!"

"Well said."

"C'mon Dante, what're we gonna do?" Kathy's face was full of confusion and not a little panic.

"I'll tell ya what you're gonna do. First you're going to listen to me and calm down. Stop acting like some kind of crazed broad, you're a cop, goddammit, an experienced detective." That wasn't nice, he could have said it in a different way. A simple "Cool down, partner" wouldn't have been too bad. Except, he thought, if she were a man she'd be less anxious, panicky, and crazed. There was no way he could work with a woman full-time.

"C'mon, c'mon Dante. What are we going to do?"

"Can't you chill out and relax a minute?" he snapped as he started up his car.

"Do you know what I think?" she said. "I think we should call the cops." Her manner changing, now strangely casual, like she hadn't a care in the world. "Why can't we ask the local cops for help?"

"Think so?"

"Why not?" Kathy went on, saying she was pretty confident they could get help without too much trouble, because what cops wouldn't love to jump a bunch of Mafia shooters?

Dante listened, and when she finished he sat in silence, looking at the vans silhouetted by a streetlight, a cement barrier wall and the ocean just beyond. As the door of the blue van opened and the driver got out, Dante ran down in his head a list of Rhode Island cops he'd met at an organized-crime conference.

Shit, the driver standing next to the van had a walkie-talkie in his back pocket. These guys were very serious.

The Rhode Island cops he'd met seemed to know their stuff, talking about wiseguys from off a hill somewhere in Providence. But they were Providence cops, no help in this town. At the same conference he'd met a Rhode Island state trooper, but he couldn't remember the guy's name. Cawley, Connelly, something like that. A huge Irish guy with a crew cut, spent the day of the conference off by himself meditating.

Dante could see without even trying that they had a serious problem here. They were alone, out of their jurisdiction, and in those vans there could easily be six, seven shooters. If they hung around and did nothing they could find themselves in the middle of a crossfire. He leaned his temple against the window and stared out at the parking lot and restaurant.

"Your cellular working?"

Kathy grunted softly but Dante couldn't tell whether she meant yes or no.

Kathy said, "Wait a minute . . ."

Vinny Rapino started up the Mercedes, backed out of the parking lot, and took off.

"Okay," Dante said, "this must be it. Your cellular working?"

"Sure."

Dante shut off his ignition, opened the car door, and began to get out.

"Where you going?" Kathy said, "Get back in here."

"Go to your car and call nine-one-one, get the locals. Tell them you're up here on surveillance, tell them your partner needs some help."

"Where the hell do you think you're going? You're not leaving me here." Kathy turned in her seat, struggling to open her door.

Dante felt a surge of impatience. "Please, just do what I tell you to do. I'll only be a minute."

Kathy made a face. "Are you nuts?"

Touched by her sincerity, Dante couldn't help smiling.

"Nuts, yeah I'm nuts. That's me, nutty Dante, probably always have been a little cracked. I'm a shitty father, a worse husband, a terrible son, and lousy friend. Nevertheless, I think of myself as a good cop. That's all I got going for me. I'm not going to sit here and watch JoJo—or anyone else for that matter—get blown away and not do something. I've got to do something, it's what I do. Something is what I do."

"I'm going with you."

"Like hell you are. You'll do what I ask and get us some backup."

"Sure." Kathy nodded, as if settling an argument with herself that Dante was not privy to. "But if you get hurt in there, I'll kill you," throwing him a faint courteous smile.

———

JoJo sat at a round table in the far corner of the restaurant, the wall to his back, a picture window on his right, through which he had a sensational view of the sea. Nicky Black sat opposite him, and Bruno beside him. He'd been sitting there for close to an hour barely touching his lobster dinner, talking nonstop, going over things with Nicky and Bruno. He'd canceled out both Nicky and Bruno as possible traitors. He never cared much for Nicky, hated the fact that he ran around with this Cuban broad on his sister, always dressed like a f'n guinea gangster, and talked out of the side of his mouth like some Hollywood goodfella. But the guy was his brother-in-law, and in truth he knew Nicky's every move. Nicky wouldn't turn on him, his world was too small a place to hide if he did. And Bruno, Christ, Bruno was such an old-timer, the guy would cut his wrists before he became a stool pigeon. His list was growing smaller, he'd already eliminated the Dwarf, that piece of work with the Puerto Rican cop was proof. And as far as that particular job was concerned, he'd never mention it again. Like he never heard of the guy, wouldn't talk to the dwarf or anybody else about it.

When he brought up the subject of Luis, the Cuban connection, JoJo watched Nicky closely, measuring the level of his concern over a prohibited drug move, deciding that he had none, which didn't surprise him too much, since it was obvious that Nicky worried little about the rules and wouldn't dare to second-guess him. He talked about his scheduled meeting the following day with Luis in Providence, about Lilo arranging the sitdown with Armond Rammino, and finally about the tip he'd gotten about the informer.

Nicky cursed the stool pigeon, saying I'd like to strangle the bastard, you know what I mean, I mean with my own two hands I'd like to rip his throat out. Then he went on about too many new recruits, never mentioning a name or making an assumption. When Bruno said he'd never put a rat jacket on Lilo, but still, he didn't trust the guy, Nicky announced that he would like to shove Lilo's head up the guy's own mother's ass. He said this out of the side of his mouth, talking cool and bad, giving JoJo a case of the creeps. Nicky had a way with words, describing Lilo as a scummer, a creep, a no good son of a fence-jumping bitch.

Bruno pointed out that it would be wise to watch Lilo close now. "Can you figure a better time for him to make his move with the Rammino's? I mean, if that's what he's got planned. The guy always bothered me but didn't bother me, if you know what I mean."

"Excuse me, JoJo," Nicky Black said, "Can I say something?"

JoJo shrugged.

Nicky rolled his shoulders and pulled at his crotch. "Why, with all the goodfellas we got hanging around, you give a kid like Vinny, Lilo's man, the break to drive you? I mean, we got good kids who'd give their right arm to do that."

"Mind your own business, Nicky," JoJo said.

"Sure," Nicky said, and went back to his chowder.

"He's doin' the kid a favor, you know your brother-in-law, he likes doin' favors," Bruno said.

"Yeah, well let me tell you something, Bruno," Nicky said. "Sometimes it's rough out there, and it's nice to get a tap on the head from the boss. Ya know, like, hey kid you're doin' a good job, something like that."

"I'm gonna give you a tap on the head you don't shut up," JoJo said.

———

Buzzed, chock full of energy, Dante walked along the seawall toward the Coast Guard House, his head throbbing with images of things to come. Each time he thought about JoJo he would sooner or later see Jimmy, arms folded, standing in the back of a courtroom shaking his head, and it was the last thing he wanted to think about. He took his gun from off his hip and slipped it into his jacket pocket, making himself relax. For the first time Dante was aware of the noise of waves breaking over rocks. It surprised him that when he purposely listened to the sound of the sea it was so loud.

He went through the restaurant door and on toward the main dining room, passing an oval mahogany bar crowded with well-dressed drinkers, a flock of them standing at the bar, men and women in soft conversation, unaware of the tense guy with the pistol in his pocket who was wondering what it was going to be like when JoJo spotted him. JoJo was sitting there at the best table in the joint in his blue blazer and silk tie, a lobster dinner in front of him, chatting with two of his henchmen. Say to JoJo, ey buddy, I've come for that meal you promised, and by the way, real soft so that no one could hear, there's about a dozen greaseballs waiting outside for you to leave, because when you do, they're gonna blow you and your friends' here asses up.

JoJo said, "Well look who's here? I don't fucking believe it."

Bruno was squinting at him, his mouth tight, looking around as if Dante were the lead man of a hit squad. Nicky in his black turtleneck sweater, black slacks, and black shirt stared at him like he was the Angel of Death.

"Are you hungry?" JoJo said.

"Starving, I can never find the time for a real meal. I'm not you, a man without a care in the world, able to sit down with good company and chitchat, drink a little wine, eat some lobsters. I've got no time for that."

"But who is this guy?" Nicky said.

"An old friend of mine from the neighborhood. Dante O'Donnell, meet my brother-in-law Nick Napoli, and this here is Bruno."

"You're not going to believe this, but I actually know who these guys are."

"From the neighborhood, huh? A neighborhood guy? I never seen ya," Nicky said.

"I've seen you."

JoJo said, "He's a cop."

"A cop from the neighborhood?" Bruno raised his eyebrows as if for verification and smiled.

"That's me, just a neighborhood guy that became a cop."

"An old street-running buddy," JoJo said.

"That was then, this is now," Dante said.

"Ey," JoJo said, "Once a buddy always a buddy. What are you doing up here? What brings a city guy like you to the sticks?"

Dante watched JoJo sitting there all smiles, his famed teeth aglow in his tan face. Dante was so goddamn uncomfortable, his stomach doing a flipflop routine, and there was a noise in his head like a helicopter dropping in for a landing. He was thinking that he just decided that he had nothing to say to JoJo, why the hell was he doing this? He should turn and walk out, let Lilo have him. He hated the guy with a passion, but why, exactly? JoJo was a wiseguy, but there were a million wiseguys, and most of them a whole lot further down on the human being ladder than JoJo. Maybe it was that goddamn smile when he was guilty of so much bad shit, but then he thought, we're all guilty of something. So maybe JoJo didn't deserve his hatred, but what did that have to do with it?

"I came to do you a favor," Dante said, looking away.

JoJo jerked his shoulders indifferently. "I bet," he said.

That's when they heard the sirens and a whooper. Patrons at other tables stood to look out the windows; two men from the bar went toward the door.

"I hope that racket's got nothing to do with me," JoJo said.

"It's got everything to do with you." Dante smiled at JoJo, feeling good.

"You're kidding me, right?"

Bruno lit a cigarette and Nicky stood up. Three tables away, a man who looked like he polished his silver hair, wearing a soft white sweater, an older man with a tanned unlined face, with a gorgeous young head at his side, left the room.

Dante squinted at the man, then slowly turned to JoJo. "I figure we all got our time to go. I believe that tonight's just not your time."

JoJo looked instantly aroused. "Yeah, well, I don't think any of us got a contract for forever, if you know what I mean."

Bruno eyeballed Dante with a half crazy look on his face, like in about a second he was going to leap up and grab him by the throat.

"Are you here looking for trouble?" Bruno said. "Because if it's trouble you want—"

In Italian, JoJo side-mouthed, "Easy, easy." To Dante he said, "You know you walk in here like it's Dodge City or something. No hello JoJo, how are you? how've you been? You're not polite, Dante. I'm going to tell you something, you always had a deficiency in the manners department. Maybe it's the way you were brought up. Ever think about that, that maybe the way you were brought up wasn't normal? Politeness," JoJo said. "You ever hear the word?"

Dante straightened up, gave him all his attention, like he alone had the power. His brain screaming *screw this guy, screw this guy, let Lilo take him out!*

"You want to tell me what's on your mind," JoJo said in a hushed voice. "Or you want to join us for dinner?"

Silence from Dante.

"You got something to say, I think you should say it," JoJo said.

Dante looked at him hard. JoJo nodded slowly, his eyes going back and forth between Bruno and Nicky Black.

"I was just thinking about you and the way *you* were brought up."

"Oh yeah?" JoJo said, looking away.

Silence again from Dante.

JoJo said, "So?"

"I figure that maybe you had no options, no other way to go. They told you life was wild, put those guns in your hands, and said this is the way it's gotta be. Maybe you're just another victim, like everybody else. Then I figure, nah."

JoJo shot him that grin again, that f'n smile of his, saying, "You don't

get it do ya? Just like your old man you got a head like a f'n rock. I'm
nobody's victim. If anything, between me, you, and the wall here, I create
victims."

"What the hell do you know about my father?"

"A whole lot more than you, you dunce."

JoJo stared at him for a long moment the silence framed by Bruno's
and Nicky Black's heavy breathing. Dante folded his arms, thinking you
know more about my father than I do? Phony bastard. And you question
why you hate this son of a bitch.

Dante said, "See, what you probably did, you probably created one
victim too many, smartass. And now you'll go down in flames. Tonight you
lucked out, but there's always tomorrow, or the next day, or maybe the day
after that. Your day'll come. It's only a matter of time."

"Enough, cop," Bruno said. "You've said your piece, now beat it."

Dante looked into Bruno's face, the guy's eyes so wide and fired with
an anger that was beyond Dante's understanding. Dante smiled at him, it
was a nice smile meant to inform, like, just try me.

Bruno took a long pull on his cigarette, too pissed off to be careful
anymore. "Ey, tough guy," he said. "Don't think that badge you got is a
bulletproof vest."

Surprised by the fury building in his chest, Dante rocked back and
forth, thinking about JoJo and Jimmy, about JoJo's naming his father—what
could the shithead know about his old man he didn't? He turned on Bruno.
"You know something Bruno?" Dante said. "You scare the shit out of me."

Bruno grunted.

"Hey Bruno," Dante said. Bruno didn't answer. He looked past Dante,
out toward the bar. "I hope you're up to date on your life insurance, got
the wife and kids all taken care of, you know. You too Nicky. Cause you're
both gonna need it. Your boss here's made some enemies, and I don't think
they're gonna take prisoners. At least, not you two half-a-humps."

Dante could see the growing anger in JoJo's face, JoJo knowing Dante
was getting to these two. He sighed, forcing himself to be cool, wondering
himself how far he was prepared to take this.

"Go," JoJo said. "Beat it while you can still walk out of here."

"Ey, JoJo," Nicky Black said, "whyn't ya let me take care of this guy?
Teach him a little respect."

That did it, Dante's adrenaline shot right up through his head. "You
skinny greaseball," he said, "get up, why don't ya? and I'll knock you into
the next f'n state."

Nicky bared his teeth and shot Dante a deadly glance.

JoJo folded his arms across his chest, sat back in his chair, and laughed a small laugh, but a laugh just the same. "You asshole, you never change. You sit still, Nicky, don't get up, because this guy will knock you down. Then I'll have to shoot my old buddy. Dante look," JoJo said, almost pleading, "will you take a hike before you really do piss me off?"

He pushed his chair back and began to rise. Dante reached across the table and poked him. A little poke, no big thing. JoJo lost his balance and fell back into his seat, throwing back his arms as he sat down, expecting to get exactly what he got. Bruno and Nicky Black jumped to their feet. Dante's hand went into his jacket pocket, and for a moment he flashed on shooting them all right here, right now. JoJo grabbed Bruno's jacket and Nicky's sweater and pulled them back down into their seats.

"Sit down, you dumbos, that's exactly what he wants. Don't give him what he wants." Then JoJo seemed to rise within himself, losing it for a moment, flying past them all and jumping to a place, his own wacky land, the region where he was king. "There's gonna be another time, another place," JoJo hissed. "Not here. Behave yourselves."

Dante was prepared to keep on pushing, get it out, go for it right here, but he saw that psychotic look in JoJo's eyes and stopped: otherwise he would have to kill him. When JoJo lost it there was no way to stop him short of a bullet in his head. And he was right, JoJo was right, this was not the place.

Dante yawned and stretched. "I'm outta here JoJo," he said.

"About fucking time," JoJo said.

"But before I go, I want to acquaint you with some facts."

"For chrissake," Bruno said.

"Let him talk, let him finish and get the hell out of here. That's all this guy was ever good for, bullshit, bullshit, and more bullshit. Go on," JoJo said. "Say your piece and then you'd better go, because I'm telling you, Dante, I've had your shit to here. You don't know how lucky you are."

"Hey, no problem," Dante said, spreading his hands. He was enjoying this. "There's a crew waiting for you," he said, and threw his thumb over his shoulder. "Out there, out in the street, and they're figuring what to do with your ashes. I tell you JoJo, you must be one important guy, all these people coming up from New York just to see you."

Bingo. The three of them turned in their seats, staring as if they could see the street through the walls of the restaurant. Dante felt good—better than good, he felt terrific. He thought for a moment that he finally had JoJo, he loved watching that slick smile fade.

"Like who?" Nicky said.

"Shut up," said JoJo.

"You three heroes know an ugly little creep named Lilo Santamaria? What about another shithead by the name of Benny Ricci, and—this one will kill ya—how about Frank Catalano?"

Dante let it float out. JoJo, Nicky Black, and Bruno were riveted.

"I figure those characters got a good reason to be here in Rhode Island. Right? It's a free country, people can go and do what they want."

"The fuck you talking about," Nicky Black said.

Dante said, "JoJo those guys are perched out in front of this place, I figure your future is in doubt. Tonight I made it my business to make sure you didn't get spattered all over the front of this restaurant, but next time, who knows?"

JoJo said nothing, his mouth fixed in a small smile. Dante felt as though he were talking to a man made out of wood. "Another thing," Dante said. "You might want to tell the cops outside about your stolen Mercedes."

Nicky Black was bug-eyed and muttering. Bruno and JoJo sat still as stone.

"Your boy took off in your Mercedes about twenty minutes ago. You got no wheels—but maybe you know that."

"Son of a bitch," Bruno said.

Nicky hissed, "The little rat fuck." He was shaking.

JoJo put a hand on Nicky's arm. Someone in the bar played Natalie Cole's "Nature Boy."

"Can that woman sing or what?" JoJo said, cool and calm. To Dante the guy was f'n mystical.

"Great, but not as good as the father," Dante said. "The second generation has a bitch of a time measuring up to the original."

"Yeah. Right. You're probably right." JoJo nodded, took a second, then smiled at him. "Buddy, who knows that better than you?"

"Ey, JoJo I ain't your buddy."

"Ey, Dante I've know that for thirty years. Now do me a favor, you've ran this boring game of yours out. Now go and take a fucking walk. I wanna eat my lobster."

"Your world is blowing up, asshole. And I love the idea that I'm gonna be around to watch it go all to shit."

JoJo and Dante looked at each other.

JoJo said. "What did I ever do to you to deserve all this affection?"

Dante winced and looked away, thinking about that. He looked back at JoJo, caught that sneaky smile. "Hey," he said, holding up his hand, "you live in your neck of the woods, I live in mine. In your life you've made something of yourself, but what you've made is my natural enemy." Dante found himself thinking of Jimmy, how his partner defended this piece of shit. He folded his arms, looking at JoJo and feeling an obscure ripple of curiosity and some envy. A firing squad waiting for him a hundred feet away, and the man cracks open a lobster claw and starts eating.

"You're a bad guy, a stone criminal, all you know is gimme." Dante sighed. He was getting real tired of hearing himself talk. "You ain't changed in thirty years. You weren't some black kid from the ghetto fighting for survival. You had choices, and you made 'em, made yourself my enemy."

JoJo nodded his head, but Dante couldn't tell what he meant by it.

Dante said slow and easy, "You're a sneaky one-way fuck, always have been. You never had the balls to do what you ask people to do for you." Then he gave the table a small wave, said, "See you guys around the neighborhood," and turned and walked out of the restaurant.

———

Police flashers lit the scene red and blue, and the avenue was alive with cops, uniformed officers and some in civilian clothes. The crowd and the noise surprised him, Kathy must have put out a call for all the cops in Rhode Island. For a while he stood out in front of the restaurant taking in the party. Two uniformed cops walked past him. One said to the other, "That smartass needed his bell rung." A party for sure.

Spotlights were trained on the vans, and the men from those vans, all shooters, stood in handcuffs, squinting into the headlights of the police cars. Dante counted twelve men in cuffs. There may have been more, cruisers were arriving, loading the prisoners, taking them off to the local station house, where he figured the desk officer must be doing backflips having to deal with all this work.

Cops with flashlights searched under and around both vans, and there were radio sounds cracking on and off from the police cruisers and from walkie-talkies. All of the cops wore bulletproof vests, some carried shotguns and automatic shoulder weapons. It was all highly efficient.

Looking among the police cars for Kathy, he lit his last cigarette and searched the night. JoJo's words came back at him, what the hell had JoJo meant, talking about his father? *I know more than you.* Then the radios and walkie-talkies were silent and he could hear the ocean, the sea crashing onto rocks. There was no moon, no stars in a sky ablaze with flashing police lights.

Kathy came out of the lights shouting his name like she was trying to warn him out of the path of an oncoming train. "Dante!" she screamed, "Dante, they shot Ray, Ray's dead!"

Dante stood frozen, his hand locked around the gun in his jacket pocket. He said the name to himself and then out loud, "Raymond," not feeling, not knowing, everything coming at him in brilliant light now, JoJo's face, Jimmy, his father, Raymond—that great laugh—Raymond.

CHAPTER NINETEEN

Vinny Rapino attempted to drive away the fear with speed, tromping on the gas pedal, hitting eighty, then ninety miles an hour, going north in the Mercedes toward Boston. The fingers of one hand drummed a cadence along the dash, he was dazed, so fearful he thought he'd puke. A sensation of powerlessness forced him to ask questions of himself as he went, the answers to which confused him even more.

He had always thought of himself as a slick guy, a man on the move, a rising star. "Shit!" he yelled at the windshield, then slapped himself in the head with the heel of his hand. He was, at that moment, a loner, off on his own, he'd skipped out on his boss, and his boss's boss. He'd challenged the both of them, told them both to get fucked. So now they would come for him, Lilo and JoJo too would come for him and kill him. If they didn't kill each other first.

He wasn't about to count on that. No more than he could count on being allowed to explain himself, his running off, his taking a hike. Vinny's heart was beating fast, and his cheeks were burning. For as far back as he could remember, his life had been governed by rules that were to be followed. And he'd ignored them, all of them and now he'd earned himself a shot in the head. Of that, and only that, he was certain. Sinatra's "My Way" filled the car, he turned up the volume thinking about where to go what to do. He figured he'd head north and find a motel, hotel, anyplace where he could hide and try to put the pieces together. Outside of Providence he slowed to the speed limit, wondering how far he could get on three hundred dollars cash and a couple of credit cards. Pretty far, he figured. Where, was the question: where could he go?

For days he had seen it coming, nothing was hidden. And so now he fled, his mind bursting in a confusion of murderous faces and recalled threats. He had thought he could figure these people and somehow snake through, keep a toe in both camps and somehow survive. But everything just came down too quick. No time to think out a good move. He knew that if he hung around that restaurant he had almost no chance of staying alive. Vinny stared at the nighttime highway. If Lilo didn't get him, JoJo would. Everything told him that he had to beat it, and maybe, just maybe, if he could put enough distance between himself and the coming shitstorm he'd be all right. Canada sounded good, it had a nice secure ring to it. About fifty miles north of Boston he pulled into a roadside motel and was pleased to find that the place had a lounge. A bright green sign announced TOPLESS DANCERS.

JoJo finished his lobster, told Bruno and Nicky to sit tight, and went over to the restaurant's door and looked out. Cops everywhere. It was interesting, groups of three and four cops getting into it among themselves, gesturing, one pointed to the restaurant. He saw Dante and the policewoman he'd met at Chaplin's in close conversation, the woman, it seemed to him, was shaken. Dante stood with his shoulders hunched, head down, nodding as he listened to her. Standing nearby listening, a uniformed cop covered with bars and gold braid like some kind of South American general looked from Dante and the woman cop to the restaurant's door. He seemed poised for battle. His hands on his hips, shaking his head, a solemn expression—My God that's terrible—on his face. He appeared to be waiting to make a move, wanting to get into the action himself.

JoJo went to find a pay phone. He telephoned John; no answer. That was not a good sign, not a good sign at all. He had told John to wait at home to take messages. He expected a call from the dwarf and from Jimmy, and from the rat bastard Lilo, who would not be calling him anytime soon. Lilo, he thought, Lilo you made your move, and now we roll it up and go to war. He leaned against the wall and went off into his thoughts, thinking about how he would hit back at Lilo and Yale. Suddenly he was anxious to be out of there, away from the restaurant, eager to be back at John's house. Lilo could have sent people there too, sent people to his brother John's house. He was amazed at how frightened he became thinking about John.

JoJo went back to the dining room, catching the eye of his waitress and asking for the check. Fifty dollars would cover it; he gave the woman two hundred-dollar bills and said, "Is there a back door to this place?"

She was a middle-aged woman with delicate girllike features. A little too much blush on her cheeks and a bit heavy with the lip gloss, but there was a soft, warm friendly look about her. Her hands were clasped in front of her.

"Can you swim?" she said.

"Sure, I could swim to France if I had to." Sounding like he meant it, speaking with more confidence than he actually felt. "Seriously, is there a way out without having to go through the front door?"

She whirled her finger in a little circle. "The cops are all around this place."

"I can see that."

The waitress stared at him in a cagey way for a long moment.

"I need a way out of here and I need a lift. There's three more of those hundreds if you can help me."

The waitress didn't answer. She frowned down at herself and brushed her uniform.

"Listen, I need some help here."

"You shouldn't bother busy people who aren't bothering you."

JoJo shook his head and looked around the restaurant. He caught a glance from Bruno that was more curious than concerned.

The waitress shrugged. "I can't afford any trouble. Besides, they got the parking lot blocked off, and that's where I have my car."

JoJo squinted as though in pain. "I've got to get out of here. And I don't need any long conversation with those cops, and that's all they want from me, a long conversation. I give you my word, I have no problem with them, it's just a long conversation they want, and I don't have the time. Help me out, will ya?"

"Where's your car? And your friends, what about them?"

"I don't have a ride. As for my friends, they can hang out here awhile, have a few drinks at the bar, enjoy the nightlife. It's only me that needs the help."

The waitress held her hands apart about six inches. "In my life," she said with a nice warm smile, "I have about this much trouble. A man looks, acts like you, can give me this much." She spread her arms wide and made little circles with her hands. "Believe me I know."

JoJo was disappointed, but it sounded honest. He needed out of the f'n joint, he needed to get back to John's. Make sure his brother was okay. He'd offer her more money if it was money she wanted, but he wasn't sure.

"Ey, from me you'll never get trouble. From me you'll only get gratitude and appreciation."

The woman laughed incredulously. "Ey," she said, "from someone like you sweet thing, I would get nothing but bad luck."

"Oh yeah, so how come you're still here talking to me?"

"It's the smile. Call me sucker, it's always the smile."

She studied him thoughtfully as though on the point of decision. JoJo looked into her eyes. They were dark brown, near black, with long dark lashes. When she spoke, she stroked her jaw with the back of her thumb. She had long, well-taken-care-of fingernails. And she smelled good, a familiar perfume, his wife Nancy's perfume, and it wasn't cheap.

"All right, go into the men's room," she said. "It's down the hall there. Go in and wait for me."

"Sounds like fun, but to tell you the truth, I've no time to play. I need out of here." He shot her his best grin.

"Just go into the men's room. Lock the door. When I'm ready I'll knock three times."

"You're putting me on?"

It was almost funny. Likely it could be real funny. He stared at the woman in amazement.

"Go," she said. "I'll be with you in a minute."

"Say, what's your name?"

"Esperanza."

"Hope. That's what Esperanza means. It fits you."

"And you, what's your name? No, wait, wait, don't tell me, I'll probably recognize it and catch a heart attack."

"You never heard of me, honey. I'm nobody important. Let me explain something to you so you understand. See, you probably think I know what's going down outside. I don't. Whatever it is, it has nothing to do with me. But I got bad luck of all kinds, and if I run into a nasty, wanna-make-trouble cop, I could have a small problem."

"Sure," Esperanza said after a moment. She walked off a few steps, turning to look back at him.

JoJo sauntered over to the table to tell Bruno and Nicky his plans.

Nicky staring at him with all the menace he could muster. Bruno sucked air through his teeth and sat rubbing his arms.

"We gotta hit 'em fast," Nicky said. "Get the dwarf and Rudy with his people. We gotta hit 'em fast and make 'em pay for this treachery."

"They'll pay," Bruno said.

"Big time," said Nicky.

"Through?" JoJo said. "You guys through? Now I want you to listen to me."

JoJo couldn't explain his feelings, not to himself, not to Bruno, certainly not to this blockhead Nicky Black. But he felt like he was about to do something great, he was going to boot ass, like he just hit the lottery and was throwing money around the street, and everyone was watching, cheering, calling out his name. There was a haunting, bitter, alarming, undeniable sense of excitement bursting in him, the likes of which he had never felt. He was a wartime boss, and he would lead the family into battle. It was f'n great.

"You'll both stay here till this heat clears. The cops haven't come in yet to snatch us, but they will. When they do, you'll go with them, you'll do what you gotta do."

Nicky waved at the wall. "Lilo's out there, you believe that? Lilo and Benny Bats and probably that ass kisser Tommy Yale, he's out there too."

JoJo nodded, thinking the kid Vinny set me up. Couldn't be any other way.

"And Rammino's man," Nicky said, "that shithead Catalano, he's loading up with them. They got a f'n army in the street here."

"Won't help 'em," Bruno said. "They blew it, and now they'll pay."

"I wanna be there when Lilo goes down, I wanna piss on his grave," Nicky said as he lit a cigarette.

JoJo put his hand over his heart. "God as my witness, on my mother's grave, I'm gonna crush these bastards once and for all. Show 'em who they're fuckin' with."

Bruno smiled, and Nicky Black cracked his knuckles.

"Okay," JoJo said. "We need to reach Rudy. Where is he anyway?"

The Dancer, Rudy Randazzo, was another of JoJo's capos. He had a crew of fifty men and operated out of an auto wrecking yard in Mill Basin. The Dancer was a shrewd piece of work, kept a low profile and ran a separate bookmaking, hijacking, loansharking, and car theft operation. His territory was western Queens on the Brooklyn border. He was crucial because his people were mostly young, rough and greedy crazies out of Bensonhurst and Sheepshead Bay who knew Lilo and Yale, the places they hung out, where they could be found. For some time now JoJo had been considering putting the Dancer in charge of all the family gambling operations. The Skipper had such faith in him that he had given the Dancer virtual independence in running the rackets under his command.

"The Dancer's in Florida. I'll reach him," said Bruno. "You gonna go out of here alone? You crazy or what?"

"I have it worked out. At least I think I got it worked out." JoJo took some of Nicky's cigarettes. "I'll reach for Rudy," he said.

Nicky said, "You gonna leave here with that big-titted waitress?"

"She a friend?" Bruno said, sounding nosy, wanting to know more.

JoJo turned and saw Esperanza standing in the hallway that led to the rest rooms. She was holding a canvas shopping bag and shrugged helplessly when he caught her eye.

"I just met her." JoJo felt a little defensive.

"And she's gonna walk you outta here?" Nicky said.

"What of it?"

Nicky shrugged. "She looks a little nuts. Has crazy eyes."

"Right, like you'd know the difference," JoJo said. "All right, I want you both to listen to me." Speaking in a whisper, JoJo laid out the plan. "I'm gonna see if I can leave with this here broad, this Esperanza, this waitress. Have her give me a lift to my brother's, and when I get there I'll reach out for the dwarf and Rudy. Tell them to roll it up and oil the guns. You two spend a little time here. If the cops clear out, make your way to John's. I'll wait for you there."

"You gonna keep the meet with the spic tomorrow?" Bruno asked him.

"You bet your ass."

Bruno nodded. "Good, good." He told JoJo soon as the cops clean the f'n street of all the riffraff he and Nicky would come to meet him. Said they would call a cab or something. He told JoJo with the weirdest grin, "Shit's on. I'm ready for a little war."

JoJo looked at Nicky and Nicky said, "Shit's on."

Satisfied, JoJo hustled back to Esperanza. She handed him the shopping bag, and JoJo grunted and nodded his head appreciatively, wondering what in hell was inside. Thinking, Nicky's right, this broad's got nutty eyes.

"Here. Change clothes, then come back into the kitchen," she said.

In the bathroom he opened the bag and found a white shirt-jacket and matching trousers, a kitchen helper's outfit. He was amazed at how calm he felt. He took off his own jacket, his shirt and tie and pants, and changed into the work clothes, folding his things neatly and putting them in the bag. Then he walked out of the bathroom and went into the kitchen. Everyone standing around stared at him, but no one stepped up to question or stop him. JoJo smiled at them, and Esperanza handed him a large green plastic bag containing he didn't know what, and not for a second did he think to inspect it. The bag was light, as if filled with dried leaves.

JoJo followed Esperanza out the restaurant's back door and into a small parking area lit by a spotlight. There were four cars parked beneath the light pole; a stiff breeze carried the taste and feel of the sea. The blazing white light brought him up like an onrushing tide. Suddenly he felt tense, nervous, on the very edge of things. He caught sight of a blue Dumpster standing alongside the last of the parked cars.

"You can throw the bag into that Dumpster there," she said casually, sounding calm. "C'mon, move like you work here."

Then she went to the first of the cars, unlocked the door, and got inside. Feeling like f'n Custer in Indian territory, JoJo tossed the bag into the Dumpster and joined her.

Esperanza had just started up the car when shit, a squat uniformed officer appeared from around the front of the restaurant. JoJo figured she'd drive off anyway, but the cop got them in his flashlight and waved them over.

Esperanza kept saying, "Okay, be cool." She pulled up alongside the cop, who stood nodding and grinning.

"Where you two going?"

"Felipe here came down with a virus or something. We don't want him to be sick all over the kitchen, so I'm driving him home. He lives in Wakefield. It's okay, ain't it?"

The cop bent to the window and shone his light into the car, he played it over JoJo's body and settled on his face. JoJo smiled faintly and shrugged.

"Sick, huh?" the cop asked sadly.

JoJo sat up straighter. He pressed the flat of his hand against his stomach and glanced at the cop's face.

"See any bad Mafia boys inside," the cop said, shooting for a laugh.

JoJo shrugged.

"Felipe don't speak English," Esperanza said.

The cop said "C'mon" and motioned for Esperanza to follow.

She drove slowly after him, around to the front of the restaurant, whispering, "Be cool, be cool. I'm going to keep moving, nice, nice." Then she smiled a little-girl smile, and JoJo began to worry.

"You're doing fine," JoJo said. "Felipe?"

Though she looked scared silly, Esperanza laughed out loud.

The cop stopped next to a white and blue police cruiser. Sitting inside was the officer JoJo had spotted earlier with Dante and his girlfriend. The door to the cruiser was open, and it seemed to JoJo that the officer must be listening to the cop, but as Esperanza drove slowly past he never turned his head or looked up from whatever he was reading. JoJo slouched down in his seat.

"Yes!" Esperanza shouted, and JoJo grinned. He reached over and rubbed the back of her neck, giving her a massage along with the directions to John's house and willing himself to sit back and relax.

They pulled out onto Ocean Road and followed it north past the town beach. John's house, the place he needed to be, was about ten minutes down the road.

As they drove, JoJo considered asking Esperanza why she'd stuck her neck out to help him but thought better of it. He flashed on John and felt that fear knot grab his throat. He was getting wild with thoughts of his brother.

No one would be crazy enough to hurt John. He nodded in agreement with himself. His brother was an innocent, you screw with someone's innocents you've got to be ready to pay with your own, your own innocents. Even Lilo was not that much of a lunatic.

And he was getting real pissed at Dante. At how he'd disrespected him, tried to make a fool out of him in front of Bruno and Nicky. Dante always the hardass. JoJo thought about the guns John kept at the house, more or less for target shooting, feeling that if he had to he'd shoot Dante himself if the guy didn't back the hell off. He wondered why Jimmy had never been able to get to the guy. Never been able to bring Dante along. He wondered what would happen if it came down to it. How would Jimmy handle it, if it came to the showdown? If Dante came down hard on Jimmy's wrong side, and if it was JoJo or Dante, where would Jimmy line up? Lilo flashed in his head like an explosion. Somehow everything, even the confrontation with Dante, seemed to be Lilo's fault. He'd kill the son of a bitch, he'd always known that sooner or later he was destined to blow the bastard away. JoJo was convinced that he needed to stay as calm as possible, easy and natural. This was his time, a wartime boss, he'd better be prepared.

Esperanza squinted at him as if trying to place him. JoJo smiled.

"You know," she said. "I've known you all my life."

"Not me." Real crazy eyes, he thought.

"Oh yeah, it's always been you. My life flies up and down the streets of bedlam and horror, I always feel as though I'm running, running for my life, and you're always there."

As she spoke her face took on a quick range of expressions, like a street psycho's.

JoJo thought uh-oh.

"I've had two husbands, both of them used me for a punching bag. Do I look like I was born to be somebody's gym set?"

JoJo laughed huskily. "Not to me you don't."

"Don't laugh, it's not funny."

"I'm not laughing at you."

"I'm not laughing at you," she repeated.

JoJo saw a kind of shadow pass over her features, and he began to get real antsy.

"My mother died last year, she had a brain tumor, they said. That's what they said. Never a day sick, a brain tumor, she's gone in six weeks. My father, six months ago, a massive heart attack is what they said. And two months ago my only kid, my Tommy, got hit by a car on the Boston Neck Road, right down here. Twelve years old with a broken back. They say there is some chance he could walk again. Some, they say."

"Christ," JoJo said, feeling the pain. He turned in his seat, glancing at her. Then he forced himself to stare out the windshield. He figured it best to keep his mouth shut.

Esperanza closed one eye and pointed at him, her hand a pistol. "You wanna hear what happened to me yesterday?"

"I don't think so."

"You'd never believe the story of my life. I should be on *A Current Affair* or some such show. Hey," she said, "ya know, I don't know your name."

"Joseph," he told her. "Joseph Paradiso."

"Paradiso Construction?"

"That's my brother."

"Oh, you're the Mafia all right. That's what that cop said, "see any Mafia bad boys in the restaurant?' That's what he said. And here I am driving one home."

"What are you talking about?"

"The Mafia! Should I spell it? M-A-F-I-A! Guinea gangsters!"

Esperanza drove along muttering, shaking her head and pointing a finger at the dash.

JoJo sat and stared out the windshield like a zombie.

Esperanza looked at him a moment, then she let out a shriek, like a f'n banshee, he thought he'd jump out of his skin. "Do you know who hit my son, do you know who crushed my Tommy?"

JoJo shook his head.

"His name is Pasquale DiLombardosi."

"Don't know him."

"Fucking dago gangster criminal. A mobster, what you all are."

She was ferocious, her eyes were wide open and glassy, her teeth were clenched. Christ, JoJo thought, can this get any worse? Esperanza leaned across and kissed his cheek. "Means I'm gonna kill ya, right? When you kiss some one it means you're going to murder them, right? I seen *The Godfather,* I know what that shit means."

As Esperanza spoke JoJo tried the door. They were doing about forty; he was not going anywhere. He was totally pissed and more than a little frightened, which he would have admitted to no one else but which he freely admitted to himself. He figured he was about a mile from John's house.

"Stop the car." His voice sounded almost childlike.

"What for?"

"Stop the car goddamm it, I gotta pee."

Pulling the car onto the shoulder of the road, Esperanza hissed with exasperation, "Who did those creeps think they were, using me, *me,* for a punching bag. I shoulda killed the both of them, poisoned the bastards. I'm gonna get Pasquale. You see him, tell him I'm gonna kill his kids."

When the car rolled to a stop JoJo jumped out and started to walk off. Esperanza sped past him, forcing him to leap for his very life out of the car's path. He rolled over in the grass and got to his feet. Then he began walking, his chin on his chest, bitterly astonished at each and every thing happening to him. Shit, he forgot his clothes in the car. He walked along the country road, a vision in white, no clothes, no cigarettes. Telling himself, over and over, you're one hell of a wartime leader, you are.

CHAPTER TWENTY

Dante came out of the bathroom and walked down the hall toward the conference room, a steady loud hum in his head like a tuning fork, wondering if there was anything more he could do tonight. Raymond, that handsome face of his, going round and round, a carousel of images in his brain. Dante could feel things starting to break loose inside him. Raymond—the guy was a husband and father, not your ordinary kind of cop, a special sort of man. But no tough guy. An outstanding detective, an extraordinary investigator. Sure, he grew up on the battle zone streets of East Harlem, but no violent guy. A gentle, thoughtful man is no match for a couple of killer bastards. A couple of punks whose hearts he would boil in oil. How frightened Ray must have been, how f'n terrified. Dante walked down the hall trying to get himself together, gathering his strength, knowing he might lose control at the drop of a hat.

Inspector Martin was talking with Jimmy and Kathy in the conference room. Dante stood for a moment outside the door, eavesdropping.

"Homicide and the Major Case Squad have done a terrific job so far. They were on it immediately, made the rounds and came up with four witnesses, three in the Bronx and one in Manhattan. What we got is two shooters, both white or light-skinned Hispanic. They were waiting up the street from Ray's apartment building. They spot him and get out of a stolen silver Pontiac that we figure was snatched in Staten Island sometime around one o'clock this afternoon."

"What are you saying boss?" Kathy said. "You saying this wasn't a street robbery? You saying it was a setup, a hit?" Giving it some thought, Kathy seemed to agree, nodding. "How can we be sure they were waiting for Ray?"

"We're not sure. But we got three college kids from Fordham, one lives in the same building as Ray. They got a pretty good look at the shooters. The best we can tell is that the punks walked straight at him, never said a word before they opened up."

Infuriated by the details, Dante entered the room. Kathy and Jimmy were seated and taking notes, the inspector was pacing.

Dante looked down at two photographs on the conference table, the first a full-length shot of Ray. He was lying face up surrounded by groceries, eyes wide open in a doom stare. Drops of blood stained his white mustache; his arms and legs were spread. The other picture, taken of the street itself, showed where the Pontiac had been parked.

"You said the college kids got a pretty good look at the shooters. Can they make an ID?" Dante said.

"The shooters were wearing hats and jackets with the collars turned up. The kids got a glimpse of their faces, but an ID? I doubt it."

"They look at photos?" Kathy said.

"All day."

"What kind?" asked Jimmy.

Inspector Martin smiled tightly at him. "Street gorillas, stickup men. Anyway, a half hour after they shoot Ray they're spotted in Manhattan under the West Side Highway and the morons are throwing gas on the Pontiac, burning it. Now there's three of them."

Dante said, "They had a driver."

"Anyone spot a third guy at the murder scene?" Jimmy asked.

"No—yeah, wait, wait till you hear this. A homeless guy, Philip Carr, a troll that lives in a box on a deserted unused pier at Twenty-third Street, he sees the whole thing. Sees three of them throwing the gas, and guess what? One of the three is a little kid. Now he sees them from about a block away, and yeah, maybe he was drunk out of his head, but he swears one was a little kid about this high." The inspector raised his arm as if to measure something waist high. He gave Dante a hesitant look, said, "What're you thinking?"

"The troll, this guy Philip, he see a second car?"

"A late model, big and black, is the best he could do. But listen to this." The inspector's voice dropped low, almost to a whisper. "Philip says the kid was driving. Now whataya think?"

"A dwarf, a midget," Dante said. Dante could hear himself, was shocked that he sounded as calm as he did. He was not cool on the inside. He felt his cautious and watchful time coming to a close.

The room was quiet. Jimmy got up, he went to an electric coffee percolator on top of a file cabinet and poured into two coffee cups.

Inspector Martin said, "Maybe you guys know something I don't."

Jimmy handed a cup of coffee to Dante and one to Kathy, told him that a half-a-hump badass by the name of Karl Marx Syracusa is a capo in the Paradiso crew. And the funny thing is, he's a dwarf. Inspector Martin said I'm way ahead of you. I thought of Karl Marx this afternoon, but then I figured no way. I've been in this business twenty years and I've never, not once, heard of a wiseguy hitting a cop. Not unless the cop was doing business with him. I know things have changed out there, but not that much. It just ain't done. And I'd stake my life on the fact that Raymond Velasquez was not doing business with any wiseguys.

Jimmy said, "Okay, if we eliminate the hit, then what do we have?" He shook his head, saying, "A street robbery, they took his gun and shield and his money. Is that right?"

"That's right," the inspector said.

Dante finished his coffee and headed for the file cabinet for another cup, he'd need to stay awake, and it was going to be a long, long night. As he poured the coffee he recalled remnants of his conversation with JoJo. Some story the devious bastard told about his father, Jesus Christ. He tried to remember if he'd told the devious bastard that he thought of him as a devious bastard or not and then thought, no need to tell him, the devious bastard knows how I feel. He returned to the conference table and took a seat next to Jimmy.

"Think about it." Dante leaned forward and reached for the photos of Ray. "Two white guys? Yeah I know they say maybe light-skinned Hispanic, only I bet they're white. And a f'n dwarf. They snatch a car, use it for the killing, then they don't just simply dump it somewhere, they burn the f'n thing. We're talking about pros, your typical dumb-shit pros, but pros nevertheless. So they grab Ray's gun and shield, carry off his money, trying to make it look good, look like a robbery. This is bullshit, this is a f'n hit. I know it."

He could see Ray, standing near his car about a week ago, smiling, then jumping into the silly Jeep of his, throwing a classical guitar tape into the tape deck. Telling Dante, ey c'mere, you want to hear the angels play, you want to hear what it sounds like to be Latin? Never again, he'd never see him again. Dante bit the inside of his mouth, bit down so hard he tasted blood.

Jimmy nodded. "How do you know it?"

"My gut tells me, and I listen."

Inspector Martin sat in a chair, got up again, went around the conference table, stood still, hands clasped behind his back. "A terrible thing. A nightmare, is what this is," he said finally.

Exhausted, Dante stayed seated, immobile.

There was a long silence.

"If there's nothing more we can do here tonight," Kathy said, "I'd like to go home."

The inspector folded his arms, "We've all had one hell of a day. Let me hear from the three of you in the morning. Maybe you won't have to come in, but call. There are no funeral plans as yet. Call in tomorrow, we'll take it from there. Okay?" The inspector stuck his hands in his pockets and headed for the door. "Oh yeah, one last thing," he said, turning back. "Which of you spoke to Ray in the last day or two? Did he talk about any problems, anything bothering the guy? Jimmy," he asked, "When did you speak to Ray last?"

Dante was curious too, he watched the way Jimmy turned and then, taking his time, looking around the room at everybody, described a talk he and Ray had had just the other day. The guy came by his apartment to rap a little and have a beer with him. Ray was calm, seemed to be at ease. He sat in his apartment and they talked. Jimmy said that Ray was getting real bored with this eavesdropping business. Said he'd been thinking about maybe making a move to homicide. Ray figured he'd find more action in a homicide squad. But wait now, whyn't he just come in and see me? the inspector said, we talked all the time. He never told me he wanted out. Dante finished his coffee and had another one while the inspector described Ray's commitment to the Intelligence Division, how he loved the fact that he had plenty of time off, could spend his off time with his wife and kids. And by the way, the inspector told them, I had a good long chat with Sarah, Ray's wife is an absolute heroine, the woman is standing up like a rock. Dante and Jimmy and Kathy sat without moving or interrupting.

Finally Kathy said, "It could be Ray kept his true feelings to himself." She was silent a moment. "I'm telling you that lately Ray was acting peculiar.

Like something was eating at him and he couldn't get to it, get it to stop. He was irritable, touchy. Nervous. I worked with him every day, and I'm saying the guy was not all right, not at all calm and relaxed."

Dante nodded. "I agree, there was something troubling Ray. Whatever it was he didn't share it with me."

"Maybe he said something to his wife?" Jimmy said. "You ask her, Inspector, ask Sarah if anything was bothering Raymond?"

Dante glanced at Jimmy, knowing in his gut that there was a massive lie here.

"Sarah Velasquez is one strong lady," the inspector said. "Still, I didn't feel I could push her, ask her painful questions. She hasn't broken yet, she will, and I don't want to feel responsible for that. We have time. I'll talk to her again."

Dante mumbled, "I'm wondering about Karl Marx, if the little bastard was involved. If he was, it don't take a genius to figure who gave the nod. Who pointed the finger."

"What did you say?" the inspector asked.

"I'm thinking about Karl Marx."

As if he could read Dante's mind, the inspector said quietly, "I can't buy that, just can't. It makes no sense. Why the hell would some wiseguy, any wiseguy, take out a cop like Ray?"

Dante went still, bowed his head and shrugged.

Jimmy Burns looked away.

"Makes no sense at all, Dante," the inspector said. "Not unless you know something I don't." He gave Dante a long look, then he picked up the picture of Ray. He eyed the photo coldly for a second and returned it to the table. "I find out who is responsible for this, the mother better duck. Dante," he said, switching gears, "what's up in Rhode Island?"

Dante sat in silence for a second, debating whether to let some of his own anger loose, then decided to let it slide. He told them he was waiting to hear from the Rhode Island police, find out how it all shook out up there. One thing was certain; the Paradiso family was going to war.

"And fuck 'em." Dante sat up, the rage climbing now. "I'd love to be the one that hands out machine guns, grenades, maybe a flamethrower or two. We could all stand back and cheer as they blow each other up. When the smoke cleared we go down to One-hundred-and-first and have a block party with balloons, whistles, and fireworks."

Inspector Martin gave him an ugly grin as if they had a mutual joke. "Okay," he said. "You three look like hell, go and get some rest. Dante, hang around a minute. I need to talk to you."

"No problem." Dante said, giving the inspector a small smile, a questioning smile.

Jimmy and Kathy stood up; Dante rose also and went and took hold of Jimmy's elbow, walking him out the door. "Buddy, whataya say you meet me in an hour at the Eighty-third Street park?"

"It's two o'clock in the morning."

"An hour and a half then?"

"Whataya, nuts or something?"

"We'll just be a minute, Dante," the inspector said from inside the conference room.

Dante held up one finger and continued his murmured conversation with Jimmy. "See, I'll only be a minute with the boss. I'll meet you in a half hour."

Kathy stood near the water fountain, fiddling with her hair, trying not to be too obvious about waiting for Dante but needing to make sure he knew she was waiting.

"All right," Jimmy said. "I'll go to the park. You wanna tell me what's up?"

"I'll see you in a half hour." Dante looked at Kathy standing there with her arms folded.

"Should I expect you later?" she said.

Dante felt a very strange mix of excitement followed immediately by plunging despair. He leaned against the wall, regarding Kathy, feeling a vague surge of tenderness rise, a good emotion. He smiled at the sensation of it.

"I'll get there when I get there," he told her.

"You want me to give you the key?"

"Sure."

When he returned to the conference room, Dante found the inspector standing near the window, his back to the room, hands on his hips. Dante still buzzing a bit from the exchange with Kathy, nervous about meeting with Jimmy, wondering just what he was going to say, going to do. He felt on the very edge of something powerful.

"You got something you want to tell me?" the inspector asked, taking his hands from his hips and running them through his hair, his back to Dante. Suddenly, from nowhere, the room was full of hostile vibrations. Dante caught a sidelong glance from the inspector.

"About what?" Dante felt a little defensive. What the hell could he tell the boss? His crazy thoughts about Jimmy? Or maybe how he was pumped about Kathy? How about JoJo, how the mere mention of the guy's name put his gut in a knot, made him feel like he had to pee. Or maybe the boss wanted to hear about his family life. He was prepared to unload a thought or two about his wife Judy, his son Danny. His and the inspector's relationship was not one of detective and supervisor. More like friends, like family. Shit, the inspector knew how he felt about Ray. So what then?

Sitting down, Dante said lightly, "You have something you want to ask me?"

Inspector Martin turned, giving him a beady stare. "No, I don't want to ask you something, I want to tell you something." He began bouncing on the balls of his feet. Dante stared at him but didn't say anything. He wondered if the boss had taken a drink.

"This afternoon I had lunch with Frank Russo."

"Yeah, so?" Dante said mildly.

"He's a good guy."

"So we're gonna be working with the feds again?" It was more an unhappy statement then a question.

"No. Well, I figure they won't be working with us for a while. See, the feds are not going to jeopardize sensitive investigations by working with us."

Jeopardize. Shit.

"Excuse me boss, but what's their problem?" Dante tried to sound indifferent. "The things we've worked together, it seems to me that we've done most of the work."

The inspector gave him a steady look, then turned back to the window. After a long thirty seconds of silence, he said, "If I found out that one of my people was double-banging me, was dirty and selling me out, had his hand out, I'd chop it off at the shoulder."

Dante chewed on that, then said, "Just what are you saying? Because if you're saying what I think you're saying, if you're accusing me of something—Inspector, I think that maybe you should come out and tell me what's on your mind."

"Something's got me right here." The inspector grabbed at his throat.

"Okay, let me put it another way. What the fuck are you trying to tell me?"

The inspector shrugged. "You know how I feel about you, I don't want to be wrong. I don't know what I'd do if I were wrong about you." He let the words hang for a minute, squeezing his lips. "We got a leak here, a traitor in the office. I'm not asking you about it, I'm telling you there is one."

"What?"

"Hear me out. I don't know who it is, but I'm going to find out. Whoever it is most likely has been burning us for some time. I don't know, maybe I'm wrong, maybe the feds are wrong. But I doubt it, I think—"

"What do you expect me to say?" Dante asked the inspector, not hiding his anger. "You've known me for twenty years, longer, knew my father too. Someone tells you something, I don't know what, and you figure Dante's a thief. What do you expect me to say, goddammit?"

"I didn't say *you* were a thief."

Christ, he is going to tell me something about Jimmy. Christ. He glanced up at the inspector, seeing him for a second as the enemy, then thought what the hell are you thinking? "You could have f'n fooled me," he said finally.

"Hear me out," the inspector said firmly.

"No. I understand what you're saying, I hear what you're telling me. And I'm telling you I'm outta here. I don't have to listen to this shit." Dante stood up.

"Sit down."

Dante remained standing. The inspector turned and threw him a hard look, unrelenting and grim. "So stand. Just don't leave, don't push your luck."

"I'm tired, I've had a long f'n day." Dante returned his stare, silently requesting that the inspector give him a break and allow him to leave. He had the distinct impression that his world, his life, the only life he knew, was about to blow up.

Jimmy, he thought. Christ, it's Jimmy. He's got something on Jimmy.

The inspector kept going. "Sitting with Russo today, you know, at Aldo's, I felt the wind shift on me. See, I've been in this job for thirty years, seen all types come and go. Pipsqueaks that come to the job to make money, others that run into money problems while on the job, nickle-and-dime guys with modest ambitions, seen them come and go too. Easy people to forget. Then there are the criminals, cops who would have been criminals if they hadn't been cops. Seen my share of those shitbirds too.

"The question is one of credibility, because you see, when I find that someone I trusted, anyone—now, I don't want to sound weepy here, or anyway, sticky. But if I discover that someone I'd bet my life on is fucking me, I wouldn't care how much I loved them, I'd go through them as fast as shit through a sick dog. From me to you, I'm not accusing you of anything. If I believed you had turned on me, I wouldn't waste my time accusing. I'm just telling you how I feel, I want you to understand my feelings is all."

"I love it," Dante said faintly. He looked at his watch and experienced a tremendous rush of anxiety. Get going. "Someone is feeding you all this shit and you're listening. The federales couldn't catch their dicks and you listen to their crap and believe it. I love it. I'm leaving."

"Go, beat it. Before you leave, one more thing. You figure Ray goes to visit your partner Jimmy often? They sit around, have a few pops and discuss life's problems? They do that all the time?"

"Inspector, you're spending too much time with the feds. Your picking up their habit of speaking in codes, not saying what you mean. If you're asking me if it surprised me that Ray talked to Jimmy about his frustration with the job, I'd say hell no, it don't surprise me at all. People talk to Jimmy all the time, he's a good listener, gives good advice, and he's smart. I don't know anyone smarter than Jimmy."

Inspector Martin threw him a bright smile. "I do," he said.

"Really? I'd like to meet him."

Inspector Martin stared at him, quiet and grim. After a moment he said, "In case you're interested, I had Harris, Tomasini, and Fritz take down the Chrysler in the garage on Fifty-seventh Street. And guess what?"

Dante shrugged.

"Flour. There was a hundred pounds of flour in the car, and nothing else. Somebody's a jokester, a game player, you have to figure that somebody is running a scam."

"Yeah, that makes sense. The question is who. The world is full of comedians."

The inspector told him right now his sense of humor was among the missing, but somebody should tell this comedian, whoever it is, that one way or another he is going to find out that no matter how funny the joke, there's bound to be somebody that just won't laugh.

Heading for the Brooklyn Bridge and Queens, Dante didn't know what he would say to Jimmy, not exactly; it was more that he wanted to see him alone and then maybe walk the old neighborhood. Like when they were kids out wandering, strolling the neighborhood and bullshitting. As if going back twenty, twenty-five years would clear the air.

He was worried about the inspector too, what the man knew and wasn't saying. It appeared the feds were on to something, and once they lined you up it was only a matter of time. Shit, maybe they had Jimmy already, maybe they were simply biding their time. That one got vetoed: the feds had you nailed they came for you and dropped the cuffs, bing-bang, that was all she wrote. It was possible they had simply heard rumors, stories from a paid informant or some such thing. In fact, it was likely that's all there was to it.

He flashed on Jimmy getting busted, dragged off in chains. The thought exploded in his head and gut, a frightful sickness in him, a weakness that made him feel small and powerless, all out of control. His buddy doing time, the six o'clock news, all that bullshit. But there was something about the thought of Jimmy sitting with JoJo, scheming, plotting and planning— laughing. The thought of the two of them together put such a terror knot in his stomach he thought he'd puke. And then there came the sick part, the feeling left out and deserted part. Lately he'd been so disconnected from Jimmy that there were times he felt like screaming at him *you're cutting me out, leaving me behind.* I'm your best friend, why would you do that to me? Was that sickness or what?

Somewhere near Sutter Avenue, about a block or two from the neighborhood, Dante found himself flashing on Ray's death so intensely that he winced at the thought of a volley of gunshots, bullets coming at him, eating at him, burning through his clothes, his skin and bone, geysers of blood from his head, bullets finishing him off, killing him, making him die in the street. He felt on his hip for his .38, the memory of how Ray went down making him want to check, and when his hand came back to the steering wheel he thought he'd get himself another gun, something with a bigger bang, more rounds than the bullshit five he carried. Maybe a Glock, or an S&W 9-millimeter automatic, anything was better than the dead lead he'd been packing for years.

His mind crammed with anxious plots, Dante pulled right, down into the playground, the place changed not at all in twenty years. Jimmy's car was nowhere to be seen. Dante tried walking about a little but he was bushed, his legs wobbly. Back in his car he sat and waited and went through cigarettes like jelly beans, and it took a good half hour of sitting there before he realized that Jimmy would not be coming. It was real late, almost morning for chrissake, he figured that Jimmy would be able to list reasons long as his leg why he couldn't take the ride from Manhattan to Queens and then back again. Nevertheless he had told Dante he'd be there, Jimmy said he'd meet him in half an hour. Jimmy doing his bail-out routine again.

Heading back to Kathy's now, Dante wondered what to do. He had this insane need to confront Jimmy, to get it out in the open. Maybe what he should do was drive to the guy's apartment, bang on his f'n door. He could be there in what? twenty-five minutes. Christ, the story Jimmy ran about his sitdown with Ray, Ray unloading about his problems with the Intelligence Division, man was that bogus. Jimmy had to know that he'd figure the story was a sham. Okay, so maybe they really did have a talk, a little get-together. But what did two guys different as day and night have to talk about other than work? He added that one, another question he'd make Jimmy answer.

Dante checked the time, near four in the morning. It would probably be a good idea to stay away from Jimmy now. Dante knew he wasn't thinking clearly, his head buzzing with this and that. And man, was he exhausted, so wasted from the day he could hardly walk straight. So what was he going to say when he finally had Jimmy alone? Hey, schmuck, what the hell's been going on? He'd need to be on his game when he got in Jimmy's face.

Coming off the Cross Bay and driving onto Queens Boulevard, Dante headed for Kathy's apartment building, a need to kick back and crash making the choice for him. Finding her street, he barely slowed down when he thought about it, the idea of spending another night in Kathy's bed had more and more appeal. So he wouldn't get to slide between her legs, wouldn't get to peel those tight jeans away from that exquisite ass. The closeness, the sense, the fresh smell of Kathy was soothing for his soul. He felt overwhelmed by his need to get a little salve for his soul.

Feeling a growing excitement, he parked the car, took his gun from his hip and placed it in the pocket of his windbreaker. He got out of the car and walked toward Kathy's building, stopping in the middle of the street to look at the sky. A clear night with the moon full, holding a cloud at one corner like a skirt. From the corner of his eye he thought he spotted someone, something, moving in the shadows, something small and quick, something without shape or form but something nevertheless. Dante moved his hand around his piece, slid his finger inside the trigger guard, thinking this little five-shot popgun wouldn't be worth shit in a real firefight. Christ, compared to the iron carried in the street these days, he might as well shoulder a crossbow.

He picked up his pace now, feeling dangerous vibes in the very air around him, starting to brood, thinking you're so goddamn cheap, go for it, will ya? Put a few hundred together and buy a real gun, for chrissake. Then thinking sure, and where you gonna find the three hundred?

Dante considered that moving around the city streets this time of the morning was to risk feeling an arm around your neck and a blade up against your throat. Even here in Queens—especially here in Queens. He found himself in the vestibule of Kathy's apartment building, now forgetting about the key she gave him, ringing her bell before announcing to himself both the obvious and the unbelievable, you're too beat, way off your game, and you're turning into some kind of ultimate victim. The once-tough street guy turned coward. Afraid on your own city streets, seeing nonexistent shadows and forms, feeling for the first time in your life like somebody's goddamn prey, when there's nothing out here to fear, no threat to you at all. But oh, he did see something move, and now he heard a noise behind him. Dante was about to pull his pistol when he felt a light touch on his shoulder, and turned to see the smiling face of Jimmy Burns.

"Whoa, you scared me."

"You, scared? What the hell could scare you?"

"Somebody sneaking up on me in the middle of the f'n night, that's what. Where the hell were you? I was waiting."

Jimmy looked away, he was unsteady, nervously running his fingers through his hair. His eyes were bloodshot and puffy.

"I told you I'd be at the park," Dante said. "The Eighty-third Street park. You never showed."

"I stopped at my apartment to pick up something. By the time I made it down to Eighty-third Street, you must have left. I figured you'd end up here." Jimmy turned partly away, his hands in the pockets of his jeans. It was as though he did not want to face Dante. "I went home to pick something up for you."

The front door buzzed, Kathy answering his ring.

"Dante?"

"Yeah."

"Anything wrong?"

He told her that Jimmy was here and they were going for a walk, he'd be back in an hour. She said hey, it's almost five o'clock in the morning. I'm going to sleep, use your key, will ya? He said it's not almost five o'clock, it's not even four thirty. She said yeah, well I'm going to sleep. Say hi to Jimmy.

Jimmy ushered him by the elbow back out onto the sidewalk. Letting go of his arm, Jimmy handed Dante a key, then began walking in circles and grabbing at his head, heading nowhere with slow, lame steps.

"What's this?"

"A key."

"I can see that, what's it for?"

"It's for a safe deposit box. Your safe deposit box."

"I don't have a safe deposit box."

"Sure you do, you've had one for years."

Dante sauntered over to Jimmy's car parked at the curb and leaned against it, studying the key, fingering it. "Hey Jimmy," he said. "What the hell is this about, what's this key?" Jimmy doing it to him again, taking over, moving all his anger, his questions aside. Jimmy Burns coming onstage. They faced each other in the warm night air on a sidewalk in Queens.

"What's happening Jimmy, you want to tell me what's going on?"

"Why, you want something to happen? That's you, you always wanting something to happen but never doing a f'n thing to make it happen."

"What I want is not important right now. Talk English," Dante said. "It's late, my brain's turned off. Don't get fancy with me, talk straight."

Jimmy didn't answer.

"I'm aching over this, I'm hurting bad, Jimmy, trying to figure what's wrong with you. For as long as I can remember I felt closer to you than anyone else in this f'n world, including my wife, my son, anyone, and you treat me like a stranger. Like someone you hardly know."

"What?" Jimmy looked stunned.

"There's nothing, not a thing in my life you don't know. I've got no secrets from you. You, *you* on the other hand, tell me shit and treat me like I'm a fucking boob."

Dante was having trouble keeping his temper from going into orbit. He blinked back tears, shaking his head. "God damn you, Jimmy. You know why the inspector wanted me to hang around the office? You want to hear what he told me? He told me there's a spy in the office, a rat. Jimmy, it ain't me, *I* know it ain't me. It better not be you. Because if it's you, Jimmy, then that simply means you chose JoJo over me. I don't know what I'd do if that were true. I think maybe I'd kill the both of you."

"Man, are you wrong."

"Bullshit."

"Dante, you know what you are? What you've been since we were kids. There's a word in Yiddish, dybbuk, a lost soul, flying around not knowing what you are or where you belong. You're a dybbuk, that's what you are." He had taken a step toward Dante, saw clearly the killer look on Dante's face and stepped back.

"You're a phony Jimmy, a f'n storyteller. I think you betrayed me, our friendship, all that we meant to each other. Tell me what this key is for, you'd better tell me what's going on."

Jimmy held his gaze steadily. "That key is for a safe deposit box, your safe deposit box," he said. "You don't know it, but you've had a safe deposit box for ten years. To be honest, I have one too, but yours hasn't been touched. There's two hundred and fifty thousand in yours. Your money problems are over."

Jimmy was having trouble keeping himself together, his face was cracking, tears building. Dante had seen that before, too, Jimmy coming slowly apart. He'd seen it after Jimmy's brother Josh was killed in 'Nam, and then again when his mother died in Florida. This was no act.

"You're kidding me, right?" Dante said.

"Hey, I'm dead serious. I've built you a nest egg, you have a nest egg, Dante. I never told you about it because I know you. I know you better than you know you. You talk big, but you're up to here in guilt with your father and all the other crap that bangs around that nutty head of yours. So I did this for you, I did it because I figured you'd want it done and not want to know about it."

Looking at Jimmy, Dante decided there was not a single truth about which he was certain. "From JoJo?" he said.

"Hey, man, you owe more money than East Germany, why the hell you getting pissed at me?"

"Are you nuts? You must have lost your mind."

"Nuts? I'm not nuts. I'm smart, smarter than you. Everyone knows I'm smarter than you are." Jimmy pounded his chest. "Me, me, I know what I'm doing." Jimmy's words faded into a thin sigh. "I always thought I knew what I was doing. I planned to wait till you retire before I gave that key to you," he said. "Only things seem to have gone out of control. Dante, how can I make any of this come out right?"

Jimmy stood motionless, staring at him.

"What have you done? You jerk, what have you done to us?"

"To us? What do you mean, to us? Correct me if I'm wrong, but ain't you the same guy that told me we should think about grabbing a few bucks if we had the chance? Wasn't that you? Or maybe I am crazy."

"Talk, Jimmy, it was talk. You say you know me, you know what I'm made of. Maybe, Jimmy, you never knew me at all."

"What are you talking about?" A choked, hoarse sound came from Jimmy, more pain in that one sound than Dante had ever heard from him. "Don't lie to me Dante, please don't bullshit me now. You've always wanted me to take care of things for you. You never came out and said it, but that's what you wanted. That is why I did it, for chrissake. Not for me, for you. I took that money and put it aside for you."

"You're a fuckin' liar." Dante startled himself. That night in the car, driving back from the Bronx after watching Freddie Miller do his rabbit routine, that night. His own words came back at him now, we should do it, if we get the shot, we should grab some money. Chrissake, everyone is, why not us? That's what he'd said. Almost begging Jimmy to be a thief.

"You wanted to take the shot, you told me you wanted to take the shot," Jimmy said in a soft voice.

"That was conversation, nothing more. And only a week ago. What you've been doing, I figure you've been doing for years. You're lying to me, you continue to bullshit me."

Jimmy said nothing, his gaze blank, his eyes trying to lock on to something just out of sight. He shrugged his shoulders.

"You want to talk about Ray? You telling me Ray came to your apartment to chat about his personal problems? You telling me that with a straight face?"

"Ray," Jimmy said. "That poor f'n guy."

Dante leaned back against the car watching Jimmy walk around, listening to him mutter curses to himself.

Dante said, "Ray wouldn't tell you anything. And you're not so special—he wouldn't tell anyone his business, the guy never said anything to anyone. I know the man, knew him a whole lot better than you, don't you bullshit me, don't you dare, I'll knock you right on your ass you keep bullshitting me." Dante could hear the anger in his own voice. He moved away from Jimmy's car, deciding to let his temper cool, watching Jimmy trying to think, to find a way of answering him that would make sense.

"You come to me now with this safe deposit key," Dante said, "and this story about putting money together for me. Figuring that's gonna do it for me. Yeah right, I need money, I've always needed money. If I had all I needed, I don't know what I'd do. Me and you are not about money, we're about tightness, friendship." To himself, Dante sounded almost apologetic.

Jimmy ran his fingers through his hair, walked off a few steps, turned and came back. Dante had never seen him so shaken, the guy was a walking nervous breakdown.

"Yeah. Right," Jimmy said as though he didn't know what else to say. There was silence for a long, long thirty seconds. "No," he said finally. "See, everything started going downhill when we opened this case. This f'n case, Dante, I told you was going to bring us nothing but grief. I told you that, but you wouldn't listen, not you, you goddamn hardheaded bastard. Not you."

"Is that right?"

"You brought this on us. You brought this all down on our heads," Jimmy declared, shaking his head.

"I did what? What did I do?"

"You brought us this grief, all this heartache, all this misery. I said we shouldn't work this case, I told you we shouldn't be involved with JoJo. Does any of this ring a bell?" He shrugged and sighed one huge sigh.

"You're telling me our working JoJo had something to do with Ray's death? You look at me and you tell me that. Look at me goddamm it, tell me this case had something to do with Ray getting shot and killed in the street, dying like some kind of fucking Mafia criminal. You tell me that, and so help me I'll knock your f'n head off, you bastard."

Jimmy greeted this news with a shrug. Dante looked at him and felt hollow, knowing. Not knowing what he knew exactly, but aware for sure that he was going to endure the worst pain of his life. It was the most frightening sensation he'd ever felt.

Jimmy smiled briefly at him, then said slowly, softly, almost in a whisper, "I fucked up. I killed him, just as sure as if I'd pulled the trigger myself. I killed the poor guy, Dante."

Suddenly bright lights blinked on and off in Dante's head, he raised his fists, screaming, "Son of a bitch, son of a bitch!" Dante let it erupt, sucking air through his teeth, he turned on Jimmy, his brain was screaming *bastard-bastard-bastard.*

"Every day of my life I will pay for it." Jimmy's voice to Dante sounding childlike, unfamiliar and foreign. He rubbed his mouth and moved away from Dante, tried getting out of his reach.

"And JoJo, he's responsible, that right?" Dante hissed.

"Sure, you're right. You're right. But it was me, I set him up. I made the call."

Dante nodded.

His slap sent Jimmy spinning, blood spraying from his split lip. Jimmy leaned back against the car, staring at Dante, sad-eyed and uncaring. He lightly touched his lip and Dante went berserk, caught him again, this time with a series of openhanded lefts. "You made the call, you made the call, you made the call," in cadence with the slaps. He pushed Jimmy away, Jimmy with his hands at his sides, never made a move. Dante unloaded a frightful backhand, and Jimmy's head bounced against the car with a sickening crack. Dante was all business, he dragged Jimmy to him, then flung him back onto the car.

Dante didn't pick his words, they flew from his mouth like razor blades. "You're his man, you've been doing business with JoJo, you backstabbing bastard." Dante was wild, not thinking, not feeling everything coming at him now, walls of neon lights shattering in his brain.

Stillness, then a quiet murmur from Jimmy, "You're right. You can kill me, I ain't gonna fight you. Maybe you should kill me, maybe that's what you should do."

Despite his calm tone, Dante could see Jimmy trembling. Dante felt as though his heart would burst out of him.

"You chose him over me, you made the choice." Dante jabbed Jimmy's chest, wet now from the stream of blood running from his cheek and nose.

"You're wrong Dante," Jimmy said. "You've always been wrong about that. It's you that I worry about, not him."

"Liar!"

"I'm not lying Dante, I'm not lying to you."

"And Ray, you want to tell me about Ray?"

"JoJo has connections, we both know that JoJo can get things done. I asked him, begged him to get Ray transferred, moved out of our office. Ray knew about me and JoJo, not everything, but enough. I wanted him out of our office, that's it, nothing more."

"Oh God," Dante said. He shook his head in infuriated horror.

"He promised me, Dante, JoJo swore he'd never hurt the man. Told me he would get him transferred, nothing more, nothing more than that."

"You believed him? You trusted that murderous bastard?"

"Ahh man, he swore to me."

Dante grabbed Jimmy by the throat with his left hand, he pulled his right back, his hand balled into a fist. Stopped. "No wait, wait, wait." Dante couldn't tell if he spoke the words or just thought them. "If I hit you again I'll kill you. I got no more in me, Jimmy, you took everything out of me. I'm done." He stepped back. "Here," Dante said. "Here, take this f'n key and shove it. It's JoJo's money in that box, ain't it?" He pushed the safe deposit key into Jimmy's shirt pocket.

"It is. I mean, yeah right. It's his."

Dante stared at the sky, a streak of pale orange light beginning to grow. Morning arriving in Queens.

"Mr. Slick's cash, huh? JoJo's money," Dante said.

"I'll do anything, whatever it takes to make this right."

Dante and Jimmy looked at each other.

"Maybe I should just go into the office and cop out," Jimmy said. "Tell the boss, give myself up. Christ, whatever they do to me can't be worse than this."

"Whataya, nuts?" Dante took a deep, shuddering breath. "Look, we'll work this out. You were stupid Jimmy, you acted like an idiot. But you're not evil. JoJo's evil. He'll pay for this. We'll figure something." A long pause, then, "A half a million bucks this guy gave you?"

"Ten years, a thousand a week."

"Whew. No wonder you never had any money problems. And what were you doing for him?"

"To tell you the truth, not a whole lot."

"Yeah, like what?"

"I don't want to get into it."

"Get into it."

"Watching his back in our office. Dante look, I said I don't want to get into it and I mean it. The whole f'n story makes me sick. Look, I did it, I'll pay for it. What else can I do?"

"You'll call JoJo. Arrange to meet him and give the money back."

Jimmy stood dabbing at his nose and lip with a tissue. He looked around as light began to fill the morning sky, glancing at Dante as if taking his measure.

"JoJo," Dante said. "That creep bastard is answerable for Ray's death, and he's gonna pay." He nodded in agreement with himself. "JoJo is a player, likes playing games," he said bitterly. "I'm gonna show him I can play too. If it's games he wants, then it's games I'll give him."

"Dante," Jimmy said, "I feel so wasted, so screwed up and lost. I never wanted to see anyone get hurt. Not even JoJo."

"I know, I know goddammit. Only it happened, Jimmy, somebody got hurt, a good man got hurt as bad as you can get."

Jimmy said, "How could I be so simple?" He gathered himself in an effort not to cry, leaned against Dante, and Dante put his arms around him, squeezed him until he felt him tremble.

"You're gonna kill him, aren't you?" Jimmy said.

Dante didn't answer.

"You want to kill me too, don't you?"

Still no answer.

Dante held Jimmy to his chest for a moment, feeling a mixture of anger, panic, and some relief, telling himself your buddy should know who you are, what's in your heart and soul, convincing himself, trying to convince himself that Jimmy was no killer and certainly no thief. He wasn't going to say something he didn't mean. He didn't know how to answer Jimmy; what he finally said was, "JoJo Paradiso is a shithead, I told you that when we were kids, and my feelings ain't changed in thirty years."

CHAPTER TWENTY-ONE

Fucking Esperanza," JoJo growled, still spooked by the nut-job psycho bitch, the way she tried to run his ass over, nut factory broad needs a beating. It was sometime around eight o'clock, coming down the blacktop of John's driveway, his arms folded across his chest, his head down, walking, rocking his head from shoulder to shoulder, wondering why he attracted so many f'n lunatics to his life, it was then JoJo noticed his brother's house bright as a Christmas tree, lights on everywhere. He hunkered down among brilliantly blooming azaleas and rhododendrons lit by ivy-covered mushroom lamps and peered out through the bushes until he spotted some movement, someone in motion, coming out the front door of the house onto the wraparound deck. His father.

Kneeling in the grass, staying out of sight, checking the lay of the land, JoJo tried to think it through. His father was there, f'n great. What was he going to do now? What could he tell the man. Christ, things couldn't go right for going wrong. Shit, was he ever gonna get a break? There he was, the old man, prowling like a lion among the herd. JoJo figured that his father must have arrived in the past couple of hours or so. Probably picked up at the airport by John, the reason his brother was not home when he tried him from the restaurant. He wondered what John told the old man. He couldn't tell him a whole lot since he knew nothing of what was going on. His brother didn't know which way was up.

JoJo left his hideout and made his way slowly along the driveway, hesitating a moment, looking for Monty Montana, the Skipper's bodyguard. When his father spotted him, they exchanged glances and JoJo gave a small wave. The old man folded his arms and nodded his head, a will-ya-look-at-you smirk on his face.

————

JoJo sat with his father on the back deck. There were spotlights stuck in the eaves, and they lit the rocks and bay below. JoJo sat and studied three crabs climbing like night burglars up the side of a huge black boulder, their goal a rotting seabird that lay on the very top, its wings crisscrossed over its head. Sooner or later the crabs would be there, atop the seabird, it was a matter of time and space, nothing could stop them, not the incoming tide or the pebbles JoJo casually tossed in their direction, getting lucky once in a while and striking their armored backs, receiving zero in response. Since he was a kid he hated crabs, hated to look at the goddamn things.

He'd spoken to his father for close to an hour, JoJo confessing, getting it out, telling the tale of the Cuban, the whole of it. His father maintained a sober expression during the telling, his only response an occasional shrug as if it didn't matter either way. Which JoJo knew was totally bullshit. But it was the old man's way, shrug and smile and listen. The man was like a mountain of steel, and there was light in his eyes, a brightness. Was it curiosity, or simply anger. Could it be he knew all along what JoJo was up to? His father did not seem shocked at all at JoJo's tale; the story of Lilo's failed ambush, the bastard's treachery brought little more than raised eyebrows and several quick nods. How JoJo had tested Barry Cooper brought no response whatsoever. How he figured to strike back at Lilo, using the Dancer and his people from Sheepshead Bay, brought the nods.

His father's eyes focused on the table they sat at. In a low drone, JoJo told him all he dared, reminding himself over and over that the Skipper was listening, not reacting to news of the drug deal, the coming war, nothing, nada. He didn't want to push his luck, so he kept the story of the Dwarf's hit on the cop to himself.

Now they both sat, JoJo emotionally drained, his father quiet, glancing at the sea and the night sky, shooting sideward glances at him, making JoJo squirm in his chair like a snake.

Lina Santangelo made an appearance every now and then to refill his father's wineglass. When she came to the deck she'd stare at JoJo, never once asking if he wanted or needed anything. Lina seemed pissed at him.

Now she made another entrance, this time carrying a bowl of fruit and a glass of wine for JoJo.

"Thanks Lina," his father said. Then he looked at JoJo, stared hard at him, waiting for Lina to close the door before he spoke.

JoJo realigned himself in his chair and leaned back. He made a conscious effort to keep his eyes on his father.

"Your brother called me this morning. Told me he was worried about you. I'm lucky I was able to grab a flight out. Well, it's off season now, it ain't that hard. He's a good guy, your brother. He loves you. I sent him on his way, told him to go and get Penny and grab a little vacation."

"Good, good. Yeah, well, I try to look out for him, keep him away from things. John's always been a worrier."

His father stared at him, he seemed puzzled. "You know," he said, "maybe I'm paranoid, I know I'm a little stupid, but even a stupid person knows when he died. When did I die, Joseph?"

JoJo hesitated, sure of what his father was saying but afraid now to respond. He reached over and took his glass of wine.

The old man shook his head. "What you've done can't be made undone," he whispered hoarsely. "Now we gotta live with it, see what we gotta do." He rubbed his forehead and stretched. "You know what you've done here, right? You understand the problems you've laid on me, you understand that, don't you?"

"Pop, I tried to do what is right here. That's all I tried to do."

"What's right? Who you kiddin'? We got rules in this family, you wait till I see Bruno."

"Jeez, Pop, Bruno did what I told him to do. I'm responsible, not Bruno."

His father gave him an are-you-kidding? look.

JoJo looked up and saw Monty Montana standing in the door from the back deck into the kitchen. Monty made a little show of glancing at JoJo, then he turned to his father, the boss. "The friends are here from Providence," Monty said. "There's a half dozen. I put two on the road, two along the driveway, and two in front of the house. The red guy sent his regards, said he'll send six more, they'll be here in an hour or so."

The Skipper raised his arm and wiggled his hand like a band leader. Monty stood still for a moment. "We're gonna leave tonight, boss? If we are I'm gonna need a couple of cars. No rush now, but if you can give me an idea—"

"When Bruno and my son-in-law get here we'll leave. I expect them any minute. Right, Joseph, they should be here any time now, huh?"

"Yeah, yeah, they should be here any minute now."

JoJo sat still for another minute or so, his hands folded between his legs, his head down. He turned to check on Monty, his father's bodyguard was gone.

"What about Lilo and Yale, Pop? What are we gonna do about those two humps?"

"You don't worry about Lilo, Lilo and his people are my concern. I'll take care of that stupid bastard."

"C'mon Pop, you need me now. Talk to me, I can help. Let me take care of Lilo."

A kind of desperation was building in JoJo. He was thinking a mile a minute. He had to keep this going and not have his father explode. "Pop," he said, "you know the kid Vinny Rapino, one of Lilo's crew?"

"I heard the name, I never met the kid." He paused, rubbing his temples with the heels of his hands. "At least I don't think I ever met the kid."

"He's been driving me for the past few days. He was with us at the restaurant, parked outside in the Mercedes."

"So?"

"It looks to me like he fingered us. Then again maybe Lilo tracked us some other way, and the kid had nothing to do with it. I'm hoping the kid spotted the cops and bolted. If that's true, he'll reach out for us. Pop, he knows where Lilo hangs out, he knows everything there is to know about the guy. He could put Lilo down for us. Tell us where we can find him, and yeah, probably Yale too."

"He stole my Mercedes, this kid?"

"It's mine Pop."

"Whataya mean *yours?*"

JoJo paused, his hands spread in bewilderment. "Mine, it's my car. I leave it at your house, but it's my car. For chrissake, I paid for it."

"The kid got it?"

"Yeah, right. I told you he was driving me. He must have spotted the cops and took off, took the car. He drove off in the car." JoJo began to sweat.

The Skipper shook his head. "Okay," he said. "So some kid stole your car. What are you saying, this kid can find Lilo for us?"

"Where are you Pop? I didn't say he stole the car, I said this kid Vinny can find Lilo for us."

"You think maybe I can't find my own captain?"

"I didn't say that. I just said the kid Vinny could help." JoJo was breathing hard through his nose.

His father leaned forward. "You said I need some kid to find Lilo. Lilo's my captain, he's been with me for twenty years. I know this shitbird like I know you. I'll find him, don't you worry." His father looked at the ground and sadly shook his head as if to suggest that JoJo was hopeless.

"You know, when we was in Florida," he went on, "I took Lina to the track. She's never been to a racetrack, so I took her. While we were there who do I run into? Uh, what's-his-name. The Biscoglia brother, the older guy, you know."

"Phil," JoJo said, "Philip Biscoglia. He was in your wedding party, Pop."

Philip and Carmine Biscoglia just about ran the garment center, the trucking and the unions, big-time loan sharks. JoJo had recently heard they were under some kind of federal indictment. He could count on the brothers for help; at least, he was positive that they would want no part of a Paradiso family revolution. They were *compares,* arrived in the States from the same village in Sicily as the old man. How the hell could his father forget their names? Carmine Biscoglia was his sister Patricia's godfather, for chrissake.

"Ey, you don't think I know that? I just forgot the guy's name. Why, you never do that? Forget names?" his father said sadly.

Monty returned to the door. "Nicky and Bruno just showed. And six more guys from Providence."

The Skipper waved him quiet. "Let me ask you something Monty. If you had to, if I told you to find Lilo, how long do you think it'd take?"

"You know boss, he's gonna jump in a hole now."

"How long, Monty? No stories, just tell me how long?"

"A day and a half, two at the most."

"Thanks." The Skipper bobbed his head. "Tell Bruno and Nicky to wait in the living room," he said. "They got a car?"

"They came back by cab. Ran into a little problem on the road with the fellas from Providence. Nobody knew who was who, you know what I mean? I think Nicky may have dirtied his pants, he's in the bathroom now all pissed off. One of the Providence guys pulled him from the cab and grabbed him by the throat. The cabdriver took off like a f'n shot. We should think about leaving, boss. Maybe that cabbie'll run to the cops."

"We got enough cars?" the old man asked, looking at Monty. JoJo shifted his weight, nervously thinking that his father might be game for all this craziness, but he sure as hell didn't seem up for it.

Monty shrugged. "We only need two. We have one of John's and we can borrow the other."

His father tilted his head, saying, "What about these out-of-town fellas? We can send them on their way, or what?"

"The red guy told them to stay with you for as long as you needed them. I don't see where we need 'em once we're outta here. Karl Marx is already at your house with some of his people, and the Dancer is on his way back from Florida. Bruno can reach another ten, fifteen people. Whataya think boss, that should be enough, no?"

"Well, I dunno. Joseph," he said, "when you come up here to visit your brother, do you go into the Providence to pay your respects to Red?"

"I will from now on." JoJo was concentrating on the glass of wine on the table before him.

"The man is a *capo di famiglia,* he deserves your respect. He's a bit of a cowboy, so you don't wanna get too friendly, but you should go and pay your respects next time."

"Sure Pop."

Finishing his wine, JoJo fought off a confusing rush of anxiety and tried to gather his thoughts. He had been so focused on telling his father the story of the drug deal, so pumped up to make things okay with the old man that he hadn't thought too much about his father's capacity to handle the coming shitstorm. He had no trouble picturing how he himself would strike back at Lilo and the others, using the Dancer and his people, Bruno and Nicky Black too. But he also had to defend his father. He doubted that the old man still had it in him to call the shots in a real war. And when you figure the way Lilo took his shot at the title, the way he did it, the bastard would need to go all the way now. The bum had no choice but to get to the old man, or he was history. Lilo would send his people, and the man had experienced soldiers, war-hardened people, Benny Bats and Yale and some of the others. And shit, if Lilo could line up the Ramminos, and the other families decided to sit this one out, the Paradisos would have problems.

Looking past JoJo's father's shoulder, Monty smiled at JoJo and sighed slightly. "You know, sometimes this kind of activity is good, gives everybody a kick in the ass, makes 'em pay attention."

JoJo shrugged and smiled at Monty, feeling a growing heat in his stomach. He was losing it, stepping aside for the old man. Bells were going off in his head, and he was afraid that what was coming would be the last round for the Paradisos. Hoping against hope, JoJo dropped the big one.

"Pop," he said. "I got this meet set up with this Cuban guy tomorrow. Maybe I should hang out here?"

JoJo thought that maybe he and his father should separate. Send the bulk of the men to guard the old man, then he could go after Lilo on his own. First he'd have to convince his father to let him stay in Rhode Island for another day or two. Kill two birds with one stone, keep the meet with the Cuban, then hunt Lilo down.

"You got what?"

"The Cuban guy, I told you about him."

"Forget it, it's a dead issue." His father waved the subject finished.

———

Dante drove Jimmy's car to the Greek's, hammering away at him about this business with JoJo. Jimmy said little, almost nothing; it seemed to Dante that the guy tuned him out. They picked up four coffees and two bagels with Muenster cheese. Dante drove to Rockaway Beach and parked at 110th Street. They sat on the boardwalk, feeling the strong sea air, drinking their coffee and eating breakfast; when they'd finished they sat there in silence. Dante watched the gulls. Jimmy was dozing, his eyes open just a slit, and for a moment Dante caught a glimpse of their blue coldness. The breeze picked up. Dante shivered.

Dante sat and thought of the days, months, and years they'd spent together. Most of his life. All of his life really. He flashed on JoJo, wanting to tell Jimmy that JoJo used you, now he's used you up. Dante thought back on all the conversations he'd had with Jimmy, conversations about JoJo, and there was a lot now to read between the lines, all of it bad. Nevertheless, he knew that there was no way he could live with the sight of Jimmy twisting in the wind. He was ninety-nine percent sure that Jimmy never intended to see Ray hurt. Sure he'd been reckless and stupid, but Jimmy Burns was not a vicious man. Dante told himself to calm down, to focus. He would need all his patience, all his poise in order to pull this off to save Jimmy and nail JoJo. The question was how.

Dante got up, yawned, stretched, and walked over to the boardwalk railing. A black couple in blue sweats was jogging in the sand at the water's edge. They'd run twenty yards or so and slap palms, in love and in matching outfits, cute. He thought of Kathy, how she ran like a teenage boy, all muscular and quick.

He turned his back to the sea and faced Jimmy, sitting now with his legs crossed at the ankles, as if he was lounging in the Caribbean under a golden palm.

"Hey Jimmy," he said. "Tell me one thing."

"Yeah?"

"Maybe I'm brain dead or something, but I can't for the life of me figure out when this love affair started with you and JoJo. Shit, we're together all the time. I never saw it happen."

Jimmy shut down, he held up his hand and lowered his head. "Oh man, I knew it would only be a matter of time. I knew you'd never let this be. Okay, you want to hear it, I'll tell you what you want to hear."

"Look man, I don't want to give you any more heartache than you already have. You want to tell me, tell me. If you don't, then forget I asked."

Jimmy took his key ring out of his pocket and began to twirl it around his finger. "You remember about ten years ago, when my mother died? You recall how pissed I was?"

"Of course I remember."

"Do you remember why? Why I got so pissed, so crazed I wanted to kill someone."

"To tell you the truth, I don't remember that. I knew you were pissed at some doctor or something with the hospital. But I wrote it off, everyone gets pissed at doctors and hospitals when someone they love dies."

"Yeah, yeah, okay. But it was more than that, much more. My folks retired to Florida, but shit, they never were the same after Josh was killed. My father stopped laughing, he had a bad heart, had a bad heart for years. I always figured it was the stress of working for those dipshits that owned the lamp factory. Those characters always playing with the cash, screwing with the books, my father spending days, weeks sitting around at the IRS. Anyway, the lamp business goes down in flames, my father packs it in after about forty years of getting up at five in the morning, walking ten blocks down to Liberty Avenue, winter, summer, taking the A train through Brooklyn, down into the city. The lamp factory goes belly-up, my old man's pension was up in smoke."

"Jimmy," Dante said, "I know all this."

"Wait, wait." He sounded apologetic. "They catch a break. My father hears about a house in Miami Beach, about a block and a half from his sister. He can pick this house up for about fifty thousand less than what he can sell his Queens house for. He's got himself a little stashed, not a whole lot, but some, and added to the fifty he could make off the sale of the Queens house, he's not in clover, but they can live, my mom and dad they can live. You know what I mean?"

Dante didn't answer, he looked at Jimmy and felt him studying him.

"Now my mother, you knew my mother, well she hated the idea of f'n Florida. Hated the heat, hated her sister-in-law, and was scared shit of all the crime she heard about. Can you believe that? The woman grew up in the Bronx, lived in New York all her life, and she was terrified to go live in Miami Beach. Anyway, she tells my father I'll go where you go, wherever you go I'm there. They don't make women like that anymore. She loved the shadow my old man walked in."

Dante nodded emphatically.

"Those people were in Florida less than six months, happy like you wouldn't believe. Turned out my mother fell in love with the place, and she got along with her sister-in-law just fine. Everything was cool, they were doing great. Then my mother goes to the doctor for her annual checkup. She gets a little dizzy at the doctor's office and says something like what the hell am I doing here? She wants to be home is all she meant, the doctor figures she's flipping out or something, he sends her for a CAT scan and they find a tumor."

"I remember," Dante said. "Sure I remember."

"Okay, okay. She's seventy-six years old, Dante. Far as I know the woman's been getting dizzy on and off for twenty years. Anyway these crepe-hanging hustling bastards, these doctors, they scare the shit out of her, and my father too, convince them both that my mother can't live without a brain operation. They don't do one, Dante—they do two. A hundred grand each."

"But she needed them, right?"

"Those doctors knew that those operations wouldn't do any good. They couldn't save her, they f'n knew it was nothing more than an exercise. Sure my mother's got insurance, but there are a few things insurance doesn't cover. She never made it through the second operation. Bam, just like that, my mom's gone and my father's broke."

Dante massaged his chin and nodded.

"I hear what you're saying Jimmy. You want to tell me how JoJo Paradiso fits into this equation?"

Jimmy seemed frightened, and the look he threw at Dante made Dante feel that Jimmy wanted him to be frightened too.

Jimmy masked his eyes with his hand. "Broke, Dante, you understand what that means? What that really means to a proud man, a man that worked all his life? A man that raised two kids, worked seventy hours a week, was religious, all that. A man that never asked another human being for any kind of help."

"Your father was a hell of a guy, Jimmy. I knew your father, he was a hell of a man, an honest man."

Jimmy gave him a dirty look, silently telling Dante yeah, and what did it get him.

Jimmy said, "Two months after my mother died, my father had a massive heart attack. He died broke and alone. I swore that wouldn't happen to me. I'd look out for myself. And for you too. I'd look out for the both of us the best way I could. Right around that time I ran into JoJo at the Sign of the Dove. We had a few drinks and the guy made me understand that I had a chance to make some money but it wasn't going to be around forever. That's all I'm saying. He asked me, back then, to talk to you, said I should tell you that he could help you live a life not crazed by money problems; if you wanted he could help."

Dante's anger filled his chest; Jimmy looked at him and smiled bitterly. "Shit, man," Jimmy said. "I knew you better. You may want to do something, even talk about it, but you'd never do it. So I did it for you. You know, I've signed your name to arrest cards, to court affidavits, to about a thousand police reports over the years. And so I signed one more time, I signed up a safe deposit box for you."

"Do you know how much I hate this bastard?" Dante hissed.

"Yeah, I do. You see, I don't hate JoJo, not even now, not even after Ray. I don't hate him because I understand him, and what I understand I forgive. I forgive things you never would."

"And the money has nothing to do with it, right?"

"Not a whole lot. Sure, it removes that pressure; you got a nest egg, a little stash, you got less pressure. But what it really is, is fuck-you money. You can tell the world to go and fuck off."

"Jimmy, you ever listen to yourself? It's the money and nothing more. JoJo is dirt, has never done a thing right his whole life."

Jimmy waved at him in disgust. "You see what you do, Dante? You're always passing judgment on JoJo, but judgment is always passed on powerful men."

That little line landed like a grenade in Dante's heart. He folded his arms across his chest.

"A powerful man, you say?"

Jimmy nodded. "You gotta admit the guy's a powerful man, Dante. JoJo can get things done."

"I don't know why I talk to you about JoJo. I don't know why I even f'n bother."

"Hey buddy, you ever think that maybe all it is is maybe, you know, simple jealousy?"

Dante slapped his leg. "You keep talking like this, so help me Jimmy, I'll lose it again and knock you down. Do you listen to yourself, you hear the things you say? The man killed Raymond. He killed him."

"For chrissake Dante, I ain't saying I love the guy. I understand him and respect him for what he's accomplished. JoJo's a neighborhood guy, no education, no real skills, and he's a f'n multimillionaire."

There was a short silence, broken only by Jimmy's sigh.

"And where would this genius be without his father?" Dante asked. "Where would he be without six hundred assholes bringing him envelopes once a week? And as far as getting things done, you're right there—he did Ray, he certainly got that done, didn't he? Ray was our friend, wouldn't hurt you for the world. For chrissake, we're talking about Raymond here."

"It was a mistake, you gotta believe it was a misunderstanding, a lack of communication."

"Tell it to his wife Sarah and their two girls."

"A f'n accident," Jimmy said.

"All right now, you listen to me, and you hear me. I gave you that key back. I want you to get that money and put it in an attaché case or something. Call your friend and tell him to meet us tomorrow night, the next night. No later than that. Tell him to meet us at the front gate of the playground at Eighty-third Street. Tell him if he's panicky he should bring whoever he likes, but tell him he'd better be there. And you too, you be there too, Jimmy."

Dante watched Jimmy slowly drop his head back, his hands over his eyes. "Whataya got banging around that nutty head of yours? What are you up to? C'mon, please don't do nothing crazy, huh?"

"What am I up to?" Dante began, then hesitated, surprised by the fear in Jimmy's voice. He was silent for a second, thinking about JoJo, Ray, and the dwarf, and Inspector Martin, the inspector not saying it but letting him know the feds are closing in on Jimmy. At least that's what he thought the inspector was saying. Telling him there's a leak in the office, a traitor here. And the feds know it. Staring at him, looking him dead in the eye and saying Ray and your partner chat all the time, do they? Inspector Martin knew something, that was certain.

"Do you ever think about going to jail, Jimmy? Ever wonder what it would be like for a thinker like you to spend three to five years in the joint?" Dante smiled.

"Sure I do."

"You gotta help me help you. Because I got this feeling in my gut, and you know my gut's never wrong. My feeling is that you're about a pussy hair away from the slammer."

"Christ, Dante, I wouldn't go to jail. Not me, I carry my escape hatch right on my hip. Nobody's putting chains on me, brother."

"Don't talk like that."

Jimmy laughed, a flush coloring his face. "Funny," he said, "but I understand your father more and more each day. I understand the man."

"Well that makes one of us," Dante said, feeling panicky now.

"Yeah, well maybe you can see some light here that I can't. I don't see any way out of this f'n jackpot."

Dante felt a flood of acid pour into his stomach. He had never considered that, never for a minute thought that Jimmy was the type that would suck on his gun. Jimmy's resolve making him real tense.

"See, the way I see it, Jimmy, you got in way over your head, but in your heart you're a good man."

Jimmy gazed at him sadly.

"I just can't accept," Dante said, "that you believe half the crap you say about JoJo. I think your mind was out to lunch when you tripped into this deal, and maybe you felt it was the right thing to do at the time. Then once you jumped, you landed in that room with no doors, no way out. I mean basically you fucked up, now we gotta find a way to bring you back, back where you belong. We're gonna clean the slate with this scheming bastard JoJo, and I know just how we're gonna do it."

Jimmy didn't say anything, didn't move, Dante thinking, Dante, you had better come up with something because right now there ain't nothing but space and boiling water in your head where your brain should be.

Jimmy nodded, just not enough to make Dante happy. "Hey partner," he said. "I'll do what you ask, whatever you think I should do. I want to do the right thing, whatever that is, I want to do it."

Dante relaxed. "Okay, that's good. That's what I wanna hear."

———

Dante entered Kathy's apartment around nine thirty in the morning. He was beyond exhausted, nervous and more than a little frightened. Confronting Jimmy the way he had, the shock of having his worst suspicions confirmed, banging Jimmy around, all combined to make him feel stunned and crazed. He wasn't sure if he could tell any of it to Kathy. How would she react, what would she do? It all confused him.

He wasn't even sure why he had ended up here, in her apartment, looking at her now asleep, her pillow over her head, a bottle of Evian water on the floor next to where she slept, shield and gun on the night table. It looked like a .380 PPK, a good German piece, a hell of a gun for the little lady. Why the water? Because she got thirsty during the night. The woman drank and peed more than anyone he'd ever known. All he could grab on to at that moment was the fact that he needed to be in that bed and get some sleep.

Dante sneaked into the bathroom. He imagined telling Kathy the story of his life, all about JoJo and Jimmy, to get some kind of outsider's view of things. He'd have to leave out the Jimmy-grabbing-the-money part, no way could he tell her that story. But he needed some advice, someone to talk to. That always had been Jimmy's role, to be his adviser, his priest. It occurred to him that he'd just begun to realize how much JoJo had stolen from him. Washing his face, brushing his teeth, he played back the conversation with Jimmy and realized that not once had Jimmy apologized. Maybe the guy didn't think it necessary, maybe Jimmy figured that Dante had to know he was sorry for both their sakes. Only he didn't seem contrite and full of remorse; if anything he continued to defend JoJo.

Jimmy. Dante couldn't shake the image of his best friend, their relationship way beyond friendship. The image of Jimmy and JoJo conspiring together, laughing, Jimmy asking JoJo what he needed done—every time Dante closed his eyes his head was full of a vision of JoJo's smile, that f'n grin of his. Dante winced, feeling that everything in his life was a sham.

"You finally got back," Kathy called out.

He went to the bathroom door. "I woke you, huh?" he said softly.

"I don't sleep so sound, wondering what the hell you're up to. Christ," she said. "Listen to me, I sound like a wife."

"Right, and I tell you it don't sound bad. It's nice to know someone's worrying about me."

He turned out the bathroom light and came back into the living room. Kathy was propped up now, the sheet under her chin. Her shoulders were bare. No T-shirt. Dante thought immediately of those great tits, that exquisite ass pushing into the mattress beneath her. He narrowed his eyes. The expectation started from the tips of his toes and ran up right through the top of his head.

"Ah, excuse me," he said slyly, "you're not wearing your famous T-shirt. Is this a signal here, am I supposed to respond? Because you couldn't have picked a worse time. I'm so tired I feel on the verge of death."

She rose a little shakily, holding the sheet tight to her.

"Are you going to show me something?" Dante said.

"Why, do you want to see something? You think maybe what I have under here is any different than what you've seen before? How's Jimmy?"

"Fine, fine. Jimmy's fine."

"Really? That why he came by here at five o'clock in the morning, to tell you he's fine and chipper. Who you kidding?"

Kathy let go of the sheet with one hand and pointed to the foot of the sofa bed. "Can you see my T-shirt? I tossed it down to the end of the bed, it got so hot in here I was sweating like a Turk."

At the foot of the bed was a balled up white quilt with embroidered triangle designs. Dante searched it and found her shirt. He tossed it to her, and when Kathy reached out to grab it the sheet fell free and a tit the size of a large pear, firm and topped by the tiniest dark brown nipple Dante had ever seen, spilled out.

"Oh damn," Kathy said, frowning and bending her head.

"You know," he said, "this is not getting any easier."

"I know, I know. I'm sorry. Maybe if you've really decided to leave your wife you should find your own place."

He didn't want to think about Judy now, his marriage, his son, but it was something he'd have to consider. He didn't know why, but Dante was certain he'd never go home again.

"Hey," he said, "the only thing I could afford is the back seat of my car."

"Don't think about that now. Just get into bed, and get some sleep. You look terrible."

Still feeling wrecked from the news of Ray's death and the head-to-head with Jimmy, he just wanted to lie still and be with Kathy, but as he kicked off his shoes and unhooked his slacks, studying her back as she twisted, hiding her tits from him, absorbing the smooth way she pulled the shirt on over her head, he was swept by a wave of downright arousal that was about to make him crazy. He stepped out of his trousers and sat down on the edge of the bed, to take off his socks. Getting under the covers, he yawned and stretched out his arms along the top of the bed, Jesus on the cross. Kathy raised her head, then dropped it slowly into the bend of his arm. The elation at the thought of having Jimmy back at his side, the rush of the coming showdown with JoJo had evaporated now and gradually even his desire for Kathy dimmed into an absolute conviction that whatever was taking place was no longer in his hands, there was another force at work here. Jimmy, JoJo, Kathy, his marriage, all were in the firm hands of fate.

Kathy sighed and rolled toward him, throwing an arm across his chest.

"Can I ask you something?" Dante said, hearing the pleading in it.

Kathy raised her head and gazed at him, an incredibly serious look. "Not again," she said.

"Can we talk about it a minute?"

"It don't do any good to talk about what you don't understand."

"Can I touch you?"

There was a long, long silence. Then, "Sure, okay. If that's what you need right now, go ahead."

Dante was not into masturbation, at least not lately, but there was something beautiful about the way she said "Sure, okay." He ran his hand across the top of the sheet, feeling the swell of her breasts. His body was ringing with a mixture of pure indulgence and self-pity. He brought his hand down the sheet, over the rise of her hip, first stroking, then pushing just a bit harder with the very tips of his fingers. She rolled slightly, surrendering a bit more to him. He could feel the top of her vulva now, he pressed for a second and she jumped, said, "I'm sorry, go on, it's okay, go on."

A very long silence. Then, "I can't. You really don't want me to." Silence again, then, "I don't understand it," he said.

"You know," Kathy said, snuggling against his shoulder, "In the Middle Ages they burned women that owned black cats."

"I think I love you," he said, felt immediately foolish and tried to cover up. "Maybe I do love you."

"Right," she said. "Can you sleep now?"

"I don't know."

"Can I help."

"How about a massage?"

"Roll over."

"How about if I don't roll over and lay real still?"

She had small hands with slender, active fingers. He lay his head back against the pillows, watching her, feeling hopeless and bewildered, and then JoJo Paradiso came back on him like a piercing agony, like a wide-awake bad dream. Kathy wet the tips of her fingers and went after him, accompanying herself with a long soft purr, sounding like she was enjoying this. When he came Kathy laughed out loud, and so did Dante.

"There," she said. "There now, feel better?"

"Wonderful, and how about you?"

"I fantasized that we were very young, a pair of virgins at summer camp sharing a tent. You were frightened, afraid of the dark woods and night sounds. I relaxed you, eased your fears, I sang you a lullaby with my hand."

"Buddies."

"Back to back, to the end."

CHAPTER TWENTY-TWO

Nothing symbolized Lina Santangelo's approach to her life more than the lunch she prepared on the afternoon following the night she left Rhode Island.

The night before, the Paradisos had bundled into two cars for the drive back to New York. Several hours later they hooked up with Karl Marx, six of his people, and three more cars at the Howard Johnson's on Bruckner Boulevard in the Bronx. Convinced that his own place was bugged and a target where Lilo's shooters would squat, Salvatore directed the convoy to Lina's house in Glendale.

In the morning sometime around nine o'clock, Lina sat across the room from Frankie F'n Furillo in a white and blue painted kitchen, Frankie holding a pad and pen, walking back and forth, looking unhappy as he listened to Lina give him shopping instructions. She was to cook meals for the gathering of capos and soldiers that were to assemble here.

Her small house was well furnished, and in the finished basement there was a second kitchen with a rather old and large gas stove that had a fine oven. The walls of the house were hung with framed photographs, a shot of Lina and Red embracing, one of their three children; pictures of her parents in the old country, one son in a military uniform, Red standing behind Jerry Vale singing at a microphone somewhere. In the pictures Lina appeared subdued, a kind and gentle woman, but to Frankie F'n Furillo the woman across from him seemed hard as nails, one no-nonsense lady.

The house was quiet. Lina got up from the kitchen table, went to a cabinet, and took out two cups. She poured coffee from the machine, black for herself and light with three sugars for Frankie. Lina said, "You shop for this stuff on Metropolitan Avenue. Don't go running to no A&P somewhere. You go to Metropolitan Avenue. It's more expensive but the stuff is good and fresh and reliable."

Not a little annoyed at his assignment, Frankie stood up straight in the corner near the door to the living room. The old man, JoJo, Bruno, Nicky Black, Karl Marx, and Alley Boy Pinto were below in the finished basement, eating breakfast around a large table.

"See," Lina said, handing Frankie his coffee, "I gotta make the food for all these people, they're gonna be hungry when they get here." She sat herself on a kitchen chair, her elbows on the table, her chin in her hands. "I'm not going to do a whole lot, this ain't no restaurant here, but I gotta do what I gotta do, a little chicken, some birds, and a whole lot of pasta."

"Ey Lina, that's plenty. Personally, I'm not too hungry."

"It's early yet. You will be."

She sipped her coffee and Frankie swallowed his and had another while Lina told him what she wanted from the stores. Frankie stood without moving or interrupting, finally holding up a hand to ask, "A dozen Cornish hens, what's that?"

"Little birds, tiny chickens. I'm gonna need four packages of stomachs and hearts for the stuffing. Two boxes of Uncle Ben's original converted rice. Two chickens, cut up. A half dozen red peppers, a bottle of vinegar peppers, Italian style, imported. Five large cans of imported tomato, whole tomato with basil. Four pounds of chopped sirloin, two pounds of ground pork, three pounds of sausage, neck bones, pork and beef, a half dozen of each."

"Whoa! Hold it. Slow down. I write fast, but there's fast and then there's forget it. Give me a break here."

Lina grinned at him, saying, "Two large containers of Sorrento ricotta cheese, two large balls of fresh mozzarella cheese, a dozen eggs, a box of Progresso bread crumbs. You can get all this stuff in the pork store," she told him. "You finish there you go to the vegetable stand across the street. Pick me up a nice head of fresh basil, parsley, onions, the red peppers, two boxes of mushrooms, a couple of garlics, nice heads, firm. You know what I mean?" Frankie nodded. "About a dozen tomatoes, two heads of escarole, two heads of chickory, five pounds of potatoes, a bag of onions."

"*Minchia,*" Frankie told her, "I'm gonna need a f'n truck."

"C'mon, c'mon, it's not so much, you too weak, bring someone to help you. Four or five bags is all. A half dozen loafs of bread, three seeded three without seeds, half these guys got trouble with their gums, seeds are bad for them." She paused a moment, took a breath, and said, "Two pounds of prosciutto, two pounds of roast pork, two pounds of roast beef, and two pounds of Genoa salami. I got enough mayo and mustard here. That's it."

"That's it?" Frankie said.

"No wait."

"*Marrone,* what else?"

Lina got up and took a peek in her kitchen cabinet. "Three boxes of penne," she said with a warm smile, "the good ones, the imported ones, you gonna find them in the market across from the pork store."

"That's it?"

"Five pounds of coffee, a gallon of milk, one quart container of half-and-half, and get me two dozen mixed pastry from the bakery on the corner."

"Ooofa," Frankie said, "Whataya feeding here, an army?"

"Ey, what else? Salvatore told me to make lunch for ten, fifteen people. These are big men, they eat. Especially when they're tense and nervous, they eat a whole lot. I'll make lunch and there'll be enough left over for dinner. I got a couple of gallons of wine my husband made a year ago— God, that stuff is terrible, it'll give everybody the runs. Maybe you should pick up some wine, huh Frankie? A little wine would be good, no?"

Frankie said, "They'll drink the homemade stuff, they'll put some ginger ale in it, it'll be great."

"Good," she told him. "Pick up a half dozen ginger ale and some club soda."

"Why don't you come with me?" Frankie said. "In case you forgot something or something?"

"No, no, no I can't leave. In case—"

"Yeah, yeah you're right. In case the old man needs something."

"Frankie, don't call Salvatore an old man. He's no old man, you should be an old man like him when you're an old man. In every room of the house Salvatore can do as good or better than a man half his age. So don't call him an old man."

"Pardon me."

"You're pardoned, now get going, for the food. I gotta cook."

————

Thinking about how badly he'd blown it, JoJo sat at one end of the table in Lina's finished basement listening to his father, who sat at the other. Karl Marx and Bruno sat opposite Nicky Black and Alley Boy Pinto, Rudy the Dancer Randazzo's main slammer from Sheepshead Bay. The old man was going on about Lilo and Yale and Benny Bats, how you gotta cut off their heads and all their tails will die, I'm not at war with their whole crew. Those are my people, confused right now, but they're under my flag, and I don't want people going around shooting everyone in sight. Understand what I mean?

Alley Boy dropped his head, said, "Shit."

"What?" The old man said.

"I got a call last night from Rudy after he talked to you. You know Rudy don't fly so he's driving back with the wife and kids from Disneyland. Anyway, he tells me we got this war and so on, tells me what happened with JoJo in Rhode Island, says to me the first chance you get hit 'em. So early this morning I sent a few of my people to cruise Lilo's club, and they get lucky, catch Paulie the numbers guy and Tommy the Saint in the street."

"What?" the old man said.

"They're gone, boss. They're gone. I mean, it was my understanding—"

"See, see what can happen here, right?" The old man's face was overflowing with a crazed hopelessness. "See what I'm talking about?"

"Pop," JoJo said, "this is a war. We gotta go after Lilo fast, can't give him a chance to lay back and make plans of his own."

Salvatore Paradiso looked around the table at each face. "What do you think, Bruno?" he asked.

"It's a war, Sal, we gotta smash these bastards."

"Karl? How do you see it?"

"There's some good people in Lilo's crew, good earners, loyal too. We gotta watch out for them."

"Hey, hey," Nicky Black said. He stood and hitched up his pants. "We oil the guns and go after them all. If we gotta, we kill their wives and girlfriends, their fucking kids. Kill 'em all, these traitorous bastards."

Frowning, Salvatore looked at Nicky Black, said, "Sit down, Nicky." Nicky said, "Sure." He sat.

"Joseph?" His father gave him a slow glance. "You used the phone here this morning, so I suppose it's okay. I mean nobody could get on Lina's telephone that quick. Am I right?" His father reached across the table and took a cigarette from Nicky Black, bent his head, and lit it. As far as JoJo knew, it was his first in about five years. JoJo saw that his father's hands were shaking. "Because early this morning I placed a call."

"The phone here is safe, Pop. I spoke to the kid Sonny the Hawk earlier, told him to send any calls he gets for me here."

"All right. Look, I want you all to listen to me. Lilo took this shot because he figured he had the Ramminos with him. But he ain't got the Ramminos. He got this bust-out hard-on Catalano, the guy's a money-grubbing hard-on. Armond Rammino ain't gonna line up with them."

"You sure Pop?"

"Not unless he figures I'm out of it all together, and as far as I know, I ain't. Unless you guys around this table got other plans." He gave them each a beady stare, then smiled.

Everyone's head, JoJo's included, jerked back. "Whoooa," they said in unison, like an Italian chorus.

"Christ, Pop," JoJo said.

"C'mon boss," Karl Marx and Alley Boy Pinto sang a little duet. Bruno said, "Salvatore?" Afraid now to speak, Nicky Black didn't say anything.

"All right, look. My *compare,* Red in Rhode Island, he already spoke to the Biscoglias, they talked to the Reninas, both those families will sit this out. And listen to this, Tommy Renina sent word that if we need any help, call. That's what he said, if we need help just reach out."

Again in unison, the Italian chorus, "F'n great."

"So come on, where is Lilo gonna go? To Armond Rammino? Armond's got so much trouble with that bullshit dope business of his, he don't need any more from us." He threw JoJo a look. JoJo dropped his head, thinking about the Cuban, wondering what the hell he was going to do now about Luis.

The phone rang. Everyone froze. Lina called from upstairs, "Salvatore," she said. "It's a friend of yours."

"Who?"

"Salvatore, answer the phone. He seems like a nice man, said he's a friend. Who else gonna have this number but a friend?"

Laughing, the Italian chorus again, "Salvatore answer the phone."

JoJo's father flicked a thumb toward the ceiling. "Ey," he said, "if all my people were as tough and as loyal as that lady upstairs, we'd have no problem, believe me."

"Salvatore," JoJo said. "Answer the phone. And when you're done you can put out the garbage."

"Don't be disrespectful," his father said softly. He went to a telephone atop a homemade bar in the far corner of the basement. Above the bar was a painting of Naples. He spoke for two, three minutes, and when he was done he leaned against the bar as if this was his usual hangout.

JoJo blew out a puff of concern. "Well?" he said.

"Lilo, Yale, and Catalano got a sitdown tonight. It's at eight o'clock, a place called Parkway Pizza in White Plains. That was Armond."

"I know the place," said Bruno.

"It's Lilo's cousin's joint," said Karl Marx.

"Beautiful," said Alley Boy.

"I'm goin', I'm there," said Nicky Black. "I'm gonna piss on the holes in their hearts."

Everyone turned to look at Nicky, who bent his head and frowned, saying, "Okay, okay, but I wanna go. I wanna be there."

"We'll all be there," said Bruno.

"No, not everybody," said Salvatore. "Joseph, my son, you'll pick the people. You'll go and take care of this."

Nicky Black tugged on JoJo's sleeve. "Don't leave me out," he said.

———————

Two hours later JoJo sat in the back seat of Bruno's car next to Karl Marx, his arms folded, his father's words going round and round in his head, *My son, you'll go and take care of this.* Riding in the Buick, sailing through Queens, his brain generated images of Lilo, his face contorted in fear and pain. In his mind's eye JoJo held two guns and blasted away at the dumb bastard's head. JoJo daydreamed of murder.

Bruno was driving along Woodhaven Boulevard, shooting JoJo glances in the rearview; Bobby Pumps Apulia, one of Bruno's no-bullshit-I'll-kill-you-in-a-heartbeat guys, was riding shotgun. He was a quiet one, a cold-blooded bastard, one of those that enjoyed the killing. With an ice pick Bobby was like a surgeon, and he always went for the heart, the pumps. JoJo had never much cared for Bobby Pumps, but he loved having him around now.

Bruno drove in silence for a good ten minutes. Turning off Woodhaven onto 101st Avenue, he said, "So we'll make a stop at the club, see who's around."

"Good," JoJo told him, too caught up in his head to have much of a conversation. He sat in the quiet of the car wondering if Sonny the Hawk from the candy store held any messages for him, reasoning that his brother

John had it made, being away from all this crap, figuring that maybe what he should think about is reaching out for Luis the Cuban, the poor guy made that trip from Spain just to see him.

Karl Marx sat back on the seat next to him reading the *Post*, his little feet dangling in midair, the fiery headline three inches high, black and bold: DETECTIVE GUNNED DOWN IN THE BRONX. JoJo glanced at the headline, then turned away, not wanting to read any of it, wanting to forget that that killing ever occurred, wondering for the moment what had happened to Jimmy Burns. He watched Karl Marx for a moment, measuring the level of his interest in the newspaper story, deciding that there didn't seem to be a whole lot.

"Am I on for this tonight?" Karl Marx said, his tone casual. "Do you want me for this?"

JoJo nodded, closing his eyes, resting his clogged head, hating now to be asked questions. What if Lilo was smart enough or lucky enough to somehow place another traitor near him? Thinking about another traitor, someone not trying to get him locked up but some bum trying to get him dead, made him feel even more tired and sad. He was overwhelmed by the thought that in this goddamn business it always turned out that you spent time thinking about renegades. When Bruno parked the car, JoJo announced the obvious to himself: you'll know soon enough.

There was no real need to go to the club. The place was bugged and tapped, and there were probably more cops around than goodfellas, and when he thought about it, what sense did it make to walk the streets now and make himself a target? Nevertheless, Bruno had convinced him that on the one hand everyone expected he'd lay low, on the other hand he was a wartime leader and wartime leaders hide from no f'n body.

He did want to grab the kid Sonny from the candy store, see if there were any messages, see if anyone's been around. He expected that he'd hear from Jimmy Burns, and maybe the Cuban; He hoped he'd hear something from Vinny Rapino, the son of a bitch running off with his Mercedes like that. There would be no business at the club. War ended business. Later tonight he'd end the war. Later tonight he'd even up with Lilo and Yale, and Catalano too. He was thinking that he just decided that what he needed was a good long vacation.

Karl Marx was the first to open his door and get out, followed by Bobby Pumps and Bruno. Bobby opened JoJo's door.

Sonny came out of the candy store and practically threw himself at JoJo, saying, "Joseph, I got messages for ya. I called over at the number you gave me, they told me you were gone. I was worried man, these messages, I got 'em. Got all your messages, Joseph."

"Good, Sonny, good, you did good. Calm down. Has anyone been around, you know, looking for me or anything?" JoJo wondered if it was safe to tell Sonny a little of what was going on, then thought what the hell for, what would be gained by that? The guy's a dumbo ex-junkie message taker, whataya thinking?

There were four phone numbers, three in code, one straight up. The straight-up number had an area code he thought was Boston but he wasn't sure. It was probably Luis, the Cuban, calling to let him know he was in town. Luis asking what the hell was going on.

JoJo walked into the candy store, went to the pay phone Jimmy Burns had told him was safe and tapped out the first of the coded numbers. JoJo nodded to Sonny the Hawk, saying, "This first number here, can you tell me anything about the caller?"

"Sure, sure," Sonny said. "That first one was from some guy at a garage."

JoJo hung up the phone. "Yeah," he said.

"That's his number, he said you can call him if you want, you can reach him there. Anyway, he left the message."

"What f'n message Sonny? The hell you talking about?"

"He said the cops came. That's all he said, 'The cops came' is what he said. That's the message, Joseph."

Bobby Pumps and Karl Marx were standing guard at the candy store door. Bruno had gone off to the club to take a leak.

JoJo dialed the second number. "Did the second caller leave a message Sonny?"

"No message, just the number."

The phone rang once and Barry Cooper answered, saying, "Jesus, Joseph, I've been trying to reach you. Are you okay?"

"Fine. What's up."

"What's up is that case of wine you ordered from Spain, you know the one, it's arrived. It's in Boston, Joseph. I'm not at all sure how it ended up there, but that's where it is, in Boston."

"Really?"

"That's right, in Boston. You shouldn't let it wait too long. Maybe you should think about taking a trip to Boston to pick it up. It's good wine Joseph."

"What number am I calling, Barry?"

"My private line."

"I know your private line, this is not it."

"I've changed it. I've been meaning to tell you that I had my private line changed."

"Will you be at the office awhile?"

"I've got an appointment outside the office at three. I'll be here all morning."

"Okay."

"You coming by?"

"Maybe. I'll give you a call."

"Do you want the number of the warehouse in Boston where the wine is being held? I have it here."

"Sure."

Barry read off a number, JoJo thinking goddamn son of a bitch, the bastard, it's him. JoJo hung up. "Karl," he said, "c'mere, will ya."

If asked, JoJo couldn't say why exactly, but he was dead certain that his lawyer, the honorable Barry Cooper, was the traitor beside him, the goddamn cancer in his family's stomach. Alarmed, JoJo smashed the receiver against the phone box. He spun on his heel and headed for the door. What was elementary, what was way beyond the worst f'n thing possible, was the panicky thought that if you figure that Barry was the rat, then what did that make Luis? Luis, the f'n Cuban, was an agent, had to be. He put his hand on the shoulder of Karl Marx and found himself walking and talking along 101st Avenue. It wasn't the brightest move, especially with Lilo loose and his shooters out cruising, looking for a target, but there he was strolling along with Karl, Bobby Pumps following, Bruno standing in front of the club, his hands on his hips, watching him go.

Maybe somewhere in his mind JoJo was hoping a car would ease up, blow him away on his own street, in front of these straight-world people who acknowledged him with quick nods and small smiles. Right then he had this heavy miserable f'n feeling he'd be better off dead than doing thirty, forty years in some federal can. Christ, Barry Cooper a stool pigeon. Was that fair, was that legal, turning your own lawyer into a rat against you? F'n government, a bunch of sneaky ruthless bastards, the man's my lawyer for chrissake.

Shit, Barry set up the drug move, and Luis the agent sucked him in. They had him, he'd walked into it, now they had him cold. He understood enough about the law to know he was facing big time, a drug smuggling conspiracy conviction would bring him home sometime in the next century. He flashed on the memory of the meeting with the Cuban, slick son of a bitch. What do they have? Recorded conversations, serious, intense conversations about bringing in hundreds of pounds of coke, swapping cocaine for heroin, shit, shit, and more shit. Bastards. Could conversation alone bring him thirty years? Hell yeah, he was a Paradiso, a made guy, big-time Mafia. He would be, putting it mildly, a goddamn media event. One hand on Karl Marx's shoulder, the other palming his forehead, he said, "Karl, I got an important piece of work for you."

Karl Marx said, "Good, good. When?"

"How about in an hour?"

"Hmm, I got that much time hah?"

"It's my lawyer."

"Shit." The dwarf winked. "I can always find time for a lawyer."

When JoJo returned to the candy store twenty minutes after Karl Marx and Bobby Pumps had left, Sonny the Hawk said, slow and easy, kind of cool and loose, "Anything you need Joseph, I'm here to help. I'll take messages all day for ya, if that's what you need, I'll be proud to do it."

"That's good Sonny, I'm glad to hear that."

JoJo tapped out the last of the coded numbers and after three rings got Jimmy Burns.

"Hey pally," Jimmy said. "What's up, whataya doin'?"

JoJo stared blindly at the candy store doorway, Bruno standing guard now. He held the phone alongside his jaw, "Talking to you, whataya think I'm doin'?"

"Listen buddy, we got us a real problem."

"No shit. What a surprise."

"I've got to see you, and it's gotta be soon."

"Huh," JoJo grunted. "I'm busy, tied up. What are you telling me?"

"I'm telling you I've got to see you as soon as possible. How about late tonight?"

JoJo could hear that Jimmy was real tense, antsy to see him. Only how? he had no time. "I'm busy tonight."

"What if it's late? You know, say one, two in the morning? How about that? You call it."

JoJo was clenching his jaw so tightly that his ears hurt. He didn't need this. "You wanna tell me what this is about?" He wanted to say hey Jimmy get off my f'n back, I'm in the middle of a f'n war here, but he was afraid to be that short with him.

"It's the other guy."

"Do me a favor Jimmy, I'm on a pay phone, where you at? Your neighbor's, right?"

"Yeah, that's right."

"Okay, so don't talk in no f'n codes. It makes me nuts. What other guy, goddammit?"

"Dante, Dante. That other guy."

"Oh for chrissake. What does that pain in the ass want now?"

"He wants to see you." That came out like a straight demand, and it made JoJo's stomach wrench.

"Yeah, about what?"

"Maybe you'd better ask him."

"Jimmy, I'm asking you."

"I don't know, tell you the truth, I got no idea. But I'll be there, and the way he put it JoJo, you should see if you can find the time."

"Where and when?"

"The Eighty-third Street park ramp. You tell me the time."

A sharp laugh from JoJo. "Say tonight, around eleven, eleven thirty."

"We'll be there."

"I can hardly wait."

"See ya later." Jimmy hung up.

JoJo hung up the phone feeling like the World Trade Center had just landed on his back. He went out to the street where Bruno was waiting. Bruno threw an arm around his shoulders and pulled him close.

"All right *compare*. C'mon, we got guns to oil, people to reach. You ready?"

They got in Bruno's car, and Bruno nodded at a brown paper bag at JoJo's feet. There were two pistols inside, automatics, new guns, wrapped in a cloth. Pulling out, Bruno twisted around to check traffic, saying, "I feel like a f'n kid, like it's my wedding day." JoJo nodded without answering. At the end of this day people would be dead, and maybe he'd be one of them.

———

That afternoon it rained for the first time in a week, the Manhattan sky an ocean of fierce rolling gray and black clouds. At twenty to one, Karl Marx valet-parked his baby blue Monte Carlo and he and Bobby Pumps walked one block west, then one block north to the high-rise office building at the corner of Fifth and Fifty-seventh Street. The first two phones at the entrance were destroyed, but the third one was working. Karl tapped out a number, and a woman's voice answered, "Law office."

"My name's Robert Tracy. My brother Richard had a twelve o'clock appointment with Mr. Cooper, I need to speak to him. I need to speak to my brother."

The woman said, "There's no Richard Tracy here."

"Don't lie to me lady," Karl said, looking around the busy street. "I know he's sitting right there. Tell him it's me, Bob."

Sounding fed up now, the woman said, "Mr. Tracy, I've no need to lie to you. There is no Richard Tracey in the office."

Karl saying now, "You know, I bet I got the date confused, I'm sorry. Say, is Mr. Cooper in?"

"Would you like to speak to him?"

Karl Marx threw a little thumb in the air, and Bobby Pumps nodded. "Not right now, I gotta run. I'll call back in an hour or so."

"As you wish."

They rode the elevator to the seventeenth floor. Bobby Pumps noticed that Karl kept making these small noises with his tongue. They walked down the hallway toward suite 1751-A, Karl in the lead, Bobby trailing. Karl looked over his shoulder and Bobby could see that the little dude had his tongue out. Outside Barry's office, Bobby reached into the pocket of his jacket and pulled out a ski mask and Colt Python .357. Slipping the ski mask over his head, he entered the office. A young black woman about twenty-five sat at the reception desk, hair cut so short he thought at first she was a he. Dressed up, wearing something red, real long and loose, lots of gold, chain necklace, earrings the size of a baby's fist, bracelets running up and down both arms. She said something like "Ahhhhh shiiiiiit" and was about to cut loose, when Bobby put his finger up in front of his lips like Santa Claus, and standing in front of her desk now, the edge catching him right at the waist, he extended the .357 eye level into the woman's face. Her name was Lee Ann McCrey, and she held tightly to the gold chain around her neck, about to scream, ready to give it all she had, when Bobby Pumps quietly hissed, "One word and you are fucking dead."

Lee Ann sat real still and quiet, her mouth open in a perfect circle. Bobby none too carefully or gently covered her eyes and mouth with masking tape, crossed her hands and taped them together. Stood her up, gave one tiny tit a little squeeze, patted her ass, and then pushed her to the floor. He then hustled to the office door and opened it, saying, "Okay, okay." Karl Marx came through the door still clicking his tongue.

Maybe if Barry Cooper wasn't half stoned from his three-Absolut-vodka-martini lunch he would have heard something, some sound from the waiting room. But he was and he didn't. Maybe if he was not listening to Mama Cass doing a hippie-ish rendition of 'Bye-Bye Blackbird,' maybe if he was off the phone for a goddamn minute, but he wasn't, he'd been speed-rapping for twenty-five minutes, trying to convince his FBI contact that no way did he want or need any of their agents with their cheap gray suits cluttering up his waiting room. He did hear his door open and was about to tell Lee Ann to use the goddamn intercom, that's what it was for, tell her for the sixth billionth time to keep his f'n door closed. "Excuse me a minute," he said into the phone, then, "yeah, yeah, and what the hell do you want Lee Ann?"

The door opened wide and he had a good view of the dwarf, standing there, just standing there looking at him, then letting his gaze slowly move around the room and then bringing it back to him. Barry sat rigid, feeling the goose bumps crawling up his legs, around his stomach, under his hair. The little bastard just standing there, his hands in the pockets of his jacket. He could hear the FBI agent, his agent, saying, "Hey, hey, Barry, you there?"

Karl saying now, "Hang up the phone." And him doing it, hanging up his telephone, in his own office, not saying good-bye to the agent, nothing. The little shit looking expressionless, standing there like maybe it was his office. Barry watched him take the gun out of his jacket pocket, a little gun with a long barrel, a silencer. "Now wait a goddamn minute," was the last thing Barry Cooper said.

Karl raised the gun, holding it with both hands, arms extended.

As Barry's palms covered his eyes, Karl shot him five times, slamming him into the back of his chair, the momentum carrying him off and dropping him to the floor.

Karl Marx dragged a chair over to the desk. Climbing up to kneel on top, he gave Barry Cooper two be-sures.

On the elevator heading for the lobby Karl asked Bobby Pumps if he was hungry, asked him if he'd ever been to the Russian Tea Room. Bobby said, "I could use a sandwich, but I hate tea, so maybe we should go back to Queens. I hear Lina is cooking a hell of a meal."

———

Lina was in a good mood, her small house filled with big hungry men.

"You know, I haven't had this many people here since my son Guido's wedding. It's nice having people around." Lina smiled happily at Salvatore, who was busy cutting and chopping chicken. Salvatore made like he didn't hear Lina and kept banging away at the chicken.

Lina bent over the counter, slicing red bell pepper, mushrooms, and onion, mincing the garlic. Salvatore was the best-looking and kindest man she had ever been with. Not that her dead husband Red was unkind; he was rough, a rough-and-tumble guy, that was Red. Also, Salvatore was tall where Red was sort of short, and he was thin, not that Red was a blob, he was heavy, stocky, you could say stocky, you'd never say fat. And good-looking, sort of good-looking. But Salvatore shaved every day, and showered and powdered himself, and smelled so good. And those blue eyes, those eyes.

When Salvatore finished chopping the chicken he put his hands on his hips and marched around the kitchen. Little circles. A real important man.

"Do you ever think of getting married again?" he asked Lina. Lina stopped working and turned to him.

"No, when Red died I promised myself I'd never wash another man's dirty underwear."

Salvatore nodded. "Yeah, when my wife died I swore to Saint Anthony I'd never buy underwear for another woman."

"Why Saint Anthony?"

"Why not?"

"Okay, I guess one saint's as good as another."

"Who said? That's not true," Salvatore went to the door between the kitchen and the dining room. Bruno Greco, Frankie F'n Furillo, Bobby Pumps, Karl Marx, and Nicky Black were seated around the dining room table playing poker. In the living room beyond, Alley Boy Pinto and five guys from his crew sat watching TV. Everyone was eating a sandwich, drinking a beer. A party.

Salvatore affected a yawn, saying, "Not all the saints are the same. They are very different, as a matter of fact."

"You tell me you swore to Saint Anthony, this and that. Ey, what for? Saint Anthony finds things, he's the patron saint of lost articles. Don't you remember in school, you lose something, the nuns said pray to Saint Anthony."

Salvatore looked at the gathering of his people. His son Joseph was in the finished basement using the phone, talking with Rudy the Dancer Randazzo or whomever. Salvatore didn't much care.

"Maybe I feel lost, maybe I'm the lost one Saint Anthony of Padua can't even find." His voice cracked a little, surprising Lina, frightening her.

"C'mon, Salvatore, c'mon. I know it can't be easy, but you have responsibilities. You are *capo di famiglia*."

"Yeah, yeah, capo di shit, that's me."

Trying to shift gears, Lina asked, "So who is your favorite saint? It's Saint Anthony?"

He turned in the doorway and stood for a second, folding his arms.

"My favorite saint, you wanna know who my favorite saint is?" For the first time Lina noticed a sort of lapse in Salvatore's speech. "For me it's Saint Thomas Becket."

"But he's not Italian."

"No, he was British, they killed him in his own house. They came for him, four men, and murdered him in his own cathedral."

"Salvatore," she said, "you know what? I think it's time we retire. I'm tired of cooking, I cooked enough in my life, enough is enough. And maybe you're tired too, tired of being *capo di famiglia*. Maybe for you too enough is enough."

"In his own house they killed him. Can you believe that?"

———

Lina Santangelo's house, from the upstairs bedrooms to the finished basement, was filled with the perfumes and fragrances of her cooking. Twelve Cornish hens, six in each of her ovens, the birds stuffed to overflowing with a mixture of cooked rice, sautéed onion, garlic, chopped chicken hearts and gizzards, bread crumbs, an egg, some parsley, the birds then set out in large roasting pans, surrounded by peeled and quartered potatoes and slices of onion, long sprigs of parsley gathered under every leg, a cup of water in each pan, they were baked until they were honey brown. These roasting aromas mixed well with the deep scent of a strong and healthy tomato, basil, and meat sauce that bubbled slowly in pots atop both stoves.

JoJo stretched, running his fingers through his hair. He went to the stove in the basement, took the lid from the bubbling pot, and stirred Lina's sauce with a wooden spoon, thinking of Jimmy Burns, what he had said: Dante wants to see you, we got a problem. He didn't know which word pissed him off more, *problem,* or *Dante.* Both together. When he finished with Lilo he'd run over to the park and see what it was that Dante wanted. Dante O'Donnell, the wacky bastard, he'd never been able to figure that guy, gave up trying years ago. He wondered if Jimmy had chosen a side, made a choice between him and Dante.

Suddenly he thought of Lilo. How many and who to bring to the pizza joint tonight? Bruno for sure, and Nicky Black, couldn't leave out numbnuts Nicky. Karl and Alley Boy, with a few of his people from Sheepshead Bay. He'd left it to Alley Boy to get walkie-talkies. Guns? Shit they had enough guns to outfit a revolution, guns were the least of his problems.

Stirring, tasting Lina's sauce, running his tongue around the wooden spoon, JoJo imagined he was in a movie, a general alone in his bunker putting together a night raid through the wire. Dim light and a ghostly sound track. No prisoners, we'll take no prisoners tonight, a body count is what I want, it's all I want. He flashed on Barry Cooper and the f'n Cuban agent. His eyes roamed the basement walls and ceiling as he listened to the voices above him, the laughter, the horsing around of his people. Thinking about Jimmy, hoping his old buddy hadn't done anything stupid.

CHAPTER TWENTY-THREE

At seven that night Bruno, Nicky Black, and Bobby Pumps rode with JoJo, Bruno driving, out the Grand Central Parkway and over the Triborough Bridge. They followed the Major Deegan north, shooting past Yankee Stadium on up to the Cross Westchester and east into White Plains. They were followed by Karl Marx with three of his people, and Karl was trailed by Alley Boy Pinto with two more slammers from Sheepshead Bay, twin brothers named Della Femina. The eleven were armed better than Israeli commandos.

By seven forty-five the caravan of killers bounced along a rutted street in the western section of White Plains, passing a movie theater that advertised *Terminator* and *Terminator 2*, a clothing store, a Thai restaurant, and a pool hall. The three cars pulled to the curb one after another, and they sat for a moment, two blocks from the pizza restaurant owned by Lilo's cousin Vincent Santamaria and his wife Paula.

Sitting next to Bruno, who was checking slugs for his twelve-gauge, putting two in his shirt pocket, JoJo went over the plan. One of the Della Femina brothers would place a call to 911, tell the local cops that a cop, one of their own, was being beaten and stabbed by a gang of wacko sons of bitches at the far end of the precinct. Every cop in radio range would think that he was needed. Then JoJo would swoop in on the restaurant with two teams of four, the first team to take out Lilo's guards at the restaurant door, the second team, made up of himself, Bruno, Nicky Black, and Karl Marx, to come right behind, enter the restaurant, and kill everyone at Lilo's table except Armond Rammino.

After checking guns and masks, JoJo sent Billy Della Femina to walk past the restaurant, check it out, make sure everyone was in place. Billy had been at Lilo's gambling joint a few times, knew Lilo by sight. He was sure that none of Lilo's crew would recognize him. The twin advanced the two blocks, crossed the street, went into the pizza parlor, and came out in five minutes carrying a Coke. He hustled back to JoJo.

"They're sitting right inside the door. Only wait a minute, there's a colored couple in back of the joint eating a pie and drinking beer. A coupla kids."

"All right," JoJo said, "if they mind their business leave 'em be." He picked up the cellular phone, dialed 911, and handed the phone to Billy Della Femina. The call to the cops made, JoJo used the walkie-talkie to tell Karl Marx, "Let's do it."

Karl pulled out, followed by Bruno, JoJo feeling a mighty blast in his chest and lungs, testing a genuine surge of craziness, nothing else in his head but Lilo's laughing face behind his eyes.

Lilo's guards were standing around, arms folded, heads on swivels, checking the street. What they saw was two cars pull up, the doors fly open, and refugees from a Halloween party at a lunatic asylum jump out. Alley Boy Pinto bolted from the back seat of the lead car, a sawed-off automatic shotgun in his hands, screaming, "Don't die, don't die, be smart you don't have to die!" Lilo's people put their hands in the air, nothing coming into their faces but horror.

JoJo was first through the door, followed by Bruno and Nicky Black. Karl Marx came after them, appearing to be precisely what he was, a three-foot nightmare in a King Kong mask, a pistol in each hand.

As if on cue, the black couple in the rear of the restaurant eating a pizza they would tell their grandkids about dived to the floor. JoJo was an arm's length away from Lilo, who sat holding a slice of pizza in one hand and a glass of wine in the other. JoJo extended his automatic, the barrel pointed at the gold medallion around Lilo's neck. The look on the bastard's face was a mixture of knowing and not believing. In that fraction of a second before the explosions poured from his pistol, JoJo thought he heard Lilo say something like, "It's all right, it's all right." Lilo's eyes narrowed, his mouth curved in a cold half smile. JoJo fired and Lilo pitched backward off his chair. Nicky Black jumped to the side, did a little jig, and took his shots at Lilo, who was rolling around the floor, trying to cover up. JoJo slipped on some spilled food, straightened up, put the automatic on Lilo again, and fired eight more times, until the slide on his gun popped.

"Not me, not me!" Armond Rammino screamed, throwing his arms in the air, falling backward off his chair. Lilo's cousin Vincent ran out of the kitchen, collided with the black couple crawling across the floor, and did a header into the soda machine. Bruno, eyes wide, had fired his double-barreled shotgun from the hip, catching Tommy Yale as he turned his head away. Karl Marx, his tongue sticking through the slit of his gorilla mask, blasted Benny Bats, who had chosen to stand and now flew back, his arms over his head, his hands stretching for the ceiling like a priest blessing the room. The dwarf moved among the spattered food and wine and upturned chairs doing be-sures; he shot Lilo in the back of the head with the gun in his left hand, Tommy Yale through the cheekbone with his right.

In thirty seconds it was over.

————————

An hour and ten minutes later the entire band was back at Lina's for coffee and pastry.

She'd set everything out buffet style, plastic cups, plates, and saucers. Lina wasn't about to wash dishes for all these characters. She put out about five pounds of *struffoli,* honey-coated pastry balls, a dozen *zeppole,* a Neapolitan deep-fried cream puff that Salvatore reminded her the Sicilians called *sfinge,* and a large cherry ricotta cheesecake.

Lina watched the young men—some looked to her like boys—troop to Salvatore and JoJo to shake hands and offer respect. Then they would take a piece of cake, a cup of coffee, sit around her living room; some went down to the basement card game. They laughed loudly, punching each other on the shoulders. It was around ten o'clock when she saw Salvatore take JoJo by the elbow, like he was a cop or something, and lead him upstairs to her bedroom.

————————

His father folded his arms and took a seat on the edge of the bed while JoJo paced, one hand over his wrist, glancing at his watch.

"You got someplace to go? You keep looking at your watch?"

"Yeah, I got an appointment at eleven."

JoJo caught an appraising look from his father, and said, "It's nothing Pop. I'm gonna go and run into my friend Jimmy Burns."

"The cop, right?"

"You know Jimmy Burns, Pop. Yeah, he's still a cop."

"So Lilo's gone."

"Yeah, and those two other humps, Yale and Benny Bats. Catalano wasn't there."

"You thought maybe Armond Rammino was going to let you kill one of his captains? You think maybe this is Christmas?"

JoJo laughed, a small laugh but a laugh nevertheless.

His father aimed a finger at JoJo's face. "Those people you clipped were my people. I lost five people today. I don't think that's funny."

JoJo nodded, surprised to find himself a little frightened. "Whose fault, Pop? These guys were coming after us."

His father squinted at him. "You remember when you came to me with this drug business?"

"Uh-huh."

"I told you no way, I told you forget it."

"I know, I know Pop. I explained, I told you what happened, how it happened. You were right, it was a mistake. Whataya wanna do, kill me? I made a mistake, for chrissake. People make mistakes."

His father looked at him and shrugged. "Anybody else but my son, I mean anybody, you're a dead man." He gazed at JoJo as if he were a walking disease.

JoJo sat down on the end of the bed, folded his hands between his legs, and dropped his head. "I'm sorry Pop."

"Oh yeah, I know you're sorry now. But if your betrayal had worked, you wouldn't have been so sorry."

JoJo started to sweat.

"You finished me," his father said.

"Don't say that."

"Turned my *consigliere* against me. Bruno and me are done, fini. How could I ever trust him again?" Salvatore Paradiso took a deep breath. "What I'm trying to say to you is, I know it's over for me. I know it, you know it, Bruno knows it. Christ, even Lina knows it. And the truth is, it's not so bad. I'm a lucky man, I can walk away from this business, this life. I mean, I can enjoy whatever there is left for me."

At that moment JoJo was so confused by his father that he stared at him, afraid to speak.

"So let's say I pack it in, what then?"

"You'll move to Florida, sit in the sun, do a little fishing. Go to the track, take Lina to a new restaurant every night. Not bad."

"No, not bad at all. And what about you? What would you do if I left?"

"I guess the first thing I'd do is reach out to Lilo's people, let 'em know it's over. They can come home now."

"And then?"

"Then go on with business as usual," JoJo said, avoiding his father's eyes. "I mean, what else is there? I ain't gonna go and open a restaurant or a bar, Pop. I'll do what I gotta do, I'll survive."

Salvatore lay down on the bed, folded his hands behind his head. "Joseph, Joseph, Joseph," he said, no warmth in his voice now. He lunged forward, rubbing his temples with the heels of his hands. "Why didn't you tell me about Barry Cooper?"

"There's nothing to tell," JoJo said, feeling acid pour into his stomach.

"The man can put you in jail."

"Excuse me, Pop, the man ain't going to be doing anything but looking up from under six feet of dirt."

"He can still put you away. You make bad choices Joseph, terrible decisions. I mean, I don't know what to do about you."

"Listen Pop, don't get pissed, but I gotta tell ya. In this business you gotta make decisions, move around. Times are changing, things just aren't the same. It's tough out there, it's murder in the street. No disrespect, but you don't know how it is anymore."

Tensed for an attack, JoJo was surprised when his father rose slowly from the bed and spoke to him in an easygoing, warm tone.

"Maybe you're right." He hesitated, giving JoJo a serious look. "I guess. Shit, I know you're right, I know, I know." His father shook his head, blew out some air. "There's things out there I don't understand anymore. I mean everybody wanting to do drugs, underbosses, *consiglieres* turning to the cops. What are we gonna have next, heads of families testifying for the government? It's nuts, it's crazy, I want no part of it."

His father spread his hands in a broad gesture of welcome. "You want me to give this all to you, this family, all of it?"

JoJo ran his hands through his hair, suddenly feeling both frightened and hopeful. He gave the question a moment, then answered before he'd thought it through. "If not me, who?"

"Well that would take some time, some thought. Who's left? Let's see, there's my son-in-law, Nicky."

"Pop."

"Not Nicky, of course not Nicky. How about Bruno? Naw, Bruno don't want it. Karl Marx, or the Dancer? Sure, Rudy would make sense. He's smart and tough, got all these wild men with him."

JoJo looked up at him as if trying to read the man's mind.

"The Dancer is *uomo di pazienza, uomo che sa pensare alla sua casa.*" His father was telling him that Rudy Randazzo was a patient man, a man who knew how to take care of his house.

JoJo began to vibrate like the strings of a piano. Angry and embarrassed, he shouted, "And me, what am I?"

He rose to his feet, on the very edge of losing it. He could feel his eyes brimming with furious tears. His father could do that to him, bring him to tears of f'n anger. He wanted to tell him, shout it out, I run this f'n family, me alone! I make the decisions. Who the hell you kiddin'? I take the worst of it, it's me, I'm the f'n boss. But before he could get the words out, his father came at him. Head up, his hands on his hips, like a real zip from the other side, the *capo di famiglia.*

"You, you'll turn it all to shit, you'll go the way of drugs." JoJo's father turned his back on the discussion and took a walk around the room. "*E di tutte cose.* It's always the same with you. You look for the easy way." He paused for a moment, looking JoJo in the eye. "Sometimes, I'm sorry to say, you are so smart, you are stupid."

JoJo grunted, and turned his head away from the stare, away from those cold, dead blue eyes.

"Stupid to become involved in dope when you knew without question I forbid it." His father regarded him for a long moment. "Stupid to trust your life to a lawyer, a man who was frightened and a drunk."

JoJo was astonished at how composed he felt while listening to this.

"The most stupid thing you do, and you've been doing it for years, is to lay yourself out to a cop."

"He's my friend, Pop, we've been buddies since we were kids. You know that. Jesus Christ, what's all this, a surprise to you? You never did business with cops?"

"You mark my words, you're gonna find out someday what kind of friend a cop makes to people like us. Sure I did business with cops, sure. I've always paid what I had to, but I never let them sit at my table, never let any of 'em near me. I told you years ago, lawyers care only for themselves, their pocketbooks. And a cop is a cop is a cop. To me anyone who even thinks about taking that job, taking people's liberty, putting people in jail, can never be trusted. You hear me?"

JoJo shrugged.

"I love you Joseph, you know I love you but you scare the shit out of me."

———

Parked in the bus stop next to Monahan's Bar and Grill, Dante kept the engine running, waiting for Jimmy, thinking about JoJo, wondering if he should have said anything at all to Kathy, knowing full well that he'd told her way too much. They had spent the day in bed, sleeping mostly, talking some, sending out for some Chinese food, rapping about the gay life, her life, giving him a goddamn headache.

He had intended to drive out to the Island and maybe see his kid, but he was so beat, he decided to stay at Kathy's, longing to take another shot at changing her mind. That little hand-job number had him hankering for more, it was the best sex he'd had in a year. Which made it pretty clear where his sex life was at. He could have sworn she was on the verge of giving in. She lay still a long time, thinking, then telling him it was Jimmy she was thinking about. "Ray had a real problem with Jimmy. I'd mention his name and the guy would sneer." Kathy definitely suspected something. So Dante felt he had to talk to her, somehow make Jimmy's case. Then maybe, who knew, she'd understand.

He didn't for one minute think that she didn't know what he was up to. Especially when he mentioned JoJo, how he was going to meet with him. Christ, he never should have told her. Kathy forcing her gun on him, telling him to carry her automatic, not that antique piece of his. And then the topper, telling him she wanted to come along, insisting, carrying on, saying she was his partner and she should be there, telling him finally that she loved him, well maybe not the way he wanted, but loved him nevertheless. Wacky broad, dynamite chick. Even so, he'd told her too much. Big goddamn mouth, thinking with his dick, wanting her to know just what a stand-up guy he was, the way he'd go back to back for a friend.

Out of the car now, walking along the sidewalk to Monahan's, he hoped that she wouldn't show up.

The place was in an uproar. Half of Queens was there, music boomed, the tables were full up, the bar elbow to elbow. Dante's first response was to wonder if Jimmy was going to show, but as he waded through the commotion he saw him sitting at their table, a pitcher of beer in front of him. Jimmy curved a finger in the air, calling him over. On the juke box Elvis was doing "Cold Kentucky Rain." Suddenly Dante felt so tense he could hardly bare to look at Jimmy. Then he saw Freddie Miller and smiled. Freddie came barrelling out of the men's room like a battleship, spotted Dante, threw out his arms and came at him. "Dante," he yelled, "Dante, I heard about your partner. Promise me, swear to me you'll bring 'em to me. Bring the mother what did it to me. I'll suck his eyes out with a straw. Promise me, Dante. I loved that little spic, I swear I did." Freddie took a drink from the bar, sniffed it once and it was gone. The drink's owner, a fairly wide and tall construction worker wearing a black T-shirt, orange hard hat, and boots, stared at Freddie, checking him out. Realizing in a flash that what he was looking at was two hundred eighty pounds of drunk nut job, he turned away and ordered another.

"I gotta talk to you, Dante," Freddie said. "We gotta talk."

"Later," he told him, and bulled his way toward Jimmy. The crowd hemmed him in, he couldn't hear, the disco was deafening, he couldn't get to Jimmy, the joint was shoulder to shoulder. There was plenty of movement but nobody was going anywhere. He caught Jimmy's eye and waved, mouthed, *Let's get out of here,* threw his thumb over his shoulder. This was his place, his bar, and he didn't know more than four or five people in the joint. He felt like he was in a snake pit.

Jimmy popped out of the crowd, crashing into him, saying, "Who are these f'n people, where they come from?"

"Outta here," Dante shouted. "We gotta get outta here, it's getting late."

Jimmy stood next to him, earnestly scanning the mob, "Hey," he shouted. "Hey, I got a friend here that can kick the shit out of any guinea in the place."

"Good, Jimmy good, that's just what we need now."

Jimmy Burns pinched his cheek. "My buddy the tough guy."

They rolled out of the place, Dante's hands over his ears, Jimmy calling back over his shoulder to Freddie Miller who had somehow managed to follow them to the door, "Not this time, Freddie. Me and the big Dante, we got important business."

Freddie staggered out of the bar and followed them to Dante's car. "Jimmy, Dante," he said, "listen to me guys. You gotta promise I'll get a shot at the bum that did Ray, promise me that."

Suddenly Dante's heart began pounding enough to make his face burn. "Yeah, yeah, Freddie I told you, you'd get your shot."

Freddie Miller extended his hand and Dante gave him a tentative slap. "Man kills a cop he gotta pay. I'll make him pay, me and the rabbit, we'll get some payback."

"Sure Freddie," Jimmy said. "Payback is what it's all about."

Dante waited by his car while Jimmy trotted to his own, opened the trunk, and took out an attaché case. Coming back, he stood by Dante's passenger door panting like a middle guard at halftime. Dante threw Jimmy his keys across the roof.

Freddie blinked and rubbed his eyes. Speaking in a drunken slur, he said, "I bet you guys didn't know that every minute, American women buy fourteen hundred tubes of lipstick."

"Guess what," Jimmy said, opening the car door and sliding in, "you're right, we didn't know that."

"Ya know something else?"

"What's that?" said Dante.

Freddie ran his forearm across his face. "Real violence is an expression of intimacy. It's sexy, man."

"I think maybe I knew that," Dante said. He had to rap on the window to get Jimmy to unlock his door.

————

On their way to the Eighty-third Street playground, on their way to meet JoJo, Dante felt an obsessive, bitter, terrifying, undeniable sense of excitement the likes of which he hadn't felt since his first rookie arrest. He was so turned on that at first he didn't notice how scared and silent Jimmy was. Earlier he'd seemed fine, now he was gulping air like a deep-sea diver. When they turned the corner of Eighty-sixth and 133rd Avenue, Dante noticed the headlights behind him. He picked up speed and took a right on Eighty-fifth. The lights followed. "Shit," he said.

"What is it, what is it?" Jimmy twisted in his seat. "We're being tailed? Who would tail us?"

Dante didn't answer, he pulled into a driveway and waited, their tail shot by, stopped, then backed up.

"Oh shit, I don't believe it," said Dante.

"Is that Kathy?"

Feeling strangely guilty, Dante said, "I'm afraid so."

"What the hell is she doing here? What is she, nuts? What did you tell her?"

"Calm down, will ya? I told her I was going to stop at Monahan's for a drink, she probably showed up when we were pulling out." Dante thought about telling Jimmy what he had told Kathy. That would flip him out, he'd have a nervous wreck on his hands, a wreck more nervous than he already was, which was saying something.

Kathy got out of her car and came toward them. Dante rolled down his window, saying, "You wanna tell me what the hell you're doing here?"

"I'm going," she said flat out.

"Where's she going?" Jimmy said.

Kathy leaned into the open window, stuck her head into the car. "I'm going with you two. Don't try and stop me, I'm going and that's it. Deal with it."

"We're going bouncing, hit a few joints, maybe pick up a couple chicks. You wanna come along, fine," Jimmy said.

"You're gonna go and meet JoJo Paradiso and I'm coming along. We're partners, I'm coming along."

Dante was suddenly grabbed by a gloomy thought. "You didn't call anyone, do anything, say anything to anybody?"

"About what, what's she gonna say, what the hell's going on, Dante?"

"Are you kidding me?" Kathy said. "What do I look like? Do I look stupid to you?"

Jimmy leaned across the seat, getting his face about a foot from Kathy's. "You look like you don't know how to mind your own business."

Dante felt anxious now, wanting to get going, wanting to see JoJo and end this thing that ate at him like some kind of clawed beast. "C'mon Kathy," he said. "Stay out of this."

"What's with that attaché case in the back seat?" she said. "What's that?"

"Drive, Dante," Jimmy said.

"No, wait, wait, wait a minute. Both of you wait a f'n minute. Look Kathy, what do you want to do?"

"Come along."

"Forget it. What else you want to do?"

"Follow you two, back you up."

"Why?" Jimmy shouted. "What for?"

"In case your boyhood buddy shows up with a half-dozen shooters. You got the radio on, you hear the news? There was a shoot-out in White Plains, Lilo Santamaria and two of his cronies got themselves wasted tonight. Say Joey boy wants to wipe the slate clean, get rid of all his headaches. Maybe you two heroes are walking into an ambush. I got a gun and a radio. Believe me, these guys don't scare me. I can help."

Dante glanced at his watch. "We're ten minutes late," he said. "All right Kathy, follow us, just stay out of sight."

"I'll hang back, I'll be out of sight. Only you two watch your asses. I don't trust this creep Paradiso. How you can blows my mind."

"Don't do anything, you hear me?" Dante told her. "Keep your distance. Things turn to shit, use your radio."

He sped off, thinking that on the one hand he didn't want Kathy dragged into this and ending up with problems of her own; he was pushing it here, knew that he was right on the edge, breaking enough laws he could end up in chains himself if he wasn't careful. On the other hand, Kathy might be right and he could end up dead. He flashed on JoJo, pictured him with that silly-ass grin of his, maybe with thoughts of setting him up. JoJo would never show alone. He'd better be ready, just in case. Dante had no idea what he was going to do when he saw JoJo. Why not shoot the bastard, just like that, bam-pop the sucker. He began to sweat out another question: if it went bad and hit the fan, where would Jimmy line up, with him or with JoJo? Dante found himself staring out the windshield, driving like a madman, thinking that maybe taking on this f'n case was not the smartest thing he'd ever done. He glanced in the rearview, watched Kathy play hell trying to keep up.

"What do you mean if things turn to shit?" Jimmy said. "What could turn to shit?"

"Maybe you know what your buddy JoJo's thinking. I don't."

Jimmy didn't answer, he sat staring, looking right through him. "You ain't planning anything stupid here?" Jimmy said finally. "You ain't . . . " Jimmy let it hang.

Dante glanced at him and asked himself the very same question.

"Wait a minute," Jimmy said. He looked at Dante as if this entire predicament was Dante's fault. "Hold on here," he said. "You told me yesterday that you wanted to see JoJo, give him this money back and tell him that I'm through with him. I mean, you're not gonna make this problem worse than it already is, are you?" You don't have any other plans? Dante, I'm talking to you, you hear me?"

"The money's in the case?" Dante asked.

"That's right, all of it, two hundred and fifty grand."

Pulling to the curb at the Eighty-third Street entrance to the playground, Dante shut the ignition and looked around. He didn't see Kathy or any other car, no one.

Jimmy grabbed Dante's arm, Dante thinking calm down, cool it will you. He shrugged out of Jimmy's grip.

"Swear to me Dante you're not gonna pull any of your crazy shit here. Swear." Jimmy was breathing through his mouth, Dante had never seen him this unstrung.

Dante crossed his arms over his chest. "I swear," he said, the anger now with nowhere to go but out his mouth. "Where is the bastard?"

The playground covered two city blocks and was surrounded by a twenty-foot chain link fence. The gate was locked at eight at night. You could enter the ramp that ran to the front gate from either Eighty-third or Eighty-first street. Some nights when Dante had one of his wacky needs to ride the swings he'd climb that fence. He'd been climbing that fence for thirty years. There was some grass, about a dozen scrawny swamp maples, a few half-dead scrub oaks, but mostly there was concrete.

CHAPTER TWENTY-FOUR

JoJo sat in Bruno's car at the Eighty-first Street entrance with Bruno behind the wheel, and Karl Marx and Bobby Pumps in the back seat, just in case. "So what are you gonna do?" Bruno said.

"I'll wait another minute or two, then walk down into the park."

"What if this is a setup, an ambush, something crazy like that?" Karl Marx said.

"Who's going to set me up, the cops, for chrissake?"

"It's not unheard of," said Bruno, taking a pistol from his belt, cocking it, sliding the safety on.

"I've known these two guys since I'm a kid. There won't be any problem here."

"I knew Lilo for twenty-five years," said Karl Marx.

"The hell do they want anyway?" asked Bruno, cautiously agitated.

"Who the hell knows? Let me go and see them, get it over with. I'm f'n tired."

"Look," Bobby Pumps said, "we need a signal or something, some way to know you're okay or not okay. Know what I mean? We need some kind of signal or something."

Karl Marx said, "He's right JoJo, what the hell did we come for if we can't look out for ya?"

JoJo envisioned a major shoot-out, everyone going boom-boom-boom. That was idiotic, he sure as hell didn't want that.

"All right, all right. Now listen to me. Only, and I mean *only* if I throw my arms in the air like I'm surrendering do you come out, come and get me. These are cops here. I don't want any of you doing something stupid." JoJo was silent, thinking, Jesus what in the hell are we doing here? He felt vaguely uneasy, there was some chance that he could be walking into a trap of some kind. But the chances of that were real slim. Except what if Jimmy Burns had lost his grip? What if the guy had some kind of guilt thing going? Then JoJo began thinking about Dante and Jimmy as if they were kids again, coming to him for a favor. Maybe Dante had finally come to his senses. Yeah, that had to be it. Shit, after all these years, possibly the wildass crazy man had seen the light.

Bruno said, "This guy, this f'n O'Donnell, he's a f'n nut job, a regular fruitcake. You look at him, Karl, you know you're looking at a wacko."

Karl Marx turned his head to look out the window, turned back to JoJo, touching his arm. "Joseph, these two guys are not doing a police thing here. You don't know what they're up to, neither do we. You be careful. You watch your ass out there."

Jesus Christ, JoJo thought, getting out of the car, feeling now as if he were walking into some kind of cowboy movie shoot-out, everyone waiting for him to step into the OK Corral. Bruno said as he started off, "Hey, hey. You got a pistol?"

JoJo told him for chrissake stop trying to make a big thing out of this, these guys are friends of mine. Bruno shot him a look. All right, they used to be friends of mine. Anyway, they're f'n cops, what are they gonna do?

He walked onto the park ramp and saw both of them coming at him, Jimmy holding something, looked like a tiny suitcase. Dante moving slowly, looking around, dude thinks he's Wyatt Earp, one hand on Jimmy's shoulder, one hand in his jacket pocket. What, was this guy kidding or what?

JoJo sauntered down the ramp trying to read the setup. He'd do this for Jimmy, Jimmy asked a favor and he'd do it. He didn't like it, but that's what he did, favors for people. Jimmy had asked him as a favor to kill the Puerto Rican cop. He didn't spell it out, but that's what the guy wanted, who's kidding who here? So now probably Dante needed a favor done. He hoped that's what this meet was all about, another little favor. But he was getting pretty goddamn tired of all these f'n favors. How about someone doing him a favor for a change, like giving him a f'n break, letting him relax for a while.

He turned to look behind him and saw Bruno standing in the street now, arms folded, leaning his back against the car, standing there with Bobby Pumps. Where the hell was Karl Marx? The light was piss poor, and the little sneak could be anywhere. Out of the corner of his eye he spotted Karl creeping slowly alongside the chain link fence, trying to find darkness. All right, if he wants to tag along fine. Just so he stays out of sight.

JoJo slowed up but kept walking, he began to play back the conversation with his father, *a cop is a cop is a cop,* then he realized that not once did the Skipper thank him for clearing up the mess with Lilo. Christ, he could have got himself killed. The old man just didn't get it, Lilo was a ticking goddamn bomb in the gut of the family. His mouth felt dry. He ran the back of his hand across his lips, pressing it against his teeth. JoJo recalled how good it felt taking Lilo out. All things considered, Lilo was a killer animal whose time had come, and that was it.

He took a deep breath and blew it out, wondering if they all had a time, the mystery growing in him now. Was all of this crazy shit out of anyone's control, all of it already written in some big-ass golden book? He wondered about the kid Vinny. Now where the hell was that crazy kid off to? Taking his goddamn Mercedes to boot. Crazy kid. That kid, the kid Vinny was a good example of another favor gone bad. It cost him his f'n Mercedes.

He was close now, close enough to see the grinding rage in Dante's face. What was it with this guy?

His destination was a twenty-foot square of blacktop in front of the locked playground gate, no more remarkable than any other piece of blacktop you could find anywhere in the city. Nevertheless, JoJo felt like he was on stage, his audience two cops, two old friends. I'm here, he thought, I'm here. If they want me they got me.

"Hey Jimmy," he said, "how the hell are ya? Dante, you look the same as the other night, raggedy-ass clothes and nutty as ever."

———

Dante watched him coming, walking kind of hunched over, moving slowly like the alley cat he was, his head moving this way and that, turning to check who was behind him, sneaky bastard. Bringing muscle with him. Dante could see two of them clear as day, standing by the car at the top of the ramp.

"I'm good, JoJo, good," Jimmy said.

Dante watched them smile at each other, his mind fragmented by a sudden chaos of anger and jealousy and no-shit hatred. He stood transfixed at the sight of Jimmy Burns and JoJo Paradiso slapping palms, and for a horror-filled moment thought that what he should do is burn them both. Chain them together and serve them both up, treat the two of them like the f'n criminals they were. He could see that these two guys belonged together, two of a kind, two of a kind. Christ, he thought, how come I didn't see this before, what's wrong with me?

Jimmy saying now, "JoJo, buddy, we got us a little problem here, the three of us. We need to straighten this out. Hell man, we know each other thirty years. We gotta find a way to do the right thing here."

To Dante, Jimmy sounded like a f'n wiseguy. His stomach started doing loop-de-loops and a muscle in his chin was going like a jackhammer.

"Fine by me," JoJo said. "It's a good idea. I hoped we'd get a chance to talk, just the three of us, if that was possible. Not get crazy or anything, you understand, just talk. What do you two have in mind?"

Dante stepped back away from Jimmy and glanced around. "Just the three of us, you say? What about the two mopes up the ramp? What about them, JoJo?"

"Friends, Dante, concerned friends, they ain't gonna let me come out here alone. This is a dangerous city man." Going over to the park fence, JoJo said. "Hey Dante, remember the game we played here against those guys from Howard Beach. I had two hundred dollars riding on that freaking game. Remember that? What were we, fifteen, sixteen? I was pitching, you were catching, and Jimmy you were playing short."

Dante went over to the fence, made it look natural. He nodded. "Yeah," he said. "Sure I remember, hot shit that you were. We were up by two in the last inning. The first guy up beat out a roller to third. You struck out the next two. Then you walked the bases loaded, you jerk. I got a hell of a memory, I'm always going back. Right Jimmy? That's what I do, I go back."

Jimmy nodded his head, he looked totally miserable.

"Jerk? Jerk? I was hot that day, the windmill was buzzing, I was burning that ball." JoJo did a little pose, rolled his shoulders, did his JoJo thing. "I was popping that ball, man, dropping those losers left and right. I can't remember, but I must have had what, fifteen, sixteen strikeouts?"

"You walked the f'n bases full in the last inning so you could show what a badass you were. You figured you'd strike out the side. Am I right?"

"Yeah, maybe. I would have, to, if my catcher didn't throw the f'n ball into center field. C'mon, you can tell me now, don't bullshit. You did that on purpose, threw the f'n ball into center field so we'd lose the game."

Jimmy leaned against the park fence, looking at JoJo, smiling. "You know," he said, "it's sort of reassuring to know that the more things change, the more you two stay the same."

Dante and Jimmy looked at each other for a long moment.

"You got that right Jimmy," Dante said, "this blowhard asshole hasn't changed a bit."

JoJo said, "Dante, you're always blaming me for things I didn't do. Whataya call that? Only a crazy person does that, blames someone over and over for shit he had nothing to do with."

Dante nodded to himself feeling a distinct, growing furor in him now, thinking of Ray, knowing at that very moment how all this had to end.

"You threw the ball into center field. Now that's the fact." JoJo pointed with his chin at Jimmy. "Tell him buddy, tell this phony bastard that we all knew it, knew what he'd done."

Jimmy shrugged.

"C'mon Dante," JoJo said, that f'n smile of his growing wider now. "Admit it, you threw the ball away on purpose and two runs scored. It was your fault we lost that game, not mine."

Dante looked from one face to the other, JoJo's stupid f'n grin, Jimmy's chin dropping onto his chest.

"It's your fault my friend's dead," Dante said slowly. "You're talking softball games, and a good man gets buried tomorrow."

Dante turned toward Jimmy and saw him smirk and shake his head with impatience.

"It don't matter who pulled the trigger on Ray. I know you're responsible, JoJo. Am I right Jimmy?"

Jimmy nodded just a little, not nearly enough to satisfy Dante. Then he shrugged. Dante flinched, wondering how he could have been so wrong for so long.

JoJo said, "Go ahead Dante, don't be bashful, tell us what you think."

"You heard me."

"I heard shit, I heard you accuse me of something. Me, I don't even know what you're talking about. You know what he's talking about Jimmy? 'Cause if you do, maybe you could help me out here."

Jimmy Burns only shrugged his shoulders again.

"Give him the bag, Jimmy," Dante said.

Jimmy bent and picked up the attaché case.

"What's this?" JoJo said. "What's going on, Jimmy? What's in the bag? This some kind of setup?"

"Ask him," Jimmy said.

"I'm asking you, Jimmy. What's going down here?"

Dante reached over and ripped the case from Jimmy's hand, he took it and threw it at JoJo, JoJo doing a pretty good job of stepping aside, letting the bag fall to the ground.

Dante paused, gathered himself. He pointed a finger at Jimmy. "Jimmy tells me there's two hundred and fifty grand in that bag." Then he jabbed JoJo's chest saying, "It's blood money. Your stink and my friend's blood is all over it."

"Hey, hey, hey," JoJo said. "Maybe you got one of those wire things going, a tape recorder or something. I don't know what the hell you're up to, Dante. But that ain't my money. Should I repeat that, make sure you get it right? That money ain't mine. And as far as your friend is concerned, he was in a dangerous line of work. Cops get killed all the time, man."

JoJo stared at Dante in disbelief. Here he was, out in the open, putting himself in the jackpot again, meeting two cops, thinking they had some kind of problem, that maybe he could help, telling himself help my ass, these guys are trying to turn me around and jam me up. Was his old man right or what? A cop is a cop is a f'n cop.

"I don't know what you two are up to. But I'm outta here." JoJo thought about his father, telling him he was thinking of turning the reins of the family over to the Dancer. What about his own son? What, was everybody out to fuck him, everybody?

Jimmy Burns said, "Wait JoJo, hold it a minute. You got this all wrong. JoJo you know that." Jimmy seemed tired, real upset.

"Take your money and go," Dante said. "You wanna walk with him Jimmy, you go ahead, and fuck you too. Only I'm telling you JoJo, I better not see you again, this is your last warning."

"Oh that's brilliant," Jimmy said. "That's f'n great. Whataya gonna do Dante, huh? You gonna lock me up, shoot me too? Maybe JoJo's right about you, maybe you are a f'n nut."

Dante shoved Jimmy aside and stepped toward JoJo, JoJo thinking, okay here we go.

"Back off you asshole," JoJo said. "I'm telling you, that badge of yours ain't no bulletproof vest. Just back the fuck off."

JoJo stared at Dante, fuming, wondering what the crazy bastard was going to do. Dante screaming now, looking like he had f'n tears in his eyes, JoJo thinking shit's on, this guy's gone, a total wack job. My f'n luck.

"Next time I see you," Dante shouted at him, "I'm gonna put a bullet in your f'n head and a gun in your hand. They'll give me a medal and a week off."

JoJo thought again of his father. Maybe he should pay more attention, listen more to the old man. He wondered what he was doing right now. Probably sitting in Lina's kitchen sipping coffee.

Dante came at him again, saying, "You hear me JoJo? The next time I see you you're a dead man."

JoJo eased back, thinking okay, just words, he's a talker, a screamer, and screamers don't shoot. This shit will pass too. I just have to ease my ass out of here.

"Dante," he said, "I'm saying good night to you, and I'm leaving. Let's not take this any further. For old times' sake, let me walk now."

Relieved to see Dante fold his arms and nod, JoJo felt as though he'd been reprieved. He turned his back on Dante and began to walk off. He felt as though he were walking down a long dark hallway with a window at the end, sunlight and a breeze coming through that window, a curtain blowing, on the other side of the window was safety. He had taken about three careful steps when all that was sane left the Eighty-third Street playground and like a thunderclap the old snake eyes made one more appearance in JoJo's life.

———————

Jimmy Burns ran after JoJo and put a hand on his shoulder, turning him. "Maybe it's better this way," he said. "It had to end sooner or later. Only you gotta understand that none of this is my doing."

Dante stood stone-faced and watched that move, realizing that this was the end of things, he could bury the both of them and live with it. Jimmy had gone bad, he'd betrayed him ten years ago, that was all she wrote, there was no more. Oh Jimmy, he thought, what the hell have you done to us? Jimmy Burns draped an arm around JoJo's shoulders and pulled him in close. That simple gesture delivered more pain to Dante then anything he had experienced in thirty years, more than the death of his own father.

He fingered the slim outline of the automatic in his pocket and startled himself. No matter what Jimmy said about setting money aside for him, all the other buddies-for-life crap, it always came out the same way. You see, he told himself, it's all bullshit and smoke. Dante let out a huge sigh, hearing himself making the case for Jimmy to Kathy, Kathy asking him over and over what about Ray? How do you explain Ray? He imagined Ray standing in the street watching the shooters that had come for him, the guy holding his bags of groceries, wondering why him? He thought of himself trying to explain to Ray's wife the reason her husband ended up dead in the street.

Now he stood like a sentinel, arms folded, observing the two of them,

feeling every single ounce of affection he'd ever felt for Jimmy Burns evaporate. Jimmy was speed-talking, and JoJo was nodding, agreeing, dipping
his head and grinning.

Dante could no longer stand to look at the pair. Turning away he
spotted a shadow near the park fence, a little shadow moving quickly. His
finger slid into the trigger guard of the automatic, a thought coming into
his mind: shoot the shadow, it has to be that little killer bastard Karl Marx,
shoot him. He killed Ray, shoot the little bastard.

———————

Angrily JoJo pulled away from Jimmy Burns, tired now of listening to his
bullshit rap, sick and tired of everyone coming at him, and him only trying
to do right by people, putting himself out time and again, always getting
screwed. He threw his hands in the air, screaming, losing it, his cool hitching
a ride to California, his temper going into orbit, all his luck going to shit,
that goddamn snake eyes again. Screaming now, "You f'n guys make me
nuts! You always made me nuts!"

Jimmy Burns looked stunned.

"Yeah, you too Jimmy, always talking to me in f'n codes, never saying
what the hell you mean. It's like talking to someone from Mars. I never
know what you're thinking. What the hell do you want from me?" Not
thinking, out of all control, JoJo felt his stomach wrench, he threw his arms
into the air, reaching for the moon. His head was full of acid, he was done
with talking.

He spun on his heel, wanting nothing more than to get the hell out
of there—then it came at him like a freight train. He'd thrown his hands
in the air. "Whoa!" he screamed in terror. "Wait a minute! Hold it!"

Dante and Jimmy stopped moving and looked at him.

No, JoJo thought, no. Hold it, I didn't mean that. His head spinning,
JoJo turning now, his arms outstretched, screaming into the night, "Everybody just cool it! I didn't mean nothing. It was a goddamn mistake."

———————

It began, the first thirty seconds of it, with everyone in and around the
playground entirely baffled.

Bruno and Bobby Pumps glanced at each other, Bruno saying, "He's
got his hands in the air." Bobby saying, "I think so, yeah, he does, holy
shit. They're gonna kill him."

Both of them pulled guns and began running down the park ramp,
yelling to JoJo as they came, wanting to do something, anything to help

their guy, their JoJo, but they couldn't, because JoJo, Jimmy, and Dante were standing where the ramp was so dark, they couldn't see much but shadows and forms, who was who, you couldn't tell. So Bobby and Bruno ran blind, their voices joining together in an eerie howl, scaring hell out of a couple of lovers who had been parked on the street two cars behind them.

———————

Karl Marx watched from the shadows, he saw JoJo in conversation with the cops. At first it seemed to be going just fine, three guys bullshitting was all. Then one of the cops got excited, the thin one, embarrassing JoJo, making JoJo—the poor guy, having to take all this shit from a pair of bullshit cops—lose that temper of his, and then, there you go, JoJo gives the signal. Karl Marx did his cross-draw, taking two pistols from his pants, he loved doing that, pulling pistols from his pants. He grew four feet with guns in his hands. Only wait a minute, JoJo was yelling, screaming, "Everybody just cool it! I didn't mean nothing." Now what the hell was that?

———————

Kathy, kneeling in a thin stretch of grass at the opposite end of the park ramp, held Dante's piece-of-crap five-shot Colt detective special in one hand and a radio in the other. Seeing Dante pull his gun—her gun—she called in a signal 10-13, assist patrolman, which meant that every cop within ten miles would be rolling their way in a matter of seconds. When she heard the first of the shots, Kathy dropped the radio and she too began running down the ramp.

———————

Dante brought Kathy's automatic out of his jacket pocket and had enough time to see the dwarf, the little bastard standing there with two pistols. Dante thought he looked confused. Dante fired three shots, pop, pop, pop, was amazed to feel no kick at all, the piece smooth as silk. Saw Karl Marx blown off his feet.

JoJo was spinning now, fumbling at his belt. Dante heard shots coming from above and behind him, a regular goddamn war. He turned the automatic on JoJo. JoJo looked at him in amazement, his hand filled with his own gun, no pretty smile on his face now. Dante jacked the trigger, jacked it again, and again. Shit! *Shit!* Kathy's automatic doing what automatics do, it jammed.

Dante raised his head and saw JoJo's extended arm, his pistol trained on him. JoJo screaming, "You stupid son of a bitch!" over and over, bringing it from deep down, snarling like a pit bull, hunching his shoulders, lining him up. Dante thinking, here it comes, closing his eyes.

Jimmy slammed into him, grabbed him and threw him to the ground. JoJo's gun went off, and Jimmy gave an astonished loud cry of pain. Dante scream-talking, saying, "You okay? Jimmy, you okay?" Falling to the ground beneath Jimmy, holding him, his face an inch from Jimmy's, seeing his mouth open in wonder, hearing more shots and looking past Jimmy's head, seeing Kathy now, running at him, at JoJo, shooting that five-shot antique of his. JoJo looking more confused than Karl Marx, shaking his head, turning, then dropping like a rock.

Dante got to his knees and took Jimmy's hands in both of his, kneeling in the grass, stretching his neck, his jaw thrust upward, squeezing Jimmy's hands as if trying to hold back the tide of blood spilling from Jimmy's side.

––––––––

Kathy leaned against the fence exhausted. She knew she had hit JoJo, hit him good, the guy caving in, falling flat on his back. She glanced at Bruno and Bobby Pumps, watched the two come to a screeching halt, turn and run back up the ramp, jump into the their car and drive off. F'n heroes taking off in a cloud of dust.

At last there were those whoopers, and sirens all on automatic, going high-low in the distance.

She took a deep breath, held it a long time, then let it out nice and easy and made her way toward Dante and Jimmy, bending as she passed JoJo to take his gun from off the ground. JoJo lay face up, and he looked to her as if he were gone, blood blossoming through his shirt, though he could talk. Joseph Paradiso always with something to say.

"You wanna tell me why this happened?" he asked sadly. And although Kathy could hear the pain, JoJo's voice was easy and smooth.

Kathy shrugged and went to the kneeling Dante, her eyes scanning the park, the street beyond, hearing those sirens coming closer and closer, her eyes now coming to rest on Dante and Jimmy.

––––––––

Dante watched the blood running in a river from Jimmy. He knew he had to do something, but what, what could he do? Direct pressure, he thought, put some direct pressure on it. He put one hand under Jimmy's neck, the other he shoved against his side. "Hang on," he said. "They're here, they're here. You're gonna be all right. You'll be fine buddy. Just hang on."

Jimmy began to shake so hard that Dante had to use all his strength to hold tight to him and make him stop. Dante felt Kathy's hand on his shoulder and he looked up at her, saying, "He put himself between me and the bullet, how about that?"

Kathy nodded silently, biting her finger.

"It was me he chose, it was me," Dante said. "In the end, when it counted, it was me."

———————

For JoJo the containment of pain, he realized, was no big thing, and it surprised him. As his pain increased he realized that he could take it, take it all. Shit, he was a Paradiso. You never knew until the moment came, now here it was and it was fine, maybe not fine, but okay. He wanted his father near him now. He'd understand, the old guy understood everything, he'd be proud of him now, the way he took the pain. He turned his head and saw Dante holding Jimmy, kneeling there with his arms around the guy, the broad standing near him, biting her finger. Dante, what a nut job. The guy always sold him short. They should have sat and had a good chat, he sort of liked the guy. Nut job. He wanted his father. Hail Mary full of grace—oh, screw that.

The woman cop came toward him, stopped and looked down at him. The sirens were real close now, maybe a block, two blocks away.

JoJo said, "Whataya think, I'm hit bad, huh?"

Kathy shrugged. "What the hell do I know? I look like a f'n doctor to you?" She turned and went to pick up the attaché case. Kathy opened it and took a peek, put her hand inside, said, "Holy shit." This, she thought, would take some explaining. She stood up straight and looked around, trying to organize her thoughts. She was holding her gun in one hand, the attaché case in the other.

The sirens were on the ramp now, blue-and-whites coming from both ends of the playground.

"Hey Kathy," Dante said. "He ain't breathing. Kathy, my Jimmy's dead."

Dante watched her. She ran a hand across her mouth, turned, and walked to the entrance of the playground. The gate was chained-locked. There was a storm sewer there, a large black hole. She slid the attaché into the sewer, and he heard it hit the water below.

"Hey Kathy," Dante called out. "My buddy's gone, my Jimmy's dead." He held Jimmy's hands tightly.

Two uniformed cops, guns in their hands, hats off, came running down the ramp toward Dante.

"EMS," Dante cried, "we need EMS here. For chrissake, will ya hurry?

It's my partner here, my partner's shot," he told the two cops as they knelt down on either side of him. "We're cops here, this is my partner, my buddy." Pointing with his chin at JoJo he said, "That bum over there, that bum, he shot him."

One of the cops stood, taking his walkie-talkie off his hip, and moved off, checking Karl Marx and JoJo, calling as he went for an ambulance, describing the scene. "We got one, maybe two DOAs here, one an MOS on the ramp of the Eighty-third Street playground." He was standing now alongside JoJo, looking down at him lying there with his arms crisscrossed over his chest. There was plenty of blood.

"You calling an ambulance?" JoJo said. "You're calling for help?"

The cop bent over him, saying, "Why should you be alive, asshole, when there's a dead cop over there?"

JoJo turned his head and looked up the ramp. Dozens of cops now, their rooftop flashes lighting the night.

The cop turned to walk off and JoJo said after him, "Wait, hold it a minute. You know," he said, "it was all a mis—" He looked at the cop's face, seeing all the hatred right there. The cop walked off along the ramp, JoJo's eyes following him, JoJo thinking I'm not going to say anything I don't mean, not now, not ever. He could see Dante looking across at him, so he shot him a nice smile, why not.

JoJo fell asleep, or passed out. He never heard the ambulances arrive, or the cops who moved above and about him, cursing his name. He dreamed of softball games and rooftop love-making, of getting high with his friends. He had sweet dreams of yesterday, the odds for tomorrow were miserable.

———

From his spot by Jimmy's body, Dante saw the uniformed cop speak to JoJo. After a moment, the cop moved off, not walking quickly, but making his way up the ramp toward the ambulance.

Alone now, Dante walked over to JoJo. He stood over him looking down, his arms folded, his head to the side. Had it really been thirty years that they'd all known each other? Dante looked around the playground, quiet again, and he was frightened by it. He felt a sudden longing for Jimmy, a longing so strong that it approached panic, not for the Jimmy twisted by JoJo's money, but for the Jimmy Burns of his memory. Self-confident, gentle, smart. His throat locked up as if he were about to cry. On the ground JoJo opened his eyes with a sigh, he was, after all, hit real bad.

"You're a moron," Dante said. "A fucking moron."